NON PUCKING STOP

On Ice #2

B. CELESTE

Print Edition

Cover Design: Aida @Algart
Editing: Proofing Style by Marla

*For the readers who can't help but love an asshole hero, a good dry humping scene, and a c*ck piercing.*

And for the readers who don't always expect marriage and babies in the epilogue because everybody has their own version of a HEA.

This one is for you.

ALSO BY B. CELESTE

The Truth about Heartbreak
The Truth about Tomorrow
The Truth about Us
Underneath the Sycamore Tree
Past the Broken Bridges
Where the Little Birds Go
Where the Little Birds Are
Into the Clear Water
Color Me Pretty
Tell Me When It's Over
Tell Me Why It's Wrong
Dare You to Hate Me
Beg You to Trust Me
Lose You to Find Me
Teach You to Love Me
Need You to Choose Me
Make You Miss Me
When It Rains
Wanted You More
Girl Going Nowhere
What's Left of Us
Three Pucking Words

PLAYLIST

"I'm the Problem" – Morgan Wallen
"Patterns" – Kelsea Ballerini
"The Diary of Jane" – Breaking Benjamin
"I Love You, I'm Sorry" (live) – Gracie Abrams
"Save Me" – Jelly Roll ft. Lainy Wilson
"Getaway Car" – Taylor Swift
"Favorite Crime" – Olivia Rodrigo
"Not Like I'm in Love with You" – Lauren Weintruab
"goodbye looks good on you" – Alana Springsteen ft. Mitchell Tenpenny
"Chemicals React" – Aly & AJ

PROLOGUE

Winter

THERE HAVE ONLY been a few times in my life that I've truly been scared. The first was when I realized my mother and father weren't coming home. I would never have my father's famous pancakes or hear my mother's angelic laugh when she heard Dad's jokes that weren't even that funny.

The second was when I graduated from high school and had no idea what came next. I had no ambitions like my older sister and no clear path that made sense to me. I felt alone in a world full of billions of people and had nobody to help guide me in the right direction.

And the third is right now, when I realize that I might *love* Thomas Moskins—a married man with secrets and a wife who loves him and a life of grandeur that is beyond what I'll ever comprehend.

This isn't some rags-to-riches story. Because at least Cinderella had parents.

No. I won't be *that* girl—the one who depends on somebody to give her a better life.

I made a promise at my parents' graves that I would stand on my own two feet and live a life they would be proud of me for.

That can't include him, because he isn't mine to love.

I'm starting to wonder if it can include anyone, or if I've been broken for a lot longer than I thought.

CHAPTER ONE

Moskins

THE SUNLIGHT CREEPING through the hotel room blinds assaults my eyes as I squint to check the time, making it hard to see the hands on my Santos de Cartier watch, a wedding gift from my wife.

Groaning when I realize I'm going to be late for a meeting with my agent, I ignore the muffled protests of the slender woman sleeping half naked beside me and throw the blankets off of us.

When the nameless blonde makes no effort to move, I say the same thing I always do to my overnight guests. "Get up, get dressed, and get out."

I stand and stretch my sore, stiff muscles and examine the sleek curves of the bartender who warmed my sheets last night. She'd made good drinks and gave good head, but frowns sleepily at me as if she expects a flowery morning greeting and pancakes. Most women know exactly what they're signing up for when they follow me to my room, and don't protest when our time together is over.

"It's early," she whines, sitting up and holding the sheets to her tits as if her nipples weren't in my mouth three hours ago. "I thought we could have morning sex and then get breakfast."

Well, she thought wrong.

I collect the clothes that I'd ripped from her body in the early morning hours and toss them onto the bed before grabbing an outfit from my suitcase for myself. "No time. I've got places to be."

I slide into the bathroom to take care of business as she starts redressing with a scowl. I'm not sure why she's pissed. She got off twice before I even got to stick my cock in her. You'd think that would put someone in a decent mood.

As I'm walking out freshly clothed, my phone goes off with Emaly's name and picture on the screen. I chuckle at the ridiculous image of her in a baggy chicken pajama onesie, holding a glass of red wine, which she set as her contact image. "I'm surprised you're up, Dimples," I greet, leaning my shoulder against the wall as I watch my visitor dress. "It's early on the West Coast."

The nameless bartender stops buttoning her shirt when she sees me on the phone, staring at me with a narrowed expression.

There's a smile in my wife's voice. "Am I interrupting something? I see you've been busy if what TMZ is reporting is true."

I snort and stare at the woman crossing her arms over her chest as she gapes dubiously at me.

"I'm just finishing up, actually," I inform her, getting a scoff from my one-night stand as she flattens out her rumpled black skirt.

My wife hums. "Let me guess. Blonde?"

I grin, giving the bartender another thorough once-over. She's shorter than I normally go for. Was she wearing heels last night? She's pretty, though. Average. Nice rack. "You'd like her," I say to the woman whose finger I slid a ring onto.

"Are you really flirting with another woman while I'm *right* here?" the bartender asks, glaring at me.

"Actually," I purr, not bothering to pull the phone away from my ear, "I'm speaking with my wife."

Emaly laughs on the other end of the phone as my lay makes a disgusted face and grabs her phone and shoes.

"You are a sick bastard, Thomas Moskins," she informs me, walking to the door.

Before she can slam it behind her, I call out, "I'll tell her you said hello."

Once I'm alone, I sit on the edge of the unmade bed and absorb the welcoming silence. After a long day of sponsorship meetings with my agent yesterday, I'm over people. Most of the jackholes I spoke with didn't seem inclined to have me be the face of their products, thanks to the tabloid headlines lately. Apparently, men's cologne and athletic wear are only for the family men of the world. Which, according to the reps of two different brands I met yesterday, I am not.

The off-season is supposed to be relaxing, but between sponsorships, commercials, and photo shoots, I've done everything *but* relax. The transition from my old hockey team in Pittsburgh to my new one in Connecticut ensures that I barely have any downtime. But I chose this sacrifice, which means I have to deal with all the PR bullshit that comes with it.

After a minute, I say, "I guess she got off on fucking a

married guy."

There's bemusement in Emaly's response. "Way to ruin her fantasy."

I crack a grin, but it quickly drops when I remember what time it is. "Is everything okay? You don't normally call this early."

The woman I've known since I was young is not a morning person. It takes an act of God to get her up before ten a.m., and even then, she needs coffee before she can hold a conversation. It's astounding to me that she can be a doctor and pull doubles, knowing what a zombie she is on her days off.

Worry cements in my gut. "Are you—"

"I'm fine," she says with a laugh.

Despite growing up in the United States, Emaly Moskins-Yokav has the faintest Russian accent thanks to her family heritage. Her parents, Mikhail and Valeria Yokav, are both from Moscow and spend a few months each year at their estate in Russia's capital. Valeria runs the country's largest artificial skating rink, where a lot of top athletes train, and they recently opened a second location solely for Olympians and their coaches.

Emaly and her younger brother, Sasha, grew up on the ice as figure skaters. Her parents expected both of them to become gold medalists like Valeria, but only one of them fulfilled their parents' lifelong dream. It's why Sasha remains in Russia, training for the next Winter Olympics, while his older sister resides in the United States under the scrutiny of her disapproving family.

My recent indiscretions certainly don't help her case

any. I'm definitely not winning them over now that my name is being plastered as front-page news on every tabloid next to a woman who is *not* my wife. Not that I particularly care to be in their good graces, despite her father's involvement in my career as of late. I may have let him puppet master my life, but it's to ensure he stays far away from Emaly's.

People can assume what they want about me, but I'll do anything to protect the people I love. And I've loved Emaly since we were kids.

My in-laws have done nothing but berate and judge Emaly from the time she was old enough to understand what berating meant. It's put a wedge between my wife and her family that's small enough where they keep in contact, but large enough not to depend on a single cent they try throwing in our direction.

Emaly never wanted their money or prestige. She's only ever wanted their approval to be her own person. But with the Yokavs...well, that's no easy task to accomplish.

Which is why they didn't even blink when Emaly chose to keep her last name and hyphenate ours when we got married. Did I care that she put my name first? No. It was her decision, and I supported it. I just wish her father could see how much that choice meant to her. Then again, I wish Mikhail Yokav would see a lot of things if he'd simply open his eyes. Life would be a lot better for all of us if he were more accepting.

"You worry too much," she chides softly, pulling me back to reality.

I scrub my hand through my hair. I really need to

schedule a haircut. "Can you blame me? The first time we were apart for this long..." I swallow, my Adam's apple bobbing at the memory that will stay with me for a long time.

I'll never forgive myself for not checking on her more. For not calling or texting her when the hockey preseason took me away for so long. If I had, maybe I would have known something was wrong. I could have seen the signs, like I'd seen them when we were younger.

Emaly must know where my head is. "It was one time, Little Bear. I'm fine now since seeing the new specialist."

Little Bear. The term of endearment is the only thing keeping me from booking a flight to California. She used to say I was as protective as her father, but with far more affection than he was capable of showing.

"It happened twice, and I should have been there," I murmur, still feeling guilty over the call I got from the hospital when one of her neighbors saw her passed out on the ground outside our apartment building.

I swallow and grind my teeth.

I should have been there.

I should have been the first one on the scene, not the firefighters. Not the ambulance. If I were there—

"I'm calling," she says, breaking through my onslaught of rampant thoughts, "because I saw what they're writing about you and wanted to make sure you're okay."

I huff out a laugh and rub a hand down my face. "You don't need to concern yourself with that, Em. It's nothing I'm not used to."

"But—"

"No," I cut her off firmly. She'll say she feels bad; tell me she can dispel the accusations. But I tell her the same thing I always do when rumors arise. "The vultures in the media will say and do anything for a headline. It's about making money for them. If they gave a shit about hurting someone's feelings, they'd have a different job. I don't want you to feel bad about what those dickwads post."

She's silent for a stretch of time before I hear her sigh softly. "We both know my father isn't going to let you off the hook so easily."

Christ. It isn't that I forgot her father is a factor in this mess, but I don't like to think about him if I can help it. Mikhail Yokav is not someone you mess with. His connections stretch much further than mine do, and so do his pockets. If he wants to make your life a living hell, he will. And while Emaly might not be their golden child, they are still protective of her.

If to protect their name only.

Up until a year ago, Mikhail had simply been my father-in-law. But after a few intense meetings with my agent, manager, and lawyer, he now all but owns my fucking life. Which means he can take away everything I've worked my goddamn ass off for.

Pissing somebody like him off is stupid. And the headlines right now are not going to paint me in a good light, regardless of how my team tries to spin it.

Emaly must know the inner turmoil waging in my body. "I can speak with him," she offers. "Perhaps he'll listen."

If he were the type of man to listen to reason, we

wouldn't be living this charade for over a decade.

Scrubbing a hand down my face, I stifle a sigh. "I'll handle it."

The woman I consider my best friend, my *only* real friend, makes a sound of protest. "You don't always have to do everything on your own, Thomas."

I want to tell her, *"I know."* But I don't bother lying, because she's one of the few people I agreed never to do that with. The rest of the world can view me as a cocky asshole. A cheater. A liar. I don't give a shit. But not Emaly. She's always seen the real side of me. The one that yearns for quiet. For peace. For love. Who would rather stay inside with a bowl of popcorn and a soda rather than go to a bar until close with the guys.

No. I won't lie to her.

So, I simply say, "I'll be more careful about staying out of the tabloids."

Because that's the only other promise I have to offer the woman I swore to love in sickness and in health—the only thing I can give the girl whom I've only kissed one time in our thirteen years of marriage after sliding a ring onto her finger. For her, I'll do better. I'll try.

She says, "I love you, Little Bear," in a soft, comforting tone that I miss hearing in person.

My throat bobs. "I love you too, Dimples."

CHAPTER TWO

Winter

THERE'S A COFFEE stain the size of Texas on my brand-new silk shirt. I'd been excited when I saw the rose-colored top on clearance for half off because it completed the I-mean-business ensemble for my first client meeting.

I check the time on my phone again and cuss under my breath as I scrub harder at the spot.

"This had to happen today," I grumble to myself, realizing that the five minutes I have left until walking into the conference room are not going to make a difference.

The outfit I spent days obsessing over is ruined because I decided to splurge on a cup of coffee, which I only allow myself twice a month because of how stupidly expensive the sugary caffeine I love is. But how can I pass up on something that tastes like heaven to my taste buds? If my father were around, he'd scoff at the drink I'm slightly addicted to and comment on my inevitable diabetes diagnosis. Unlike me, he preferred his coffee black and bitter.

But I deserve it. At least, that's what I told myself when I handed the barista my last ten-dollar bill and cringed at how little change I got back.

Today is the first day I get to shadow and assist Janel

Starr, my boss, as she takes on a "delicate" PR case. I have no idea what I'm walking into, or who will be on the other side of the table. All I know is that Janel thinks this client can be difficult, and cleaning up his reputation may not be as easy as the other cases we've taken on here at Starrs Strategy.

Defeat weighs on my shoulders as they slump at the pitiful sight of me staring back in the reflection. I got up early just to braid back my pin-straight blond hair and hide the hot-pink tips my sister helped me dye. Pink is a happy color—a positive one. It matches the color on my fingers and toes, but hardly fits my personality. Not anymore, at least. I'm more of a black kind of girl these days. Optimistic to a point, cynical to a fault. It's hard not to be when you've gone through the amount of loss as I have. So, I choose to surround myself with happy colors.

Today it's pink.

I spent extra time making sure my makeup is neutral, highlighting my mossy-green eyes and full lips with liner I don't normally wear. My outfit is—*was*—cute and classy. The gray slacks aren't tailored, but they fit my short legs better than most of my jeans, and the rose-gold top tucked into the waistband emphasizes my hourglass waist in a professional manner. Before the coffee incident, I felt…good. For once.

When I looked at myself on the way out of my apartment this morning, I didn't feel like a twenty-five-year-old orphan on her way to her first *real* job. Well, my first real *meeting*. I felt confident. Older. Excited.

"You had to get a stupid coffee," I scold myself, throwing the damp paper towel into the trash bin by the sink. I usually drink water at work because water is free. If I spill it, the most I have to worry about is a wet shirt. Not *this*.

I give myself one last glance in the mirror before groaning loudly and walking back out to my cubicle. Sometimes I keep a sweater at work because of the draft above my desk. I could slip that on to hide the mess splattered over my boobs and save the day.

"What on earth happened to you?" Janel asks me halfway to my desk.

I wince as she eyes my shirt. "I went across the street for a coffee on my break and then promptly spilled it on myself trying to avoid being run over by a guy on an electric scooter."

She stares at me unblinking before shaking her head. "Do you have something to change into?"

Janel has always been a laid-back boss who rarely cares about what we wear. Case in point, her short hair is currently bright purple and matches her dress. I don't need to hide the pink in my hair or wear business-casual outfits, but I want to be taken seriously by the clients we represent. I've only done the backend work at Starrs Strategy—making calls, fetching coffee, writing meeting minutes. But I've heard about the people who come in here needing our help. I don't want to come off as anything other than professional to the multi-millionaires who have money to throw at their reputations.

"I thought I had a sweater, but I think I took it home with me," I answer, frowning as I go through my desk drawers. My spine straightens as I turn to her. "Please don't make me sit this meeting out. I'll sit on the other side of the room and take notes. The client won't even be able to see the stain."

One of Janel's dark eyebrows pops up. I wonder why she didn't dye them too, but I don't bother asking that because I've got better things to concern myself with. "Winnie, the people in the building across the street from us can see that stain. There's no missing it."

All of the hope and excitement I'd woken up with deflates. "I understand," I murmur, sitting down and glaring at my shirt.

Janel remains by my cubicle. "Why are you sitting? Our client showed up two minutes ago. We've got to go."

I blink at her. "But…" I'm speechless for a second. "You still want me to be there?"

She rolls her eyes. "Winter, I went to a meeting last week with spinach in my teeth and mascara smudged under my eye. I looked like somebody had punched me. We're only human, and our client could use the reminder that he is too. Let's go."

I'm quick to follow her as she turns and heads down the hall. The room she booked for today is private, unlike some of our other conference rooms with glass walls that modernize the building. It means that whoever is sitting inside is a high-profile client, not some random CEO under scrutiny of a tweet gone wrong or an office affair at a Coldplay concert.

We stop outside the closed door, and Janel turns to me. "Teeth check," she says, baring her teeth and running her tongue over the pearly whites.

"All good," I say after careful inspection, getting an appreciative smile from her.

"Before we go in," she begins, gesturing toward the room, "I want you to remember not to react. Whatever happens in this room is confidential. We're not here to judge, we're here to listen and help."

My smile slips a fraction. What exactly am I walking into? Did this person commit a murder? Something worse? What's worse than murder? It could be a self-defense thing. Or maybe they were protecting their family or pet *John Wick* style. I can totally get behind that.

"I can see the wheels turning," she observes with arched brows. "I need them to stop. You can't go in there with any preconceived notions. There's a reason why I picked you for this case and not one of the others."

If she willingly chose me over Cody or Farrah, that probably means it's a celebrity. Most likely an athlete or actor. She knows I'm a safe bet because I know very little about sports, which means I won't fangirl or try sliding my number to someone known in the game.

Rolling my shoulders back, I nod at her. "I can do that. No judgment."

Unless he hurt an animal. Then there will definitely be judgment. I'll just keep it to myself.

"Good," she praises. "And try not to let him get under your skin. He's good at that."

Janel opens the door after the heeded warning, leading me inside the large room with a walnut conference table and expensive office chairs surrounding it in the middle. Above the polished wood hangs a chandelier that looks oddly out of place compared to the crisp, clean aesthetic below it. There's a drink bar set up off to the side with coffee and water on top next to the crystal glasses, and alcohol inside the glass cabinet that looks well-stocked. The paintings hanging on the walls are minimalist and make no real sense to me, but I don't pay them much mind. Not when I see the man sitting casually at the end of the table with a scowl on his ruggedly masculine face.

"Mr. Moskins," Janel greets, setting her laptop down on the opposite end of the table. "It's nice to see you again. Will your agent and manager be joining us this afternoon? I can wait for them."

His eyes slide from Janel to me, dragging along the front of my body. I can feel his gaze like a heated touch, and the pin prickles of heat travel from the crown of my skull down to my painted pink toenails stuffed into a pair of white heels that are a size too small for me and bound to leave blisters. There isn't a centimeter his focus doesn't graze with curiosity, and I feel it all.

Goose bumps cover my skin as he appraises me like a sculpture he wants to put a bid on, and I'd be lying if I said the feeling wasn't nice. Men have noticed me before, but their gazes always feel slimy. His is curious, maybe a little calculated, but overall cautious.

Good. He should be.

Janel notices where his attention is too. She puts a hand on my arm and says, "This is Winter Bronte. She'll be assisting me with your case. Winter, this is Thomas Moskins. He's a hockey player with Connecticut's new NHL team, the Fireflies."

Ah, a professional hockey player. I'm not familiar with many of them, but he certainly looks athletic. Bulky and muscular in all the right places, like he can take a hit and still play. I've heard hockey is a violent sport, but his body is definitely built to handle it. I'd read that Fairbanks was getting its very own pro team in the league a year ago, which is supposed to boost the local economy when they officially start playing in the fall.

"Bronte?" Thomas repeats, studying me with his arms crossed over his broad chest. He's not nearly as dressed up as I am, but he wears his long-sleeved shirt well. It isn't baggy and hugs his torso and arms like he needs to size up.

Not that I'm complaining.

Isn't he hot? It's got to be at least seventy-five today. Summers in Connecticut aren't brutal, but I'd be sweating through that if I were him.

"Like Charlotte," I offer sheepishly when I realize I haven't replied to him.

He stares at me blankly.

I shift on my feet, trying not to wince at the pinch of pain from the heels. My sister was right. I should have gone with flats. "You know. The author?"

He remains silent because, of course, he wouldn't know who Charlotte Brontë is. I'd taken a class on her work in college and developed an interest in her novel, *Jane Eyre*. Maybe because her character is an orphan girl too, simply trying to survive in a world that tries its best to chew her and spit her out.

I swallow nervously. "Not that there's any relation," I babble, waving my hand in the air. "I don't think there is, anyway. I've never done a DNA test or anything, but—"

"What the fuck happened to your shirt?" he asks, cutting me off.

I stop yammering and flinch when I remember what I must look like. A mess. All that work I'd done this morning was for nothing thanks to the wet stain. "Uh, I had an unfortunate incident with my coffee on the way to the meeting."

Our client stares at me for a moment longer before turning his chair toward Janel with skepticism written all over his face. "You expect me to believe *she's* put together enough to be on my case? My manager said your agency was the best possible team to help me wipe my slate clean. She can't even carry a cup of coffee without messing up."

I withhold from dropping my jaw at the asshole who clearly isn't going to offer me the same courtesy of a judgment-free zone. "I was attempting not to get run over by a scooter. I'd like to see twenty-six if I can help it."

He deadpans before closing his eyes and pinching the bridge of his nose. "Christ. They hired a child to clear my name."

This guy has got to be kidding me. "I'm *twenty-five*," I inform him firmly. "I've got a dual bachelor's degree in public relations and online media management. The reason Janel hired me as a communication strategist is that I'm qualified for the job and know what I'm doing."

Janel pats my arm in comfort before lowering her palm. "I can assure you, Mr. Moskins, that you'll be well taken care of. Winter was hand-selected for this specifically. Her ties to the community will enable us to provide the best results for your predicament."

He leans back in his chair and studies me carefully. I can't quite tell what color his eyes are—they aren't entirely blue but mixed with gray. What I can tell is that they're intense. I don't know what he's looking for or what he sees, but I can tell he isn't impressed.

The feeling is mutual.

"Look," I tell him honestly, "I may not be what you were expecting, but I'm probably what you need. Because who better to take charge of your persona than a millennial girl who grew up in the digital age? I know exactly what people want to see, and it's not"—I wave a hand in his general direction—"this. Clearly, your charming personality isn't winning you any favors, or you wouldn't be here. So you can either sit down and listen to our pitch, or you can walk out and find another agency with half the reputation that we have."

Janel stills beside me, but she doesn't speak up or scold me. Instead, she lets Thomas Moskins mull it over. Maybe I could have been a *little* nicer in my delivery, but I don't owe him anything if he's going to be a dick to me.

And, frankly, I'm not lying. Starrs Strategy has won numerous awards since Janel started it almost ten years ago. Her client list is expansive, and the connections she has with agents and managers means that our clientele will grow. She's trusted not only in Fairbanks but on the whole East Coast.

It feels like far too long before the slowest grin curls up the right side of his mouth. "Okay," he says, leaning forward and resting his crossed arms on the edge of the table. "You've got my attention, kid. Better make the most of it before I lose interest and find someone else."

I don't let him bait me with his nickname. "I saw the way you looked at my chest, *Mr. Moskins*. You don't think I'm a kid at all."

His shoulders square back, but he remains silent as I sit beside Janel and open up the folder she collected on the notes and previous calls she's had with his team.

Eventually, he mumbles, "I was looking at the stain."

We both know that's a lie. "You can call me Winter since we'll be working together." I scan over the notes my boss gathered over the past month, leading up to this meeting. It's no wonder his agent reached out to us to help bring him back in favor with people. He's got quite the rap sheet going for him.

Adultery.

Rumored divorce.

Public indecency.

Public intoxication.

Career probation.

I look up at him through my lashes. "It looks like you have a stain too," I note. His eyes go down to his shirt in confusion. Before he can say anything, I continue. "Lucky for you, I can fix yours. It'll take time, but if you want to win back the trust of your new team, you'll have to let someone take control."

When I meet his eyes, his bluish-gray hues flash with something unreadable that tightens my stomach. "And you're the type of woman to take control?"

From kid to woman.

Interesting.

"I've had to take control of my life a long time ago," I inform him, not that I owe him anything. "So, yes. I am."

Janel clears her throat. "We think we're quite capable of handling this situation with a few tweaks to your…lifestyle. At least, your lifestyle as the public views it. We'll organize a few events, some interviews and photographs, and get ahead of whatever online narrative is being formed."

Thomas doesn't look at Janel as she speaks.

He stares at me.

With far, *far* too much interest in his smile.

His head cocks as his focus dips to the top half of me, visible above the table. His lips curl up higher at the corners, and he says, "Good. When do we start?"

THOMAS MOSKINS, AS I learn, is trouble with a capital *T*.

After our meeting ended and he left to do God only knows what, Janel gave me a stern talking to regarding my people skills. Specifically, how *not* to let someone like Thomas get under my skin.

While the scolding made me flush and apologetic over my behavior, I could tell Janel was secretly impressed by my ability to bite back. She turned to me with an arched brow, told me she didn't know I had it in me, and…smiled.

It's the only reason I held my tongue rather than begging her to remain on the case despite how I acted toward the hockey MVP. Was it unprofessional to give him attitude? Absolutely. Would I do it again if he spoke to me with disrespect? I sure as hell would.

Which is how I wound up with a six-inch binder full of everything I need to know about the two-hundred-and-twenty-pound professional right-winger. According to his file, the thirty-five-year-old has won a lot of awards throughout his career—everything from the Calder Memorial Trophy as a rookie to the MVP Hart Memorial a few years ago. He's good, based on whatever standards these awards are measured by. I'm certainly not going to YouTube the inner workings of his sport to figure it out, but I don't need to.

My job isn't to praise him on the ice and remind people why he's an amazing hockey player. The world already knows that. His stats prove it. My responsibility is far harder.

It's to make Thomas Moskins look like a decent human being.

And based on every tabloid printed out in front of me, that is no easy task.

Perhaps taking this on is biting off more than I can chew. Maybe I'm overzealous for acting as if I can fix his reputation, like all it needs is a bubble bath and a pretty bow slapped on top of it. Scrubbing a hand down my tired face, I lean back in my dining room chair and sigh. "What did you get yourself into, Win?" I ask myself before glancing back down at the latest headline.

NHL right-winger Thomas Moskins is seen leaving the Yokav Center in Fairbanks, Connecticut, following the accusations of his latest affair reported by TMZ. There are rumors that Mikhail Yokav, owner of the Fairbanks Fireflies and father-in-law to Moskins, plans to suspend the one-time MVP award winner after images of him leaving a hotel with a mystery woman went viral three weeks ago. A source close to Moskins claims there is no tension between him and his wife, Emaly Moskins-Yokav. However, it appears the meeting with the Fireflies owner did not go in Moskins's favor as seen in the images below.

I cringe at the pictures taken in rapid succession of Thomas knocking down a planter and then kicking a dumpster so hard it looks like he dented it.

With the current tensions rising between the right-winger and his father-in-law, it doesn't appear that the star offensive player will start in the Fireflies first season with the NHL without a major overhaul to clear Moskins's name.

I can understand why Janel told me not to judge when she started discussing the reasons Thomas needed our assistance. It also makes sense why I had to sign a nondisclosure agreement that was as thick as his file.

Based on all the articles about him, this is the third time over the last year and a half that he's been seen with women who aren't his wife. A year before that, he'd been seen with the same blonde over the course of six months in Boston. The year before *that*, during his last season with New York's team, it'd been a brunette he was constantly spotted out with in Seattle.

None of them his wife.

In fact, most interactions between him and Emaly Moskins-Yokav seem to be strictly online. There are cute selfies and candid pictures posted between them with messages that are equally adorable. She never posts anything about the alleged affairs, and only ever praises and supports him throughout his hockey seasons.

It's a bit…strange.

It also means that if I'm going to help him like I said I would, I'm going to need to figure out their dynamic. Something tells me getting that information will be as easy as giving medication to a cat. I have the scars to prove how hard that actually is. Thomas Moskins is about as open as the sealed exercise bike still sitting in its box in the corner of my bedroom, waiting to be used.

So, yeah.

I may be screwed. And not in a fun way.

Standing and stretching my stiff muscles, I walk over to the sink and fill a glass of water. A picture frame sits on the windowsill, filled with smiling faces that hit me square in the stomach.

What once used to be a family full of love and laughter got torn apart when a thirty-six-year-old decided to get behind the wheel of a car drunk. One choice turned my life upside down and took both of my parents from me.

Kourtney, my sister, was old enough to take me thanks to our nine-year age gap. If it weren't for her, I would have had to move out of state to live with our aunt and uncle in Detroit, Michigan—a far cry from Fairbanks, Connecticut.

My sister had lived in a tiny one-bedroom apartment that wasn't much bigger than the one I'm currently renting. She slept on the couch in the living room and gave me the only bedroom there was. We learned to cook together and count on each other. She continued with college to become a teacher, and we helped each other with homework and tests as they came and went.

The picture on my windowsill is the last family photo we took during the holidays. I hated wearing matching Christmas sweaters with my mom, dad, and sister at the time, but I would do it all over again if it meant having them here.

Walking back over to the table, I pick up my phone and go through the text threads I have with Kourtney. She's busy with her seven-year-old son, Luca, and adapting to the new fifth-grade curriculum she switched to from second grade this year.

Me: *I miss you*

Despite the chaos of her life, she responds within five minutes.

Kourt: *Have you been abducted by aliens? Are you dying? Is this your way of saying you've been kidnapped and need me to call 911?*

I roll my eyes at her theatrics, but grin as I thumb out a reply.

Me: *If I were kidnapped, I'd make it way more obvious. Like 'tell Mom* *and Dad I won't be home for dinner tonight'*

Kourt: *Morbid*

Kourt: *But smart*

I settle into my seat, ignoring the mess of papers scattered in front of me. It's been a few days since I've heard from my older sister. We both acknowledge that we're busy and try checking in when we can. But today…Today, I miss her.

Me: *Can't I miss my favorite sister?*

Kourt: *I'm your ONLY sister*

Me: *Tomato, potato*

Kourt: *It's tomayto, tomahto*

Me: *Turn teacher mode off, sis. I'm not five*

I scowl at the memory of Thomas Moskins calling me *kid*. The nerve of that guy is astounding, but after reading over his history, I'm not surprised. He's entitled. Arrogant. Annoying. I suppose he could have called me worse.

Kourt: *Is everything okay?*

She's always known when something bothers me, even if she can't see my face. It's her sixth sense. Or maybe it was her maternal instincts getting honed to prepare her for Luca.

Me: *Just busy with work and thinking about Mom and Dad*

Most days, I don't allow myself to think about their passing. It's been twelve years since the accident, but it doesn't feel like that much time has passed at all. Sometimes, I swear I can hear Mom's laughter. When I do something dumb, like forget to change out my winter tires or check my oil, I can sense Dad's disapproving stare somewhere in the distance.

Kourtney did everything a twenty-one-year-old college student could. We had shelter and food, and she made sure I got to school on time and passed all of my classes. She helped me with college applications and essays, and never once discouraged me from taking random classes until I figured out what I wanted to do. She gave up her social life for me and never once complained.

Me: *We should go out soon and get drinks. Make Brad watch Luca for once*

I don't necessarily blame myself for Kourtney's less than stellar relationship, but I do wonder if she settled for the sake of stability. We'd spent years wondering if we could make ends meet, and her meeting Brad Fisherman seemed to help ease those worries. I'm sure there's love there, and they have the cutest kid ever. But I don't know if she's truly happy.

Kourt: *He's out of town for work. Dinner instead? Luca can be good*

I'll never pass on the opportunity to love up on my nephew, even if it makes me irritated that her husband is gone *again*. I still don't fully understand what he does, but apparently, it requires him to be gone. A lot.

But it's none of my business.

Me: *You can choose the place*

Kourt: *You already know where we'd go. Luca won't eat anywhere else*

Me: *It's a good thing they're cheap*

After we make plans for a date and time to get dinner together, I stare at the three bubbles dancing along the bottom of the screen. My heart warms when I see the last message she sends.

Kourt: *I love you, Winnie*

I swallow.

I don't remember telling Mom and Dad that I loved them the night of the accident. I'd begged them to stay home instead of going with them to run errands. They reluctantly agreed and told me to behave myself—that if there was any emergency, I was to call them or Kourtney. But did I tell them I loved them? It's a blank space in my mind that I don't recall and that has tortured me for over a decade.

I've made sure to let people know how much I love them ever since, because I learned the hard way that you never know what can happen.

Me: *I love you too. Give Luca a tight squeeze for me*

Long after we stop talking, I'm staring at the piles of paper pertaining to our newest client. Who does *he* love? If online fodder is right, his wife never goes to any of his games. Neither do his parents. Does he have siblings? People who support him? Or does he make it a habit to push them all away?

I tell myself I shouldn't care.

But I do.

For work purposes, of course.

CHAPTER THREE

Moskins

THE FIVE-THOUSAND-SQUARE-FOOT TUDOR-STYLE home located in Fairbanks's only gated cul-de-sac is complete overkill. I would have been happy with a condo or penthouse suite, not two acres of land that I have no need for. I'll give the small city some credit, though. The area is nicer than where I lived in Pittsburgh, and not far from Greenwich, where I grew up, and some of my oldest friends still live.

Although I suppose friends is a loose term. I'm not one to reach out very often to my small group of confidants. I keep in touch by liking their online posts from my burner account. That way, I don't have to worry about random pick-me girls coming out of the woodwork to harass me or reporters digging through my shit and asking for exclusives. I get enough of that on my professional pages.

A few of my former teammates with the Penguins would give me shit for being a bad texter. What they didn't know is that I usually just ignored them whenever they'd ask me to come out with them or remind me about team plans. I went to what I had to and only entertained them with my presence when I felt like it. If I really needed a drink, I preferred pouring myself one in the comfort of my own home, where temptation and scandal couldn't find me.

I'd like to think that's where I differ the most from my parents. I could say no to a stiff drink—I knew my limits. Socially, I'm more tempted to have one too many. But never, *never* have I let myself cross the line I saw my mother and father step over too many times to count.

So, yeah. I've become a homebody.

Especially since my meeting with Mikhail and my agent, Ashton, went exactly as I expected it to. Which was bad. Very bad. If it hadn't been for Bodhi Hoffman, the head coach for the Fireflies, stepping in during my father-in-law's long-winded rant about every reason why he should fire me on the spot, I'd probably be fucked. Then I would have bought this house and left a team I loved for nothing.

So, solitude is the better option. It's the *only* option. Even if the halls echo with my wandering thoughts, it's better than putting my ass on the line solely for an orgasm or two.

My phone goes off as I walk into the kitchen to find something for dinner, and I glare at my agent's name on the screen. "What?" is the way I greet him. I've learned that when he calls past five o'clock in the evening, it's usually about nothing good.

Thankfully, Ashton doesn't care. "Hello to you too. My night was good, thanks for asking."

I roll my eyes. "*You* called *me*. I'm not going to entertain you with small talk."

He snorts. "Of course not," he muses. "My mistake.

I'm calling to find out why you asked for details about Winter Bronte. The message you left was vague."

Since when does he care? "You've done background checks for me without needing an explanation. Why question me now?"

"Because," he says smoothly, "those were for women you wanted to sink your dick into. This is someone who's supposed to be helping save your ass before your father-in-law throws you out onto the street. You can't fuck her."

That's why he's really calling me. To tell me where I can and can't put my cock. "I never said I wanted to," I inform him, even though the thought definitely crossed my mind.

Attitude is like foreplay to me, and Winter wasn't hesitant to dish it out when I called her a kid. The second she stood up straighter and pinned me with those fierce green eyes, my dick stood to full attention. All I could picture was how good it would look in her mouth.

So, no. I don't think she's a kid. I don't think she's anything close. But did I like the offense written all over her face when I called her that? Hell, yeah, I did. And what I liked more was her all but telling me to fuck right off.

"I'm simply curious about her," I explain to the man who likes to tell me what's best for my career. If it's not him being a pain in my ass, it's my manager. Both of them would tell me to stop thinking about the blonde with a sharp tongue and focus on what's more important. My contract with the Fireflies. My brand deals. Getting new sponsorships since the old ones have chosen to distance themselves from my less than stellar rep.

Too bad for them, I don't like listening.

Ashton sighs. "There isn't much to tell. She's new to this position, but she's qualified. Janel is the type of person who only hires the best. I've worked with her before. Anybody who she thinks isn't a right fit for her company barely makes it past the first month before quitting. Winter being there for a year means something."

This is the first case she's on, according to Janel. She must be picky if she waited this long to assign her. Lucky me for being the chosen one.

"There's more," I state. I know Ashton well enough to tell when he's holding back information. "What aren't you saying?"

There's a brief pause before he sighs again, this time sounding withdrawn. "She's ten years younger than you, Tom. The last thing she needs is to be wrapped up in your personal life in any way other than professionally. The kid has gone through enough."

My nostrils flare. He's forty-eight, so he's allowed to call her that and mean it. "So you just called to tell me not to fuck her and mess up her life?"

For once, he doesn't hesitate. "Yes."

Asshole. "I'm not a monster, Ash."

"I know you're not," he affirms, sounding more genuine than he typically does. "But there's a lot she doesn't know about you that she'll have to figure out if she's going to clear your name. Let her do her job without giving her a hard time."

He's never been this firm about who I allow in my life. It isn't like he encourages me to go after women, but he'll turn a blind eye after telling me to wrap it before I tap it. This time seems different.

My eyes narrow in suspicion. "Do you know her?"

I don't like the silence I'm met with.

"Ashton," I growl.

He's relatively local to Fairbanks, so it isn't out of the realm of possibility that he knows her. Or knows *of* her. And that doesn't sit well with me.

"No," he eventually says, but his voice doesn't sound right. It's forced. Distant. Hard. "I don't know her. Not personally."

But he does know *of* her, and I want to know how. "Care to elaborate?" I press, grinding my teeth.

Suddenly, I want to know less about her and more about how my nearly fifty-year-old manager is attached to my latest obsession. He's from Connecticut—a Greenwich boy originally whose family made it big as investment bankers in the city. According to him, he spent a lot of time in Fairbanks because of an old fling, so he has ties to this city. If Winter is local too, it would make sense that they may have crossed paths before.

Ashton does something I least expect. Turns me down. "No. I don't. I'm simply calling to tell you to keep it professional. That's it. Don't put your dick anywhere near her. Use someone else if you need to get off, but not her. Understand?"

It shouldn't bother me that I'm being warned away from her. But it does. I've never been a fan of being told no, and it's not often I hear the word. I acknowledge how that makes me sound, but I don't give a fuck. "You're really not going to—"

I don't get the question out before the dickhead hangs up on me.

"What the fuck?" I mutter, staring at the blank screen. I try calling him back, but it goes straight to voicemail.

If he thinks this is going to squash my intrigue over Winter Bronte, he's dead wrong. He just fed a whole new interest that I *will* find out one way or another.

I WAKE UP in the middle of the night to the sound of footsteps creaking the aged floorboards in the hallway. The layout of the house isn't as spread out as it might look from the outside. I've made downstairs my main living space, claiming the only bedroom on the first floor despite it being the smallest of all the rooms. The master is upstairs, along with an attached walk-in closet and bathroom that's double the space. It's too much room—a luxury I don't deserve.

My ears perk up to the footsteps nearing my closed door. It would be my luck if I purchased a haunted house. As if my career being threatened to crumble around me isn't enough, I get to deal with Casper the goddamn ghost haunting my ass.

I grab my lamp and rip the cord from the wall because the mid-weight metal is about as good a weapon as I can find on short notice.

And when I hear the doorknob jiggle, I hold my breath to be as quiet as possible. The room is bathed in darkness thanks to the blackout curtains I hung on the windows, so there isn't easy visibility for whoever opens it.

When the door cracks, I hear the softest voice call out, "Little Bear?"

Wait a second. I know that voice.

"*Emaly?*" I ask, lowering the lamp. I'm instantly out of bed and walking over to the door to turn the light on. After my eyes adjust, I see the five-foot Russian woman in all her dark-haired, flawless beauty standing at my doorway. "What the hell are you doing here?"

I finish the question with a hug, pulling her into my body and listening to her soft chuckle against my bare chest. It's a reminder that I'm only in a pair of boxer briefs because I get overheated easily when I sleep. I would feel bad about the lack of clothes, but it isn't the first time that she's seen me naked. It is, however, an improvement over the last time.

At least now I'm not stripped down to nothing but skin while she slathers ointment on my ass from the poison ivy I'd gotten while camping the one and only time she convinced me to slum it in the woods. She'd spent the entire time laughing at my expense and joking about selling the pictures of my inflamed ass cheeks to the highest bidder.

I press a kiss to the top of Emaly's head, which smells like the same jasmine and honeysuckle shampoo it always does. Floral and clean and…her. My best friend. "What are you doing here?" I ask again, peeling away and giving her a thorough once-over.

She smiles at me, making our fifteen-inch height difference comical as always. "I tried calling and texting you, but you didn't answer."

I look behind me at my phone, which isn't plugged into the charger. I'd gotten so fed up trying to search for Winter's social media that I must have forgotten.

"My bad," I tell her sheepishly. "Are you—"

"I'm fine," she cuts me off knowingly. Her hand comes up to cup my jaw, her thumb rubbing against the stubble covering my chin. "But I know the meeting with my father didn't go well, so I wanted to come see how *you* are."

She called and asked how it went the second I'd gotten home. My bet is that she tracked my location from the sports complex to the house. I didn't bother to sugarcoat the truth. Things between her father and me aren't good. But I don't want her to concern herself with something that I did to myself. This is on me and only me.

"I told you not to worry," I remind her, putting my hand on top of hers and leaning into her palm. "You didn't need to come all this way."

We have a house in San Diego, California, where she usually resides. It's not often that she travels, because she has everything she needs on the West Coast. She'd visit me at my place in Pittsburgh once in a while or see her parents when they stayed at their Queens estate in the city. But over the past few years, her trips have become few and far between.

In her parents' minds, that's my fault.

This trip comes not long after helping me move into this place, which is exactly why she knows where my bedroom is. It's surprising that she'd leave work so soon after taking time off to help me settle in.

"Where is Ronnie?" I ask, looking behind her. The house is quiet—too quiet.

Emaly's smile is sleepy. "In California. I wanted to come alone. I figured I would spend time with you and then see my parents. Perhaps I could calm my father down a bit." Her throat bobs with a swallow. "Is it…is it true he's trying to fire you?"

Damn the media for blasting those stupid reports everywhere.

I shake my head. "It isn't that simple. There's a board that has to decide the fate of the players on each team. Most of them agree that this isn't an infraction of my contract, but a personal matter that should be handled off the ice. While some of them agree I need a reality check to stop spreading negative press that overshadows the Fireflies' first season, they don't think there's a justifiable reason for me to lose my position."

Her chest deflates with a relieved breath. "I was hoping you'd say that." Her lanky arms wrap around my waist in a tight hug. "I'm going to talk to him anyway."

I frown. "And say what exactly?"

She can't tell him the truth.

As if she knows that, her shoulders go limp and her hold on me loosens. "I don't know," she admits. "I haven't thought that far ahead. I tried to come up with something on the plane, but didn't get very far in the planning process."

When she pulls away, I look down at her with interest. "How far did you get?"

"Well, first I was going to fly here," she tells me with a sheepish smile.

"Accomplished," I note.

"Then," she continues, "I was going to make sure you were okay and maybe convince you to make me breakfast in the morning. I can't get my scrambled eggs as fluffy as yours."

Chuckling, I nod along. "Lucky for you, I just ordered groceries."

She beams. "Then…" She wets her lips. "I guess that's it. I haven't even thought about what I'd say to my parents besides 'hello.'"

My eyebrows quirk up. "You never were very good at strategy."

She scoffs, swatting me. "Be nice to me, Thomas Xavior Moskins! I rubbed ointment on your ass. I deserve respect."

I knew she was going to bring that up. "When are you going to stop using that against me? It was *your* fault I had to shit in the woods. We both know I'm not the camping type."

Her giggle warms my chest. "I thought you'd like it. I didn't realize you'd find the *one* patch of poison ivy at the campsite."

I roll my eyes because we've had this discussion. There was a lot of poison ivy around, we just didn't know it. "I prefer indoor plumbing and toilet paper, but I appreciate the adventure."

Emaly grins at me. "You're too soft for the wilderness anyway, Little Bear."

I'd take offense to that, but she's not wrong. "The beds are made upstairs. You can pick whichever one you want. Do you need me to get any of your bags?"

I know her well enough to assume that there's more than one suitcase waiting for me in the foyer. She doesn't go anywhere without at least three bags packed to the brim.

Emaly waves me off and walks into the room, sitting down on the edge of my king-size bed. "I think I'll choose this one. It's already warmed up for me."

She peels her shoes off and tosses them onto the floor before smiling at me and curling into the spot I'd just been sleeping. What a pain in the ass.

"Comfortable?" I ask, brows arching.

She settles in. "Yes."

I roll my eyes and join her, not about to give up my bed. We've had sleepovers before. It started when we were teens, not long after we first became friends. Everyone assumed we'd been doing more than talking until we fell asleep, and neither of us ever denied it. We both knew people would think what they wanted, regardless.

It isn't until a few minutes later that she asks, "Where is the lamp?"

I grin in the darkness, turning onto my side and closing my eyes. "Don't worry about it."

CHAPTER FOUR

Winter

LUCA SPOTS ME before Kourtney does, and beelines in my direction the second I step into the Chuck E. Cheese entrance. "Aunt Win! Aunt Win!"

I grunt when he barrels into me, barely able to keep myself upright as I wrap my arms around the seven-year-old's lanky body. "Have you grown since I last saw you?" I ask skeptically when I realize he comes up to my chest. In hindsight, that's not hard to do. I'm only five foot three, but still.

He laughs. "Mom says I'm a weed."

"*Growing* like a weed," my sister corrects him, rolling her eyes over the top of his head as she approaches us. "It means you're growing fast."

Luca peels himself away from me to look at his mother. "Dad says I'm small for my age."

The frown that curls my lips doesn't compare to the one weighing on Kourtney's mouth. "Your father is confused," she says through gritted teeth. Apparently, she's as done with Brad's bullshit as I am. Maybe that's a conversation we'll have today while Luca plays.

When we're done ordering a cheese pizza and fries, because it's the only two things Luca will eat right now, we sit down at a table by the arcade games.

Kourtney sneers at the mouse mascot high-fiving a group of kids. “I hate that stupid mouse,” she grumbles.

I snort. “You’re still traumatized by the time Melvin brought that mouse into your bed, huh?”

Her face darkens at the reminder of our childhood cat. He was a mighty rodent hunter. Except that he rarely actually *killed* them. Melvin simply liked showing them off by bringing live mice into the house, and sometimes, into Kourtney’s bed.

“I’m glad he passed away before Mom and Dad, because I would have put him up for adoption if it were my choice,” she seethes, crossing her arms over her chest.

No, she wouldn’t have. “I loved Melvin too much for you to do that to me. Remember how much I cried when Dad told me he was gone?”

Kourtney’s face pinches. “You made us have a funeral with a eulogy and everything. Do you know how hard it was for me to come up with something nice to say about that pain in my ass? Once, he brought a half-dead *bunny* into the house. There was blood everywhere.”

I cringe. Okay, so I didn’t know that. “What happened to the bunny?”

“You don’t want to know,” she informs me, moving on. “Anyway, what’s going on with you? You’ve got that look on your face.”

My brows pinch. “What look?”

She sips the soda our waitress brought over and waves her hand in my direction. “The one that says there’s something on your mind. Spill.”

I want to talk about her and Luca and Brad, not me. "Is there something going on with *you*? It seems like you're mad at Brad."

She shrugs limply. "When am I not?" she counters, setting her drink down.

Okay. True. "Do you want to talk about it?"

The only response I get is her deadpan expression that says, *Do I look like I want to talk about it?*

So, I move on. "Do you remember when I went to the semi-formal dance in middle school with the new kid from my grade?" I ask her, folding my straw wrapper into an accordion.

She thinks about it for a second. "Jason? Is he the one who made you cry in the bathroom when he danced with that mean girl who bullied everyone?"

I nod. "That's him."

"What about that douche?"

I see she still hasn't forgiven him for hurting me. That's sort of sweet. "You told me to kill him with kindness—"

"No," she cuts me off. "I told you to fill his locker with garbage and dirty gym socks, and you told me you weren't doing that."

I snort. "Okay, but *after* that, you told me the second-best option was to kill him with kindness. So, I was always nice to him. And he eventually apologized for ditching me for Marni and asked to be friends."

Kourtney sighs. "I still can't believe you agreed to that. He was a loser."

"We were twelve," I remind her.

She doesn't reply.

"Anyway," I go on, "I have a work thing that I need advice on. Because I don't know if killing him with kindness will work. Our client is..." An asshole. Dickhead. Douchebag. All of the above. I filter those names out. "...stubborn."

"Who is it?"

I give her a look. "You know I can't tell you that. I signed an NDA."

"Celeb," she theorizes. "Cocky, probably. Let me guess. He's either in a cheating scandal, a paternity lawsuit, or hit someone he shouldn't have and is facing charges."

I blink at my older sister and her dry delivery. I can speak about the case hypothetically as long as I'm not naming names that would give his identity away. "To my knowledge, he hasn't fathered anyone or hit anybody."

She hums. "Cheater. Got it. Okay, so he's under fire for a cheating scandal, and you need to boost him back up. Don't you just have to make up stories that put him in a good light? You don't have to pretend to be nice to him."

I wish it were that easy. "For me to figure out how to put him in a good light, I have to study him and learn his behaviors to train him on what *not* to do. My boss basically wants me to do PR 101 with him until I can come up with a few stories that could change people's perspective of him. Then there are the events he'd have to do to further that image, which can be hard if he's not believable. And that's only *if* he agrees to go that far. Some people prefer press releases online or statements on their Instagrams with half-assed apologies that they don't mean."

My last meeting with Janel was not fun. Especially

when she told me that Thomas Moskins wanted me to work with him one-on-one without Janel present. The only thing she's concerned about is me calling him a dickhead, which is going to be hard. But I'll manage.

Probably.

"I'm not sure what advice I can give you that you don't already know," Kourtney eventually tells me. "If you can't kill him with kindness, then just make sure he knows his place since actual homicide is frowned upon."

I glare. "That's all you have?"

One of her shoulders lifts. "People who are used to getting their way aren't going to change overnight, Winnie. I wish they did." Her frown twitches her lips, and I wonder if she's thinking about her husband. "But they all have soft spots and weaknesses. If he's going to be a stubborn prick, make sure to knock him down a peg. Match his energy. If he didn't need you, he wouldn't be in your life. Right?"

I slowly nod. I'd basically said as much to him during our initial meeting. A great first impression, but clearly one that didn't scare him away. "Yeah..."

"So keep reminding him of that," she finishes. "You're Winter-Freaking-Bronte. You've gone through too much to let some rich dick try to tear you down. You're here to make his life better, not to let him make yours worse."

Would he try making mine hell? That's the last thing I need. "What if I fail?" The thought isn't one I like having, but it's a real possibility.

Sometimes, these people come to our agency, do well with the first few steps of our process, and then go right back down the rabbit hole that got them into trouble in the first place. Then all of our hard work goes down the drain because they don't know how to be decent human beings.

Like Kourtney says, they don't change overnight. Some don't change at all.

"Then that's his problem," she informs me firmly. "Not yours. You're only paid to try making a difference in his public perception. It's up to him to actually change for the world to believe it."

I blow out a breath when I realize she's right.

"If you have to do events together," she adds casually, sipping her drink. "Make them something important to Fairbanks. You know what this community is made of. If you're stuck babysitting this guy, you might as well find ways to give back and use him to do it. He probably has money and a fanbase regardless of whatever scandal he's in. It sounds like giving back to Fairbanks is the least he can do."

This community *has* done a lot for us. And if Thomas Moskins is worth what his Google page says he is, then he can afford to give back to the city that is now home to his new hockey team.

Luca comes running back with a long line of paper tickets trailing behind him. "Look! I can finally get that giant dragon."

My sister hides her wince when Luca points to the stuffed animal that I'm not sure will fit into her car. "Great," she murmurs.

She doesn't enlighten me about her relationship, work, or anything personal, the rest of the day. That's Kourtney for you. Closed off and far too focused on everybody but herself.

But when I get back home after our dinner out, I compile a list of ideas for Janel's approval that could make a big difference to both Thomas Moskins *and* the people of Fairbanks.

I CAN SMELL my coworker Cody before he actually appears at my cubicle, thanks to the rancid cologne he bathes in. When I turn from my computer to see why the twenty-something-year-old is leaning against the wall of my cubby, I'm met with an arrogant smirk that I want to smack off his face.

Ever since I was hired, he's been the bane of my existence. We went out on one measly date not long after I started, which I left early with a made-up excuse about a family emergency. I've never entertained him again, and I'd like to thank my frontal lobe fully forming for that wise decision.

My decision to let him take me to dinner has been one of my biggest regrets in the past year. But as someone who was broke and just starting out, the thought of getting a free meal from him sounded too alluring to pass up. It's why I went on a lot of first dates and not a lot of seconds.

To me, the man currently poisoning my space with off-brand Axe body spray was a meal ticket and nothing more. But I learned my lesson, which was cemented by a scolding conversation with my sister after realizing Cody wasn't getting the hint about my lack of interest.

"You don't shit where you eat, Win," Kourtney says over

the phone. "Never date a coworker. Not even for a good steak."

I'd gotten chicken that night, but I understood enough to promise I'd never do it again.

"Can I help you with something?" I ask the office pest, waving my hand at my computer screen. "I'm a little busy right now."

His eyes move from me to the screen. "Is that the Moskins case?" he asks with way too much interest as he pushes off the wall and steps into my personal space.

I quickly turn the screen away from him and power it off. "It is, but we both know I can't say anything about it."

I don't like the mischievous spark in his eyes. He's up to no good, and I don't trust him. Especially when he sits on the corner of my desk like he owns it.

Prick.

"How did you manage that anyway?" he asks, stretching his legs out in front of him. "You go from fetching coffee and doing meeting minutes to being part of a high-profile case for someone you probably didn't know existed five days ago."

My eyes narrow. He's right, I had no clue who Moskins was, but what does that matter? It clearly gave me the advantage. "Your point?"

He huffs out a laugh. "I'm clearly better suited to be on his case. I know him, his stats, and everybody signed to his new team. It's strange that you got assigned to it, and I'm not the only one who thinks so."

All I can do is blink. Is he implying that I somehow bribed my way onto this case? With *what*? I literally agreed to go on a date with him for food, which means I have no money to my name. If I did, I'd have a stocked fridge at the apartment and no reason to agree to the amount of overtime I do. There isn't anything else I could offer to convince Janel to assign me to this specific case.

"Have you ever thought that if you were a decent person, you might have gotten picked for this?" I question with a bite to my tone. He deserves it for trying to accuse me of shady shit. "I know for a fact that you were pulled from the Shiba Humphrey case because you flirted with her and tried to get season tickets out of the deal."

Defense instantly squares his shoulders. "I was *joking*. Nobody can take a joke these days."

Oh, please. "The only thing I did to get assigned to this case is earn Janel's trust. If she trusted you, you and your vast knowledge of all things Thomas Moskins would have been on it."

His glare would turn me to stone if it could, but I don't care. Nobody is going to come into my space and tell me I haven't earned something that I work hard for every single day.

"I come in early," I tell him, lifting my thumb. "I stay late," I add, lifting my index finger. With each point, I add a finger to emphasize the list of reasons why I deserve this more than he does. All while locking eyes with him. "I don't gossip. I don't flirt. I have the decency to say hello to everybody here rather than giving them the cold shoulder. You can be mad all you want, but it doesn't change the fact that I'm on Moskins's case and you're not. That's not going to change."

Just as he's about to say something that would probably

border on harassment, a new gravelly voice cuts into our conversation. "She's right. So get the fuck out of her space."

It doesn't come to me who the person is until we both turn to see Thomas Moskins standing there. His eyes aren't on me, but on Cody. And they're narrowed into unimpressed, inquisitive slits. It's not an expression I'd want on me if I were my coworker.

Cody pushes to his feet, completely morphing his face into a fake expression of professionalism as he extends a hand to the hockey player. "It's so nice to meet you, Mr. Moskins. Winter and I were—"

"You," he cuts Cody off, "were just leaving."

Cody's smile drops when the professional athlete ignores his outstretched hand and gestures behind him. He's not going to shake it. He's not even going to pretend like he gives a shit.

I have to curl my lips back to hide a smile as Cody grumbles under his breath. That is, until I realize that he's mumbling what sounds oddly like, "…clearly sleeping with her client."

My heart drops at the accusation.

And I'm not the only one who hears it.

Before Cody can storm off to whatever bridge he crawled out from under, Thomas Moskins grabs hold of his arm to stop him. "The *fuck* did you just say?"

My eyes widen at the venomous tone that even has Cody looking wary.

"I-I—" My coworker stumbles over his words as he stares wide-eyed at the man he clearly wanted to work with.

I wonder if he's second-guessing that now.

My new client pulls Cody toward him, so there's barely any distance between them. It's only then that I realize how tall he is compared to my coworker. He towers over the man who, only seconds ago, crowding my personal space. I wonder how *he* likes it. "If I ever hear you disrespect another woman, I will make sure you don't have a goddamn job to come back to. Feel me?"

Cody is quick to nod vigorously.

It's enough for Moskins to let him go and shove him away. As Cody scurries off, Thomas calls out, "And lay off the fucking body spray. You smell like a douchebag."

All I can do is gape at the right-winger as he turns to me with a deadpan expression.

I blink.

He blinks.

I swallow.

He stares.

"Do we have an appointment?" I ask, frowning down at my calendar. I'm meticulous about updating it. He's not on here until Wednesday, when he's supposed to come in to speak with Janel and me about our game plan. I'm still making cold calls and cementing all the little details to propose to him.

"Come on," he says, grabbing the jacket I have hung up on a hook outside my cubicle. He tosses it to me, and I barely catch it before it hits me in the face. "Let's go."

I don't move an inch. "Ugh…where?"

"Out," he answers dubiously, staring at me as if I'm an idiot for not following. His chin dips to my coat. "Put that on, it's raining outside."

Why is he so bossy? "I can't just leave. I'm working. What is this about? You're not supposed to be here for another two days."

Apparently, he doesn't love being questioned. "Do you always push back this much?"

I can't help it. I lift my shoulders casually and nod. "Sometimes."

He tries hiding it, but I see the slightest twitch on his lips. "We're getting something to eat. We need to talk, and I'm hungry."

That sounds way too serious. "Janel has a meeting in ten minutes, so we can't go until—"

"I don't want Janel," he informs me, not bothering to let me finish my sentence. "I'm here to get you."

Confusion makes me sit silently as I gawk at him. He's not here to speak to Janel. Weird, but okay. Why me? "She's still the main lead on your case, Mr. Moskins. It's better if she's there if you need to discuss things relating to it."

Boundaries, I remind myself. *Set boundaries.*

He rolls his eyes at me as if I'm being ridiculous. "First off, don't call me that. Secondly, I already cleared it with her. She knows you'll be stepping out. Like I said, we need to talk."

My stomach tingles as I process his demand. Do I believe him? Not really. I have no reason to. But it's almost my lunch break anyway, so I can always take it early and make sure I'm back within an hour. If I go over, I'll stay late again. No big deal.

Except, it *feels* like a big deal.

"This is a work meeting, right?" I ask him as I stand to slide my jacket on and zip it. Grabbing my purse from my desk and draping the strap over my shoulder, I collect my notebook and a pen in case there's anything I need to write down.

His only reply is, "What else would it be, Bronte?"

It sounds like a challenge.

One I do not take.

So all I ask is, "What *should* I call you then?"

Slowly, his lips curl into a grin that would make anybody nervous. "I have a few ideas, sweetheart."

My spine straightens. "Do not call me that."

His grin only spreads. "Touch a nerve?"

I don't respond.

He chuckles. "Let's go."

He still doesn't tell me what to call him.

CHAPTER FIVE

Moskins

SHE WON'T SIT still. It's fucking annoying watching her squirm in the private booth far from the public eye. I always request a section where people can't snap photos or video me. The occurrence has become far too common these days, thanks to my face being a regular feature on people's social media with ridiculous clickbait headlines. Suddenly, everyone wants to be a citizen journalist documenting my every goddamn move.

"Would you sit still," I grumble, flexing my fingers around the water glass. "You act like you're about to get tortured."

She frowns. "Aren't I?"

I snort, loosening my grip before I break my cup. "If I wanted to torture you, I'd take you back to my place to do it more privately."

Her face, which I've spent way too much time studying every feature and angle, turns red. It takes me a minute to realize her mind must have gone to a dirty place, which makes me grin in approval.

"Mind out of the gutter, Bronte," I bemuse, making the color in her cheeks darken. She's got a pretty face with round, doe-like green eyes and a full, pouty mouth. I can picture doing vile things to those lips, but I refrain from telling her as much in fear she'd use her cutlery in retaliation. "I don't have whips and chains there."

Toys, on the other hand, I do have. I don't plan on sharing that with her, because I'm not sure she could handle it.

Winter clears her throat. "Now that we've established that you're not the next Christian Grey, can you enlighten me as to why I'm here?"

"I don't know about that," I challenge, my grin growing. "I'd hate to be discredited for my unique tastes. I'm sure if they wrote a book about me, it'd make twice as much as *Fifty Shades of Grey*."

One of her brows quirks. "I don't know if I should be impressed or scared that you know what I'm referring to. You don't even know who Charlotte Brontë is."

I refrain from laughing or disagreeing with her. What she doesn't know is that my house contains shelves full of leather-bound books with gold foiling on every piece of classic literature from the nineteenth century. Collecting them is a hobby of mine that not many people know about.

Charlotte Brontë sits alongside other greats of the period. Jane Austen. Charles Dickens. Walt Whitman.

I'd rather she assume I'm just another airhead jock, like most people write me off as. It's easier to live under the presumption that my narrow-minded ways are nothing more than surface-level. Trivial. To everybody, I only like booze, women, and sports. They don't know about my actual interests. Sure, women and sports are on that list, and I enjoy a good drink now and again, but that isn't all

I'm made up of. Books, documentaries, and a good cup of hot coffee are what make me happy.

Days where I can be alone with my thoughts, no matter how rocky those may be, make me happy. I don't always like isolation, but I've come to appreciate it when the rest of my world is deafening from the noise.

But none of that is what I brought her here to talk about.

Changing topics, I hit her with the first question that's been on my mind since hanging up with my agent. "Do you know who Ashton Dessen is?"

The ass hasn't been replying to my texts or calling me back, so I figure it's best to go right to the source for answers. However, the source seems confused.

A little line forms between her brows. "Uh…who?"

"Ashton Dessen," I repeat. "He's my agent."

It's obvious that she has no clue who I'm talking about, which only furthers my distaste for Ashton's reaction on the phone.

Eventually, Winter shakes her head. "Sorry, no. Should I? Janel is the one who usually works personally with our clients' teams, so I'm sure she's spoken to him before. She keeps records of conversations in her notebooks if you need to check something."

I lean back in my chair and stare at her. I'm fairly sure that she's telling the truth, and I don't know why that irritates me. Maybe because I can't outright ask about her past. Well, I could. But I have a feeling she isn't the type to indulge me. If I were nicer, if I left a better first impression, I would have stood a better chance of getting any piece to her puzzle.

"Why are you staring at me?" she asks, deadpan.

I make her uncomfortable.

That's probably a good thing.

"What's the deal with that prick from your office?" is my next question. I'm not owed an answer, but I want one.

Her nose scrunches. "Cody?"

She neutralizes her expression, but I can tell there's a level of distaste there. It was written all over her face when I saw him making himself at home on her desk. I don't know what they were talking about before I stepped in, but it made her shoulders rigid and her face hard.

Winter's focus stays on her untouched soda, staring at the bubbles lingering on the top. "He's innocent enough. All talk, really."

That doesn't answer my question. "He shouldn't be talking to you like that." My reply comes out like a low growl, earning her attention.

She peers up at me through her lashes, parting her lips silently as she gawks at my tone.

"Nobody has a right to say shit like that," I tell her firmly. "If he continues, you need to report it to your boss."

I've been around dickheads like him who think they're more important than they are. He's a walking sexual harassment violation.

"Why do you care?" she counters, shaking her head as she studies the way my fingers clench on to my glass again.

I lift a shoulder. "I don't like women being disrespected, and I don't like people like him."

Her eyes narrow as she soaks in that reply. She doesn't believe me. Or maybe she finds it hard to. I wasn't exactly Mr. Rogers during our first meeting. But I also wasn't spitting hateful accusations at her like her coworker.

Cody. Internally, I sneer at the name. I'll make a mental note to speak to Janel about him before our meeting, because I have a feeling Winter isn't going to.

"I can handle myself," she informs me, meeting my eyes. There's reluctance in her gaze before her shoulders slump a fraction. "But I do appreciate you stepping in. Cody can be a bit much sometimes."

That's putting it lightly. "Does your boss know?"

Her lips curl downward. "That he's annoying? Yeah, I'm sure she does."

I gape. "Does she know that he harasses you? I'm sure a guy like him isn't only bothering one person. If he's a nuisance, somebody needs to inform the boss and get it taken care of."

Truthfully, I shouldn't give a shit. It isn't like Winter means anything to me. But I've seen Emaly in her shoes before. She'd been harassed by one of her attendings at the hospital she'd done her residency at, and came to me crying after a month of nonstop comments from him. It'd taken everything in me not to show up and beat the pulp out of that guy when she admitted he'd cornered her in the on-call room one night. Instead of hurting him, I'd gathered enough proof to report him to the hospital director and get his ass canned so he couldn't do it to her or anybody else again.

Maybe Winter reminds me a little of my wife. She's got

a hard exterior, but it's a front. Inside, she's much softer. Sensitive. I want to know why.

Winter takes a long sip of her drink to stall, and I try not to focus on how her lips wrap around the straw. She's not wearing makeup today, and I almost like her better for it. The first day we met, she looked like she was trying too hard to impress someone.

When she has no other reason but to answer, she sits back and toys with her straw wrapper. "I feel like it's partially my fault that he acts that way," she admits, biting her bottom lip.

I want to rip it from her mouth and smooth my thumb over the spot her front teeth are digging into. "Why is that?"

She's suddenly sheepish. "We went out once."

I instantly scowl. "You went out with *that* guy? He smells like he walked through the perfume section at Macy's three times to avoid having to buy the scent."

The laugh that bursts past her lips is unexpected and lightens her face. It's a nice sound that almost makes me smile.

Almost.

"To be honest," she tells me, "I only went out with him because money was tight and I didn't have any food at the apartment. I got a meal, split it in half, and took my leftovers home for dinner the next night."

I blink at her. "You date men for food?"

She makes a face. "You make it sound like I'm prostituting myself out. I don't go home with them. I never do."

I'm hardly the person to judge what one does in their

sex life, but that doesn't mean I like the idea. "Going out with him doesn't earn him the right to talk to you that way at work. Have you told him you're not interested?"

Her hesitation makes me want to pinch the bridge of my nose.

"Not in so many words," she murmurs, her quiet voice making me shake my head. "I've told him it's not a good idea that we go out on a second date. If I wanted to, I would have. It seems obvious enough to me that means no."

Well, he's a guy. An arrogant guy. They need far more basic terminology. Like 'fuck off, I'm not interested' for one. "You can mouth off to a professional athlete during your first meeting with one, but you can't tell your coworker that you don't want to date him?"

She frowns. "It isn't that easy."

My brows go up in doubt.

"I have to work with him," she explains, pulling her drink toward her and tracing her finger along the condensation on the sides. "If I make him mad, I have to see him every day. If some cocky client comes in and mouths off to me, I can dish it back because they aren't going to be around for long."

All I do is stare at her pointedly. Because I'm right here. Across from her. Living and breathing flesh. "How'd that work out for you?" I quip.

She glares.

My grin returns.

"Is there a point to this meeting, Mr.—"

"You can call me Moskins," I cut her off. "I hate the

formal bullshit."

Her head tilts inquisitively. "Not Thomas?"

"No."

"Not Tommy?"

"Absolutely not." That reply comes out harder than I intend.

Her eyes light up. "Okay then."

Something tells me she's going to use that name regardless of my hatred for it. "What do you go by? Winter? Certainly not Ms. Bronte."

She shakes her head. "I'm not one for formality either. Ms. Bronte sounds so...old." It's a reminder to me of how young she really is.

Twenty-five, I tell myself.

"Most people call me Win or Winnie," she finally says, lifting her shoulder. "I don't have a preference."

Win has a nice ring to it. Then again, I've always liked that word. It's been ingrained into my blood ever since I started playing hockey as a kid. Losing isn't an option. I'm competitive and cold-hearted, and I have no regrets about what I do in order to secure a victory.

Something shifts in her, and her nerves are back. She shifts in her seat and twiddles with her wrapper again. "If we're going to work together," she says softly, "I'm going to need to get to know you a bit better. I can't help you unless I understand you. If the world is going to believe that you're trying, it needs to be genuine."

Isn't PR fake? "Do you get to know all your clients so...personally?"

She wets her lips, and dammit, I follow that movement

a little too closely. "You're my first client," she admits, wincing as if it's information she hadn't planned to share.

I already knew it, but I understand. That information puts her at a disadvantage. Some people would probably want her off their case because of her lack of experience. But not me.

My lips curve. "So I'm popping your cherry."

Her eyes snap up to me and widen.

I can't help but laugh at the face she makes as she spits and sputters a response that never comes.

"Calm down, Bronte," I muse, sipping my water and leaning back. "I don't do virgins."

I BARELY GET any information out of the twenty-five-year-old over the hour and a half I keep her at the restaurant. I watch her split her food in half, knowing she's taking the leftovers home to have another meal tomorrow. I slip the waiter a fifty to put an extra meal in the bag without her knowledge—chicken parmesan, because the only valuable thing I did learn from her is that poultry is her favorite, especially when it's smothered in cheese and sauce.

I spend the short drive home white-knuckling the steering wheel, angry that I care about her past with her coworker. It was one date, so why the hell do I care? I've been on plenty of dates, if you call what I do "dating." I suppose it's more casual than that. Sex, mostly. It's probably my lack of sex that's aggravating me so much. My appetite for a good orgasm tends to steer my thoughts in directions it wouldn't usually go if I'm without a decent lay for a while.

One thing is true. I'm attracted to Winter. More than I should be. Hell, more than I *want* to be. She's ten years younger than me, with a lot less experience if her embarrassment over the word "virgin" is any indication.

Her innocence makes me hate my body for reacting to her—for liking when she mouths off or dishes out sass. She doesn't look her age. She isn't baby-faced or lacking curves where I like them most, but it still feels dirty.

The shit I've gone through has aged me in ways I don't wish on anybody. My time in foster care shaped me, but not as much as the years I spent with my biological parents in that trailer park. I suppose asking about her past is hypocritical, since I have no intention of divulging anything about mine. It's why I'm cautious about those I let around me. The fewer people who ask questions, the more secrets I can hold on to. And people like Winter, young and curious, would definitely ask questions.

Plus, choosing not to surround myself with younger people means there isn't a constant reminder that I have one foot out the proverbial door in this career. I'm not sixty, but even Tom Brady was considered geriatric before he retired from football in his early forties. Hockey is a brutal sport that does serious damage to the body, and I know my time is coming to an end soon enough. I don't feel like being reminded that I'm not twenty-five anymore and full of hope that the world has more to offer me.

Emaly bombards me with questions the second I walk into my house, breaking me from my train of thought.

"How did the interrogation go? Do we like her? What do we know?"

We. She's always considered us a team, even when she's twice removed from a situation. "I didn't interrogate her," I state, eyeing her as I toss my keys into the bowl in the foyer and head to the kitchen with her hot on my heels. "And *we* didn't learn anything."

Besides her favorite food, which I add to the mental folder with her name on it. Alongside her love for poultry is her appreciation for caffeine and how clumsy she apparently is. Hardly anything to go on.

The long sigh that comes after that is full of defeat. What did I expect? I'd hoped to get information directly from the source before hiring someone to dig into her for me. Is it any of my business? Absolutely not. Has she captured my interest enough to spend the money? Yes.

"Other than her having bad taste in men," I mumble more as an afterthought before chugging half a bottle of water and wiping my mouth off with the back of my hand. I look around. "Did you reorganize my kitchen?"

"It was messy," she says, shrugging. "But back to her bad taste in men. I'd like details. It sounds juicy."

I deadpan, "You need a hobby, Em."

She smiles. "Gossiping *is* my hobby outside of saving kids' lives. And Ronnie is in surgery all day, so you're stuck entertaining me for now."

Lucky me. "I take it you haven't spoken to your parents yet, *Dr. Moskins-Yokav*? Do they even know you're in town?"

She rolls her eyes at my mocking tone, then frowns

when my question sinks in. Emaly claims she's here for me, but I can tell there's something more to her story. She loves me and cares for me, but I recognize the brokenness hiding behind her smile. She's hurting.

So, I indulge her in conversation. "Winter," I tell her, when she makes no effort to give me an answer, "has a coworker who reminds me a little too much of Dr. Porter."

Her wince at the asshat's name who cornered her makes me nod. "Oh."

My jaw clenches as I think about the asswipe's comment mumbled under his breath. I hate the kind of people who assume the only way for women to build their careers is by sleeping with the higher-ups for sway. I hate even more that Winter looked mortified and glassy-eyed from it. He was going to make her *cry*, and I'm not okay with that.

"She went out with him for food," I muse. If he realized that, it probably wasn't a great stroke to his ego. It also didn't stop him from trying to get more from the deal. "Doesn't seem to realize that she's not interested."

Emaly watches me carefully before a small, secretive smile tilts her lips. "And what about you?"

I stand up and give her my back to go through the fridge for nothing in particular. "What about me?"

She snickers. "Are *you* interested? She's blond, isn't she? You like blondes."

My attention whips to her to see her eyebrows wiggle suggestively. "How do you know what her hair color is?"

I'm not about to admit I tried finding her social media to no avail, so I can't help but wonder how she managed to.

"Starrs Strategy's website has professional shots of all their employees," she states, leaning her shin on her propped palm that's leaning on the counter. "I wasn't totally sure if it was Winter you were all bent out of shape over, but I had a feeling. You said she was younger, and the other two women on their team list aren't your type."

I swear, this woman could join the FBI and track people down faster than most trained agents. It's a superpower I'll never understand. "I don't know if I'm impressed or not that you even bothered looking."

"I was curious."

"Why?"

"Because you *hate* when PR people come into your life and try dictating what you can and can't do," she replies with a knowing look. I can't argue with her, and she knows it. "How many times have Ashton and Scott tried convincing you it was the best idea to clean up your online footprint? You always told them to screw off."

I did do that. Scott, my manager, was never happy when I'd hang up after he suggested involving a professional to handle what I liked to call a "hazard spill." Whenever I did something stupid, whether it was being seen out with a woman or getting into fights at bars when guys would be a little too handsy with women, my team would call me up and tell me their plans to get it taken off the internet. Not an easy feat in this day and age. Most people I know hire companies to manage all of their social media pages, but not me. I'm a control freak.

"But you're allowing her to," she concludes, her smile growing into an annoying one.

I hate to point out the obvious, but I do. "I'm allowing them to step in because my career is on the line, Em. Your dad is *pissed.* And while the board might decide to keep me, they still consider me a risk between my age and the fact that they're too new to be riddled with scandal."

The smile on her face drops, along with her shoulders. "But there is no scandal."

I wet my lips. "They don't know that."

They don't know a lot.

I walk around the island and pull her into me. Emaly's mood is shifting to dark territory, and I don't want her to make herself sick. "It's okay," I murmur, kissing the crown of her skull. "It's *going* to be okay."

She starts shaking her head, but I don't want her to argue.

We're quiet for a long time.

Until she hefts out a breath against me and peels away. "I'm sor—"

"Don't," I cut her off. "Don't apologize. This whole thing was my idea, right? We both agreed. What's happening now is the consequence of *my* actions. This isn't your fault."

She wants to disagree, but she's smart enough not to. Instead, she says, "Are you really going to pretend you're not a tiny bit into Winter, though? I can totally see it."

I glare at her.

She blinks up innocently at me. "I'm just saying, I could make that happen for you."

"Emaly," I growl.

She holds up her hands. "Fine, fine. I'll leave it for

now. But I expect all the juicy details the next time you see her."

That is one hundred percent not going to happen.

Now is a good time to turn the tables. "Are you going to tell me the other reason you came? You've barely talked about work, and I know how much you love your kids."

Her kids are her patients. As a surgical oncologist in the pediatric unit in San Diego's best children's hospital, she's surrounded by illness and death. But there are times, not as often as she'd like, where she's also surrounded by remission and hope. The weight on her shoulders has to do with something that happened with a patient, if I had to put money on it.

She evades my eyes. "I don't know if I want to talk about it yet." Her voice is quieter than usual, so I don't push her.

"Okay."

She lets out a small, contemplative sigh before she picks her gaze up. "Work has been…difficult lately. And things with Ronnie have been hard because of it. It's my own fault. I make everything more challenging than it needs to be."

I start to disagree, but she doesn't let me.

"I do," she insists. "Ronnie is upset because I can't be honest with my parents. And I'm upset because I can't help my patients or their families more than I already do. It leaves a lot of strain on our relationship. And then there's you—"

"I'm fine," I remind her.

"Your career is on the line," she says. "Another obstacle

because of me."

This time, I don't let her finish. "Things with Ronnie will work out. And I know you. You go above and beyond for every single patient you have. Their families are lucky to have you assigned to their child's case. And I *am* okay. It will all be fine, Em. I promise."

Sadness dwells in her eyes.

I rub her arm. "It will work out," I repeat one more time, as softly as possible.

Eventually, she nods. And I can see that she's starting to believe it too. "I just needed some space to breathe. To..."

I understand. "You're always welcome here."

"Even if I pester you about cute blondes?"

My cheek twitches. "Even then."

"And make you do facial scrubs with me?"

My skin has never been softer. "Yes."

"And—"

I laugh at her insistence. "You're always welcome here, even when you annoy the hell out of me. Like right now."

"You love me," she replies with a bright smile that washes away the shadows previously on her face.

"Whatever you say, wife."

Her laugh echoes in the hall as she goes to the bedroom she claimed upstairs. "You know I'm right, husband."

CHAPTER SIX

Winter

WEDNESDAY ROLLS AROUND too quickly, and I don't like the nerves pecking at my conscience as my afternoon meeting with Moskins approaches.

When I got home on Monday night, I noticed that my leftovers were joined by two other to-go boxes. I wanted to believe it was a mistake—or maybe a twist of fate that meant I got at least *three* extra meals out of one lunch. But my assumption that the waiter put someone else's order in my bag by accident was quickly dispelled when I saw that the other half of Moskins's lunch was in the third box. It wasn't a coincidence that I wound up with more food than I ordered, especially not after telling him about Cody. Or, evidently, my love for chicken.

Because the second meal is the chicken parmesan, which I didn't want to order at lunch for two reasons. One, because it cost twice as much as the chicken tender basket I'd inevitably gotten. And two, because I didn't want to risk getting the sauce on my shirt and proving to the professional athlete that I am, in fact, a mess.

But there it was, proof that the sarcastic man who I'd sat across from for nearly two hours listened. It was oddly…nice. I blame him and his stupid, thoughtful consideration for the buzzing under my skin since I woke up this morning knowing I'd see him today.

Thankfully, I've managed not to dump coffee on myself. When I walk into the conference room, I'll be stain-free and professional. And maybe, if he doesn't piss me off, I'll even thank him for what he did.

That one act of kindness made me confident my plan for him could work. Because deep down, I think Thomas Moskins is a good guy who pretends to be bad. Why, I'm not sure. I could also be totally wrong. My dating history would indicate that I am a *terrible* judge of character. But that's beside the point.

I gather my things and walk over to Janel's office at the other side of the room, knocking on her open door and smiling when she looks up from her computer. "I'm about to go set up in the conference room. Are you ready?"

She checks her watch and curses under her breath, pushing herself to her feet. "I didn't realize it'd gotten so late."

Janel isn't often frazzled, but she looks discombobulated today. "Is everything okay?"

The small smile she offers me is tired and not at all convincing. "I had a lot of calls to deal with this morning because we're a bit short-staffed."

My brows knit together. "What do you—"

"Come on," she urges, gently pushing me out of her office and guiding me to the conference room. "How are you feeling? Good? Nervous?"

Like I want to pee my pants, is the answer I want to give her. I definitely do not say that though. "I feel great."

My chipper tone is clearly as believable as her phony smile because she gives me an arched brow.

I tone it down. "I'm a little nervous, but I feel good about what I've come up with. It's mostly up to him to agree to do these events. That's going to be the hardest part."

Janel hums her agreement as she unlocks the door and flicks on the lights. "You came up with a solid plan. We haven't even considered partnering with some of these local organizations before."

I blush at the sound of her approval. I'd worked tirelessly to create a list of places for Thomas to make appearances. Organizations that our community appreciates. If they see one of their newest members helping the less fortunate, it could give him a boost that he desperately needs right now.

"Moskins—" I start to say, before Janel's eyebrows dart up at my informal address of him, making me wince. "Er, I mean *Mr.* Moskins. Uh...Thomas—"

"I told you I don't go by that," the man himself says, walking in with his usual scowl. Does he ever smile? He sort of did during lunch. It was more like a smirk, but same difference.

"It's Moskins," he says, dropping into the spot he sat in last time. "I'll accept 'Royal Liege,' though. Once, I was nominated for Sexiest Rookie of the Year, so I'll also answer to that."

Before I can help myself, I ask, "But did you win? Because you can't claim that title if you didn't earn it."

His cheek twitches like he's refraining from smiling,

but he shakes his head. "Alas, I got second place."

I make a thoughtful noise. "Then I guess you're *not* the sexiest rookie of the year."

Janel clears her throat. "Moskins it is then," she says, bringing the conversation away from who is or isn't sexy.

His eyes are on me when he replies, "Good."

I force a smile that feels stiff, and the prickles traveling along my limbs spread to my stomach until heat settles there. This man, who looks far too casual and closed off, is not the same one who bought me food to take home. He's cooler. Stiffer. On guard. A different persona.

What are you hiding? is on the tip of my tongue, but I hold it there until I suffocate my curiosity.

"Hi," I greet, my voice a pitch higher than normal as his eyes remain on me.

So much for the confident professional woman I planned on being today. At least there's no coffee stain.

Moskins doesn't greet me back as he leans back in his chair and drums his fingers along the edge of the table. "Let's see these grand plans that you spoke so highly of during our last meeting. My team is talking about benching me during our preseason games, and I don't want that to happen for obvious reasons. So these better be good."

No pressure there, I grumble to myself. What happened to the playful version of him from thirty seconds ago? Did he forget Janel was in the room? Is this a big game for him? The longer I'm around him, the more questions I accumulate.

I walk over to him and place the sheet down with a schedule of events over the next month and a half. Six weeks isn't a lot of time to work with, but it's the only availability he has between now and when the Fairbanks Fireflies start their preseason matches, according to the game schedule on their website. I had to cross-reference to triple-check the dates worked and confirm with his manager, Scott.

Moskins scans the sheet with an unreadable expression before I see the slightest movement in his jaw. "These are charities," he states, finally glancing up from the paper. "And...Furrever Home?"

He's not addressing Janel.

I stand tall and nod. "Furrever Home is an animal shelter. Fairbank's largest one."

"I would hope so," he says. "It'd be an unfortunate name for a nursing home."

I ignore that remark. "The rest are local nonprofit organizations that mean something to our city. They've done a lot of good in our community—helped the less fortunate, offered comfort and support when people needed it the most. If you want people to take you seriously, then you need to participate in the culture here. Perhaps if you do it first, you can convince the rest of your team to hold an annual event at some of them to raise awareness together. You know, hand out holiday meals. That sort of thing. Consistency is good for image."

Moskins blinks. "Is this a Hallmark movie or something? I'm a professional hockey player, not a kitchen server. I've donated to charities before. This is nothing new."

"That's where I disagree," I tell him calmly, earning a

skeptical look from him. "There's a difference between signing your name on a check for a hundred dollars and actually *showing up* to participate in events that benefit people. Everybody needs to see you in action to understand that you're *willing* to step up."

"I write checks with far more zeroes than that, sweetheart."

There's that name again.

At least he's not calling me kid. I don't react to the pet name as much as I want to. I also refuse to let myself soak in the fuzzy feeling that settles into my stomach hearing it, despite warning him that I don't like it. "Good for you. I'm sure the organizations you've donated your hard-earned money to are thankful. But this isn't just about a tax break anymore. It's about making an actual difference. You can start by giving up your weekend plans to serve food at the soup kitchen this weekend."

Janel, who's been watching us like she's tuning in to a tennis match, steps in. "The community believes in building strong foundations. Now that you're signed with a professional team attached to our city, it means showing them you want to do the same."

His jaw tics. "What if I don't want to build strong foundations here?"

Before Janel can answer, I say, "Then you made a mistake by signing your contract."

My boss doesn't scold me. Mostly because she probably would have said the same thing. She's never one to mince words, even if she does it lightly. Janel might not kiss our clients' asses, but she takes a more political stance as the person in charge.

"It's no secret that you've given a lot of money to charity," I add, sitting down and pointing to my folder. I've done my research on him. I've seen the praise from old headlines that emphasized how much he's given away. But that was then. This is now. "But Fairbanks is the type of place that does more than throw money around. We care about our people. When something happens, we come together. When tragedy strikes—" I swallow, remembering what Fairbanks did for my sister and me when my parents were killed. "They help their own. You signing with the Fireflies means you're part of our community now. They'll be a lot more receptive to you if they see you're willing to show up the way others do."

When Kourtney and I lost our parents, the local churches and food banks donated meals and groceries to help us get by. A few of the neighbors even raised funds from the community to cover the first year's bills, since they knew my sister was taking guardianship while in college.

Fairbanks is a small city with a huge heart, and I can't imagine being anywhere else. Not even with the sad history carved into the town and city borders.

Janel knows that I'm referring to my family and gives me a comforting smile before turning to Moskins. "It's not often we send our clients out on this many appearances, but she has a point. With the Fireflies being new to the area and bringing a lot more attention to our city, it's going to be important for the team to make a lasting impact. If the players are seen out mingling with long-time residents, it'll go a long way. To the people here, you won't be the headlines that the media make you out to be. You'll simply be one of us."

I can see him mulling it over. He doesn't want to do it. If he says no, we can't force him. But I think he'll be making a mistake if he rejects this plan.

Apparently, he thinks so too. "The team's board is up my ass to make good on polishing their reputation in the media," he tells us, staring down at the paper. "I may not like this, but I don't think I have another choice at this point. If I keep pissing them off, it's only a matter of time before they find a reason to push me out."

It's a selfish reason, but one that gives us the green light. So, I don't care why he's going through with it, as long as it allows me to move forward.

Before I can say anything, Moskins pins me with a look and slowly curls his lips up. "I have a condition."

The victorious excitement within me quickly deflates.

It's Janel who slowly asks, "What is your condition?"

He points to me. "You have to do these events with me. If they're that important, surely you wouldn't want to miss out."

I stare at him for a brief second before shaking my head. "That is *not* a good idea."

"Too good for a little charity work?" he quips, trying to bait me.

Unfortunately, it works. "That is not it at all. If you haven't forgotten, you being photographed with women is what got you into this mess. The last thing you need is to be pictured with me for the internet to run wild with."

Even the thought makes my skin crawl. There's a reason I deactivated my social media accounts. They're more trouble than they're worth. The last time I braved one of my platforms, it was nothing but negativity. Pass.

"While you have a point," Janel tells me, tapping her fingers on the table thoughtfully, "it may actually not be a horrible idea to go with him. As a point person. Someone who's familiar with the community and can make the introductions."

I was already going to connect Moskins with the right people. That doesn't mean I have to be there to hold his hand through it.

"Yeah, Winter," Moskins goads, that annoying smirk still high and tight on his stupid, attractive face. Why does he have to be good-looking? His jaw could cut glass, and his eyes could make even Mother Teresa drop her drawers. "I'll need someone who's familiar with this small-town Hallmark community you seem to love so much."

He's mocking me. I get it. Maybe he wasn't hugged enough as a child and doesn't understand what it's like to be part of a community. Perhaps he has an aversion to kindness because he's never truly experienced it before. "You can make fun of Fairbanks all you want, but you're going to realize that they'll see right through your little facade as fast as I did. So when we go to the soup kitchen on Saturday, you'd better slap a smile on that pretty boy face and do your best to seem like you want to be there. Or this will all be for nothing."

His smirk quickly drops, and his infamous scowl returns.

Janel clears her throat. "Any questions?" she asks Moskins.

His nostrils flare. "Looks like I have all the information I need right here," he says, swiping the paper from the table and standing. "I'll make sure to meet you at eleven sharp, princess. With a giant fucking smile and all."

With that, he walks out the door.

First *sweetheart*, and now *princess*.

I got under his skin.

The thought makes me smile.

"Well, that went..." Janel's words fade. "I don't know how that went, actually. Can I even trust you two to be alone together?"

I gape at her. "It was *your idea* to back his brilliant condition," I defend, dumbfounded. "I would have been fine organizing everything and staying in the background."

Amusement takes over her face as she leans back in her chair. "If I didn't back him, do you think he would have agreed? Men like Mr. Moskins—*Moskins*—prefer things to go their way as much as possible."

She's probably right. If she'd pushed back on that, he could have told us to fuck off. "Fine, you have me there. And we won't be alone anyway. There are always at least ten other people at the soup kitchen every weekend."

That seems to relieve whatever internal tension is building in her shoulders. "All right. I trust you with this, Winter. It's him I'm a little iffy with. He likes to get a reaction. And you..."

I feed into it. "I can hold my own."

She stands, smiling at me. "I know you can. I'm just

afraid you'll eat him alive before we can officially get paid."

I snort. "Now I see your real concern."

Janel brushes my arm. "You'll be okay going there, right? I know those organizations are very close to your heart."

That's why I chose them. "They need a face like his to get more media attention. It's a win-win. He'll be seen as the golden boy, and donations will flood in from hockey fans."

My motives are selfish too, but I don't feel bad about them one bit.

She hums. "Okay."

That's all she says, and I wonder what the twinkle in her eye means when we walk out of the conference room.

IT'S FIVE MINUTES to eleven when I check my watch for the fourth time since pulling up to Our Open Table, Fairbank's largest soup kitchen that serves over twenty thousand meals a year to those in need.

A message from my sister pops up on my watch's screen, making me smile and pull my phone out.

Kourt: *Good luck today, and give Vinnie a big hug for me*

Me: *Will do!*

Bubbles appear at the bottom of the screen, but I yelp when knuckles rap against the window and startle me. I drop my phone between the seat and center console, cursing as I peek through the crack where it's laying on the dirty carpet. Is that a Cheerio? I haven't had cereal in at least three months.

Man, I really need to vacuum this car.

I'm broken from the thought when I see Moskins staring at me from outside the car door. He's expressionless as I turn the ignition off and step out, offering him a sheepish smile.

"I dropped my phone," I tell him, gesturing toward my seat. "Give me a second, and we'll head in."

Before he says a word, I'm crawling back inside and trying to reach the awkward place it slipped. I cuss as I get my hand jammed before victoriously pulling it out.

"Got it!" I tell him, waving it in the air as I turn around.

Moskins isn't looking at my phone.

He's looking where my ass was.

"Were you staring at my butt?" I accuse him, frowning.

There's no shame on his face as he shrugs. "It was there," is all he says. "Are we doing this or not? I don't have all day."

Actually, he does. His schedule is clear for this event. Janel spoke to his agent and manager to confirm as much. "Come on," I say, walking toward the entrance. "I'll introduce you to the owners. Their names are Beverly and Vincent, but they go by Bev and Vinnie. You'll love them. This place is their passion project."

I'm not paying attention to whether he's listening, because I'm excited to see the people who acted like grandparents to Kourtney and me. If it weren't for them, my sister and I would have struggled more than we did. A lot of people refer to them as Fairbanks's grandparents.

As soon as I step in, I'm wrapped in the same cozy atmosphere that smells like lavender, sugar, and spices. It's a good thing I ate this morning, or my stomach would be rumbling right now. Then Bev would force me to sit down, lecture me about being too skinny, and make me eat at least half a meal before letting me help.

I smile and wave at a few familiar faces lingering at the tables off to the side, already eating their late morning meals. "Hi, Abe. Hi, Babette."

The elderly couple lifts their hands in waves as I make my way to the back, where I know the main group of volunteers is.

I can feel a pair of eyes on me the entire time, but I pay no mind to Moskins. He'll see how tight-knit everyone here is and understand why it's easy to remember names.

When I push the kitchen door open, I ignore the photographer and journalist setting up in the corner. Instead, my focus goes to the white-haired woman whose smile is big and broad and wrinkling her aged face.

"There she is," Bev greets, opening her arms for me.

I ditch Moskins by the door and walk over to hug Beverly. Warmth fills my chest the second she wraps her arms around me. For someone so petite, her strength is overwhelming. I swear one of my ribs pops from the pressure she squeezes me at, but I don't mind at all. I love hugs. I miss them. My parents used to be the best huggers in the world, and that trait didn't rub off on Kourtney. She's not unloving—she's the most loving person I know. She's just not a physical person, which makes my heart a little sad sometimes.

"Hi, Bev," I say into her shoulder, absorbing a few more seconds of warmth. "Thank you for letting us come here today."

Beverly and Vincent Walters used to be a power couple in New York City until they retired and moved to Fairbanks fifteen years ago. They've had a summer house and family ties here most of their lives, and wanted to give back to the community they've considered their home after years of successful stock trading in the Big Apple. Their son, daughter, and all their grandchildren are here too. The entire family, kids included, will come during the holidays to help serve huge turkey and ham dinners for those who need it most.

Since Kourtney got married, she doesn't come as often. Apparently, Brad doesn't like her being around "*these people*," as he refers to them. But nothing could make me stay away. It doesn't matter if it's Thanksgiving or Christmas, I'm bundled up in my holiday best with a smile on my face and a ladle in my hand.

Screw Brad.

"You and your friends are always welcome here, sweetie," she answers, pinching my cheeks lightly.

I don't bother correcting her about who the man behind me is. If she wants to believe we're friends, then I won't tell her otherwise. It's easier than explaining the real reason the six-foot-three hockey player is standing in her kitchen. When I suggested this little setup, she knew it would involve a camera and a journalist, but she didn't ask any questions. Knowing Bev, she'll try getting a story out of him at some point today. She's good at that.

To my surprise, Moskins appears beside me with his hand extended. "It's nice to meet you, Bev. I'm Moskins."

Bev is five feet tall on a good day, so it's comical watching her look up, up, up at him as they shake hands. "It's nice to meet you, dear. We're always happy to have extra hands on deck. It's been a busy summer for us."

Vinnie comes in with his usual purple frilly apron tied around his waist. It was a joke gift from Bev that she never thought he'd wear. But he dons it proudly every single day with a smile on his face.

"I see you brought an entourage today," Vinnie greets me, pulling me in for a one-armed hug and kiss on the temple. He pulls back to study Moskins. "He looks sturdy. I have some boxes I need moved around, and he looks like he can get the job done."

"Moskins," I say, "this is Vinnie. Vinnie, this is Thomas Moskins. He is at your service today. We both are."

The plans for today are simple. After we get a good few photos of him serving the clientele, we'll talk to the journalist to answer some questions and spend the rest of the time helping out. It's clear-cut. Easy. As long as he plays along.

Vinnie shakes Moskins's hand. "It's nice to meet you, son. Welcome to Our Open Table. We appreciate you taking time out of your busy day to help us out."

The familiarity in Vinnie's words tells me he knows exactly who Moskins is. I suppose I'm not surprised. He's always talking about sports to whoever engages him in conversation.

"Kourt says hi," I tell Vinnie, seeing the fondness on his face grow. As someone who took in his own siblings after their parents left, he has a soft spot for my sister. He sees a lot of himself in her stubborn demeanor.

"She better stop in and see me soon," he says, pinning me with a look. "Her boy too. It's been too long."

I know it's not Brad he wants to see, but Luca. I'm pretty sure we're on the same wavelength when it comes to believing Kourtney can do way better than the man she married. But neither of us is willing to say it because she's unyielding about her choices.

Moskins watches me as I smile at the older man. "I'll drag them here myself."

He tweaks my nose the same way he did when I was thirteen, before turning to Moskins. "Shall we get started? The lunch rush is going to come any minute. Best to prep."

Ten minutes later, I'm being glared at by Moskins as he adjusts his hair net and rubber gloves. The photographer is still setting up, getting ready to snap some photos, so I gesture toward my lips and trace a smile in the air for him to remember he can't scowl in the pictures.

It only makes him scowl harder.

I snort. "It's policy," I tell him.

When Vinnie passed him a hair net, Moskins stared at it for a solid minute before my favorite eighty-year-old said, "It's for your head," before walking off to help someone else.

I point to my head. "I have one too."

"But you have hair," he grumbles.

My eyes go to his head, which very much has brown hair on it. It's shorter on the sides and longer on the top, but it's still hair. "So do you. And nobody likes getting hair in their food, *Tommy.*"

The name makes his shoulders stiffen. Then he grumbles under his breath something unintelligible about looking ridiculous. I don't pay much attention to his complaint. Mostly because it's not true. A tiny hairnet and rubber gloves don't make him any less attractive, like I wish they did. He's still hot.

Not that I'd ever say that out loud.

"All right," the photographer says. "I'm ready whenever you guys are. I got the list of shots to get, and then I'll get out of the way so you can go about your day."

Janel got a list of photos we can take of Moskins approved by his team, so they know we're not going to make him randomly strip down for the cameras. While I'm sure Thomas Moskins serving the homeless in his underwear would garner a lot of attention, it's not the kind we want.

Plus, Vinnie is strict about proper clothing in the kitchen. If he doesn't allow anyone without a hairnet to serve, I can't imagine he'd let someone without pants in his kitchen.

Bev, on the other hand…

She'd totally be okay with that.

"What's that smile for?" Moskins asks, making me realize I have a very detailed mental image of him in his underwear in my head. Tight briefs on thick thighs and all.

I wave the pleasant image away. Far, far away. "Nothing. Let's start! We'll get a few shots of you alone, then you with some workers. Everyone here has agreed to be photographed and signed consent forms to be posted."

"What about you?" he questions as they open the doors to the kitchen for people to start forming a line at the end.

I rock on my heels. "What about me?"

"You're supposed to be doing this with me."

"I'm here, aren't I?" I quip, gesturing around us.

His eyes narrow. "Are you just going to watch or make yourself useful?"

Bev steps in, winding her arm around mine. "Winnie always makes herself useful when she's here. Her presence alone makes everybody lighter."

I beam at her compliment. "I try." When I turn back to Moskins, I can't help but see an odd bit of...softness to his face when he looks between Beverly and me. "After you get some solo pictures, I'll hop in and help serve. Then you can go help Vinnie move whatever he needs in the back. They get bulk shipments every Saturday morning, so it's probably heavy items that he'll struggle with. It's good if you can help him out with that."

Bev nods along. "His back isn't what it used to be."

I smile sadly at her. "We'll help," I promise. "I don't want him throwing it out again. He was cranky sitting at home for a week to recover last time."

She groans. "I swear I was two seconds from suffocating that man. The only thing that stopped me was the realization that I wouldn't survive in prison. And orange is not my color. It would wash me right out."

I'm not sure all prisons have orange jumpsuits, but

that's beside the point.

The snort that comes out of me is big and embarrassing, making my cheeks warm when I see Moskins's raised brows at the sound.

I direct my focus to the photographer as people make their way down the line, getting soup from one volunteer, rolls from Moskins, and vegetables from a third person. I nod at him to start taking pictures, making sure I'm out of frame.

Despite agreeing to do this, I still don't want to be in any photos. It would fuel a fire I'm trying to put out. I'm sure his team would agree.

Forty minutes later, the photographer has seemingly gotten everything he needs and shakes both Moskins's and my hand before leaving us. I stepped into the serving line twenty minutes in to make conversation with some of the locals I've spoken with before. Asking how their days are. Asking about their kids. Little things that seem to brighten their days.

One thing I learned a long time ago is that you never know how far kindness can go. One smile can make somebody's day. One compliment can save somebody's life. So no matter how badly I want to let my inner demons win, I smile anyway.

Moskins watches me contentedly throughout each interaction, sometimes chipping in and even offering his own greetings once he warms up to those walking in. I'm sure he's not used to conversing with the people that Our Open Table brings, but he seems like a natural as time goes on.

"This one," Ridley, a sixty-something man who frequents Our Open Table, says to Moskins while pointing to me, "is a troublemaker. Best watch out for her."

I gasp dramatically at his playful accusation. "I thought we were friends, Ridley."

"You beat me at cards last week," he harrumphs, accepting the roll I pass him with my tongs. "Haven't forgiven you yet."

I laugh at his theatrics. "It was a no-stakes game of Go Fish. If it makes you feel better, we can have a rematch soon."

His eyes light up. "Today?"

I smile sadly at him. "I can't today. But I'll swing by next weekend. How's that?"

Ridley is a kind soul who lost his fortune to addiction. He's been clean for years, but never quite got his life back in order. It's better than it was, but something is holding him back from truly putting the pieces together permanently.

He hefts out a sigh. "Fine. I'll see you next week then."

I wave him off and frown when I see the skeptical stare Moskins gives me. "What?"

"How often do you come here?" he asks.

I lift a shoulder. "Every week if I can. Sometimes every two. It depends on how busy I am. Janel usually offers me overtime if I come into the office on weekends to help her, and the money is decent."

He blinks.

Blinks again.

The line is pretty much gone now because everybody is

eating, with a few stragglers coming in here and there.

His weighted stare makes me shift on my feet uncomfortably. "What? Why are you looking at me like that?"

"I'm trying to figure you out," he says casually.

I make a face. "Why?"

"Because you intrigue me."

Despite the tingling in my stomach, I don't like the sound of that. "I'm not that hard to figure out, Moskins."

He huffs out a laugh. "On the contrary."

We serve a few more people, making idle greetings and small talk with them before we're alone again.

That's when I quietly say, "I never got to thank you for the food. You didn't have to do that."

He doesn't deny what he did, which I'm grateful for. In fact, he doesn't say anything in response.

I lick my lips. "Why did you do that?"

I've been wondering ever since I realized what he'd done. It hasn't bothered me, even though I don't like feeling as though I owe somebody. He'd pissed me off too much to say anything about it during our last meeting, but he's been surprisingly great today. Humble. Kind. It could all be an act, but I don't think it is.

That is, until he replies, "Didn't want you to have to go on any more dates. You clearly don't have a great radar for decent men."

I glare at him.

He smirks.

And then Vinnie comes and pulls him away to help him in the stock room. Which is probably a good thing. Because I'm two seconds away from throwing a dinner roll at his head.

At the end of the lunch rush, I help Bev and a few others take the empty trays and plates to the sinks in the back to be washed. Cleanup between meals usually takes at least an hour, but we've become a well-oiled machine in our routine to get it done as quickly as possible.

Bev nudges me with her shoulder as we scrub plates in the soapy water. "He's quite the looker."

I know who she's referring to, but I don't play into whatever this is. "Don't let Vinnie hear you say that or he'll ban Moskins from stepping foot in here again."

Not that I think he'll come back willingly after this obligation is over.

She chuckles. "I'm just saying, you've got a good eye. And he was a natural today. Some people will come in and judge those we serve for what they wear or what they look like. He didn't have an ounce of judgment in his eyes. I don't know his story, but I bet it's an interesting one."

I'm surprised she didn't try getting it from him today. In the few hours we've been here, she'd only come over to praise him for his work. And that one time she told Thomas that he had a nice smile and should do it more often. I swear I saw his cheeks turn pink. It was kind of...cute.

Nope. Nope. Nope. Nope.

There is nothing cute about Thomas Moskins and an overinflated ego. That kind of charm is exactly why he's here. It's what he uses to get girls into his bed. I will not be next.

"This is a professional relationship," I explain to her

softly. It serves as a good reminder to me as well. "Nothing more."

She hums like she doesn't believe me, continuing to wash the dishes. After a minute, she says, "That's a real shame."

And I think, *I know.*

CHAPTER SEVEN

Winter

GROCERY SHOPPING IS the seventh level of hell that reminds me of two things: that I am horrible at math, and that I am broke.

Cheeks flaming as I try to recount the bills in my hand, I clear my throat. "Isn't the chicken on sale? There's a yellow sticker on them for half off, but I'm not sure it rang up that way."

The teenager sighs heavily, looking like he wants to be here as little as I do. "Do you have a coupon?"

A coupon? Was I supposed to bring one?

My voice hitches, pointing to the bright yellow sticker that reads NEW MARKDOWN in bold black letters. "But there's a sticker..."

God, this is so embarrassing. I double-checked all the prices as I crossed items off my list. I'm good at figuring out how to budget. It's something Kourtney and I became pros at because we had no choice. Math is not my strong suit, but being frugal is. I should have enough money for this.

"Well, the sticker isn't scanning right," the boy informs me dryly. "So do you have the money or not?"

I swallow nervously. For someone who majored in

communications, I am *so* not a people person. My confrontation button only activates around six-foot hockey players, apparently, not pimply-faced teenage boys. Sigh. "Can you talk to someone about that? Like a manager who can fix the price in the system. Technically, you're supposed to sell things as marked, or it's considered faulty advertising."

I hear someone in the line grumble, "You have got to be kidding me."

It only makes my cheeks grow hotter as I admit defeat. Swallowing my pride, I stand a little taller and decide that my dignity is not worth a package of half-off chicken breasts that are probably days away from going bad. "Can you take off the chicken and yogurt please?"

The same person cusses under his breath behind me, making me feel bad for holding everybody up. I'm about to apologize for no reason other than pure embarrassment when I hear, "Shut it, asshole. We've all been there before. Move."

Then a small dark-haired woman who looks vaguely familiar appears in front of me, shoving the bulky man aside with her hip. Her smile is bright. "I've got you. How much do you need?"

She's pulling money out of her wallet before I even know what's happening. "Oh my God. No way! I can't—"

"You can," she reassures, looking from her wallet to me with soft eyes. "It's fine. I insist. And not because I'm an impatient dick like *some* people, but because I've totally been in your shoes before. Med school was brutal to me. I counted change to make ends meet a lot."

When she realizes I'm not going to budge, the cashier says, "She needs twenty more."

I watch the stranger pass him a twenty-dollar bill before closing my eyes.

A hand rests on my arm. "Don't be embarrassed. I'm all about passing it on. I've had people do some really amazing things for me in life, so I like paying it forward."

I open my eyes and swallow, having to force a wobbly smile. "Thank you. I..." I don't know what to say. "You didn't have to do that. I appreciate it."

She takes the change from the teenager who seems glad to be done with me. "No problem. Seriously."

After my bags are loaded in the cart, and I thank the stranger for the umpteenth time while avoiding eye contact with the rest of the line, I make my way out to my 2004 Subaru Outback with way too many miles on it. It takes everything in me not to soak in my wounded pride as it simmers in my chest. I suppose things could have been worse. At least I didn't have a card rejected like I did at the dollar store once. The woman who'd been standing behind me that day snickered as I walked out with nothing I'd come there for. All because I'd forgotten to cancel my free trial to an audiobook app. I've made it a point to mark on my calendar when to cancel things since.

I remind myself that payday is coming next week, so I'll be fine until then. I have food for the week, gas in the car, and all my other bills are paid for the month.

"It could be worse," I whisper to myself, cementing the sentiment in my head as I roll the cart into the corral.

I'm halfway back to my car when I hear a familiar voice

call out, "Hey! Wait a second!"

Looking over my shoulder, I see the woman from the store jogging toward me with her own bag of groceries. I swallow down my embarrassment and try offering her the same smile she's giving me. "Hi," I say, rubbing my arm. "Thank you again for what you did in there. If you have Venmo, I can pay you back when I get paid on Friday. I'll be good for the money."

She rolls her pretty brown eyes, and it's a playful gesture that seems light-hearted. "I meant what I said. I've been there, and I know how tough it is to accept help. It was only twenty dollars. You do *not* need to pay me back."

Shifting on my weight, I loosen a sigh. For some people, twenty dollars isn't a big deal. I can't wait until the day I can go grocery shopping and pick out whatever I want without having to look at the price tag or weekly paper for coupons.

"I'm usually better at calculating how much groceries will be, but they must have increased their prices again." Despite what she says, I can't help but add, "Are you sure I can't pay you back somehow?"

She goes to answer, probably to tell me no again, then stops herself. I'm not sure what she's thinking, or why there's a small smile slowly curling her lips as she stares at me. "Actually," she tells me, making me nervous, "I have an idea. We should go get coffee. It can be quick, so you can get your food home and put away."

I treat myself to coffee twice a month, and I splurged twice already. Granted, one of those times left me wearing half of the drink, but still. I refuse to be ashamed about my budgeting tactics because it's how I survive, but I don't want anybody—even a stranger—to think it's weird.

So, I fake it 'til I make it. "Sure." It's the least I can do if this is all she wants.

She points toward the café across the street. "Want to walk there so we can keep our cars parked here? I'd love to chat."

I'm not used to a stranger being so personable. I give her the briefest once-over to figure out why she looks familiar, but it isn't coming to me. She's beautiful—her porcelain skin is flawless, and her round, dark brown eyes match her nearly black, shoulder-length hair. She's shorter than me by a couple of inches, which makes me feel tall for a change at five feet three. I'm average compared to her. Average height. Average appearance. My blond hair is thinner but longer. My green eyes are brighter, but narrower. And I lack the same curves she has—mostly because food is expensive and I've got student loans that chew up most of my paycheck every month, because the scholarships I got only covered a minimal fraction of my tuition.

Still, I have no idea where I know her from.

And she must notice that curiosity. Because she sighs and says, "I get it now. You're pretty. And you have a kind soul. I can tell."

My brows pinch at the comment.

Before I can ask what she's talking about, she winds the arm not weighed down with a grocery bag around mine and starts guiding us to the coffee shop. "My husband always had a good eye," she says as we approach the glass doors with coffee beans painted on them with their hours in white lettering.

I frown. "Your husband?"

Her smile grows as she opens the door and looks at me. "Thomas Moskins."

My heart drops as I freeze in the middle of the doorway.

That's why she looks familiar.

Emaly Moskins-Yokav is Thomas Moskins's wife. I saw a few photos of them together while I was going through his file. Most of the images are old social media posts that are filtered with sappy posts attached to them.

And she knows me. What could she possibly know about me though? Unless she thinks…

"Oh my God. I-I—" I sputter my words, forcing myself to shake my head. "He and I aren't like that. We're not—"

"Sleeping together?" she guesses, bemusement dancing in her eyes. "I know. Come on, I need a caffeine kick. I've been exhausted adjusting to Eastern time again."

She tugs me in when my feet refuse to move, and I have no choice but to follow her. We wind up in line, and tension builds in my shoulders as I wait for whatever this is to unfold.

Emaly looks up at the order board and scans the options with the same contentment that's been on her face this whole time.

What the hell is happening?

When it's our turn, she pulls me up to the young woman at the cash register. "I'll have a large caramel macchiato with whipped cream, please. What are you getting, Winter? It's on me."

The sound of my name on her lips seems so familiar that it takes me off guard. "I, um…" I wet my lips and wince at my awkwardness. This whole situation is so confusing. "Just tap water for me. Thanks."

Emaly's smile slips a fraction like she wants to tell me to get something else, but I'm grateful when she doesn't as she hands over her card to pay.

It's not until we're sitting down at a table in the corner that she giggles. "You can breathe. I'm not here to attack you or dump my drink on you."

I toy with the cup of water they gave me. "I don't really understand what's going on right now. Did you know who I was in the grocery store?"

She shakes her head, wincing as she rubs her temple. "Not right away. It wasn't until I looked at you for a minute that it clicked. You look pale. Are you okay?"

I take a sip of my water. To stall. And because I feel parched suddenly. This woman is married to a man riddled with adultery scandals that I've been hired to fix, and she knows my name. That's not a coincidence. Does she think I can help her? Feed her information? Help seek vengeance?

Emaly starts digging through her bag and produces a bottle of Advil. "Sorry," she apologizes with a shy smile. "I've got the worst headache."

I notice the slight shake to her hands as she tries opening the cap, so I reach out to help her. She accepts the bottle and cap graciously, pouring two pills into her hand and swallowing them with her drink.

Clearing my throat, I squirm in my seat. "I have an NDA that tells me I can't speak to anyone about your husband," I explain slowly. "Not even spouses or next of kin."

The chortle she gives me is half-snort, half-laugh as she dumps the pill bottle back into her bag and settles in her seat. "I figured as much. But don't worry, I wasn't going to try making you give me any information on him. Actually, it's *me* who wants to offer *you* some intel that I think can help."

I blink at her. "Like…For revenge?"

That has to be what this is, right? The scorned wife goes to someone to feed them information on their cheating husband. But if she really wanted to do that, why not go to the press directly? Media would have a field day with any information she'd share with them on Moskins. I'm sure TMZ has reached out to her numerous times before to offer her a good payout.

Her grin widens. "I can see why you'd think that, but no. Our situation is a bit complicated. And I'm not really at liberty to say how because that goes deeper than we have time for me to explain. But I want you to know that he's more than he seems. He comes off as a dick, but he's not. Not really."

Should I be entertaining this? It can't be good, considering it's a conflict of interest. Or is it? He's my client, who I'm tasked to get into people's good graces. Who better to help me with that than his own *wife*?

So, I bite. "He wears a mask," I reply.

It's not a question, but an observation. He was good

with everyone at the soup kitchen. He did something nice for me. But he's snarky. Unfiltered. Sometimes, I can't tell which version of him is the real one. Can *she*?

Emaly nods. "I blame his manager and agent for a lot of that. Ever since he was a rookie, he's had to present himself in a certain way in public. And when you're young, it's easy to mold yourself into what people think you are. And people see him as a closed off, entitled playboy. He's run with his reputation because it's easier than convincing people otherwise."

Is she saying that his reputation is false? I've seen the proof. "If that's the case, then I feel bad for him. But my job isn't to deep dive into his psyche, it's just to make him look…better than he has been."

You know, where it looks like he isn't cheating on you? Is she really not going to say anything about that? You'd think she would. If I were in her shoes, I'd be livid. Once, when a guy broke up with me, I'd let my emotions win and posted that he had a small penis on an anonymous forum. Kourtney and my first taste of alcohol may have influenced that decision. Needless to say, he'd been pissed about it, and I took down the post a few days after the damage was done.

But Emaly doesn't seem like the type. According to the articles I read and the research I dug into, she's never commented on his affairs or scandals. There's nothing about her opinion regarding their relationship that paints him in a bad light. I'd bet money, as little as I might have, that it's because Moskins's agent convinced her not to.

"I can see it on your face," she says gently, watching me

a little too closely. "You believe the side of him that everybody else does. I get it. He's a great actor. But you'll see. He's not that way. He's different."

"They always say they're different, Win," Kourtney says, passing me another tissue so I stop using my shirt to dry my tears. "Men will literally say that two seconds before sticking their dick into another woman. Trust me, he isn't worth it."

Those words hit me like a brick. I'd sworn to my sister that my ex, my first real love, was different. It'd been a rocky relationship that ended with him cheating on me because I wouldn't sleep with him and me drunkenly posting online about his penis. Which I'd never actually seen. But I had thought, naively, that he was the infamous one so many people seek to find.

Turns out, he was just a douchebag who wound up getting another girl pregnant while we were seeing each other. They had three kids, got married not long after, and are divorced now.

Karma is a bitch.

"Look," I tell Emaly. "It's not my position to see him a certain way. He's my client. So whether he is one way or not doesn't matter to me."

Thomas Moskins is a paycheck.

A means to an end.

He's not my friend. Not my confidant.

I don't owe him any benefit of the doubt.

Emaly frowns. "It's not my place to say, but I think you'll be pleasantly surprised if you get the chance to know him."

This whole conversation is giving me whiplash. Why

does she even care? Why would she want me to get to know her husband? So I won't judge *her*? So I won't wonder why she stays with him? It's none of my business.

"That's the thing, Emaly." My smile wavers as I sit straighter. "I don't want to."

She nods, looking down at her drink.

Did I upset her? I shouldn't care, but I do.

Her sigh is light. "Okay. I just wanted to say that he's a good guy. Not many people see the soft side of him like I do. Maybe not teddy bear soft but…" A tiny smile plays on her lips as her eyes brighten. "But more like a cute bear cub."

Her comparison makes me snort before I can stop myself. "Sorry," I apologize, covering my face when I see her grin. "I wasn't expecting you to say that."

She shrugs. "Like I said, Thomas is a mystery to a lot of people. But he's transparent to those he lets get to know him."

Well, that won't be me. "We'll only be working together for a short amount of time before he starts his season. Hopefully, my job will be done by then."

She hums thoughtfully before reaching into her purse and pulling out a piece of paper and a pen. I watch curiously as she writes something down before sliding it to me. "If you decide you ever want to know more, that's my number. *And* his."

Her lips twitch upward as mine part in shock at the two lines of digits in front of me.

If Janel knew I got a client's number, even indirectly, she would *not* be happy. God only knows what would happen if Cody found out. Although I haven't seen him at work lately, I know he would use this to fuel his accusations that I got this case because I'm sleeping with Moskins.

Emaly slides off her seat and squeezes my arm once lightly. "It was nice formally meeting you, Winter. I'll see you around."

She says it so confidently, it makes me wonder where we'd possibly see each other.

Emaly starts walking away and stumbles slightly. I'm able to catch her arm to steady her, earning me an apologetic smile form her. "Sorry," she says, squeezing her eyes shut. "Got up too quickly."

Her voice sounds off, and her lips fight a frown as she rolls her shoulders, releases a deep breath, and rubs her temple.

"Are you all right?" I ask.

She nods, wetting her lips. "I will be" is the last thing she says to me.

She's still rubbing her temple when she disappears from the coffee shop. I glance down at the paper, wondering what to do. Then, despite my better judgment, I slide it into my purse.

CHAPTER EIGHT

Moskins

I MUST BE going deaf, because there's no way I'm hearing her right. "Pardon—the fuck—me?" I ask my wife, staring skeptically at her.

Her smile is sheepish. "I finally told my parents I'm in town, so they want to have dinner. The four of us."

The four of us. Together. This sounds like what my nightmares are made of.

I stop washing the dishes to give her my full attention. "Are you sure that's a good idea? I'm still on your dad's shit list. Maybe you should go without me. Or tell them you have a headache."

It isn't like the last thing would be a lie. When she got home yesterday, she was so pale I knew she had one. She'd barely said two sentences before curling up in my bed with the lights off and windows blacked out. It'd been hours before she came out back to her usual self.

"I'm fine now," she insists, brushing off the valid concern.

Emaly has been full of good ideas lately. Like giving both of our numbers to the blonde who I've been having repetitive sex dreams about. Last night, I woke up hard as steel after a vivid scene involving me bending Winter over with a toy against her pussy and velvet rope securing her wrists behind her back. She'd been begging me to fuck her, and I'd woken up right before getting to the grand finale.

I'd had to wrap my hand around my cock and take care of the problem myself, coming harder than I have in a while. I imagined her naked in my bedroom and soaking my sheets. Her sweet face had been contorted with pleasure, and her body was writhing for more.

I'm not mad that Emaly gave her my number. In fact, I'm intrigued to see if she'll use it. So far, it's been two days with no contact other than an email she copied her boss on regarding our plans for Friday to attend an event hosted by the local animal shelter. Apparently, images of me holding puppies are supposed to simultaneously clean up my image *and* get some of the animals adopted. I don't get it, but I'm not about to pass up spending a handful of hours petting dogs. People who don't like puppies are psychopaths. That is one thing I am not.

What I am *not* happy about is our dinner plans tonight. "Em, I don't think I should go. I've been keeping a low profile. We both know that it won't go well if I attend."

She knows how quickly this can go awry, but I can tell she wants me there anyway. For support. For comfort. I may not be her main person, but I am *one* of her people. Just like she's been mine since I was young, back when the only thing I had to look forward to was skating on that frozen pond with her. I didn't have a lot in my childhood, but I did have Emaly.

And for her, I'd do anything.

Which is why I close my eyes, pinch the bridge of my

nose, and sigh. "Fine. Christ. This is going to be bad, but fine."

Emaly's eyes light up at the idea of me coming, so I know I'm making the right decision, even if it's going to take a lot of liquor to ease my nerves the entire night.

It'll go how it always does when I sit down with Mikhail and Valeria. They'll talk up Emaly's brother, Sasha, offer her backhanded compliments about her career as if she isn't doing the world's hardest fucking job as a pediatric oncologist, and then turn their attention to me. That's when things usually go downhill fast, thanks to my lack of patience for their bullshit.

I'd like to think I'm not a totally unreasonable guy. Their feelings toward me are warranted, given my past. To the world, and to my in-laws, I'm a lying cheater who doesn't deserve his wife. I'm sure my father-in-law has done his homework on me well beyond my years being married to his daughter. He knows how deep the wounds go—what my family did. I'm sure he thinks I'll wind up like them and wants Emaly far away from that. I'm fine with that, because I know I'll never be like them. I've worked hard to ensure I go down a path that will lead me into a life I never could have forged myself if it weren't for Emaly's friendship and encouragement.

Mikhail can't hurt me with his commentary because I already know every flaw attached to my existence. I draw the line at them picking *her* apart, though.

Emaly gives me a hug. "I appreciate you, Little Bear. It's one dinner. They know I'm going back to California in a few days, so we'll only have to suffer through a few hours of their company."

If she's going back to the West Coast, she must have made up with Ronnie and accepted it's time to go back to work. "Please tell me dinner isn't at their house."

She grins up at me. "We're meeting him at his favorite restaurant, so it'll be very public. You know how he feels about keeping a squeaky-clean reputation. He wouldn't dare cause a scene where he likes to dine every week."

At least I'll have that going for me. "Unless the waitstaff stops refilling his glass," I mumble, making her pinch my side. I hiss and jerk back, and she giggles. "What was that for? You know it's true."

She jabs her pointer finger at me with narrow eyes full of phony anger. "Yeah, but I'm the only one who's allowed to say it."

I chuckle. "Whatever you say, darling."

Emaly bats her lashes at me. "I know, sweetheart."

Sweetheart. Coming from her, it sounds comical. It doesn't garner any reaction like it does when I call Winter that. Her distaste for the name only makes me want to call her it more.

Shaking my head, I lean against the edge of the sink and cross my arms over my chest. "I'm sure Ronnie and the hospital will be happy to have you home."

Her face morphs from amusement to love and something dimmer that isn't quite readable. "I miss them," she tells me softly, eyes not meeting mine. "The kiddos at the hospital have been asking for me. After the last case…" She quiets, her throat bobbing with a thick swallow. She'd told me about the patient she lost over dinner the other night, explaining why she had to step back for a little while. I could tell there was more to the story, but I didn't push it. "It's been hard to be there and even harder to stay away."

I lift her chin with my finger. "You can't save them all, Em. No matter how hard you try."

Her eyes turn glassy, but she blinks rapidly to fend off tears. "I know. It doesn't make it any easier, though."

There's no denying that.

She stands taller and brushes her hands under her eyes before forcing a smile. "Anyway, when is the he-devil getting here? I need to make sure I'm hiding in my room when he arrives."

I give her a pointed look. "Why do you and Ashton hate each other so much?"

Emaly's nose scrunches. "Because he's annoying. And *he* started it! He clearly doesn't like me."

My brows arch at her reasoning. "So that makes you instantly not like him?" She can get along with anyone if she needs to, she just chooses not to with Ash.

"You know I've done everything I can to make him like me," she argues, frowning at my audacity. "The only thing that would work is divorcing you."

I can't help but snort, knowing she's probably right. "It's a good thing he doesn't get a say then, huh?"

She harrumphs. "I swear that man would do anything if it means I'm out of your life. To him, I'm a liability who—"

"Don't," I cut her off. "Don't call yourself that. If anybody is a liability, it's me. That's not what this is."

I know what she'll say. *He doesn't know that, though.*

And he doesn't. Nobody knows the truth regarding our situation. Just because he's on my payroll doesn't mean he's privy to it either. Although he likes to disagree.

Which is why he's always up my ass about why Emaly and I are married when we live separately. He used to ask a lot more questions in the beginning before he realized I wasn't going to give him any answers. That's part of the reason he's acted sour toward her. I've made sure to correct that behavior whenever they're around one another because I'll be damned if anyone disrespects her in my presence. It's bad enough Em's own parents do it, I'm not going to let someone I pay partake.

"Ashton doesn't know that, though," Emaly responds, making me internally snicker at the commentary I knew was coming. "And since you refuse to inform him why we're married—"

"He doesn't need to know."

She deadpans, "Little Bear, he is supposed to help you grow your career. And because of me, you've had backlash that's made it harder to get brand deals. I understand why he doesn't like me. But maybe if he understood the situation better, it would help you."

I knew she was going to bring this up. "Em, it doesn't matter."

Her frown deepens, wrinkling the corners of her mouth. "It does to *me*. I hate seeing people tear you apart."

"Then stop reading those stupid tabloids," I tell her for the umpteenth time. "They're not going to get any better. People like them are paid to report the worst about others. Nobody wants to read about how ridiculously in love a couple is. They're going to click on the article that highlights every reason people are toxic."

Her shoulders drop. "That's so sad."

"It's the truth." It's also a conversation I'm sick of having, but I'll keep having it until she gets it. "You and I are both fine. We're happy. My money isn't in jeopardy because I'm lacking new sponsorships. I'm smart with my investments, Em. I've got my salary. Most of my signing bonus is still in savings. You are *not* to blame for my deals drying up. You didn't make me shove my dick into other women."

She pins me with a sad expression. "I fell in love with somebody, Thomas Xavier. I'm to blame for a lot of things."

The admission isn't one spoken often. Not because it's a secret—there are few things we keep from each other. Her falling in love is not one of them. We've always had that close bond where we've been open about our lives. And seeing her find her person… Shit. It's one of the best things I've gotten to witness.

Unfortunately for her, that love is the one thing that's off-limits for others to know.

"He doesn't need to know," I repeat.

End of discussion.

The doorbell rings, making her sigh. "I love you too, Little Bear. You know that, right? I can love both you and Ronnie equally."

I've never questioned it, although the love she has for me is far different. "I know that. You show me how much you love me all the time. Why else do you think I married you?"

Her next hug is brief. "I'll go upstairs and leave you and Ashton to talk. Dinner is at seven. We're supposed to meet my parents in the city."

As she heads for the stairs, I call out, "Looking forward to it," as sarcastically as possible.

When I get to the door, my agent is impatiently waiting on the other side. "About time," he grumbles, shouldering his way in.

It's a damn good thing I like him eighty percent of the time, or that would piss me off. "Please, come in," I muse dryly.

He heads to the kitchen with his satchel containing the same shit as it always does. His laptop, a notebook, and an ungodly amount of paperwork. "We've got business to discuss, especially before your next little PR stunt."

Ashton begins setting up at the kitchen island, so I make myself comfortable on one of the stools and grab an apple to snack on.

He glares at me when I bite into it, not caring how loud I am. I'm not saying I enjoy ticking the guy off, but it's certainly a pastime that entertains me while he's here.

"You've got your serious face on," I say with my mouth full.

Ashton mumbles something under his breath as he turns his laptop screen toward me. "Your photos from Our Open Table event got good traction, and a few big outlets have picked it up. But the PR team and I have had to do a lot of work to change the narrative and do damage control."

"I thought we were all on the same page. Me going to

these *is* damage control," I point out.

He levels me with a look. "The whole idea of you doing these things is to create positive press, not the kind that calls you on your bullshit."

I take another obnoxious bite of my apple and shrug. "People aren't dumb, Ash. They're going to call it like they see it. Celebrities in deep shit are going to wear a temporary halo and write hefty checks and kiss babies if it makes them look good. We didn't invent the wheel."

He rubs a hand down his face. "Then you need to be more believable. The pictures you posted to your social media got a lot of engagement, but you aren't filtering out the comments that are shifting the bigger picture."

Of course I'm not. "Everybody is going to have an opinion. Isn't it you who said no press is bad press?"

Ashton mumbles, "Fuck me," under his breath as he closes his eyes. "Usually, yes. But we both know the press surrounding you is usually not the good kind. It would be helpful if you deleted some of the comments since you refuse to let anyone take over your accounts to do that for you."

It'll be a cold day in hell before anybody touches my socials. "The second those negative comments go away, I'm going to be called out for getting rid of them. Then it'll be less about all the good I did dumping soup into bowls and more about how I'm censoring the public's opinion of me."

He's quiet. There's no point in arguing because we both know there's a lot of truth to the statement. Not everybody is going to be happy with the work I'm doing. It's impossible to please a majority of the public, so why bother?

"The general consensus is positive, right?" I question, wiping my mouth when apple juice drips down the side.

He passes me a napkin with a sigh. "I suppose. Yes."

"Good. Let's focus on that then."

My manager rubs his lips together, which means he has more to say. Go figure. "Did you have to post the picture with *her* in it?"

There's only one person he could be referring to, but I play dumb. I toss the apple core into the garbage. "You'll have to be more specific. I worked with plenty of women that day. Bev was a real spitfire. You would have liked her if you showed up. Remind me again why you bailed at the last minute?"

His glare is back because he obviously doesn't want to talk about the woman in charge of Our Open Table or why he decided not to attend despite being so concerned about where I stick my dick. "You know damn well I'm talking about Winter Bronte. Out of all the photos that were taken, why did you have to include one with her beside you in your carousel post?"

He acts like I posted one staring at her tits. "I posted all of the ones you and the team deemed appropriate and tagged the necessary people. Why are you bitching if I added one more?"

It's clear that Our Open Table means a lot to her. I haven't figured out why, but she definitely has a personal connection to Vinnie and Bev. They were too familiar for her not to be invested. All the questions they asked her made them seem close. Familial.

Since we tagged their organization, I wanted to make

sure Winter was acknowledged for everything she did that day. I'm sure it'd come as a surprise to Ashton, but I didn't do it solely to piss him off.

"Tom, you can't be posting images with her. This is the one and only time," he informs me with an expression that seems both concerned and irritated.

What is his deal? He's always touchy when it comes to her. For someone who was on my ass about behaving at the event, he made up some lame excuse about checking in on other clients not to come.

"If you post more of the two of you together at these events, it'll form a pattern that people will put together," he informs me. "Then forget about the censorship angle. People will only be talking about you with yet another girl. Do you want her to look like a notch on your belt? Is that the reputation you want to leave her with?"

He has a point. "Are you going to tell me how you know her? Because this seems deeper than concerning yourself with my playboy image."

"No," he answers with no hesitation, the vein on his forehead pulsing. "Next order of my business."

I groan because I don't want to talk about business. I want to get to the bottom of what he's clearly holding back.

He ignores me. "I had a call with Janel and Scott today about your Furrever Home visit and suggested Winter sit this one out."

My shoulders square. "You don't have a right to tell her not to be there when she's the one who organized it."

"This is exactly why I don't want her there," he says, gesturing to my clenched fists. "I don't know what your obsession is, but I don't like it. You need to focus on your career, not getting your dick wet. If she winds up being in more photos with you, it's going to be a bigger problem than it needs to be. Not only for you, but for her. Do you want that lifestyle for her? For her to be mocked and judged?"

"Of course I don't," I spit at him. "I don't want anybody to be part of that. But do you really think it's fair to make her sit out events *she* planned?"

"She's still getting paid," is his response. "It isn't like she's not getting the credit for setting this all up. Her boss understands where I'm coming from and wants to protect her too."

Why didn't he confront *me* about this? "You didn't even ask me first. *I* pay *you*. And it's my money on the checks to the PR company, is it not? You had no right going to Janel and asking her to take Winter off the project."

"For Christ's sake." He groans, swiping a hand down his tired face. "It's for *one event*. Maybe two. I didn't ask to have her removed altogether, so don't get your goddamn panties in a bunch before I change my mind. Why are you so worked up about this?"

"Because you didn't run it by me first."

"I didn't think I had to!" he blasts back. He takes a deep breath and lets it out, pinching the bridge of his nose. "I'm going to ask you this once, and you're going to be honest with me, no matter how much I don't want to hear it. Did you fuck her?"

He thinks I'm doing this because of *that*? I've never

even had sex with my wife, and I'd go to prison for that woman. "Have *you*?"

Ashton reels back, like the question doesn't just disgust him, but offends him. "What the hell kind of question is that?"

"You don't care about the reputations of the other women I've screwed," I say matter-of-factly. "I find your vested interest in Winter's well-being suspicious too. And, for the record, no. I haven't fucked her."

Ashton stares at me for a long time, trying to determine if I'm lying or not. Whatever he sees must be enough to convince him to trust me. "She'll be around for other events. Just go to the one on Friday without her. Be convincing, pet some fucking puppies, kiss a kitten, and answer the questions we've gone ahead and approved them to ask. I'll come and make sure everything goes smoothly."

I mentally note that he's only coming because *she* isn't, but I know he won't divulge why that is.

I stand, thoroughly pissed off. "Fine."

"Where are you going?" he asks as I start leaving the kitchen. "We're not done. I've got a new brand deal that could work in our favor."

The last thing I give a shit about is brand deals, but I know he won't leave me alone until I've heard him out. "Is it for something lame?" I ask, turning to face him.

Amusement lifts his lips. "Actually, your little obsession brought it up to her boss as a joke. She said that we could play on your current reputation by making a lighthearted jab at your expense to amuse people. But I decided it wasn't a bad idea, so I reached out to a few companies to see if they'd be interested. I heard back from one within three hours."

I should probably tell him not to call her that, but I don't. I'm almost scared to ask about what deal Winter could have suggested, but I do. "What is it?"

His grin makes that wary feeling inside me grow. "Trojan condoms."

WHEN THE UBER pulls up to the front entrance of Sparks Steak House in midtown Manhattan, I'm quickly reminded of the establishment's infamous history attached to its name. Do I think Emaly's father is going to hire four Russian assassins to gun me down the way they did Paul Castellano in 1985? Probably not. But he's got connections in his home country that I wouldn't be surprised if he tried using to off me the way the Gambino family did to their mob boss.

Allegedly, of course.

Emaly's hand comes down on my arm, covered in one of my nicer suits that I usually only wear on occasion. I know if I showed up in anything less, it would instantly be picked apart by the man who may or may not try to get rid of me one way or another. Even though it's custom-tailored to fit me, the neckline feels too tight and the tie too constricting.

"What are you thinking?" my wife asks quietly, her brows furrowing as I tug at the collar of my button-down. "You look worried."

My eyes trail to the sidewalk through the car window. "I'm thinking that I don't want my brains splattered on the cement like Big Paul's were back in the eighties."

Her hand slips away. "My father isn't part of the mafia," she chides, eyeing the driver, who I'm not even sure is paying attention to us. "I'd rather that rumor not be spread."

My brows inch up. "Do you know that for sure? He's always talking about the people he knows back in Russia. I doubt he'd tell you about them if he did have connections."

She rolls her eyes and opens the door. "Just tip the driver and let's go. It's going to be easier to get on his good side if we're not late."

I pay the man with cash and slide out of the car after her. "We showed up ten minutes early last time we met up with him, and he *still* accused us of being late."

She de-wrinkles her dress. I'm not used to seeing her dolled up. She usually lives in sweatpants and a stolen hoodie of mine with her hair thrown up into a bun and no makeup on. It took her almost two hours to get ready today, all to impress people who probably won't have many nice things to say anyway.

"You look good," I tell her, grabbing her hands as they tug on the hem of her dress that lands just above her knees. "It's not going to get any longer by fidgeting with it."

Her sigh is heavy as she rubs her temples. "I should have worn something else. My mother—"

"Will survive if she sees your kneecaps," I assure her, putting my hand on the small of her back and guiding us to the entrance. "They have way more to focus on than the scandal of your dress length. I can bring up the last TMZ article that highlighted every woman I've been seen with over the past two years, and they won't even remember what you're wearing."

She swats my chest with an easy laugh that makes me smile. "Don't you dare!"

"Headache?" I ask suspiciously as she rubs the back of her neck and rolls it.

"Slept wrong," she lies. "There's a knot. I'm fine."

"Em—"

"Not now," she cuts me off. "I'm *fine*. It's not…that. People get headaches all the time."

True enough, but she's not most people. "I'm only letting this go because I don't feel like hearing your father accuse us of holding him up. But you and I both know your headaches aren't like others."

Her eyes go to her shoes for a moment. "I know," she murmurs.

I press a kiss to the top of her head and sigh into her hair. "Come on, Dimples."

Once the hostess brings us to the table in the far corner of the main dining room, Emaly's playful smile morphs into a serious expression that hides the very dimples for which she gets her nickname. It's another reason why I hate her family. The carefree, beautiful woman whose laugh can light up a room is silenced in their presence. She's an entirely different person with them than when she's around me or Ronnie or any of our friends.

"It's about time you two showed up," Mikhail greets with a blank look on his face. He doesn't bother standing up to shake my hand. Instead, I come to him with an extended palm to be as civil as possible.

Even though we're not late, I say, "Sorry. Traffic was backed up. It took longer than normal to get here."

Valeria stands to give her daughter a hug and a kiss on the cheek. "We are just happy you made it," she tells Emaly, before turning to me and offering me a stiff hug that barely lasts a second.

Her mother is softer with Emaly but untrusting of me. Understandable. I wouldn't be surprised if she's gone through a cheating scandal or two with her husband and finds herself feeling a little too sympathetic out of personal experience.

Mikhail hums. "We ordered drinks and appetizers already because we didn't feel like waiting. We've been here for a while."

Typical.

I force a smile. "Thank you."

"I ordered you water," he informs me pointedly. "I didn't think alcohol was the best decision. It allows for too many bad choices. I'm sure you're well aware of that."

I have no doubt that's in reference to my parents, who spent far more time with bottles of booze than they did with me. "I am," I agree tightly. "Alcohol can make you do regretful things."

My eyes dip to the scotch glass he's holding on to, which I bet is his second one. Perhaps he blames the Macallan for his brilliant idea to start the Fairbanks Fireflies and hire me. Or possibly his mentality is to keep his friends close and enemies closer. He's never been a huge fan of mine. He has, however, seen me as a good investment. I may not be the right person for his daughter, but he knows I'm the perfect man for his team.

That kind of skewed loyalty is all anybody needs to know about Mikhail Yokav and his priorities.

When he came to me with the offer to sign with his new team, I wanted to laugh and tell him to fuck right off. But when he brought up Emaly and made veiled threats to interrupt her life in California if I didn't agree, I didn't have much choice.

He knew Emaly was the perfect bargaining chip to get me to do what he wanted. He was willing to use his own damn *daughter*. So, I signed on the dotted line. But not before my agent made sure to get more money out of him. If I were his golden pawn, he was going to pay for it.

"Where did you get your dress, dear?" Valeria asks Emaly as soon as we sit down. Her nose twitches as she examines the burgundy color. "It's a bit short, no?"

My jaw tics at the condescending tone. "It's to her knees," I reply before Emaly can. "Half of the women in here can't say the same."

My wife's hand comes down on my knee under the table, squeezing it. I'm not sure if it's in warning or appreciation, so I choose to change subjects.

I turn my focus to Mikhail. "I seem to be missing my emails with the training schedule. I've been keeping up with my conditioning on my own, but I know how important it is to train with the team. Clarkson said you've been having them come in twice a week at the stadium gym."

Jesse Clarkson, the Fireflies' captain and my former teammate in Pittsburgh, has been hounding me about when I'm coming in. What he doesn't know is that I had no idea they were meeting. Which means Mikhail has been intentionally leaving me out of the loop. Needless to say, he's still pissed about the latest scandal.

Mikhail studies me for a moment before sipping his drink. "Strange," he says. "Perhaps it's a system error. I'll be sure to pass your concern on to IT, but it may take a few days."

He's playing a dangerous game to punish me, but we both know it'll impact him as much as me if I'm not on the same page as the others.

"Clarkson also informed me that the head coach has been wondering where I am." The mention of Bodhi Hoffman should be of no surprise to him. Formerly with the Rangers, Hoffman retired due to a recurring shoulder injury to coach this team instead. He, like myself and Jesse Clarkson, were personally selected to come play for the Fireflies. A powerhouse trio, according to ESPN, when the Fairbanks Fireflies were officially announced as part of the Eastern Conference.

Too bad they won't see us in action if Mikhail-Fucking-Yokav doesn't pull his head out of his ass soon.

I've known Bodhi for years as a rival and have only seen him a handful of times since he became the coach. It's a strange dynamic change that's only been made manageable because of Jesse Clarkson joining me as captain of the Fairbanks Fireflies. And by manageable, I mean, Clarkson is used to whooping my ass into shape when I act out. I basically came with my own babysitter.

Apparently, it's not news that the head coach has been asking about me. I would be too if I were in Hoffman's shoes. He can't coach a team if the star players aren't all present. And much to Yokav's dismay, I *am* one of the stars.

"We both want to make a mark on the NHL, right?" I ask Mikhail, ignoring the quiet side conversation happening between Emaly and her mother, which seems murmured and tense. "The only way to do that is by burying the hatchet and letting me train with them so I'm not behind. I'm doing what I can to make things right. I agreed to go to Starrs Strategy. I'm doing the events they lined up for me. I don't go out anymore. I don't party with anyone. I don't drink—"

"I do not trust you," he cuts me off matter-of-factly, lifting one of his broad shoulders.

I lean back in my chair, doing everything I can not to scowl. "You trusted me enough to sign me on to your team. Winning means the same to you as it does to me. Without me, there's a good chance your first year in the league is going to be unremarkable. And I know you better than to accept that sort of reputation. You want to stand out. To show your investment pays off. Can you really do that if you let one of your best right-wingers sit out and watch all season? You didn't pay me that seven-figure sum just so I can watch us get decimated by the other, more established teams. I know what it takes to win, what the other teams' weaknesses and strengths are, just as much as Clarkson and Hoffman do."

He's more prideful than I am. The Yokavs don't spend their money on things they think are a waste of time. If I weren't married to their daughter, perhaps I'd still wind up on his team. I'd still have the stats that prove I'm a worthy investment. Whether he likes it or not, he's stuck with me, and very little can void that contract.

His fingers flex around his glass because he knows I'm right, and he hates it.

Emaly must have been paying attention the entire time, because she clears her throat and interjects, "He's right, Daddy. You need him. Let him come in and get to know his new teammates. If you isolate him from the others, he won't be able to give his all on the ice when the season starts. They won't be compatible or in sync. Isn't that as important in ice hockey as it is in figure skating?"

I cover her hand that's still placed on my knee as a silent thank you. She hates bringing up skating because it's a path she never went down, like her family wanted. The topic is a source of contention between them. But she makes the point anyway for me.

"I'm not asking for a lot," I tell her father. "But you already sent me the money from the contract, so you might as well use me."

My father-in-law is quiet for a long time as he looks between his daughter and me. He doesn't like me, and he never will. Not for Emaly. Probably not for anybody. But he'll be placated if I can bring us a win on the ice. That means being allowed *on* the ice.

"I'll make sure you get the schedule by tomorrow," he tells me, finishing off his drink and lifting his empty tumbler for the waitstaff to see.

As if on cue, a waiter comes over with as much grace as possible for someone speed-walking and takes it from him. "I'll be right back with your next one, Mr. Yokav," the twenty-something-year-old says, before heading to the bar for a refill.

Drink number three, if I had to guess.

Emaly's hand squeezes the spot above my knee when her mother says, "Now that's settled, we should discuss the foundation dinner coming up. You're both expected to be there. I'll make sure you have something appropriate to wear, Emaly."

Backhanded compliment number one of many. Maybe it's a good thing I'm not allowed to drink tonight, or it'd become a game that neither Emaly nor I would be able to walk away from without severe alcohol poisoning.

"Looking forward to it," Emaly tells her mother with a secretive smile that only I understand.

Because it's the same insincere response I gave her when she told me about dinner tonight.

I hide my smile behind my water glass.

Emaly leans her chin on her palm and asks the one question that's always bound to take the attention off of her and me. "How is Sasha doing?"

CHAPTER NINE

Winter

I DON'T USE the phone number given to me, no matter how much I want to. Because what the fuck. What. The. Fuck.

It'd taken me a week of nonstop calls to the director of Fairbanks's animal shelter to agree on a date and time for Moskins's event, only to get booted. The director is a seedy older man with very little enthusiasm about the situation, despite the kind of press it could bring for their organization. Which, frankly, could use the donations. They're overfull and underfunded and need someone like Moskins to come in and save them.

He acted as if I was asking him to give away free animals and do surgeries at no cost to the public. I'm trying to run them into the ground; I want the opposite results. I'd been flipping off my phone receiver the entire time he questioned what he would get out of it.

All that work. Gone.

And if I had to guess, it's because Moskins is mad at me. Or maybe he's angry at his wife for giving me both of their numbers.

Kourt: *Let's egg his car*

I snort at my sister's reply after explaining that my Friday is now clear, thanks to my client getting his manager to pull me from my own event. It's all Thomas Moskins's fault. His agent called Janel, saying he thought it was best if I stayed out of the shelter event—that he would ensure everything ran smoothly. Janel, to her credit, fought for me. Her confusion matched my own when he told us that it was better I didn't wind up in any more photos together. Neither of us knew what he was talking about.

Until Farrah had shown us an image of me and Moskins that was posted on *his* account.

Not a picture I took.

Not one I posted online and tagged him in.

But I was still paying the price for his choice.

So, did I want to call him up and bitch him out? Yes. But did I want him to have my number and use it as leverage to get me kicked completely off his case? No.

He would not win.

He *couldn't.*

Janel told me to take the day off after the unexpected change of plans, even though I could tell she was swamped with work. When I asked where Cody was, because I hadn't seen him lurking around, she'd gotten quiet and said he took time off. Then told me to enjoy the day, dismissing me from asking more questions.

And, frankly, I don't want to be there anyway. I'm still getting emails and calls about the event, which I've had to direct to Janel and add to her workload since I'm not allowed to participate.

The problem with having a sudden day off is not

knowing what to do with it. I'm so used to working, I don't usually get to have a life. My version of fun is watching *The Secret Lives of Mormon Wives* using my sister's Hulu account and playing free games on my phone because I typically can't afford to do anything else.

I'm not much of a reader. I used to go to the library when I was younger and use their computer to play games, not pick out books. The head librarian tried to convert me into a bookworm, with no luck. She'd given up after the third time I failed to return one on time, and eventually waived the late fee when Kourtney came in saying she didn't have the money to pay it. Then I'd felt bad for stressing my sister out and stopped going entirely.

I enjoy listening to audio books, but they get expensive. Kourtney buys me audio credits for my birthday so that I can enjoy all my fairy smut—her words, not mine. Not that she's wrong. I love book boyfriends with large wingspans as much as the next girl.

But the credits from my last birthday were used a long time ago, so I'm back to zero. Which means no wingspans for me.

What do poor people do for fun? Cook? I don't have food at the house, unless you count Hamburger Helper, eggs, and ramen noodles. Work out? I snort at the thought. The only workout I do involves running my mouth to Kourtney when someone pisses me off.

Which reminds me.

I type out a message.

Me: *Eggs cost way too much money*

Me: *Would ramen have the same impact?*

Kourt: *It would smell delicious, not bad. We could raid the fish market for carcasses. Luca would easily fit into a dumpster*

I laugh at the thought of her telling him to climb into the trash to dig out fish bones. She would too. If Luca knew someone had hurt my feelings, he'd volunteer in a heartbeat if it would make me feel better. God, I love that kid.

Me: *Don't do that to my favorite boy*

Kourt: *You're right. Then I'd have to smell him*

Me: *We'll think of something*

Unfortunately, there isn't much revenge to be had that wouldn't backfire on me. I got banned from an event for doing nothing. I can't imagine what Moskins would do to me if I did something to his car. Would he call the cops? Have me arrested?

Revenge is not worth that.

I suddenly wish I'd done better at keeping up with friends. I still talk to a few people I went to college with. Once in a while, I even have dinner with my high school bestie, Rayna. But everyone has lives now. Nobody prepares you for how hard making new connections is as an adult. It can be isolating trying to exist in a world without friendship.

Sadness engulfs me, then more anger.

Because I shouldn't be bored or pity myself for not having more people in my life. I should be at the animal shelter helping set up and petting cute puppies and cuddling with fluffy kittens. I was even thinking about adopting, dammit!

Okay, maybe adopting would be too far. Sure, I've always wanted a kitten, but I can barely afford my own food. There's no way I'd make a cat suffer with my lifestyle.

I told myself that when one of my student loans is paid off, I can get something for myself. Ideally, a car that isn't covered in rust with two hundred and fifty thousand miles on it. But a feline companion sounds nice too. Maybe that's not the responsible choice, but falling asleep with someone soft and warm sounds pretty good to me.

When I get home, I kick the front door closed and drop my things on the small kitchen table pushed against the wall. My space is small, a little cluttered, but clean. Mostly because I'm sick of my sister complaining whenever she comes by for movie nights. But it beats going to her place and listening to Brad moan about our poor movie choices because it doesn't involve the military or someone being abducted. In hindsight, maybe I need to have a serious talk with Kourtney the next time she's over. Because what the hell is with that?

I'm not sure why I'm pulled toward the piece of paper I hung on the refrigerator, or why I even kept it to begin with. I should have thrown it out the second I got it. Dumped it in the coffee shop trash on my way out the door.

But I didn't.

I stare at the two numbers jotted down in smeared ink from where I'd accidentally rubbed my hand against it. The numbers are still legible—too legible.

And maybe it's loneliness.

Maybe it's the need for an explanation.

But I type the second number into a new message thread and hover over the keyboard in contemplation.

"This is a bad idea," I murmur to myself.

I send the message anyway.

As soon as the text delivers, dread fills my chest. I drop my phone on the table and close my eyes. "What did you do, idiot?" I chide myself.

I start pacing, wondering if I can unsend the message. As I reach for my phone, it dings with a new message that drops my heart to my butt.

"Oh my God."

Dumb. Dumb. Dumb.

"You should have gotten a kitten," I grumble to myself, slowly opening the new thread to see the message on the screen.

Emaly: *I'd love to meet up! I can pick you up in an hour. Send me your address*

This is a bad idea. A spectacularly stupid one, in fact. I blame my friends for all having better things to do. I blame my sister for having a full-time job and a child.

And I definitely, one hundred percent, blame Thomas-Freaking-Moskins for taking away my one and only distraction that helps me forget how lonely I really am.

But it's too late now.

Wetting my lips, I thumb out a reply that contains my address and send it to my client's wife, hoping this doesn't come back and bite me in the ass.

EMALY MOSKINS-YOKAV IS prettier than I remember. She's also nicer than anyone I've ever known. However, that's not hard when the only real person I have to compare to is Kourtney. And I'm pretty sure my sister was born with frown lines on her face.

The sleek silver Equinox I slide into looks fresh off the lot and far too nice for someone like me to be sitting in. I almost feel bad that my flip-flops probably have dirt on them when I study the pristine mats laid out.

"It's a rental," Emaly explains, earning back my attention. She smiles from the driver's seat. "That's why it's so clean in here. Trust me, the one I have back home is storage for lost lip glosses, hair ties, and phone chargers. There's also chips in the glove compartment and pretzels in the side door because I get hangry if I skip meals."

I crack a grin. "Emergency rations," I say approvingly. "Smart."

She pulls away from the curb as soon as I'm buckled in. "I'm happy you reached out. I was hoping you would before I left."

Left? "Where are you going?"

She pauses for a moment, contemplating whether she

should give me any details. "California," she finally answers. "I work in San Diego at a children's hospital. I've been gone to spend some time with Thomas and my family, but it's time to go back to the kids."

My eyebrows go up. "Wow. That must be hard."

Her smile wavers, and I worry that I've pressed too much for something that's none of my business. "I'm a surgical oncologist. And it's a very tough job."

So she's beautiful, kind, *and* smart. What the hell is wrong with Moskins for cheating on someone who's the entire package? "I don't know anything about that, but I'm sure it's difficult seeing sick children."

Emaly nods, worrying her bottom lip. "It is. But it can be very rewarding when you become one of the reasons that they get better. Unfortunately, it's not always the case. That's when…" Her voice cracks, and she clears it. "I needed a bit of a break. It was nice coming back here for a little while, but I know I can't hide forever."

So she came here because of her job, not for her husband. There's far more about their relationship that I don't know and probably never will. Even being here is crossing lines that will more than likely get me reprimanded at work.

But, unlike Emaly, I'm not smart.

"Can I ask why you texted me?" she prods, slowing for a red light. "Not that I'm unhappy you did. I'd just assumed you threw out the numbers the second I gave them to you."

She thought I would do that and still gave them to me? "I debated it," I admit honestly, sitting on my hands so I can't fidget with them. "But I couldn't bring myself to. I don't know why. Not until I got home early from work and realized…"

This is going to sound pathetic, isn't it?

Emaly gives me her full attention as we wait behind a line of traffic.

I sigh, realizing I have nothing to lose. If she had the nerve to give me a phone number, the least I can do is have the guts to answer her question. "I don't have much in my life. I'm so used to working that I've never realized how little I have outside of it. I've got my sister. Maybe a few surface-level friends I can grab food with and talk about trivial things once in a while. But I'm…"

It's hard admitting the truth.

That I'm lonely.

That I'm sad.

That my life choices are why I have to isolate myself from so many people. More than that—that *other people's* life choices have closed me off from the world.

Would I have been more outgoing if my parents hadn't been killed? If Kourtney wasn't forced to take care of me, and I could be more carefree and adventurous? I didn't participate in sports because that cost money, and so did school-appointed trips to new places. I tried not to burden my sister with anything I knew she couldn't handle, and I never complained. Not once.

But my upbringing wasn't like that of most of the peers I went to school with. To them, I was the sad, orphaned girl whose parents died. The poor kid. The introvert. Was I that way because of circumstance? Or because it's simply who I am?

"I'm lonely," I finish, my voice nearly inaudible as I look out the window at the buildings and trees that pass by. "I'm twenty-five and barely have anything to show for it. I work so much that I sacrifice friendships. My family is—" I stop myself, the words lodging in my windpipe. Shaking my head, I swallow them. "I don't have anyone besides my sister, who has a husband, a child, and a stable career that keeps her busy. And when I got an unexpected day off, I didn't know who to reach out to or how to spend it."

Pathetic.

A comforting hand comes down on my arm, causing me to lower my gaze to the slender fingers resting on me. "Take it from someone who understands," she says in a gentle tone. "Work is important, but it can't be everything. I have lived and breathed this career for the past decade of my life, and I don't regret anything because it's what I've always wanted to do. But that's in large part because of the people in my life who I can fall back on. We are humans who need connection and companionship to survive and stay sane. There needs to be more than work. You need to find ways to do more than exist."

I follow her arm from where it's extended in my direction, up and over to where she's focusing on the road. I know she's right. I'd like to think that once upon a time, I had more people in my life. But where had they gone? Had I tried that hard to keep them around? No, I hadn't.

Perhaps because I've never believed I'm close to anybody—that I'm forgettable. Unimportant. I can barely recall half of the names in my class, and I spent my whole life in Fairbanks. If I can't remember them, I'm certainly not on anybody's radar of former classmates to check in on.

It isn't my place to ask her how she can fall back on a person who doesn't seem very trustworthy, but the curiosity eats me up inside. "And Moskins is someone that keeps you…sane?"

If I were in her shoes, I'm not sure I could rely on him for that sort of security. I'm not very experienced in terms of dating, but I know when I deserve better. I've been cheated on before, and it isn't a good feeling. Yet, Emaly is here on an entirely different coast from the one she works on because her husband is here. She could have gone anywhere to take a break from her job, but she came to the one place Moskins is.

It makes no sense.

Emaly's laugh is light. "I get why you'd think that seems asinine, given what people report about him. But our relationship isn't what people think it is. Thomas is very private, and he's kind. Like I've told you before, he wears a mask to present himself a certain way to protect what he values most."

A crease forms between my brows. "Which is what?"

"Me." Her answer is casual. Simple. The smile on her face warms. "*And* the people he loves. They have always mattered most to him. In his eyes, the public won't try to dig into his life to learn about him if they think there's nothing to see beyond some broody, entitled hockey player. They see an asshole as an asshole and deem him a lost cause."

I start to reply, but take a minute. I've seen the articles and pictures. They don't seem photoshopped. And who would edit images to make themselves look bad, even if it's to hide some deeper truth? "So are all those cheating scandals and pictures of him walking out of hotels and closets with other women set-ups? Are you saying they're fake?"

They didn't look fake to me. Not between the ruffled clothes and hair like they'd just got caught doing something they shouldn't have been through a professional lens.

There's a pregnant pause where she doesn't offer me an answer. Then she lets out a quiet breath. "No. They're not fake at all."

A crack forms in my heart for her.

She knows he's been cheating. And…she accepts it? Somebody as smart as her can't possibly want to settle for that. Right?

Sadness sweeps up any self-pitying feeling I have and brushes it under the rug. "I'm sorry, Emaly," I tell her quietly.

She shakes her head as she pulls up to the curb on a familiar side street, putting the car into park. "Don't be," she says, turning to me. "Having Thomas's love is one of the best things that has ever happened to me."

I have a feeling I'm not going to get any answers to alleviate the confusion, which only deepens the more this conversation continues.

"Come on," she urges, turning the ignition off and opening her door. "Follow me."

I open my door and gape at where we are. "I can't be here," I tell Emaly as she approaches the side door of the animal shelter. "I was specifically told not to come to the event today."

She scoffs. "Screw what Ashton says. You were the organizer of this event, so you deserve to be here for it. We'll make sure you're not seen. I promise."

What on earth is happening right now? "Me reaching out was more of a 'let's get coffee' type of thing, not a 'let's smuggle me into an event' kind of deal."

She laughs and holds the door open for me. "But isn't this so much more fun?"

No. No, it isn't.

Reaching out to a client's wife is bad enough. Coming with her to an event I was strictly pulled from is worse. Way worse.

"I'm so screwed," I whisper, following her when she shows no effort to stop.

She presses her fingers to her lips as we enter a hallway where people are talking in the distance. Then she looks both ways, waves me forward, and tugs me to keep pace with her as we jog toward a closed door at the end of the narrow corridor.

"Why are you doing this?" I whisper, trying not to get caught. My heart is racing, and my hands are clammy as she releases my palm and reaches for the doorknob.

"Because," she whispers back, "I love my husband. I want what's best for him, so I'm going to do everything I can to make that happen."

My brows pinch together.

She opens the door and says, "And he's lonely too," she concludes, pushing me inside the room and closing the door behind me as I tumble forward. I hear her fleeting giggle from the other side of the door.

"Whoa," a gravelly voice says, before warm flesh smacks into me and strong hands appear at my biceps to steady my falling body.

When I look up, Thomas Moskins is standing shirtless in front of me in all of his six-pack ab glory.

"Hello there, sweetheart," he all but purrs, those piercing blue-gray eyes looking down at me.

They're rimmed with blue and nothing like I've ever seen before. Intense. Heated. Beautiful.

And despite my naivety with most men, I know for a fact they're filled with interest.

I blink slowly.

Then blink again to make sure I'm seeing this right.

Because for the millionth time today, I ask myself what. The. Fuck?

CHAPTER TEN

Moskins

IN ALL HONESTY, I have no clue what the hell is going on. But I'm also not about to complain when I feel the warm flesh of the petite blond against me as I steady her.

My mood has been shitty since getting here, when some seventy-year-old tried blowing smoke up my ass as if my appearance was his idea when we both know it wasn't. One look at him, and I knew he'd never seen a game of hockey in his life. He probably thinks we have quarters and touchdowns, not periods and goals.

Ashton made me play nice, force a smile, and shake hands while the man, whose name I had no interest in remembering, told me all about the schedule. Probably to distract me from quizzing him on anything game-related, because there is no way in hell he knows who I am. I'm pretty sure the douchebag called me Timmy.

His prattling on about what to expect pissed me off more. It shouldn't have been my manager or him telling me what to do and where to go; it should have been the woman currently standing in my arms.

"Hello there, sweetheart," I purr, watching as her face grows crimson.

When Emaly told me she was on her way with a surprise, I'd been expecting a cup of coffee or something for breakfast since Ashton rushed me out the door before I could make something to eat. My stomach has been rumbling for the past two hours, and the meat stick Ashton produced from who knows where hardly did the trick to silence it.

Winter quickly straightens, putting space between us like my touch burns her.

Get in line, sweetheart.

"I don't suppose you have a muffin or a cup of coffee, do you?" I ask, crossing my arms on my bare chest to cut some of the tension clearly coiled in her shoulders.

Her green eyes go to my abdominals that I've worked relentlessly to get. Growing up, I'd been a lanky kid and got bullied for my chicken legs and scrawny arms. If my bullies could see me now, they'd run the other way.

"My eyes are up here, baby girl," I tease, gesturing her locked gaze upward until her red face darkens and she winces at getting caught.

It's not the first time I've been ogled and certainly won't be the last. I like her focus on me. A little too much.

"So…muffin? I have a secret sweet tooth, so I like chocolate chips in them. But I'd accept anything at this point. Even a dry-ass corn one."

One of my eyebrows pops up when she gapes at me. Is she breathing? I'd hate to be the reason for oxygen deprivation that will inevitably kill her brain cells.

"No muffins?" I bemuse. "Coffee then? Can you speak, or have my abs struck you speechless?"

Once she realizes she hasn't answered, she snaps out of

her train of thought. "They didn't put anything out for you? There was supposed to be something in your room. Bagels. Coffee. Fruit."

She looks around, trying her hardest not to make eye contact with me in her search. It's cute how she actively skips over the spot I'm standing in just to make sure her gaze doesn't land on my exposed skin.

"My cock isn't out, you know."

She chokes on air as she flinches at the blunt statement. "That's…good. You should probably keep that in your pants."

I snort. "A lot of people would agree with you there," I retort, walking over to the chair in the corner and sitting down to give her some breathing room. "Are you going to look at me?"

She doesn't. "Are *you* going to put a shirt on?"

My lips stretch into a wide smile, and I slide a hand down the ripple of muscle covering my torso. "Do my abs offend you? I've been praised a time or two for them. Pretty sure they've won awards online. Once, a woman told me they were lickable."

She's still not looking.

Which only makes this more fun for me.

I study her for a microsecond. Her neck is slender and feminine. Soft. It would look good with my hand wrapped around it. "You're quite the prude, aren't you? Let me guess. You were raised in a covenant. I already told you that I don't do—"

"I'm not a virgin," she snaps defensively, finally meeting me with cold, offended eyes.

There she is. "My mistake." I raise my hands in surrender with quirked lips. However, I have an odd sense that she's lying. "They were doing test pictures when one of the puppies got a little too excited."

Interest takes over the irritation on her face. "Excited as in…?"

I chuckle. "It peed on me."

A surprised laugh bubbles out of her when I lift the white shirt I'd shown up in. It's got a bright yellow pee trail across it. "Are they going to get you a new one?"

Is that look in her eye because she's hoping they *will* or *won't*? "If my manager gets his way, he'd have me get a few shots like this before anybody delivers me something new to wear. I'm sure a shirtless man holding puppies would stop people from scrolling away from an article about what a do-gooder I am."

Despite her best efforts, her eyes dip down to my chest, then further south. I flex, knowing damn well she likes what she sees. I may be cocky, but I'd like to think the hours I spend at the gym weekly earn me a right to be.

Winter rips her eyes away before walking to the opposite side of the room and putting as much distance between us as possible. "It would get attention," she relents, nodding. "But I don't think it would give the kind of vibes we're going for. Unless you think more women thirsting after you is going to solve your problem."

Is that jealousy I detect in her tone?

I rest my elbows on my bent knees and smirk at her. "Does the idea of women *thirsting* after me upset you, Winter?"

The sound of her name makes her top teeth dig into her bottom lip. "No," she says with a bite to her tone that wasn't there a moment ago. "But I'm not your wife. Maybe you should ask her."

I swipe a hand over my mouth to hide my wavering smile. "What *did* you and my wife discuss on the way here? My nefarious ways? Is she writing a memoir titled *Married to a Professional Man Whore*? Is she prepping for a *60 Minutes* interview to go over every way I've wronged her?"

Her glare is comical, but she's silent.

I hum. "You're right. That book title makes me sound like an escort. I get my taste for free. Perhaps I should charge for my services. What is your advice on that?"

Winter's head shakes. "That's called prostitution, and it's illegal in all states."

"Except for Nevada," I chirp.

She blinks at me. "I'm not surprised that you know that. You're disgusting, do you know that?"

I shrug. "I've been called worse."

By my own family, even.

But I don't like to think about them.

She deadpans, "I'm sure you have, Tommy."

My jaw tics. "Don't call me that."

"Why not?" she prods.

"Because I don't like it," I growl.

They called me that name.

I will never be Tommy again.

I do my best to calm my tone and change the topic to something safer. "You're in a particular mood today. Now I really am curious what you and Emaly talked about."

Winter pushes off the wall and stalks over to me with a deadly, narrow expression. "Are you really wondering why I'm in a bad mood after what you pulled? I worked my ass off to organize this event and all the others on your stupid apology tour, all to be told *not to come.*"

The smugness on my face drops when I see the genuine hurt lingering in her eyes. It makes the pretty green color dim. "I had nothing to do with you getting taken off this project," I say, softer than either of us expects. It takes her off guard. "That was my manager's doing. If Ashton had come to me first, I would have shut it down before he ever went to your boss."

She scoffs. "You expect me to believe you?"

One word. "Yes."

She rolls her eyes, and from this close, the mossy color has specks of gold in them. They're beautiful and forgiving, even when they're full of distrust. "Well, I don't. If you were that pissed about me getting your number—"

I bark out a laugh, silencing her.

"Is that what you think happened?" I muse, studying her stricken face. It is. She thinks this is some sort of act of vengeance for Emaly passing her my number. "If anything, I'm upset you *didn't* use it."

She crosses her arms on her chest, and I can see how the movement pushes her tits up in her tee. The curve of her breasts peeks over the V of her neckline, and I have no shame in admitting that I like what I see. Her boobs may not be big, but they'd be the perfect handful—a perfect mouthful too. That's all a man really needs.

"Stop staring at my boobs!" she snaps at me.

I slowly look from her chest to her eyes unapologetically. "I was just returning the gesture. You looked first."

Her nostrils flare in irritation. "I wasn't exactly expecting you to be shirtless when your wife shoved me in here."

My lips curl up at the sides. "Feel free to even the playing field and take yours off. I'd love to see what's underneath."

Winter gapes at me, as if she's actually shocked I would suggest such a thing. "I am not taking my shirt off. What is wrong with you?"

"That list would take too much time to go over, sweetheart."

Her fists clench and unclench from where they're tucked under her armpits. "Don't call me that. I'm not your sweetheart. Or your baby. Or your anything. I'm Winter. *Only* Winter to you."

It's hot when she's bossy.

My eyes drag along the front of her. From the bright purple color on her toenails that matches the one on her fingers, all the way up to her blond hair resting in loose waves past her shoulders. I flick the pink strands. "I like this," I compliment. "New?"

She stands taller, touching the piece that my fingers brushed. "No. I hide them for work meetings to look more professional."

My lips flatten. "Your boss has purple hair."

"It's a personal choice of mine. I want to be taken seriously so clients don't think I'm incapable of handling my job."

It's a jab at my commentary during our first meeting

that clearly still gets under her skin. "Why pink?"

"Because I like it."

She doesn't seem like a pink kind of girl. She'd been warm and bubbly with Bev, Vinnie, and the others at Our Open Table last week, but there's something hiding underneath the surface. Pain. "Is pink your favorite color?"

The question leaves her skeptical. "Why do you care?"

I lift a shoulder. "I don't. I'm simply curious. Is there anything wrong with asking questions? *You* barged in on *me*, after all."

She grumbles under her breath, and I swear I hear her cussing out Emaly's name. I do my best to hide my amusement by schooling my features and stretching my legs out.

"Mine is black," I tell her. "If you accept black as a color. I know it's technically not, but I find myself liking it anyway. It makes sense, I suppose. I prefer my coffee black, my whiskey straight, and my chocolate dark."

Winter stares at me. "So you're a bitter person. Shocker."

My smile returns. "You could say that. *You* don't strike me as bitter, though. Even if you pretend like you are."

Her lips part. "I do not!"

"You're certainly not sweet. Not to me."

"You haven't earned that right," she counters.

Touché. "What do I need to do then?"

Her lips open to reply, then close when she comes up with nothing. Her tongue drags along the seam of her lips to wet them, and I can tell she's thinking.

I stand and slowly approach her. Her frame is tiny

compared to mine, but she's slightly taller than Emaly, so the height difference doesn't feel as dooming. "Do you want me to beg for your forgiveness? Would you like me to get on my knees right here, right now?"

My low spoken words are slow and steady, and a small breath releases from her when my shoes nudge the tips of hers. Her eyes peer up at me through thick lashes and are glazed with something I'm all too familiar with.

Lust.

"Do you want me to get on my knees, Winter?" I repeat the question, watching her crane her neck to look up at me with flushed cheeks.

Her throat bobs with a swallow that tells me I'm not the only one who's interested.

Good to fucking know.

"You don't—I—" Her sputtered words get stuck, and that red in her cheeks returns. Forget black. I think I like that color more.

I lift my fingers to her chin, pinching it between them to hold her gaze. "I would have chosen you to be here over Ashton or that condescending asshat who runs this place. It wasn't me who suggested you stay out."

Her eyes don't move away from mine. "I thought..." Her throat bobs again.

She thought I'd done it intentionally.

To hurt her.

To get back at her, somehow.

Slowly, so slowly, I sink to my knees. "Is this what you need, Winter?" I'm at eye level to the waistband of her jeans, but I look up at her so I don't get any ideas. Like unbuttoning her jeans and pulling down her zipper. She's staring down at me now, her bottom lip between her front teeth. "I wanted you here. I even told my agent I wouldn't do it if you weren't involved."

She sucks in a breath. "What? W-why?"

"Because, contrary to popular belief, I'm not a total asshole. And there's nothing I hate more than when people take credit for something they didn't do," I explain, ignoring the bite of pain in my knees from being on the hard floor.

My sincerity must be written on my face, because she offers me a singular nod to acknowledge me.

How many times had Emaly called me upset that someone in school or at her internship had taken credit for an idea or project? Too many. I saw how much it upset her to be discarded after putting in the work for no reward. I won't see it happen again. Not to her. Not to Winter.

"It hurt my feelings," she admits, more to herself than to me.

"I didn't mean to do that."

She stares at me, her throat bobbing.

"I very rarely get on my knees for just anyone, Winter," I say, eyes roaming over her until I meet her eyes. "The next time I get on my knees for you, it'll be to taste you."

She sucks in a breath. "Who says I'd let you?"

My lips kick up. "Who says you wouldn't?"

"I—" She doesn't get a chance to tell me one way or another, not that she needs to. I recognize the look in her eye. The interest. The curiosity. She wants to know what my mouth would feel like on her, she just won't admit it.

Before she can lie and tell me I'm wrong, I hear Ashton's voice from down the hall. I bolt up and walk us toward the furthest wall away from the door. When her back hits the drywall, she lets out a sharp breath that gets cut off when my body completely presses against hers to hide her from view. "If you want to make sure my dumbass manager doesn't rat you out for showing up today, follow my lead."

Her body is stiff against me. "I don't know what you—"

I gather her hair in my fist to hide the pink strands, so Ashton doesn't see them when he opens the door. "Do you want to get caught?"

"No!"

"Then go with it and don't kick me in the balls," I say with my lips pressed against her ear. Her body shudders from the briefest touch.

Before she can object, my mouth is on hers.

And the *sound* she makes.

The fucking *sound.*

It has the potential to be my undoing.

What I'd classify as a surprised moan goes straight to my cock. The kiss is unexpected. Hard. Awkward at first. But, to my surprise, Winter's body melts into mine as I place my free hand on her waist and massage the flesh there. Her hands grip my sides before smoothing over my obliques and moving around my back as she opens her mouth for me.

The door opens, and Ashton curses as soon as he sees us. "For fuck's sake, Tom. I leave you alone for thirty minutes to find you a shirt, and you're already trying to screw one of the volunteers?"

I peel my lips away despite the sound of her protest just enough to growl, "Out," to Ashton before dipping my head back down and closing the space between us.

Winter tastes like sugar and watermelon and feels like goddamn heaven against me. I barely hear the door slam closed because all I can focus on is the next moan that escapes her as I roll my hips forward for the friction that my hard cock wants.

She closes her lips around my tongue and sucks as her arms wind around my neck. I'm steel in my fucking jeans thinking of what those lips would feel like around my dick. Would she be a good girl and take the lead, or would I need to help set the pace? I would happily tell her what to do. Where to touch me. Where I wanted her tongue and fingers as they worked me.

It's a fantasy of mine I've been thinking far too much about in my short time since meeting her.

Her fingers clench my sides, not to push me away but to pull me closer. We get lost in the moment, neither one of us paying attention to the fact that we're alone again.

Another sound rises from her throat as she grinds against me. I would strip her naked right here and sink my cock into her warm pussy against the wall if I could. But anybody could walk in, and the things I want to do to her would take far more time than we have.

But I'm not done yet.

"Please," I growl against her mouth, desperately needing something. I'm not entirely sure what I'm asking for. But more than *this*.

My fingers rise to circle around the nape of her neck and squeeze lightly. "The things I would do to you, Winter..."

Her arms tighten around me as I lift my thigh to brush between her legs. She whimpers into my mouth, so I do it again, applying more pressure where she wants it. Her fingertips dig into the muscles of my shoulders, and I like the bite of pain that comes with her nails sinking into my flesh.

My hands move down her body and rest on her hips to start guiding her to use my leg to get off with. If the door had a lock on it, I'd strip her jeans off and bury my face in her cunt until she came at least twice. But I don't have the luxury of a lock or time before Ashton, or God knows who, comes back and disrupts us.

"That's it," I coax, watching her face morph with pleasure as she rocks against me. She already looks close. So responsive. So *mine* at this moment. "Come on my thigh, Winter. I can see how badly you want to."

It's easy to see that she's on the brink. I want to dive under her shirt and bite her nipple and slide my hand into her panties and play with her clit. But something tells me if I go out there smelling like I'd just gotten freshly laid, it would cause some problems.

So I do neither of those things.

I do, however, press my thumb against her over her jeans. And the jerking motion that thrusts her hips forward as she tips her head back and opens her mouth into an *O* tells me that's all she needed before going over the edge.

"Christ, you're so sensitive," I praise as she rides out the orgasm. Watching her come is an ethereal experience. The stiff, guarded expression usually on her face is now long gone and replaced by bliss and sedation.

It's too goddamn much.

I set her down and barely have time to undo my jeans before I'm coming in my hand. I stabilize myself on the wall as my head tilts back and hot cum spurts onto my stomach as I picture her falling apart on repeat.

"Christ," I mumble, catching my breath as I examine the mess I made of myself. If she could do this to me with our clothes on, I can't imagine the destruction of my sanity when I'm inside her.

From beside me, I hear the quietest, "Oh my God."

When I glance over my shoulder at Winter, she's staring at me with glassy eyes and parted lips. Her focus is on the cock still hard in my hand, not that she can see much from her angle. If she did, her eyes would be a hell of a lot wider at the silver piercing.

"Oh my God," she says again, this time more panicked. As though ice water had been dumped on her, she slams into the wall and covers her face.

"Winter—"

"You're *married*," she rasps, shame filling her tone as she shakes her head against the palms covering her eyes. "You are a married man, and I—And *we*—"

I tuck myself away, grab a tissue from the table off to the side, and wipe away any evidence of what we'd just done. Anybody who comes in will be able to smell the sex in the air. But I don't care right now. Not when she's on the verge of a full-blown panic attack.

"Winter," I begin again, turning to face her.

Her face is still cupped in her hands, hiding from the reality of the situation. "I'm a horrible person. If Hell really does exist, I'm going there. Oh my *God—*"

I pull her hands away from her face. "Look at me," I demand, giving her no other option. "I need you to look at me, Winter."

She swallows, lets out a shallow breath, and then slowly lifts her gaze to meet mine. Guilt is weighing on her face as her nostrils twitch and her eyes rapidly blink to fend off the tears building behind them.

When I know she won't look away or shut down, I say, "I'm going to tell you something, and I need you to listen and repeat it to nobody. Do you understand?"

Confused, she nods slowly.

"Good girl," I praise, running the pad of my thumb against her bottom lip and feeling a shaky breath brush against the pad. "Emaly and I are not together."

Her eyes widen. *"W-what?"*

"We're married," I confirm, only making her confusion grow. "But we're not together…like that. It's complicated, and not fully my story to tell. But I am free to do what and who I please. And that information needs to stay between us for obvious reasons."

Her silence is deafening, and I can tell she needs time to process. Understandable, given my reputation. Given everything she's ever read about me, the truth probably isn't easy to accept.

"So you're not a horrible person," I reassure her firmly. A small smile tilts my lips. "And if you *do* go to Hell, it won't be because you let a married man make you come."

A new wave of heat covers her face, and I can't help but chuckle to myself over the embarrassment resting there.

An impatient fist bangs on the door, startling her. Whether she means to or not, she hides behind me to mask herself from anybody seeing who's in here with me.

And the primal part of me wants nothing more than to protect her. "I need to go out there before they barge in," I tell her, wanting to do anything but. "I'll make sure the coast is clear for you to sneak out. Wait at least thirty seconds after you stop hearing us before you leave the room. Go to the diner across the street and wait for me."

Winter stands taller. "I'm not—"

"Emaly isn't going to be able to drive you home because she's on her way to the airport," I explain. "Unless you want to call someone else, let me get this over with and then come to you."

I can tell she wants to argue. To tell me no.

But her curiosity wins her over. "Fine. But only because I have questions."

I smirk. "I have no doubt, sweetheart."

Her jaw grinds. "It's Winter."

My grin widens, and I shake my head. "I know what you look like when you come. You're not just Winter to me."

I DON'T EXPECT her to be there when I show up an hour and a half later. I figured she would have gone right home or maybe waited for twenty minutes before leaving a note with the waitstaff that said "fuck off" on it.

But there she is.

Sitting by herself in a corner booth, staring out the window with a faraway expression on her face. She looks contemplative and lost, her brows pinched together and her thumbnail in her mouth.

"You'll ruin the polish," I say, sliding into the booth across from her. It looks like she's already chipped at the purple on the nail she's withdrawing from her mouth as she takes me in. Her eyes slowly go from me down to her hand, as if she hadn't realized what she was doing.

When they lift back up, they take in my green T-shirt with the shelter's logo on the breast pocket, then rise to the backward baseball cap covering my short hair, and the sunglasses I have yet to slide off.

"Does that getup usually work for you?" she questions with a frown. "Wearing sunglasses inside doesn't make you look inconspicuous. It just makes you look douchey."

I snort at her bluntness, glad that her orgasm hasn't melted her brain the way it did mine. I take off the glasses and toss them onto the table with an amused smile. "Better?"

Her throat bobs as she glances at me, but averts her gaze quickly to the glass of water she's hardly touched.

She can't look me in the eye.

"Why purple?" I ask, gesturing toward her nails. It's a pastel shade that reminds me of Easter. "You like bright colors."

Her eyes go down to her fingernails. "My world needs a

little color in it," she replies, her brows furrowing again in thought before she loosens a sigh and turns back to the window.

She doesn't explain any further, but I don't need her to. My world may as well play out in black and white. Watching it in Technicolor is a privilege that not everybody has. No amount of money in the world could afford me to forget about my past and the things I've done to get where I am.

So, I get it.

"Maybe I need a better favorite color," I say with a limp shrug. "But black is all too fitting."

I can tell she wants to ask me why when her eyes peer up through her lashes at me, but she refrains from speaking her curiosity. I go easy on her and say what she needs to hear instead.

"What we did isn't the end of the world," I tell her nonchalantly. "I didn't even see you naked. I didn't even get to touch a tit."

Her whole face blossoms with heat. "Keep your voice down," she hisses, glaring at me. "It may not be a big deal to you, but it is for me. I was hired to help you have a better online presence after your affairs came to light. What we did crossed a huge line. I'm supposed to make sure your name isn't being associated with all of that negative press, not—"

"Let me pin you against a wall and make you come?" I finish for her.

Her eyes dart somewhere behind me, probably checking to make sure none of the employees are listening. "Stop saying it so loudly. I cannot believe I let you do...*that.*"

I tilt my head to study her. "Give you an orgasm? Most women would thank me for that experience."

Her nostrils flare in pure frustration. "I am not most women. You're married, for crying out loud!"

"Ah." I nod slowly. "Yes. That."

"*That.*" She scoffs, rubbing her temples. I hear her mutter a countdown from five under her breath. Then she lowers her hand to her lap. "It's a big deal, *Tommy.*"

"I told you I don't want to be called—"

"Does it look like I care what you prefer being called?" she cuts me off coolly. Her shoulders are rigid as she turns to the window, closes her eyes, and calms herself. "I don't like being called pet names, but you still do it. So you can suck it up, buttercup."

I hide my wavering smile the best I can by the time her attention is back on me. "I told you that my marriage is not what it seems."

She shakes her head. "You could just be saying that to get what you want."

One of my eyebrows arches. "And what is it you think I want?"

Her cheeks grow darker as she squirms. "It seems pretty obvious to me. You want..." Her tongue drags across her bottom lip as she gestures between us. "You want to have—"

"Sex?" I finish for her. "It isn't a bad word."

Before she can reply, a middle-aged waitress comes over with a less than amused look on her face. "Do you want anything?" she asks me, holding a notepad. "You've been keeping this one waiting long enough. I thought for sure she'd been stood up."

From the corner of my eye, I see Winter flinch.

The waitress's eyes narrow on me, and something resembling familiarity fills them as she takes me in. "Do I know you from somewhere?"

I'm not recognized as often in Connecticut as I was in Pennsylvania, but thanks to the tabloids blasting my photos everywhere for the past two months, it's become a common occurrence. Especially among the population of Fairbanks that enjoys online fodder and pop culture gossip. This woman definitely indulges in TMZ articles in between customers.

"I doubt it," Winter answers for me. "He just got out of prison yesterday. That's why he was late. He's a bit out of sorts in the real world."

I snort at the explanation that she makes, and the waitress's eyes widen. Her examination of me becomes more judgmental, going to my arms, then my face, before turning to Winter.

"You're far too pretty to be wound up in whatever mess he's gotten himself into," she chides to the blonde across from me. "I'd leave while you still can."

Winter forces a smile. "I will certainly do my best."

I chime in with, "I'll take a Coke and a menu…" My eyes scan her nametag. "*Linda.* And I'd appreciate it if you could take it easy on the advice. I'm trying to get laid here."

Winter makes a choked noise, and Linda narrows her eyes before walking off to, hopefully, get me a soda and a menu.

"Seriously?" Winter quips.

I drape an arm over the back of the booth. "I could have said worse. And prison? Really? That's going to be a hell of a headline. I look forward to seeing what your boss thinks of that contribution to my reputation when it comes out as front-page news."

She rolls her eyes. "Nobody recognizes you."

All I do is hum. Unlike her, I know when I'm seen. People aren't as subtle as they think. Within the next thirty minutes, Linda is going to be pointing her phone in our direction and emailing TMZ for an exclusive.

We fall quiet, and she shifts again.

I lean forward and drop my voice. "Do you regret doing it? Or do you regret that it made you feel good?"

Her body freezes at the question, her eyes remaining on the table in front of her as she sucks in a long breath.

I soak in the silence before filling it. "Guilt can be a bitch when you let it eat you alive. I've learned a long time ago that isn't the way to live."

When she picks her eyes up, I can't read what's behind the glaze in them. "The difference is that you clearly don't care who it can hurt."

My jaw tics. She has no fucking idea. No. Goddamn. Idea. "If you don't know what you're talking about, I suggest not saying a word."

The snarled warning makes her swallow and press her lips together.

Spine straightening, I clench and unclench my fists before forcing them on my lap. "Let me ask you something, Ms. Perfect."

Witner scowls.

"Why did you let it go that far if you didn't want it? You could have said no and told me to stop. You could have kneed me in the balls and yelled for help. But you didn't do any of that. So are you mad at me or are you mad at yourself?"

Her throat bobs, and I know I got her.

If she wants to feel guilty for what we did, have at it. But I won't be dragged into her pity party. I've got better things to do.

A Coke gets placed in front of me, along with a straw and a menu. Linda is staring between us inquisitively, sensing the tension in the air. She simply shakes her head and walks away, leaving us to deal with the mess we've made.

"She said you were lonely," Winter eventually whispers, staring into her lap.

My brows furrow, and some of my anger dissipates. "Who told you that?"

Another few seconds pass, and she spends them fidgeting with her fingers under the table. Then, offers me a quiet, "Emaly."

Ah.

When she peeks up at me, there's no guilt. Only shyness. "She said you were lonely too."

Too.

Now I understand why Emaly brought her to me. Because she sees the same thing in Winter as I do. A mirrored reflection. Somebody holding on to a million pieces of themselves, unsure if they can be put back together. We are walking shards of broken pasts, bleeding and praying to push aside the things holding us back to get…something. Anything.

Relief.

Happiness.

A distraction at best.

My muscles relax, and I lean back in the booth to settle against the cushion. "That certainly sounds like something she would say."

Emaly has always been observant. Half the time, she sees things before I do. She claims it's because she's an empath and in tune with people's emotions. If that's the case, I don't envy her. I'm a sad bastard to be around.

"So it's not true?" Winter questions.

I pick up the menu and scan it, reading through the burger options. "I didn't say that." I pause. Then, "You're going to eat, right?"

When she doesn't answer, I look over the top of the menu to see her gaping.

"What?" I ask casually. "The breakfast burger looks good if you're not opposed to eggs on it. They have other options though."

"You…" She blinks, shaking her head. "Is that really all you're going to say?"

I lower the menu down. "What would *you* like to talk about? Everything I suggest you don't seem to have an interest in speaking about. Like how your face scrunches when you—"

"Stop," she squeaks.

I grin. "My point exactly."

"We're in public," she murmurs.

"We were in public against that wall too."

Crimson may be a permanent color on her, but it looks good against the blond. "I still have questions. What you said is big. Huge. It could change so much about the work we're—"

"Nobody is going to find out about what I told you," I cut her off with no argument in my tone. "I meant what I said, Winter. That stays between us. The only reason you know is because you looked two seconds away from jumping out a window and into oncoming traffic. I had to figure out how to stop you from doing that."

Her glare is oddly refreshing. "I wasn't going to do either of those things. Hyperventilate? Maybe. Start going to church to repent my sins and ask for forgiveness? Perhaps."

I huff out a laugh. "And now?"

She's staring at the menu on the table between us, reading the words upside down. "I don't know," she admits, lifting a shoulder. "You asked why I didn't stop you. Why I didn't tell you to stop. And the truth is…"

Winter pauses, her words fading before she closes her eyes. "The truth is, I don't know why I allowed that to happen. I don't know why I let myself enjoy something that I knew was wrong. The only explanation I can come up with is that I'm lonely. And I needed…something to make me forget that I'm sad for once. And to answer your other question, yes."

My eyes scan her face. "Yes, what?"

"Yes, I'm mad at myself," she confesses, her throat bobbing as she moves her eyes away from me once more.

"But I'm always mad at myself, so what's new?"

I watch her for the longest time before accepting her answer for what it is. Because I know exactly where she's coming from, which is why Emaly brought her to me.

So we both can be a little less lonely together.

So we can both take a break from hating ourselves, even if it's a temporary fix.

We are two halves of a broken whole, with a crack down the middle that nobody may be able to repair.

But what a journey to try.

"You're too young to be this mad at yourself," I tell her delicately. How did she get here at twenty-five?

Her eyes trail over my face for a moment as if she's looking for something specific. "I could say the same about you."

"I'm thirty-five," I point out. "Not exactly the poster child for the fountain of youth. I have plenty of reasons to be mad at the world. It's no way to live."

Her eyes go down to her drink. "Anger doesn't have an age limit. Neither does grief."

Grief.

She lost someone, but who?

I want to ask, but I know she won't tell me.

So, I pop a straw into my soda, take a long sip, and say, "I'm thinking about adopting a dog."

CHAPTER ELEVEN

Winter

I SHOULD HAVE known Monday was cursed the second I got into my car and heard a new noise under the hood. My typical reaction is to turn up the radio so I can drown out the sound. Unfortunately, my radio stopped working too.

When I got to work, there were no parking spaces anywhere near the front entrance. Which meant walking in the pouring rain without a rain jacket or umbrella because I'm dumb and left mine at home. By the time I made it to my cubicle, I looked like a drowned rat undergoing cosmetic testing. Because yes, I choose to believe testing makeup on animals involves putting the actual product on cute little mice until they're dolled up to the nines with false lashes and rouge. It makes me happier than accepting the alternative that usually involves—

Nope. I will not think about it.

It isn't until I'm sitting down after attempting to dry myself off and fix my running mascara that things get extra sucky.

"What is wrong with you?" Farrah asks, standing with her hands on her hips.

It's not even nine in the morning, so I have no energy

to have a conversation like this. Because there's a lot wrong with me.

For instance, I haven't done laundry in a week and a half and ran out of clean underwear. And instead of simply throwing a load in like a logical person would, I opted to go commando today.

Or maybe she's referring to the fact that I didn't tip the woman at Starbucks this morning. I felt bad about it, but all she did was take a croissant out of the display case and put it in a to-go bag. I'm pretty sure it was an old pastry anyway, because they gave it to me for a discount.

She could be referencing my unethical behavior over the weekend, which had me anxious from the moment Moskins dropped me off in front of my apartment. I think he wanted to come inside, but I was *not* about to let that happen. What we'd done was bad enough. My limbs are still weak from the intense orgasm I had just from rubbing on his leg.

His *leg*!

Moskins had been cool as a cucumber the entire drive to my place, telling me not to worry about people finding out I'd all but humped him like a dog in heat. Those were his words, of course. To which I'd flipped him off, got out of his Nissan Rogue that I'm still surprised isn't a fancy Mercedes, and ignored the way he laughed.

There is no way Farrah could know something happened between him and me. She wasn't there. I'd been able to make a clean exit without anybody noticing, thanks to him distracting everybody inside. And unless the brunette staring at me was hiding in the bushes, that means she has zero clue what occurred.

"You have nothing to say?" Farrah goes on while I have a mini meltdown internally. Her hands go from her hips to her chest, crossing pensively.

I rub my eyes. "I'm not entirely sure what I'm supposed to say," I admit to her. "Did I do something?"

Something other than letting our client give me the fastest orgasm of my life?

She scoffs. "You got Cody suspended!"

"I—" I stop myself, trying to figure out if I heard her right. "I'm sorry. Wait. What are you talking about?"

She throws her hands up. "Have you not noticed that he's been gone? Seriously, Winter. Open your eyes. Whatever you said to Janel and HR got him put under investigation while they dig into claims made against him."

And she thinks *I* did it? "I didn't say anything to Janel or HR. Did somebody say I did?"

Farrah sighs heavily. "We all know you don't like him."

Everybody knew that except for him, apparently. I lock that comment away, though.

"And since *I* didn't report him…" she adds, staring at me accusingly.

I pinch the bridge of my nose. It's too early for this. My brain isn't computing the information. I haven't had coffee yet. Or my potentially stale croissant, which—

Dammit.

I left my pastry in the car. Even if it was one of their older ones, I was going to eat it. The chocolate-filled goodness is a weakness of mine, and I need a boost today.

"I didn't report him, Farrah," I repeat, finally looking

at her again. "I don't know what you're talking about. If someone spoke up about him, then clearly it's for a reason."

She has to know how slimy he is, doesn't she? I've seen him around her cubicle before. There is no way she welcomes all his creepy come-ons and bad pickup lines.

Farrah does not look happy with my response. "We were working on a big case together. Now I'm stuck doing all the heavy lifting because Janel is too busy with her own load. So thank you very much for making my life harder."

Before I can reply, she storms off with the sound of her heels clicking against the floor the entire way back to her workspace.

I stare at the empty spot she occupied.

Then I walk over to Janel's office, where she's eating her usual yogurt bowl from the organic smoothie shop down the road, and knock on the open door. "Do you have a minute?"

She lowers her breakfast. "Sure. What's up?"

I look behind me at the open cubicles facing us. Including Farrah's. Then I close the door behind me and lean on it. It doesn't really matter, given the huge glass wall that separates us. But I'd rather have a private conversation that nobody can listen to. "Did something happen to Cody? I just heard he's under some sort of investigation."

My boss's eyebrows dart up. "Who told you that?"

I don't bother lying. "Farrah. She seems a bit…stressed about the work he left her to deal with." It's as kind as I can put it without calling her out for being a total bitch.

Janel sighs. "I can't go into details, of course, but yes. He's on a leave of absence at the moment. We're *all* a little busier because of it."

Even though I know she can't tell me, I ask the obvious question anyway. "Who brought it to HR's attention?"

Her lips rub together as she sets her bowl down on the desk and folds her hands together. "I did, actually."

My eyes are about to pop out of my head. Had Cody been harassing his own boss? "Did he..." How do I even ask that? "Did he do something? Say something?"

Janel's head tilts. "I should be asking you the same question."

Her retort straightens my spine.

"I like to know about what is happening in my office, Winter," she goes on. "I understand that some things may be uncomfortable to bring up, but I would like to think I'm the type of supervisor who is open to any tough conversations my employees want to discuss."

I nod. "You are."

"Then why did I have to hear about Cody harassing you through Thomas Moskins?"

Everything stops.

Thomas Moskins did *what*?

She gestures toward the seat across from her desk, and I slowly lower myself into it. "Winter, I know things like this aren't easy to bring up. But I wish you had come to me directly."

I cannot believe he would go to her about Cody. *When* had he done that? The day he told Cody to get out of my cubicle? After our lunch that day? Recently? Did he do it after we...?

I can't even think about that.

I shake my head. "I didn't want to make the work environment awkward. Cody was a lot, but I know how much of an asset he is to the team."

"*You're* an asset too," she informs me with stern eyes. "And I do not want you thinking that what he's doing is okay. It isn't. When I asked around after Mr. Moskins made the claim, it became clear to me that he's been doing this for a while. Not only to you but also to others. Clients included. And I cannot have that here."

Cody has been here the longest out of any of us, and I've heard the rumors about his flirtatious conversations with some of our clients. They're usually not met with interest. "I'm sorry I didn't come to you. It isn't because I didn't think I could. I'd hoped that if I ignored him, he'd get the hint."

A sad, sympathetic smile pulls at the corners of her lips. "He's a man, Winnie. Men need detailed diagrams drawn to understand things. Cody has always been a little too confident for his own good. *I'm* sorry that I didn't see it sooner and do something about it."

Guilt washes over me for not bringing it to her attention. Then irritation and something else, something lighter, washes that away when I think about Moskins stepping in.

Wetting my lips, I ask, "When did Thomas Moskins come to you about Cody?"

She leans back in her chair and picks up her yogurt. "The morning of our meeting with him to go over the schedule of events."

Why hasn't he said anything to *me* about it?

Because you've been too busy getting off to him to ask the right questions, dumbass.

I internally cringe at that inner voice.

"Is he going to be fired?" I ask, unsure if I want to know the answer. If he does, will it be my fault? I mean, I know I'm not the one telling him to hit on everyone in the office, but I *did* go out with him. I gave him the impression I liked him for some chicken and pasta. Which was so not worth it. The chicken was drier than Cody's personality, and the pasta didn't have enough sauce.

"I don't know yet," she tells me earnestly. "It doesn't look good. I'll have the final say, and I'm not entirely sure what my choice is. For now, I'm letting him sweat it out. That being said, I want you to know that your opinion matters to me. Everybody here needs to feel safe. If, for any reason, Cody makes you feel otherwise, I would like to know. I'd planned on coming to you about it soon, but now is as good a time as ever to talk about it."

It isn't that Cody makes me feel unsafe. Just grossed out. But do I want to be the reason he loses his job? "I don't appreciate his lack of personal space," I tell her carefully. "Or his taste in cologne."

A small smile tilts her lips.

"But he doesn't scare me or anything necessarily," I add, lifting my shoulders. "He's just...a lot. Maybe if he gets scared straight and does some sort of mandatory sexual harassment course, things will be better. I don't know."

It's the best I can offer her right now.

Thankfully, she accepts it. "Okay then. I'll talk to a few more people and figure it out. Thank you for being honest with me."

I stand and go to the door.

"Oh. And, Winnie?"

I turn to her.

"You'll be expected to go to this weekend's event at the food bank with Mr. Moskins," she informs me, not looking up from her computer. "I confirmed with his agent this morning."

I don't know if the tingly, fluttery feeling in my stomach is good or bad. But something tells me I'll find out on Saturday.

KOURTNEY PASSES ME the plate of steaming food before dropping into the spot beside me on the couch. She props her feet up on the coffee table with a groan of relief. "It feels so good to sit down. I've been prepping my classroom for the new school year and chasing Luca around all day."

I don't bother asking where Brad is because I don't really care. It's nice to spend time with just her and Luca. It means we can eat on the couch and put something trashy on the TV that usually involves finding love behind walls or the lives of Utah wives.

"He's got a new fixation," she tells me with her mouth half-full of the rice she stuffed in it.

My eyebrows go up. "What is it now? I thought he'd just gotten interested in car washes. I even bought him that toy where the cars change colors in cold water."

Kourtney loads one of the streaming services and starts searching for our show. "He still likes car washes, but he's more interested in how vending machines work. He asked for one for Christmas this year."

I snicker. "A vending machine?"

"He doesn't even care if there's candy in it," she retorts, face scrunched at the thought. "Or soda. Or anything fun. He just wants a plain old vending machine so he can figure out how it functions."

I can't help but laugh. "I love this kid," I muse, snorting at the idea of him with his little toolbox that I got him last year for his birthday, and taking apart every mechanism inside.

Luca—sweet, smart Luca—is on the spectrum. He's always been a brilliant kid, but he's had a struggle with reading social cues. But he's truly one of the kindest souls I know. And when he loves, he loves hard.

"So, are you going to get him one?" I ask, poking my pork chop with my fork. "Because if you're not, I'll find a way."

She eyes me. "How? By stealing one? Do you know how expensive those things are? I had to Google it. Go on. Guess."

I don't. "There *is* one at work that nobody uses because the only things left in it are trail mix and strawberry Pop-Tarts."

I'm not sure who is supposed to stock it, but they've neglected it all year.

My sister is contemplative. "I liked the strawberry ones."

I don't comment on that because then I'd have to point out that she's always had bad taste in things. Like men.

"I'm just saying, we could probably figure out how to take the one from work. It's in an alcove, but—"

"We're not stealing a vending machine," she says, laughing as she tosses a piece of carrot at me. "Those bitches are heavy, and we have no vehicle to transport something that size."

She's totally considered stealing one. "I guess you're right," I mumble defeatedly.

When I glance down at where Luca is sprawled on the floor, I see him hyper-focused with his blue headphones on and his iPad in his hand. He's watching a YouTube video on machine mechanisms, looking fully enthralled by whatever the narrator is saying.

"See?" Kourtney says.

I nod. "He could be into video games," I point out. "Or saying six-seven and laughing hysterically, even though nobody knows what that even means."

A scowl that reminds me a little too much of Moskins appears on her face. "Don't get me started. The number of eleven-year-olds that I'm going to hear that from this year is going to drive me mad."

I do not envy her.

"So, what's going on in your life?" she asks me after we turn on an old season of a reality show we love. "You haven't said much since getting here."

Damn her for being perceptive. "I don't have much to say," I lie, not sounding very convincing to myself.

I could tell her about my recent revelations regarding my coworker, who still hasn't returned. Or the fact that my *other* coworker is mad at me for it. Or probably the juiciest update in my life, which is that I had an orgasm that wasn't self-induced for once.

But I do not divulge any of that to her, because then she'd ask for details. And I wouldn't be able to tell her for two reasons.

One being my NDA agreement.

And two being that I don't *want* to tell her.

Kourtney isn't usually one to judge. She'll be the first one to tell you when she's done something stupid. That doesn't mean I want to admit I made a bad decision that has eaten me up since it happened.

I've been thinking way too much about how Moskins's thigh felt against me. How heat spread throughout my body. How badly my nipples ached as I got closer to the edge.

It's been a long time since anyone has touched me, and he barely did. Maybe I should be embarrassed by how easy it was to get me off. One kiss, one touch, and I was detonating.

And since then, it's been a recurring thought I can't get out of my head, no matter how hard I try. Then I wind up with a hand between my legs and very dirty thoughts replaying in my head.

"Spill," Kourtney demands, pausing the show and turning to me with suspicious eyes. "You're all flushed. What happened?"

Why do I have to be so obvious?

"I'm not," I squeak.

"Win," she says slowly, "you are a terrible liar. Do us both a favor and stop doing that because it's cringey."

I frown because she's right. I've never been good at lying. One look from our parents as a child, and I would break. I hated disappointing them, and they knew it. Apparently, I haven't honed that skill all these years later.

But I really, *really* don't want to tell her about what happened.

"Winnie," she says expectantly.

I weigh my options. If I don't tell her something, she won't let it go. Then it's going to be a long night. A painful one. I'll have to excuse myself early, which means going back to my apartment and sitting in silence.

"Winter!" Kourtney bellows, snapping her fingers in front of my face. "Get with it. What aren't you telling me?"

So much.

I'm not telling her so, so much.

And I feel bad about it because she's always been there for me when I needed her. But I don't need her right now. Not when it means coming clean about what I did with a married guy.

We're not together like that, Moskins told me.

Do I really believe him? Emaly certainly doesn't seem heartbroken over his transgressions. It would make more sense if they had some sort of…arrangement.

Oh my God.

Oh. My. God.

Am *I* part of some sort of arrangement between them? I'm trying not to judge, because to each their own, but what the actual fuck? Maybe this is a game for them. Maybe they're in on this together.

Kourtney hits me in the face with a couch pillow, and I

almost spill my dinner all over the floor. "Hey!" I whine, steadying my plate. "That was rude."

"Ignoring me is rude too," she counters unapologetically.

Fair point.

I go with a half-truth. "I think I may have accidentally gotten my coworker fired. Well, not me directly. But my client did. And it's made work a little…" I think about all the dirty looks Farrah has shot me this week. "Tense."

Anger instantly takes over my sister's face, like she's ready to fight for me without any more context. "Did they do something to you?"

Her mama bear energy is coming out, which warms my chest. "Cody—"

She groans at his name. "The guy you went out with? You said there was no policy against dating coworkers. Why would he be fired?"

"There isn't," I relay, scratching the column of my neck. I never told her that he'd still been hanging around and acting weird. Then she would have murdered him. Or done inhumane things to his favorite appendage. I'd hate for her to be punished for protecting me. "But he's been persistent, and I've been persistently bad at telling him to fuck off because I was trying to keep the peace."

You know, so things *don't* get weird at work like they have been. Clearly, a failed attempt that was all for nothing.

I rub a hand down my face. "I know it's partially my fault for not being more direct with him, but—"

"Fuck that," she spits out. "This is a grown-ass man, Win. He's more than capable of making his own choices.

He knew you weren't interested and didn't care. If he gets fired, that's on him."

Logically, I know she isn't wrong. It's what Janel said too. And if I bring it up to Moskins tomorrow, if I gather the courage to, then he'll say the same thing as them. "I don't like being the reason someone may lose something they've worked hard on."

Being responsible for life-changing events places a heavy burden on people's shoulders. If I lost my job, what would I do? Where would I go? I have bills. Rent. Student loans. I'd have to default or pause my payments. Then interest would only rack up what I owe, and I'd be double-screwed. I'd probably have to move in with Kourtney, which means hearing Brad bitch about there being no privacy.

"I don't want to put somebody at a disadvantage where their life turns upside down," I murmur, staring at my food.

My sister's hand is gentle when it touches mine. "This is nothing like what happened to our parents, if that's what you're thinking. You went out on a date with someone who's too arrogant to see his own faults. You didn't get behind the wheel of a car. Cody is the one responsible for his own demise, just like Adam Burgess is responsible for what he did to Mom and Dad. Don't blame yourself. They wouldn't want that for you."

Hearing that name sends shivers down my spine. For months after the accident, I'd had nightmares of squealing tires and sobbing screams, even though I wasn't there. I would picture our family's car being hit, then the person responsible speeding away.

Seeing Adam Burgess in court didn't help. Kourtney told me not to go, but I wasn't about to let her go alone. We'd both lost people, and I was going to face the person who caused it and be strong like she was.

That name…I haven't let it infect my life in a very long time. I've refused to acknowledge it after it did so much damage. This is the first time I've heard her speak it in years.

My appetite wanes, which is sad because I rarely have full meals like this.

"Tell me you know I'm right," she insists. "If you still feel bad for what happened to Mom and Dad, I need you to know it's not your fault. Just like your coworker being a seedy motherfucker isn't."

I know there's nothing I could have done to stop what happened. If I'd gone with them, I would have simply been victim number three. Kourtney would have lost everyone. Our grandparents on both sides passed away from a mixture of old age and illness, and we never had a lot of contact with aunts and uncles. We've heard from some of them on and off over the years, especially right after the accident, but even that fizzled out as time went on and they stopped feeling guilty about our parents' deaths.

Finally, I nod. "I know it isn't my fault."

"Good," she says firmly. "I hope Cody loses his job. Guys like him skeeve me out," she replies nonchalantly, pointing to my food. "Now eat before it gets cold."

I roll my eyes at her motherly tone. "Yes, *Mom.*"

She flips me off.

I blow her a kiss.

Luca sits up, turns to us, and says, "I changed my mind. I want a claw machine for Christmas instead. Look how cool they are inside!"

CHAPTER TWELVE
Moskins

THE BALL OF black and white fur hisses at me when I bend down to pick up the feather toy laying next to her. Then a paw darts out and swipes at me for a third time in a row.

"Ow!" I growl, retrieving my hand without the toy and glancing at the scratches left behind.

My arm looks like I put it through a meat slicer. Some of the wounds are fresh, others are days old. All of them are thanks to the demon staring up at me with beady yellow eyes.

I can handle two-hundred-and-thirty-pound men coming at me on the ice and smashing me into the boards. But cat scratches are an entirely new pain.

I jab my finger at the kitten. "What pit of Hell did you escape from? It's no wonder they suggested I take you."

Her sharp, high-pitched meow is accompanied by a little butt wiggle before she pounces on my shoe.

The feline, appropriately named Oreo, has black fur with little patches of white down the middle of her back, just like the cookie. According to the shelter, she's the last of her litter to be adopted. Now I know why.

"I should have gotten a dog," I mumble, peeling her

from my jeans that she's trying to climb up.

Oreo makes another noise, batting at my fingers as loud rumbles come from her.

I gawk at her. "Do you enjoy torturing me?"

She meows again, still purring.

That's a yes.

Sighing, I check the clock and realize I'm going to be late to meet with Winter at the Fairbanks Food Bank.

Problem is, I don't know what to do with my new family member. Can cats be alone? They can, right? As long as they have food, water, and their litter box. I set everything up the second I brought her home. I'd released her from the carrier they'd given me to transport her home in, and she tore ass through the living room and hid for hours. I spent forty minutes trying to figure out where the pain in the ass went, only to find her in the room Emaly claimed. She'd puked on the carpet and stained it orange.

At the last minute, I decide to bring Oreo with me. I'll feel bad leaving her in her carrier, and I don't know if I fully trust her to be home by herself. Which might be tricky, considering I doubt Hoffman would allow me to travel with a cat all season long.

I'd gotten to go to the Yokav Stadium and see the team twice this week. Once for a group workout in the stadium's gym, and once for conditioning on the ice. I got the training camp schedule for September and the schedule for all our preseason games. I'd be lying if I said I was confident that the Fireflies stand a chance at getting anywhere near the championships, but I'd work my ass off to get us close.

When I pull up to the food bank, I turn to see the kitten staring at me through the crate bars with big eyes. She pawed at the door the entire drive, wanting out. But I learned the hard way what a bad idea that was when I brought her home. She'd not only gotten car sick on me, but she kept trying to get under the gas pedal.

At least she didn't puke this time.

I don't think twice about grabbing her carrier and bringing it with me, listening to her squeaky protests as we head to the building's entrance, where we'll spend the day sorting and distributing groceries to the community.

"What is that?" Winter asks as soon as I step inside. She's pointing a pen at the carrier dangling in my hand, gaping skeptically at the kitten's array of noises. "Did someone dump a cat outside? Oh my God, that poor thing!"

She quickly comes over and squats down to see inside, her whole face brightening at the sight of the she-devil wrapped in cute black fur.

"Don't let the cuteness fool you," I tell her, setting it down in front of Winter. "She's a devious little shit."

Winter gasps. "Don't say that! She was abandoned and probably scared. I would be t—"

"I adopted her."

My statement stops her, and she slowly looks up at me with a confused expression painted over her features. "You…what?"

A small smile appears on my face. "I adopted her from the shelter. Went back a few days ago. I was planning to get a dog, but they said cats are easier to care for if you have a busy schedule because they're more independent. Since I live alone and will be gone a lot, it'd be easier for me to have a cat."

Winter continues to gape at me in utter disbelief. This shouldn't be that shocking. I told her I wanted to get a dog at the diner. She just chose not to take me seriously.

Eventually, she closes her mouth and glances back down at the carrier. "Can I…?" She gestures toward Oreo, and I nod.

"Be careful, though. She's a feisty one."

The blond sinks onto her knees and opens the carrier door. She's cautious, trying not to scare Oreo as the kitten slowly makes her way out and looks around her new environment.

Her little pink nose reaches toward Winter's extended hand, sniffing her once. I expect her to lash out. Scratch her. Hiss. The same shit I've endured since bringing her home.

But then I hear it.

Not the sound of haughty distrust.

The sound of approval.

"Is she fucking *purring*?" I ask, frowning as Winter picks her up and cradles her against her chest without any fight from Oreo. The kitten nuzzles Winter's chin, making the blonde giggle.

Unbelievable. "That thing hates me. She only purrs after causing me bodily harm."

Winter carefully stands, still holding Oreo close to her chest. "Maybe it's because you refer to her as a 'thing.' What's her name?"

There is instant love in both of their eyes that makes me jealous of a fucking cat. That's low even for me. "Oreo," I tell her begrudgingly.

She repeats the names to herself, barely making a sound. Yet I watch her mouth form the word a little too closely.

When I step toward them out of some sort of invisible draw, Oreo hisses at me. "See!" I exclaim in frustration, glaring at the cat. "She hates me."

Winter continues to soothe the fur on Oreo's back, hushing my cool tone. "I'm sure this isn't the first time a pussy didn't like you. Huh, Oreo?"

The retort makes me freeze.

We're quiet for a second.

Two.

Winter sheepishly peeks up at me.

Then I burst out laughing.

Her grin quickly grows, and she joins in while still fussing over the kitten in her arms. "I'd say sorry, but I'm not."

I shake my head. "I wouldn't have accepted it anyway," I reply easily, huffing out another laugh. "Seriously, though. I think I chose the one animal that doesn't want me around. At this rate, you should keep her. It's obvious she has favorites."

Winter straightens, her eyes flicking to me. "I cannot have a cat."

The indignation in her tone has me staring at her skeptically. "Why not?"

She levels me a look. "Thomas, I date men for food.

Remember? If I can't afford more than ramen on my own, I'm not going to be able to budget for cat food and everything else she'd need to live happily."

The reminder makes my fingers tighten into fists. And apparently, I'm not the only one who wants to continue that conversation.

"Did you really go to Janel about Cody?" she asks quietly, not looking up from Oreo to avoid my stare.

I drop my voice so the people gathering at the other end of the room can't hear. "If you're asking, you already know the answer."

We're quiet.

She focuses on Oreo.

I focus on her.

"He could lose his job," she whispers.

All I say is, "Good."

When she peeks up at me again, I can see the way her lips part to say something before she inevitably decides not to.

My eyes go down to her hands. "Your nails are yellow today."

Another happy color.

Her throat bobs. "Yellow represents healing, optimism, and clear mental focus." Her fingers flex around Oreo. "And it was my mother's favorite color."

Was. I take the reference to her mother in the past tense as another piece of the puzzle. I don't tell her I'm sorry for her loss because I don't think she'd want to hear it. "What does purple mean?"

"Creativity and spirituality," she answers after a moment.

I cock my head. "And pink?"

She doesn't answer me. Mostly because a woman who can't be that much older than me walks up with a big smile on her face. "Welcome! You must be Thomas." She sticks her hand out to me, and I dutifully take it with a well-trained smile.

Before I can correct her, Winter says, "He prefers Moskins, Kaleigh."

The woman, Kaleigh, nods in understanding as she inspects me with an inquisitive eye that seems to hold more than curiosity. "Moskins," she tests out, a small, flirty smile tilting her painted pink lips as her gaze rakes over me. "Well, it's very nice to meet you. I'm Kayleigh, the executive director here. Anything you need, please feel free to ask."

I'm sure she'd give me anything I want if I give her the right smile. Unfortunately for her, she isn't the woman I want something from. "I came with my own expert, so I think I'll be well guided."

My hand comes down on Winter's lower back, just hovering enough to feel her body heat soak into my palm without actually touching her. Nonetheless, she stiffens and stands a little straighter.

Her eyes bounce from me to Kayleigh before clearing her throat. "Our original photographer had a family emergency, so our backup is running a little late," she explains to the executive director, still giving me bedroom eyes.

Kayleigh's focus is on where my hand is, and I can tell she isn't very happy with the current placement. "Why don't you wait here to make sure we don't miss them, then? I'll show Moskins around to familiarize him with our setup and explain how today is going to go."

I begin to protest, but Winter steps away from me with a nod. "That's fine. I'll meet you as soon as they arrive."

Kayleigh puts a hand on my arm, and the touch is a little too forward. Normally, I like that with women. There's no point wasting time if all two people want is to get off in the end. I'd rather they not mince words or expect pretty pleasantries.

But her touch isn't the welcome one I want.

So, I move my arm away and reach over to brush Oreo's fur despite the bastard's protests. "I will be right back. Take care of my cat for me."

Kayleigh perks up. "That cutie is yours? She is—" She jerks back when Oreo swats at her with her murder mittens. Guess I'm not the only one she doesn't like. "—adorable."

Her voice is strained and forced when she finishes off the very fake compliment. We both know that's not what she's thinking.

But I say, "I know," anyway.

All while staring at Winter.

DODGING WOMEN'S ADVANCES isn't necessarily something I'm used to, so I deserve a gold medal for the work I do to avoid the director's more than friendly touches throughout the day. I don't like it. Just like I don't like the dark colors on her nails that aren't bright or fun or meaningful like they are on Winter's. She probably painted them for fun. Winter painted them for a purpose.

It's easier to avoid Kayleigh when the photographer, who happens to be none other than my head coach's wife, shows up full of repetitive apologies and her service dog trailing beside her. "So sorry, everyone. I'm a last-minute fill-in for today because the original photographer had to pull out."

Honor, with the golden retriever standing next to her with his service vest on, sticks out her hand to me. "Hi, Moskins. I hope you don't mind that I stepped in. When I heard today might not go as planned, I offered my services. Don't worry. I won't make you pose or force you to smile because I don't want your scowl to break my camera."

I huff out a laugh at her sarcasm. I've only been around the redhead a few times, and it's easier to see she's become more comfortable in social settings. She used to be more reserved. Civil, like she didn't want to say the wrong thing. I like that she isn't holding back. She'll need that, being surrounded by a bunch of brutes like us.

"That's good," I muse. Because the cold shoulder I've been getting from Winter since Kayleigh pulled me away hasn't particularly put me in a smiley mood. Part of me likes that she's jealous enough to react. The other is pissed off that she won't even look at me. If she did, she'd realize I'm not returning the advances.

"They better be paying you good money to do this," I say, making small talk with Honor. "Bodhi mentioned how busy your studio has been lately."

Honor beams as she sets up her camera, testing it by snapping a few pictures around the room. "I don't mind doing side gigs like this because it keeps my connections fresh. If someone I know hears about certain events happening, they'll refer me as the photographer. So if it means moving around my schedule a little, then it works out in the end. A paycheck is a paycheck."

Bodhi Hoffman talked more about his wife's success when I met with him to speak to Mikhail a few weeks ago than he did about his own. It doesn't matter that he's heading his own NHL team and getting mad money for it. The only thing he really cares about is Honor's booming studio photography business.

I get it, though. My old team didn't know much about my personal life, but they sure as hell knew that my wife put herself through medical school. She didn't expect me to contribute, even when I got my contract with the Penguins. I saw the grueling hours it took for her to get where she is now, and I didn't let people take away the credit where it was due. I may have helped her study a little, but her success is hers and hers alone. That's exactly how Bodhi is with Honor.

Winter is silent more than she isn't after Honor starts, only speaking to our famed photographer when she needs to. It's easy to see that she's mad at me, and the reaction is comical at best.

It tells me exactly what I want to know. That she's impacted by me as much as I am by her. I want to say, *it's not fun, is it?* I want to make a comment that will make her blush. Maybe one that will make her glare and flip me off.

Instead, I behave like the good little boy I am, no matter how much I want to mess with the glowering blonde watching from the sidelines in frumpy clothes that do little for her figure. Is she trying to seem unappealing? Because not even the oversized shirt tucked into the worn pair of pants can make me uninterested at this point.

I shake hands and smile, and even sign a few pieces of paper when young fans come in. Outside of the professional shots Honor gets, I take pictures with a couple of the volunteers for their social media and a few kids who tell me they plan on buying my new Fireflies jersey once it goes on sale because I'm their favorite hockey player.

It's a gentle reminder that people give a shit, despite what Mikhail or the media thinks. I may not be the best person, but I'm a damn good player. The fans who watch know that I've got something not everybody has. I need to make sure I don't totally fuck that up.

I go about the day helping sort through donations to check their expiration dates, stock shelves, and assist between the drive-thru and in-person distributions, all while Winter watches me with my kitten in her hand and her lips pressed into a line that tries not to give too much away.

Sucks for her because that expression says more than she wants to admit.

She's jealous.

Especially when Kayleigh or one of the other girls comes up and offers me their fakest laughs and biggest smiles as if I get off on fake pleasantries.

It sucks for them. A month ago, I probably would have

invited both of them to a hotel room with me. We could have enjoyed each other's company and gone our separate ways, feeling satisfied and victorious.

It's too bad for them that a five-foot-three blonde with permanent pink on her cheeks has burrowed under my skin and stayed there like a nuisance.

When it's the end of the day, and Honor is packing up her things, I walk over and lean on the wall. "Did your husband tell you I'm working with the team finally?"

I have no doubt in my mind they're the kind of couple who tell each other everything. I'm sure when they both get home, they share gossip while rubbing one another's feet with googly eyes full of love plastered on their faces.

I'll never forget the first time I went to a barbecue at their house with the rest of the guys from the Fireflies shortly after the news broke about the new team. It was similar to what Bodhi and I have gone to in the past with our former teams. It's a bonding experience, as if we don't see the boys enough during the season to begin with. It was obvious watching them that Honor and Bodhi are in the sickening kind of love.

Honor zips up her camera bag and throws it over her shoulder before reaching down to scratch between her dog's ears. I'm trying to remember what kind of service animal he is without coming out and asking like an asshole.

Saying, *"Hey, what's wrong with you that you need a dog?"* probably doesn't come across very well. Not that I'm known for my politeness, but I like Honor.

"He did," she confirms. "He's relieved that Mikhail agreed to have you come in. He was starting to worry that you wouldn't see ice time."

It'll be a cold day in hell before I let that happen. "I was feeling the same way," I admit, feeling a pair of eyes on me from across the room.

I don't turn to Winter or let on that I can feel her staring. Instead, I gesture toward the golden retriever sitting idly on the floor. "Do you mind if I ask what he's for?"

I'm pretty sure Hoffman told me once, but I'll be damned if I can remember. I'll be the first to admit that a lot of conversations I have with people are in one ear and out the other. I can't always find the energy to care. If I'm at big events, I'm usually thinking about when I can finally leave them.

"Puck is a seizure detection and alert animal," she explains with an unoffended smile. "He's been a big part of my life for years. Huh, buddy?"

The dog looks up at her with his fluffy, dark yellow tail brushing happily against the ground.

Seizure detection. It rings a bell hearing her husband explain it to a few guys and me when we went over to their place earlier this year. "How did you get him?"

The question is out before I can process it, and the surprise and concern on her face are evident. Her voice lowers when she asks, "Are you okay? Is there—"

"I'm not asking for me," I quickly explain, studying the dog's vest that has "working dog" and "do not touch" in bold lettering on the back. Wetting my lips, I peel my eyes off him and back over to Honor. "I'm just curious."

We both know I wouldn't be asking if it didn't matter to me, but she indulges me in an answer anyway. And only when Honor passes me a piece of paper with a website to look into and phone numbers I can call do I feel satisfied enough to stop pressing for information.

"I'll see you around," I tell her, slipping the paper into my back pocket and waving her and Puck off.

When I walk over to Winter, there's a shadow on her face. "We'll wrap up, and then you can go." She passes me Oreo, who looks none too pleased to be given to me. "Here. I'll let you deal with her. If you haven't already, it wouldn't be a bad idea to post with her and show that you adopted from the shelter. It'll make you look better."

I shake my head. "I don't care about that."

She deadpans, "The whole point of this is to make you look more human and less—"

"Douchey?" I guess, knowing that's one of her favorite descriptors of me. "I didn't adopt Oreo to come off more believable."

Winter pauses, hesitating with a nibble to her inner cheek as if she doesn't want to ask me the real reason. Curiosity wins out. "Then why did you get her if not for the attention?"

"To be a little less lonely."

I deliver the answer with a limp, nonchalant shrug that she gapes at.

"But," I add quietly, running a hand down Oreo's spine, "you already knew that. It's just easier for you to see me as the bad guy."

She closes her eyes. "I never said that."

I tug on a strand of her hair lightly, only enough to get her to look at me again. "You didn't need to."

This time, she says nothing.

Doesn't apologize.

Doesn't argue.

Doesn't make excuses.

Her eyes lower. Not to the ground, but toward my legs. I'm not sure what she's thinking because she shakes off whatever thought she had and suddenly looks angry. "I'm going to confirm we got everything and then head out. Thank you for coming. It was a successful day."

Her tone is too professional.

Civil.

Like we're strangers.

As if she doesn't know one of my biggest secrets.

It takes everything in me not to reach out and wrap my palm around her arm to stop her from storming off, but I manage to control myself.

Not here, I think to myself.

Not in front of all these people.

So, I let her go.

CHAPTER THIRTEEN

Winter

NO, NO, NO, *no*. Not today. This could have happened at any time, and my car chose *this* moment to stop working.

"Please, not now," I whine to my Subaru, trying unsuccessfully to turn it over for the fifth time since climbing in. It's been a long day, and a hot shower, clean pair of leggings, and an oversized shirt are all calling my name. I want to sulk and eat my weight in knock-off Frosted Flakes while binge-watching an old season of *Grey's Anatomy*.

Although my favorite medical drama has been compromised since meeting the dark-haired woman whose husband I have the audacity to be mad at for flirting with another woman. What the hell is wrong with me?

Too much, I've decided.

Emaly deserves better.

And I need to go back to therapy. Except therapy is expensive, so bettering my mental health will have to wait. Again.

I close my eyes and lean my forehead against the top of my steering wheel when I realize that my car may officially be gone. I'll have to have a funeral for it, like I did for Melvin the cat. I bet Kourtney would have nicer things to say to my trusty vehicle than she did to my precious feline companion. Like how she lost her virginity in the back seat, which is a story I wish I could unhear all these years after she shared it with me. Or how she used to tailgate at parties that Mom and Dad never knew about because, unlike me, she's good at being stealthy. She definitely loves the Outback more than Melvin, and that makes me miss him way more.

I yelp when someone knocks on the window, and I hate the way my face crumples when I see Moskins standing on the other side. When I make no move to open the door, he does with arched brows as he studies my slumped body.

"Car problems?" he guesses.

All I do is nod silently.

"Got in the way of your dramatic exit, huh?"

This time, it's me scowling.

His lips tug at the corners. "Come on. I'll give you a lift. We can call a tow truck on the way."

He's nonchalant as he turns with Oreo's carrier in his hand and heads toward his car. I still find it hard to believe he drives a Nissan Rogue and not a Mercedes or Porsche. Something flashy and...*douchey.*

Sighing, I weigh my options before realizing I have very few. I can call a tow truck and wait for them here and, hopefully, get a ride home with them, or...

I can go with the man whose butt looks way too good in those jeans. And screw me for noticing. And screw *him* for looking over his shoulder to see if I'm following at the very moment my eyes are plastered to his ass.

Why is the world against me?

I tell myself the only reason I follow him to his car is because of Oreo. Her loud, vibrating purrs will soothe my anxiety about what's bound to be a very expensive and unexpected repair bill. I know I've been biding my time with my car, but I love it too much to let it go. And new vehicles, or at least new to *me* ones, are expensive. Janel told me that she and her husband both have car payments upward of seven hundred dollars a month each.

Seven. *Hundred!*

I could never. I will learn the bus schedule and pay my dues to the Fairbanks public transit before I ever get something that equals my rent.

"Care to explain why you're pissed at me this time?" Moskins asks, breaking me from my faraway thoughts. "I'm losing track of reasons. Last time, it was because I inadvertently got you pulled from the shelter event and then made you come against the wall in apology. What did I do *this* time?"

Flaming heat works its way up my face and settles under the skin in my cheeks. "Is that what that was? A pity orgasm to shut me up?"

He huffs out a laugh. "It was a lot of things, sweetheart. But it did work, didn't it?"

My chest tightens as I stare out the window and listen to Oreo in the back seat. She doesn't seem very happy being stuck in her crate, and I'm right there with her.

"I'm so glad I could help contribute to your quota of pity fucks this year. Your charity work knows no bounds," I reply sarcastically, staring out the window and praying that traffic doesn't slow us down. The quicker I'm out of this car, the better.

Unfortunately for me, there's a long line of red lights that really seem to love us as we approach them. One after another, the greens turn yellow, which then turns into the same color as the flags I seem to attract the most.

Bright-ass red.

"There's one problem with that assessment," he remarks, not seeming fazed at all by my biting tone. His casual nonchalance pisses me off that much more.

I deadpan, hating the knot in my chest that feels a lot like jealousy, "And what would that be?"

"I haven't fucked you yet, Winter."

I suck in a sharp breath at the words that soak in a little too deeply.

He hasn't fucked me *yet.* That three-letter word grabs hold of me for dear life, and I hate how much it stirs something inside my lower gut.

Yet.

His lips quirk into a knowing smile. "Do you like the sound of that?" he guesses, studying me as we wait for the light to change. It's not an actual question he needs an answer to. "If you want to get to know me, here's a fact. I don't *fuck* out of pity. I fuck to feel good. I fuck so my partner feels good. I *fuck* because I like it, and I like it when my partner does too."

He's not looking at me as he drives, but I know his eyes are intense as they focus on the road. His fingers are wrapped tightly around the steering wheel—the skin is pulled taut around his knuckles and white. His jaw grinds, and a slight tic of his jaw tells me that he's holding back a lot more than he's saying.

And what I may hate more than my reaction to his initial statement is the way my heart leaps in my chest when he says the word "fuck" like it's a prayer.

His mouth wraps around the word like I imagine it wrapped around my—

Oh my God.

"Stop," I blurt, not sure if I'm talking to myself or him.

"Stop what?" he asks, still grasping the wheel tightly as we drive down the long stretch of Main Street. "Stop the car? Stop telling you the truth? You're the one who wants to get to know me, so I'm letting you know who I am. I'm a man who has a healthy appetite for sex. I have no shame about that. I love the feeling of sinking my cock into a wet pussy. I love the sound that women make when they come around me. I love—"

I swallow past the lump in my throat as I fidget in the front seat. "Stop talking like that," I cut him off, feeling my heart drum wildly in my chest.

"Can't handle it?" he challenges.

My nostrils flare as I finally look in his direction. "Do you ever feel like a jackass hearing yourself talk, or do you get off on it since you love the feeling so much?"

To my surprise, some of that intensity melts into amusement. "Who says it can't be both?"

I shake my head and wrap my arms around my stomach in a hug to keep my hands from fidgeting. "You may have no shame, but that doesn't mean I have to be like you. I can feel bad about—" I cut myself off before admitting to him the reason I'm mad.

The annoying green monster nags at my soul after seeing him slip that piece of paper into his back pocket earlier. After watching Kayleigh, who's notorious for being a little too friendly with people, all but grope him all day, it was hard to watch him flirt with the pretty photographer.

It's even harder for me to accept that I'm upset about it. I have no claim to the man. In fact, I have no right at all to feel this way. But that's always been the problem with me and my stupid anxious-avoidant attachment. The second someone starts to give me attention, it's like I hold on to it for dear life to forget that I'm normally on my own. My old therapist said it was a trauma response to losing my family—that I crave attention and validation. As I got older, I shifted to avoidance. When people gave me attention, I wouldn't give them the full me. Because if I don't even like me, how can anybody else?

If I still went to that kind, older woman that I'd met with once a week for almost two years after my parents' passing, she'd tell me I'm forming a pattern. Maybe she'd even tell me that Thomas Moskins is not the type of man you fall in love with. He's the kind that your mother warns you away from because he'll break your heart. After all, I don't have a mom to heed those warnings.

I want nothing to do with heartbreak. Losing my parents was the biggest one I could have faced. Adding an unavailable man to my life would cause nothing but trouble.

It would be really nice if my body got on board with that sentiment before I let him do something stupid to me.

"You can feel bad about what?" he presses, his voice

uncharacteristically soft compared to before.

I close my eyes and realize I backed myself into a metaphorical corner. "Nothing," I say, hoping he'll drop it.

He doesn't. "Tell me."

Bite me, is what I almost say in retort. Problem is, he'd probably grin and say, *happily*. So I hold that response in and swallow it like the bitterness I felt all day long.

"Winter," he says slowly. "Tell me."

When I peek at him, he's staring at me.

Hard.

We're stopped at another red light, the last one until we turn onto the street that will take me to my apartment. His eyes pin me to my seat, the blue-gray color fiercely impatient.

I let out a shallow breath and give in because I have a feeling he won't let it go otherwise. "I was jealous, okay? Happy now?"

For once, he's quiet.

Too quiet.

Contemplative.

His lips rub together until someone behind us honks at the light that's finally green.

Moskins nods once and starts driving again.

But we don't turn onto the street that leads to my place. We keep going straight.

"You missed the turn," I tell him, looking out the window with a frown. Is this where he takes me to the woods and tortures me? Rats me out to Emaly for being jealous? Goes to Janel?

I turn to him, worried. "Moskins, we missed—"

"I know," he cuts me off, staring forward and not giving me his attention. "And I don't want you calling me that anymore."

My brows pinch. "What? You said you prefer being called—"

"From now on," he says, cutting me off, "it's Thomas to you. Just not…not Tommy. Please."

Concern blossoms in my chest, and I regret being honest with him. What is he thinking? Why does he look like that? Pained and…and sad and *angry*?

"Where are we going?" I don't call him by the name he wants me to. I can't. It feels too intimate.

That concern blooms into something completely different when he says, "My place."

I DON'T KNOW why I follow him into the house that seems even bigger inside than it does from the brick exterior. It's a beautiful home, full of warm woods, open space, and a cozy ambiance that seems so unlike anything he would enjoy. I never pictured where he lives, but it's certainly not *this*.

As soon as the door is closed behind us, he sets Oreo's carrier down and lets her loose. She shoots out and runs as fast as her little legs can go until she's out of sight.

"Fucking cat," Moskins mumbles, shoving the crate off to the side.

I'm studying the pictures hanging along the walls when I feel his focus turn to me. But I can't take my eyes off the black-and-white image of him and Emaly laughing as they lounge on a checkered blanket in the grass. They both look younger—his face is lacking any stubble, and his features are less defined, as if he hasn't spent the same amount of time at the gym as he does now. There's something smeared on her face. Frosting? Whatever it is, it also happens to be smeared on his hand.

Body heat soaks into my back as Moskins walks up behind me. He doesn't touch me, but he might as well have. My skin tingles from his closeness, and my heart beats wildly in its cage so hard I worry he can hear it. "That was our engagement shoot," he tells me, voice sounding distant yet nostalgic.

My eyes go from where frosting is painted on her cheek down to her hand. Then her *other* hand, when I assume I'm looking at the wrong one. Except there's no ring on any of her fingers. There isn't one in a box or strategically planted in leaves or other aesthetic places either.

He must know exactly what I'm looking for, because he says, "There isn't one."

I don't need to ask what he's referring to, so I look over my shoulder at him in hopes of an explanation.

Moskins gives me one without me having to ask. "We agreed that I didn't need to spend money on a ring. At the time, we were in our early twenties. I was just getting scouted by the NHL, and she was still in college and applying to med schools. Our finances were limited."

I know very little about Emaly, since her background isn't what I had to look into in my initial search of her husband's extracurricular activities. What I do know about her is that she comes from a very wealthy family.

I debate asking the question at the forefront of my mind before just doing it. "Did her family not…help?"

A shadow casts over his features, hardening them. "Her family and her aren't as close as she'd like them to be. Emaly has always been independent. She's never wanted their resources to be the reason she's handed things. It's been her goal to establish a future for herself on her own terms. To *earn* it. If she accepted help from her mother and father in any way, it would come with a steep price and steeper consequences. Neither one of us wanted that."

The more I learn about Emaly, the more I like her. And the more I feel like utter garbage for feeling the way I do.

"I shouldn't be here," I say aloud, swallowing down the guilt rising up my sternum and rubbing my clammy hands down my thighs.

Moskins tips my chin up when I refuse to meet his eyes, forcing me to look at him. Then he produces a piece of paper from his jeans and flips it over for me to see the ink across it.

It contains two things.

A phone number.

And a website.

All written in feminine handwriting.

"I didn't get Honor's phone number," he informs me matter-of-factly. "That's the redhead's name who you stormed out because of. That's the head coach's wife. She was giving me information that I intend to pass along to someone else."

My eyes flicker between him and the paper, eyebrows pinched. "A website about service animals?"

The photographer, Honor, had a service dog who'd stayed with her the entire time. He quietly stuck by her side as she worked, never getting in her or anybody else's way.

It's not my business to ask who he plans on sending that information to, no matter how much I want to know.

He dips his chin once and lowers the paper down on the foyer table beside us and encompasses me in the scent of sandalwood, laundry detergent, and something masked by the overbearing perfume Kayleigh wore.

I do everything I can to not react the way the little green monster inside me wants to.

His eyes look grayer than blue as he stares down at me. The storm raging inside them melts me to the floor, and I have to lean against the wall to put even the tiniest distance between where our chests nearly brush.

He leans an arm against the wall and cocks his head. "Ask me what you want to ask me, Winter. I know you've got questions."

It's hard to process any of my thoughts when he's this close. How does he expect me to voice them when all I can smell is Kayleigh's stupid floral perfume? What could I possibly say that he would want to hear anyway?

"I shouldn't be—"

"You already said that," he cuts me off unapologetically. "But just because you *shouldn't* want something doesn't mean you *don't* want it. So ask me what you want to know."

I suck in a sharp, quiet breath and let it flood my lungs. If I thought my heart was racing before, it's nothing compared to when he reaches up and tugs on a loose strand of pink hair that escaped the updo I put it in. It's not a painful pull, but one that grounds me as he twirls it around his finger.

Eventually, I swallow and gather what little focus I can despite what he's doing. "Why didn't you get her a ring after you signed your contract with Pittsburgh's team? I know what you made back then. I've done my research. You could have bought her hundreds of expensive rings by now."

He hums, leaning forward to close the gap between us until his mouth brushes against the shell of my ear. "Because," he says, his lips grazing me, "we agreed when we got married that we wouldn't spend money on something that important until it meant something to us."

His answer is as confusing as the way my nipples harden in my shirt. I blame his hot breath echoing against my earlobe, and the husky tone of his voice that vibrates me to my core for the reaction I wish I didn't have. Can he see what he's doing to me? I hope not.

"That's…" I'm at a loss for words.

Because I don't understand. Not fully. There is so much of their story that I'm clearly missing, and I know I have no right to fill in the gaps.

I shouldn't be here.

I really shouldn't be here.

But damn, do I want to be.

The next question out of my mouth makes me want to find his bathroom and drown myself in the tub. "Are you going to kiss me again?" It's asked in a breathy, choppy tone that gives away how much I want to be in this position.

His lips slowly stretch into a half-grin as he studies me far too closely. The finger with my hair wrapped around it tugs again, this time getting my head closer to his until our mouths are a centimeter apart.

Then he says, "No" and backs away.

I sink against the wall, heart dropping into my stomach. There are so many questions I want to follow up with. Like why? And what the hell? And what am I doing here then?

I don't ask him any of those.

Because he slides his hands into the pockets of his jeans and tells me, "The next time we kiss, it's going to be because you're begging me for it. And make no mistake, Winter. It won't feel like I'm pitying you. Not at all."

If my heart could stop without killing me, it would with his promise. Because that's what this is. Not a warning. Not a threat. Not a taunt. He is promising that it *will* happen. That I'll cave. That I'll finally admit I want this. Whatever the hell this is between us.

Nothing good.

Nothing permanent.

He didn't even buy his own wife a ring.

"Why did you bring me here, Thomas?"

His lips tilt at the use of his name, but the smirk quickly vanishes. "That's a great fucking question," he mumbles, more to himself than me. "I guess I like torturing myself."

He turns on his heels and walks into another room, but not before I see him adjust himself where the denim of his jeans is tented.

CHAPTER FOURTEEN

Moskins

I'VE MADE A lot of mistakes in my life, but none of them are as painful as the one currently walking around my house. My balls are at risk of turning blue and falling off, and it's nobody's fault but my own. I could have dropped Winter off at her place and forgotten everything she said. I could have ignored her jealousy and pretended it didn't matter.

But I'm a goddamn masochist.

Winter strolls into the home office, where I store my first-edition novels and spend time alone. I enjoy the smell of wood and leather and find myself hanging out in the armchairs or at my desk more times than I can count. Usually, I'm dicking around on my phone or staring at the bookshelves that line two out of the four walls.

The prized collection of classics cost me an ungodly amount of money, and the ones strategically placed on the built-in shelves are only *some* of them. The rest are still displayed in glass hutches and entertainment stands in two other properties. I let Emaly choose which ones she wanted to keep in San Diego, and I am still sad she wanted the only editions of *Little Women* and *Frankenstein* that I could find.

"Wow." I hear her breathe as she runs her hand along the edge of the shelf. When she gets halfway down the line of nineteenth-century titles, she stops and stares at one in particular.

I know exactly which one she's reaching for before she even turns to me with a skeptical arched brow. "You acted like you didn't know who Charlotte Brontë was," she accuses, holding up the copy of *Jane Eyre*.

I do my best not to look like I've been caught in a lie and lift a shoulder. "Must have forgotten," is the answer I settle with.

One she doesn't believe. "You like books." It's not a question, or even something she expects confirmation over. It's a simple statement as she carefully puts the novel back in its place and then continues scanning the other titles. "Have you read all these, or is this just for looks? There must be hundreds here."

I debate whether or not I want to be honest, but I've admitted more about myself to her than to anybody else. "I've read all but three," I admit, trying to act casual about it even when she shoots me a surprised but impressed glance. "English has always been my favorite subject. When people were bitching about having to write a report on *The Scarlet Letter* or *Moby Dick*, I was diving in and highlighting everything I could."

She mock-gasps, a hand flying to her chest. "I hear writing in books is punishable by death."

My cheek twitches with the threat of a smile that takes everything in me not to give her. "That is only for the heathens who dog-ear book corners."

Winter plays along. "And you'd never dare."

"Never," I tell her with a flicker of amusement.

She opens another book to inspect the pages, frowning at the lack of highlighter or ink smudges in the margins. She won't find any on these. Other editions, sure. But not my collection.

"These editions cost too much for me to write down my thoughts in them," I say, still sitting behind my desk. I needed the distance from her—the block of a large piece of polished walnut to separate us before I did something stupid.

Stupider than bringing her home.

Dumber than pinning her against a wall.

Again.

I scrub at my jaw, wiping away the thought before my erection comes back in full force. "I find reading to be a peaceful escape from reality when I no longer wish to live my own life." I gesture toward the shelves. I love the various colors. The gold foiled font on the spines that stands out against the dark, aged wood. This space may be my favorite. "Why live one life when you can live thousands?"

Her eyes soften, but there's still some level of skepticism in them. "Is your life so bad that you need to escape it?"

I lean back in my chair. In her eyes, I probably sound like a privileged crybaby. And in many ways, I am. I'm lucky to experience wealth and good fortune despite my upbringing. But I've had to work past a lot of shit in order to be content with where I'm at. "We all have things we try to escape," I reply, tilting my head. "My past is mine."

I don't elaborate, and she doesn't press.

Smart girl.

She nibbles on her bottom lip, and I can tell there's another question coming regardless. "Do you openly try to hide this side of you for a reason?"

"And which side is that?"

Winter lets out a small, quiet breath. "The human one. People can relate to that. It isn't a weakness, Thomas."

I've never liked anybody calling me anything other than Moskins because it reminds me of *them*. Of the very past that I want to brush away and lock up in the deepest pits of my mind and never think about.

But coming from her mouth, it feels right. As right as when Emaly calls me by my name. My skin doesn't crawl. My stomach doesn't sink. No. She causes the opposite reaction.

"I never said it was a weakness," I huff out, crossing my arms and resting them on my chest. "Maybe I just don't give a fuck what people think of me. Have you ever thought of that?"

She's contemplative, her body turning away from mine as she gives her full attention to the pricey novels. "If you didn't care about what people thought, then you never would have met me. One day, you'll have to be honest with yourself."

Fat chance that will ever come to fruition.

"What do you think I'm lying to myself about, oh wise one?" I quip, not seeming to faze her with my sarcasm.

She still doesn't turn when she answers, "If I had to

guess, everything."

For once, I'm quiet. And the more I think about it, the more I become annoyed. Because who does she think she is to assume she knows anything about me? She doesn't.

She doesn't know the sleepless nights.

The endless training.

The counseling sessions.

The foster homes.

The secretive midnight phone calls with Emaly using the prepaid phone she'd gotten me when my mind trapped me in nightmares.

I praise Emaly for the work she put into becoming a doctor. There are kids who dream of being under her care. But I don't offer myself the same courtesy because then I'd have to remind myself of how far I've truly come. And that means acknowledging the people who could have prevented me from this path, and the trauma that instilled.

I swallow.

"That's quite the hypocritical comment," I tell her, leaning forward and setting my elbows on the edge of my desk. "Since you've been lying to yourself this whole time about not wanting me when it's obvious you do."

The remark hits exactly where I want it to, and her nostrils flare as she soaks it in.

"You don't know me," I inform her. "You will never know me. Not fully. There's only one person who can."

I want it to hurt. I want it to make its mark so she stops trying to dig her way in further than she already has. Because if she keeps going, she'll discover everything I've worked so hard to keep hidden away. She'll hit the vault

I've let sink into the abyss and try opening it.

Once that happens, I don't know what will be left of me.

Winter faces me, her shoulders stiff and square. On guard. Mad, perhaps. But her face is softer than it should be. Like she…pities me.

What the fuck?

"The only person who knows the real me is my sister," she says calmly. "And sometimes, I'm not even sure she knows me at all. Because there are pieces of me that I'm still trying to figure out myself."

I stare at her.

She stares back.

"You can try to hurt me," she adds, her voice far too soothing. "But I see right past it. If you wanted to seal yourself off from everybody in the world, you wouldn't have brought me here. You wouldn't have hired me. Because you wouldn't have felt the need to prove anything to anybody. So, you're lying. You do care. And that pisses you off. But guess what, Thomas?"

I'm silent, fisting my hands together and clenching my jaw as she psychoanalyzes me.

She smiles, but it's empty. Void of any emotion that's usually molded into the curve of her lips. "Nobody can hurt me by being cruel and hateful because I already torture myself enough by being the same way."

A lump in my throat forms that I try swallowing down. "You shouldn't."

"I can say the same," she counters. Then she produces her phone from her pocket and looks down at it. "My Uber is here."

She ordered a ride? "I could have driven you home, Winter."

Her empty smile widens only by a millimeter, looking suddenly tired. "You could have," she agrees. "But I'm saving us both that headache."

She barely makes it past the threshold of my office before I call out, "You know more of my secrets than I do yours. It's only fair you even the playing field."

Winter studies me for a moment before shaking her head. "Who's to say I haven't shared just as much with you? It's about being receptive to the information."

What does that mean? "One thing," I all but beg her. "Just one."

She stares at me for what feels like forever before she looks away. "I miss being hugged. I miss the comfort. I miss feeling…loved. I don't know what that's like anymore or if I'm capable of it."

That's all she leaves me with before walking out, the front door opening and closing behind her as my front door camera pings from my phone.

I stare at the space she occupied only seconds ago, trying to decipher what secrets she divulged, all while wishing I could chase after her. Beg her to tell me more. *Hug* her.

But would she let me?

EMALY'S GAPING FACE takes up the phone screen, and I worry her eyes will dry out if she doesn't blink soon. "You did *what*?" she asks.

Sighing, I pick up the fussy feline and show her off to the woman on videochat. Oreo has forced me to lie on the couch with her for the last hour because she didn't want to move from where she's been curled up in a ball on my chest.

It's not often I'm so sedentary, but my first training day with the team kicked my ass. Even though I kept up with my workout routine at the gym, it doesn't compare to the grueling work we do on the ice. I'm sore in places I didn't know existed before this sport.

"Her name is Oreo, and she used to be Lucifer's pet before he decided he didn't want to deal with her anymore," I explain.

Oreo yowls at the commentary, then starts purring. She's gotten used to me enough to stick around instead of hiding, but that doesn't mean she doesn't still get on my nerves.

"And I wasn't the first one you told?" she reiterates in disbelief, staring at the black and white kitten licking its paw on me.

"No," I confirm, watching Oreo. "You weren't."

Neither was Ashton. Or Scott. They don't know that I adopted a demon from the shelter because they'd be pushing me to post about it for clout online if they did. At least when Winter suggested it, she let it go when I told her no. My manager and agent won't be so relenting when they come over and see the cat tearing ass around the house like the menace she is.

Emaly hums thoughtfully, studying the new edition to my family. There's love in her eyes. Fondness. She's never liked cats, even though she's never had one. Her mother claims the whole family is allergic, but I think she only said that to avoid getting one and dealing with the shedding.

"Interesting," Emaly says, a secretive smile on her face.

"It's really not," I deadpan and pet the cat. Her smile is mischievous until I ask, "Where is Ronnie?"

Only a small amount of guilt pangs in my chest when her lips drop. "At the hospital," she answers dryly. "Like always. So, what made you decide to get a cat? You struck me as more of a dog kind of guy. Remember when you talked about getting a corgi? Those things were your entire personality throughout high school. You had a name picked out and everything."

I chuckle. I'd told everybody I knew that I was going to get a Corgi named Cooper, but it never happened. I never had the space, time, or money. "I still stand by them being fucking adorable," I reply easily. "They're walking loaves of bread, and I will get one someday when I have the time. And don't think I'm going to gloss over you changing the subject. Are things better between you and Ronnie, or is there still some tension?"

Emaly groans at my redirection, but it's on her. She's the one who called me, so I'm going to interrogate her the same way she would with me. "Do we have to talk about this? You never answered my question about getting a cat."

"They're independent," I answer plainly. "Now that that's out of the way, spill. You always call me when you want to talk. So talk."

"Maybe I just miss you."

My answer is easy. "I miss you too. But you've only

been back home for a handful of days, which tells me something is going on. You worked a double yesterday, and you're not sleeping right now. No offense, but you look like shit."

She glowers. "All offense taken. Never tell a woman she looks like shit. You're only ever supposed to compliment us."

"Duly noted for next time," I bemuse. "Now tell me what this is really about. Because if I hadn't distracted you with a cat sleeping on my chest, you would have divulged what's on your mind by now."

She frowns because she knows I'm right and can't figure out how to get out of it. "You're annoying when you're bossy."

She means I'm annoying when I'm right.

Blowing out a breath, she leans back against the chair that she's nestled in. I recognize it from our house in San Diego. That recliner was my favorite because it was long enough for my legs and tall enough that I could rest my head back without it fucking up my neck. I'd wanted to bring it with me, but it's another sacrifice I left behind because it's her favorite too.

"We're not doing good," she admits, closing her tired eyes and pinching the bridge of her nose. There are bags under them that indicate she's in desperate need of sleep but fighting it. "And I get it. Ron is upset about our situation and doesn't understand why I let my parents dictate my life when I'm not close with them. Whenever our future comes up, we're always disagreeing. Then one of us goes to work and spends way too much time there just to avoid the other. It doesn't get us anywhere. We're…stuck in a cycle that I don't know how to break out of."

I frown. This is the first time she's mentioned how serious they are. I've asked how things have been going, but she tends to avoid the topic when I bring up engagement and marriage. "Em, if you two want to get married, then—"

She cuts me off, "You know it's not that simple. My father and his ridiculous ways would never accept it."

While I understand that obstacle, I also point out something obvious. "You've always done your own thing, and it's gotten you this far. You met the love of your life, Dimples. Are you really willing to let your father ruin that? It's not fair to either of you."

Her silence weighs in the air between us.

The answer: yes, she is willing to do that.

But *why*?

"You know I'll do anything for you," I tell her softly, earning her attention back. There's a glaze to her eyes that I can't tell if it's tears of exhaustion or both. "But I don't want to see you blow up your life because of something, or someone, that your parents don't approve of. You don't need them. Would it be the end of the world if our charade ended so you could start over? We've accomplished everything we set out to do."

We agreed that we would let this last for as long as we needed to and support one another through thick and thin, as any married couple should. We've been loyal to our vows, loving each other in sickness and in health. Being there when we need it most. I love Emaly, and I want nothing more than for her to thrive. Which is why I won't be the one to hold her back. Not like her parents do.

When she put herself through college, her parents threatened to cut her off. They told her they wouldn't pay for an apartment or her health insurance, or anything. They'd had a path paved for her that she derailed from because it wasn't what *she* wanted. And I wasn't going to stand for that.

It's obvious she doesn't need me now. Not like she did back then. I'll always be here for her when she needs advice or to vent. She's got an amazing job with even better health benefits than I do, and a person who loves her unconditionally.

Maybe it's time for us to call this.

"What would that do to *you* though?" she doubts, her frown deepening. "You're playing for my dad's team. If we get divorced, he could use that against you. He's already tried to use all of these allegations in the media to screw you over."

He could do his worst, but it would hurt him more than it would me. "All due respect, Em, but your father is too selfish to ruin his chances at winning a Stanley Cup. Until someone comes into the league with my stats, he knows he can't replace me. He backed himself into a corner."

Sure, fresh-faced rookies come in every year. Some of them with talents that I'm easily jealous of. They're younger, faster, and have better chances of recovering from injuries than the seasoned players like me who have gone through years of rigorous abuse on the ice. I know, like any athlete, my time in the professional league is limited. But I'll be damned if I don't milk that for all it's worth while I can.

I stroke Oreo's fur as she settles back down on my chest. She's been cuddly the last few days, and her loud purrs ease some of the tension coiled deep in my chest. "You don't have to worry about me all the time. I'm a grown boy."

"Isn't it my job to?"

I smile easily. "According to your degrees and certifications, your job is to save sick children's lives. How about you focus on that instead of prioritizing me? I'm fine, Dimples. I want *you* to be too."

She's quiet for a long moment, repositioning in the chair before nodding and rubbing her temples.

I frown. "Do you have another headache?"

"It's nothing," she tells me, a little too quickly. "Stress. I'll think about what you said. There's a lot to consider. Ronnie will have to be patient with me until I come up with a decision that benefits everybody."

I shake my head. "That's the thing. You can't please everyone. I don't want you stressing yourself out trying to placate the people in your life. We're all adults who can handle ourselves."

I want to tell her that patience can only go so far before it's stretched too thin, but I don't think I need to remind her of that. She and Ronnie have been having trouble for a while, so there's no need to point out the obvious.

"Think about who will make you happiest," I add softly. "No matter what, I'll have your back. I will be the dude of honor at your next wedding. Hell, I'll be the flower girl. You can call me whenever you need to bitch about something or complain about your job. You know that. But if you push Ronnie away..."

Well, I don't need to tell her what will happen. It'll destroy her.

"I know," she whispers, her voice cracking.

"Everything else is okay, though?" I ask lightly. She hasn't brought up the information I passed along from Honor since I sent it. "Did you talk to the specialist about getting a service dog? You should have enough medical history by now to show them you qualify. And the hospital wouldn't be able to limit your access to a service animal. There are protections in place."

Her smile is sad. "Little Bear, it's not that simple. Getting a service animal takes time, and I'm not even sure it's right for me."

"But if you have another—"

"I haven't had a seizure in almost two years," she says firmly. She finally stops massaging her temples. "Ever since I started seeing the new neurologist, I've been monitored closely. The mass hasn't grown, and my symptoms have been manageable. I have time, and I'm going to use that time to make sure I help as many people as I possibly can before I need more help myself."

Time is relative, but I'm not the person to tell her how to spend it. "I worry about you a lot. With you working so much, and Ronnie being gone a lot too, it concerns me when you look so exhausted. That can't be good for you."

"Says the man who used to only sleep for three hours a

night," she muses.

I crack a small smile. "Only in the offseason. Trust me, the game wipes you out. I pass right out depending on how much ice time I get."

And if I play my cards right, it'll be a lot during our first game. Hoffman seemed impressed when I practiced our drills. There's still work to be done, but I've proven my asset to the team. As long as Mikhail doesn't get in the way, I should be golden.

"I'm sleeping plenty," is what she tells me.

"You're way too stubborn," I grumble, not believing her for a second.

Does she pretend her diagnosis doesn't exist? Is she pushing it away as if it won't be there for tomorrow? "I'm glad your neurologist is on top of it, but that doesn't change things. Being stubborn isn't going to alleviate the problem. Your form of MS is rare, and I feel like you refuse to acknowledge that."

Her laugh is bubbled with surprise. "You're one to talk about stubbornness. You refuse to even say Winter's name when we both know she's always on your mind. Is avoiding *her* helping *you* any?"

I don't refute it. She's deflecting again. "Not the point, Em."

"Does *she* like cats?" my wife asks knowingly.

I glare at her but say, "Yes."

A victorious smile brightens her face. "It'll be good to have someone who can come over and help take care of Oreo when you're playing away games then, huh?"

My lips flatten. "Don't get any ideas."

"Too late. I have *so* many ideas," she chirps far too enthusiastically. An evil grin splices her face. "With my very functionable brain. Because, despite what you think, I know that I was graced by the gods with a rare form of multiple sclerosis. And I know that makes it harder to treat. And I *know* my life is going to get harder." She gives me a pinned look. "But I can't stop living my life. I can't put everything I've worked for on the back burner. I'm not going to let this disease win. I'm going to be successful and happy and proud until the day this stupid tumor tells me I can't. Until I need more intense medication to alleviate symptoms. Until my hands shake too much to do surgeries. Dammit, Thomas. That day isn't here, so let me live my life for a little longer."

I swallow at the elephant in the room she's finally addressing. The elephant shaped like a large lesion in her brain that resembles a tumor. After years of medical problems that were ignored, she'd finally found out she had tumefactive multiple sclerosis. It's not a common form of the autoimmune disease that causes breakdown of the protective covering of the nerves. Which means it's harder for doctors to treat. When they determined the tumor wasn't cancerous, it was simply a monitoring game to make sure it didn't grow and impact her.

It explained the seizures she'd had in the past. The struggle she had with coordination as a child. The back pain. The headaches. It all made sense. Every reason that she couldn't be the athlete her parents wanted her to be wasn't because she lacked motivation or skill, it's because she's sick.

And having that answer changed her for the better. She stopped blaming herself for not being the daughter of her parents' dreams and chose to move forward with her schooling to prove to herself she could.

"I just don't want you to forget to take care of yourself," I explain. "I love you, Em. I want to make sure you're going to be okay."

Because I can't be there.

Because I wish I could be.

Because she won't *let* me be.

"I am," she reassures me. "I promise."

We're quiet for a second.

Her smile grows again. "Is now a good time to tell you that Winter and I talk?"

They *what*? "What do you talk about?"

Is it about me? It's got to be about me.

She grins. "Wouldn't you like to know."

"I would. That's why I'm ask—"

"Oh, shoot. Look at the time. I should get going," she says, glancing at her wrist that's void of a watch. "It was *great* talking to you, but I really need to sleep. Love you, bye!"

She hangs up the video call before I can respond, making me glare at the screensaver of her in that stupid chicken onesie. "Why are the women in my life such pains?" I ask Oreo, watching her stretch out her leg and knead her claws into my shirt.

Why am I talking to a fucking cat?

Maybe I need *my* head scanned.

Setting my phone down, I stare at the ceiling. I really

should get up. Work out. Cook something for dinner.

But I find myself closing my eyes and letting myself melt into the couch cushions. This time tomorrow, I'll be wiped out from practice. The only plus side of the sore muscles I'll undoubtedly have is that they'll be a welcome distraction from the girl I can't stop thinking about.

Especially now that I know she still talks to my wife.

CHAPTER FIFTEEN

Winter

IF I EAT another bite, there's a possible chance I may spontaneously combust in the middle of Our Open Table. Then Vinnie will be mad at me for making a mess of his establishment. Although I'd be dead, so I guess it wouldn't be my problem.

"I think you cheated," Ridley accuses with narrowed eyes, before turning to an elderly woman sitting between us. "Don't you think she cheated, Beth?"

Beth sighs, setting her cards down. "You always think she cheats when you lose. Ain't nobody accusing you of playing tricks whenever you win."

Ridley harrumphs. "I still think she was hiding draw fours in her sleeve to use on me. How many usually come in a pack?"

I snicker and pass him the deck. "You shuffle them to make yourself feel better. I'll even shake out my sleeves to reassure you that I'm not hiding any secret weapons in them."

He frowns. "I don't have time for another game."

Last I knew, he had nowhere else to be. But I play along, knowing it has more to do with being a sore loser than a busy schedule. "I should get back to the kitchen and see if Bev needs any help anyway. I'll see you later?"

He nods begrudgingly, making Beth roll her eyes at him. I pat his shoulder in comfort as I walk around him, offering him the friendliest smile I can muster. Despite his trying to be mad, I know he can't stay that way.

When I walk into the kitchen, I immediately put my hair into a ponytail and ask, "Do you need any—"

My question stops short when I see who's standing at the oven next to Bev.

Thomas Moskins.

Vinnie comes over and puts a hand around my shoulders. "Look who came back to help! I told him he should have brought his fancy camera crew because I'm having a good hair day."

My eyebrows go up as I glance over at his balding head, but I choose not to rain on his parade. Instead, I turn my focus back to the man whose house I left days ago. "What are you doing here?"

He stops stirring whatever is in the pot on the burner. "I wanted to help. Bev and Vinnie told me I could come back whenever I wanted."

Bev bobs her head. "Yes, we did. I told you before, Win. Any friend of yours is welcome here."

"But we're not—" I stop myself from finishing that sentence and collect my thoughts. Amusement curls Thomas's lips, but I do my best not to react. "I wasn't expecting you. That's all."

"Well, we're glad he's here," Vinnie tells me, dropping his arm. "We had a pallet full of canned goods come in this morning that weighed over one hundred pounds. We needed the manpower."

Shipments usually come on Saturdays, but sometimes the loads are split into two. I suppose an early delivery isn't uncommon, especially if they're stocking up for the colder weather coming in a handful of months. It means more mouths to feed and shelter. "Why didn't you call me? I would have come earlier if I'd known you needed help."

He waves me off. "You have a life, kid. I can't always call whenever I need something. We have other volunteers."

"Plus, have you seen these muscles?" Bev chirps in, gesturing toward Thomas's arms. "If he can't move 'em, none of us can."

I swear I see the faintest shade of pink dot Thomas's cheeks at the attention. Since when is he embarrassed by people complimenting his looks? He usually gets off on it.

"Now that you're here," Bev continues, coming over and guiding me to the oven, "you can help him finish with the pastas and sauces while Vinnie and I go set up the serving station. It's nearly dinner."

Before I can protest, Vinnie passes me a hairnet and follows his wife out of the kitchen.

"Well, that was…something," I murmur, securing the net over my hair and studying the pots on the stove. One contains pasta, one has red sauce, and the other has white sauce. "Ah. Italian night."

I can feel Thomas's eyes on me as I check the pasta to make sure it's not overcooking.

"You're staring," I state without having to look at him. In fact, I don't want to. I'd rather dunk my hand in boiling marinara sauce than meet his gaze.

"Am I making you uncomfortable?" he asks, bemusement in his tone.

I grind my teeth. "No." It sounds unconvincing even to my ears. "What are you doing here?"

He puts his hand over mine to get me to stop fiddling with the pasta boiling. "I already told you," he replies, taking the spoon away and setting it onto the counter. "I wanted to help."

I finally turn to face him. "Why here?"

One of his shoulders lifts. "Because I enjoy cooking and I was hoping you'd be here."

The admission is so casual, so nonchalant, that I almost think I heard him wrong. "Me," I repeat slowly.

He dips his head once.

"You came here," I drawl out, "for *me*?"

Typically, I only come on weekends. But because we have the charity gala coming up, it means preparing for that rather than coming here. I like popping in every now and again during the week to help out and be around people. It drowns out my inner thoughts.

But Thomas doesn't know that I only come on weekends, which makes me wonder how many times he's shown up before today.

Thomas chuckles. "Yes. For you. And here you are. Which means we can talk, because I've been thinking about something you said the other day before you left."

A long stretch of silence lasts between us as my ears ring with anticipation. What could he have possibly been thinking about? I didn't say anything interesting enough for him to dwell on.

"You said you weren't sure if you were capable of being loved," he finally says, voice uncharacteristically soft.

Heat warms my face and tingles in the back of my neck at the reminder of those regretful words. Out of everybody I could have admitted that to, why did it have to be him?

"I get it, Winter," he tells me, brushing his knuckles against my arm until I'm peeking up at him. "More than you know. But I've decided something."

That doesn't sound good. "And what is that?"

"It's bullshit."

My lips part in shock. "Excuse me?"

"The notion that you're unlovable is bullshit," he repeats casually. "If there's one thing that I've learned from Emaly, it's that there are different kinds of love. If you think you're not capable of any of them, you're lying to yourself."

The nerve of this man. "You really have the audacity to say something like that to me?"

"It's not audacity," is his easy retort. "It's called the truth. Take it from someone with firsthand experience."

Is he saying he knows what it's like to be unlovable? "Thomas, you and I are nothing alike. You have a wife who loves you regardless of what you do and fans who literally wear your name and number. You're loved by thousands of people."

He stirs the sauce and shakes his head. "I'm inclined to disagree with you. We're not that different, whether you want to admit it or not. So, how about another secret? Tit for tat."

"I don't want to play any games, Thomas." I groan, rubbing my tired eyes. I haven't been sleeping well, and it's catching up with me thanks to Cody's absence at work, adding on to my to-do list.

"Neither do I."

The seriousness in his tone makes me drop my hands and loosen a sigh. "Fine. You go first if you want a secret in return so badly."

I expect him to argue, but he doesn't. "The worst kind of love is the unrequited kind," he says quietly, lowering the heat on the pot and moving on to the other saucepan like he knows what he's doing. "You can be married to someone and realize that the love you have with them is different than the one you wanted."

I'm not sure what secret I was expecting from him, but this one…I swallow, feeling a pang of hurt in my heart for him. "You said that you and Emaly weren't together like that. Why?"

He never gave me the details, but it's obvious that he loves her. And there's no doubt in my mind that she loves him too. She wants him to be happy, to have companionship. Why not give him those things herself?

Thomas shifts his attention to me, a small smile on his face that isn't sad but…reminiscent of something equal to acceptance. "Because she's in love with somebody else."

That pang of hurt grows into more, and I can practically feel the weight of those words as if they're free weights sitting on my chest. "I'm sorry," I tell him. "That must be hard."

To my surprise, he shakes his head. "I've accepted it by

now. I'm not the person who can give her what she wants. I love her. I'll always love her. And, sure, a part of me, a younger version of me, expected more from us. She's been my best friend for a very long time. But it's a different kind of love we share. I'm grateful for any that she can offer me."

Who is this person? I've never seen this side of him before, and I don't know if I like it or am scared of it. Because he seems too…human. Normal. Vulnerable.

"Truth is, sweetheart," he says gently, "you can be loved and adored by thousands of people and not feel worthy of it. So, I'll take whatever scrap I can get from anybody important."

The room falls quiet, save for the hum of the refrigerators and the sauces bubbling as they heat. If I listen carefully enough, I may even be able to hear my heart crack.

"That seems like more than one secret," I finally say, voice quiet as I take him in.

His lips curl up higher at the corners. "The others are a bonus. I just want one."

"Why?" It isn't that I'm unwilling to give him one in return, but I need to know why it matters to him. It's not for blackmail, not like I'd originally suspected. No. This is something else. Something deeper.

His tongue drags along his bottom lip before he looks away at something above my shoulder. His face turns contemplative, as though he's trying to come up with the right answer.

When his eyes come back down to me, there's something soft in them. "Because maybe we stand a better chance at happiness if we lessen the burden on our souls. Nobody knows what I've told you. Not even Emaly knows what I thought of us in the beginning. That secret is yours to keep. It's ours."

I can see it then. The need to stop feeling the way he does. He's hurting. Badly. And I don't think it has to do with Emaly's unrequited love. After all, they're married. There has to be a reason she hasn't left him for the other man she's in love with.

So, I offer him something that equals his truth. "I don't think I deserve love, because I took advantage of it when I had it. I didn't appreciate it, and then it was taken away. And I can't..." My throat bobs as I try to swallow the pain coursing up my windpipe, trying to steal my words. "I can't change what happened. I can't apologize. I can't make amends. So, sometimes it's easier for me to accept that my punishment is loneliness. Because maybe that's what I deserve."

I'd been such a brat the day my parents died. I'm eighty percent positive I didn't say I love you when they left, even when they agreed to let me stay home. My therapist said it's survivor's guilt that makes me feel this way, but I'm not so sure.

I think it's a reasonable punishment. Fair. My parents loved me unconditionally, and I never got a chance to thank them for it. It doesn't matter how often I go to their graves when I'm upset to talk to them, to tell them now how selfish and blind I was to their love, because it's too late.

Thomas tips my chin up. "Nobody deserves that."

I close my eyes to fight off the tears burning in the backs of my eyes.

Then, I'm encompassed by heat and muscles and a scent that's woodsy and something masculine that I can't put my finger on.

Thomas Moskins is…hugging me.

And I melt into his body and soak it up because I need it.

I miss being hugged.

My last secret. Now he has another to add to the stockpile between us.

One of his hands comes up to my head and strokes my hair. He doesn't say anything. He doesn't need to, and I'm grateful for the silence.

When he pulls away, he swipes at my cheek with the pad of his thumb. It's only then I realize the tears escaped their ducts despite my best efforts to keep them at bay.

Then, he simply turns back to the oven and continues the work we were assigned to.

Just like that.

We exchanged secrets.

Shared a moment.

And now we're back to…this.

Comfortable silence.

And my chest feels ten times lighter as I help him finish dinner and serve it.

CHAPTER SIXTEEN

Winter

CODY WALKS BY Janel's office flanked by two of the building's security guards, with a box in his hands and a scowl that could rival the one always on Thomas Moskins's face. It makes sense now why my boss asked for an impromptu check-in without any notice.

At first, I thought she'd found out about the very unethical experiences I've been having with our client. But her face was far too friendly for a conversation like that when I walked inside her office to chat. I assume if she ever hears about what Thomas has done to me, it will involve a deep, disappointed frown and someone from HR present to explain why it's not okay to go to clients' homes and get pressed against their walls.

Is having wall kinks a thing? Because I think I may have it, given my last two interactions with Thomas, walls, and me being put against one.

Why am I sweaty right now?

"Are you okay?" Janel asks, snapping me away from staring out the glass wall that separates us from a very angry man.

Cody's obvious anger radiates through the office space, which helps bury my previous thoughts.

"He's been fired," I state, trying not to frown.

If Cody was let go, it's because there was proof he was doing something wrong that went beyond his inappropriate flirting. I keep reminding myself that it isn't my fault, even if I have the slightest inclination to feel guilty.

Mostly because I'm putting myself in a similar situation. Sure, I'm not doing it at work. I'm also not forcing myself on anybody who isn't interested. That's the problem. Thomas may call me out for what I want, but it's obvious he wants this too. And I hate that the tension between us is palpable and far too dangerous.

Janel's sigh is light. "We heard all we needed to hear to know about Cody's indiscretions. He made his bed; now he has to lie in it. The reputation he has here will inevitably follow him no matter where he winds up. All I can hope is that he's learned his lesson."

I'm quiet for a long time, fiddling with my fingers in my lap as I watch him collect his belongings from his desk. The guards stand on either side of his cubicle, making sure he doesn't do anything.

Could that be me if she finds out what I've done? The escape I've allowed myself to have? I know it's wrong, and I know I shouldn't entertain a playboy like Thomas, but…

I'm intrigued.

Curious.

There's so much to him I don't know.

More secrets he hasn't shared and may never.

Why is he married? What do they have to gain from one another? Is it an open relationship? Is she with the love of her life? Why haven't they divorced?

I love my husband and want him to be happy.

That's what she said the day at Furrever Home before shoving me into a room with him. Was it her way of telling me to…what? Give me the green light to start something? Imply that it's totally fine with her if I rub against his leg like he's a genie's lamp about to grant me three wishes?

He's right. I'm mad at myself. Because I do want him, and I don't know why. Maybe because he's unobtainable. Disposable. He's somebody who can make me feel good—a temporary fix to a bigger problem. A Band-Aid on a bullet wound that will end in casualty, even if it's a delayed reaction.

I want to close my eyes.

Sink into myself.

Be ashamed.

But I…can't.

I miss being hugged. I can't believe I admitted that to him. What's even more unbelievable is that he'd willingly hugged me at Our Open Table—that he volunteered his own free time just to see me and help Bev and Vinnie. It's been a long time since somebody simply wrapped their arms around me because they wanted to. It's been even longer since I've allowed myself to search for a person willing to do so.

I don't have time for a relationship, and I'm certainly not in the headspace for one. I need to focus on work, on paying my bills. Not on finding a partner who can cure my fractured heart. Truthfully, I'm not sure anybody is capable. Even after what Thomas and I discussed.

In hindsight, my minor obsession with Thomas

Moskins makes sense. Temporary means that I can have fun and let it go when the time comes. It means not expecting more than the bare minimum from him, so I don't get hurt.

"It seems as though things with Mr. Moskins are going well," she comments, snapping me away from the dooming thoughts echoing in my head to look at her.

"What?"

One of her eyebrows lifts at the pitch of my tone. "Mr. Moskins," she repeats slowly, eyeing me for a moment with a frown. "I've been monitoring the articles about him, and they're starting to turn around. There's certainly some more work to be done, but when you search his name, it's the events he's been doing around Fairbanks that comes up first. People are looking forward to seeing him start for the Fireflies this fall. There have even been pictures of him entering and leaving the stadium with his team, which is far better than the old ones of him leaving hotels with women."

Relief massages at my tense muscles, and I try to relax in my chair. "Right. Yes. I've noticed that too. After our next event this weekend, we should only have to monitor the media and push the narrative we want. By then, I'm sure the negative press will have been buried."

It's a trained, robotic response. Professional. I've heard Janel say the same thing when it seems like our work is successfully doing what it's supposed to. Two weeks from now, I won't have to see Thomas or his adorable kitten again. I can rip the Band-Aid off and go about my life as though I never knew who he was.

And that's for the better after where we left things off. Whenever I'm around him, my brain short-circuits, and I do reckless things. Like follow him inside his home. And word vomit things he has no right knowing.

Did he need to know I basically hate myself? No. He could weaponize that against me. But part of me knows he won't. Because if he wanted to ruin me, he would have by now. He hasn't said a word about what happened at the animal shelter to anybody, after all. There's a chance that he's doing this because he's intrigued by me and the stormy rain clouds always hovering over my head, because they match his own.

"I'll admit, I thought this would be harder," she muses. "It seems as though he surprised us with his cooperation."

I'm not sure I even register what she says before I blurt, "He got a cat."

Her brows pinch. "Who did?"

I clear my throat. "Moskins. Thomas. He adopted a cat from the shelter. Her name is Oreo, and he took her to the food bank with him. They may have gotten a photo or two of her, although he asked to keep them away from the portfolio they were compiling to send to his agent."

Maybe that's too much information, but my filter doesn't seem to work when I'm nervous.

"Why would he bring a cat to a food bank?" she asks, just as confused as I was seeing him with the carrier.

I shrug as casually as possible. "Apparently, he didn't realize he could leave her home. I don't think he's ever had a pet before."

Janel hums, then picks up her phone and starts typing

something in. "He hasn't posted about it. I'm surprised his agent hasn't said something to him about posting a photo of her. It would be great press. People were receptive to the images the shelter shared, but there was a sixty-forty split in his interview questions when he spoke about his plans for the future. Barely anybody brought up the scandal and asked more about if he adopted any of the animals."

I saw the pictures when they were shared on Furrever Home's page. They'd tagged his Instagram, which had photos of him in a bright yellow shirt holding a cute pug puppy that was licking his face. He looked so boyish in them, so carefree compared to normal. In those images, he wasn't the superstar athlete who got paid millions to play hockey. He was simply a man enjoying his time with some animals.

The only problematic question that was asked, despite it being off the approved questions list, was whether or not his wife would be coming to support him at his first game. He'd simply said, "Next question," while scratching between a pit bull's ears.

Anything pertaining to his wife was off-limits. Except, apparently, when it came to me. He's told me things nobody else knows. So why do I feel jealous whenever somebody gets close to him like he's mine to claim?

I cringe, thinking about the jealousy I felt when it came to Honor slipping him the piece of paper. When I got home that day, I logged onto an old social media account I hadn't used in years and started searching for her name. Sure enough, Thomas wasn't lying to me. Honor Hoffman is married to the Fireflies' new head coach and is the daughter of the Rangers' coach in New York. She's an advocate for epilepsy awareness, has adorable photos of her service dog, Puck, and is an amazing photographer. Plus, she's gorgeous. And so, so kind. Which made being pissed at her that much worse.

It was bad enough watching Kayleigh go after him, but seeing him go to Honor had been a punch to the gut I had no right feeling.

I'd felt…used. Like I was simply any other girl he'd ever been with. Wanted until he got what he wanted and disposed of. It reminded me of how little I open myself up to people, because then they have the opportunity to hurt you. Worse. They have the opportunity to get to *know* you. And the more Thomas learns, the more he'll understand how truly messed up I am.

"He didn't want it to be posted about," I explain to her, trying to brush off the heaviness sitting on my chest. My heart feels like it's jammed in my throat.

Janel looks up at me with a blank expression.

Rubbing my lips together, I sit a little taller to try to relay his reasoning. "He didn't adopt her for attention. He wanted a pet to…" *To feel less lonely like me.* "To fill his space."

She blinks, then lowers her phone to the desk in contemplation. "I suppose that's better than filling his home with women. Not quite what I expected of him, though."

"Me either," is out of my mouth before I can stop myself from saying it. But Janel doesn't seem to think too much about it, so I continue on with my shameless ramble. "He's a bit unexpected. An ass, for sure. But definitely not what I was anticipating."

Just like I wasn't anticipating being attracted to him. Go me.

My boss nods, as if she understands. "I've worked with clients like that before. You see a different version of them sometimes. Other times, they're exactly as they seem. What's that saying? Don't meet your heroes. I've certainly been let down by too many people to believe in them the way I used to. You have to err on the side of caution in this job, because you never know who will come into your life or how they'll change it."

She says it so casually, but there's an undertone to the words that sink in a little too deeply. I chalk it up to a guilty conscience and try not to seem fazed.

"Yeah," I agree, wetting my lips. "You're probably right."

"I'm having a meeting with his agent today, if you'd like to sit in," Janel offers with a kind smile when I meet her eyes. "That's actually why I invited you to talk. Ashton will be here any minute. I figure you're an important part of this project, so you deserve the credit for all you've done. Even after he had his reservations."

Excitement mixes with nerves at the invitation, and I suddenly wish I'd worn something better than the old pair of leggings and cute polka-dot tunic I found thrift shopping. I know I have nothing to prove to this man, because Janel's approval is all I need. But according to Thomas, this is the same man who pulled me from the Furrever Home event, which means he doesn't like me. Which *also* means that he may know things I'd rather he not.

I swallow down my nervousness. "Do I need to prepare anything?"

She shakes her head. "It's just a little debrief and next steps, so they know what to anticipate for their client's upcoming schedule. Since we only have the charity gala left, it's vital we speak to them about what comes after he's done making appearances. We can try doing meet-and-greets at different locations over the following two weeks after those events are over, but he'll be busier than usual from now until the start of the season. It'll be harder to schedule that on top of his other PR obligations. That's why it's imperative we speak to his agent."

I noticed some of the photos he took with fans were going viral. His smile wasn't forced in any of them. They were genuine. So was the way he spoke to the kids who raved about hockey. Not only about him playing, but also about others. I didn't realize how passionate he was until seeing him interact with fans.

"So we're almost done," I theorize, wondering why I'm not more relieved to wipe my hands of him.

"With the hard part," she replies, gathering papers and putting them to the side. "Now, it's about consistency. I have a basic formula I use on all of our clients after they're done making plans. You'll hear more about it when—Oh! There he is. Come in, Ashton."

I turn as a man enters the room in a suit that probably costs more than my rent. But I barely have time to appreciate the designer material before I see his face.

Fair skin. Angular jaw. Almond eyes. The features are basic enough, but it goes beyond that.

And I'm not sure who's paler as we soak each other in.

"Oh my God," I whisper, taking in the face I haven't seen in person since that day in the courtroom.

"Winter?" Janel asks in concern, a hand falling to my arm. "Are you all right?"

I stand, feeling dizzy and nauseous all at once. "I need to go. I'm sorry. I'm—" I shake my head and bolt past the man who looks like an older version of the one I'd last seen getting put into handcuffs after being charged with vehicular manslaughter in the second degree.

I will never forget the face of Adam Burgess or the way he tried to apologize to Kourtney and me for killing our parents.

Saying sorry wasn't going to bring them back. Neither were his alligator tears. He wasn't sorry for killing people. He was sad that he threw his life away and had to face the consequences.

My name is being called by two different people, but I don't stop. I continue to my cubicle, grab my jacket and purse, and make a quick exit out the side door, so I don't have to see that haunting face again.

All while my chest feels like it's caving in.

THE TEARS DON'T come until Kourtney ushers me into her classroom, where she's been working on setting up her bulletin boards with punny kid-appropriate science jokes that would make me roll my eyes if I weren't in the middle of a breakdown. As soon as she sees my face and asks what's wrong, the floodgates I'd managed to keep closed open with a vengeance.

"H-he's back," I blubber through hearty sobs that produce a heinous amount of snotty tears.

Kourtney guides me to the chair behind her desk and sits me down, passing me a few tissues with both rage and worry on her face. "Who is back? Is it that asshole you work with? Did he do something to you? Do I need to go over to your office and kick his balls in?"

I try my hardest to collect myself before she commits a crime on my behalf, but I can't seem to breathe. The oxygen won't make it to my lungs, where I desperately need it, and I find myself gasping between words.

"Not…him." I wipe my face and keep the tissue pressed against my damp cheeks to absorb as much as I can. When I finally suck in a long breath, I clench my eyelids closed and repeat, "Not him."

I blink rapidly, hoping it'll dry my eyes and let me see her properly. Or at least look at the stupid, nerdy posters she's taping on the wall. I bought her some of them, knowing she and the kids would find them funny more than lame.

Like the one that says, *Did you know oxygen and magnesium got together?* Beneath it are the two elements that spell out O M G. Or the one with beakers full of liquid that says, "Chemists have all the solutions." Will fifth graders get it? Maybe. I guess that will be up to her to teach them enough to understand them by the end of the year.

But staring at cringey posters can't distract me from the overarching problem lingering. "It's Adam. Adam Burgess.

I *saw* him, Kourt. He stood in front of me, looking like *he* just saw a ghost."

My sister gapes at me. Then she blinks. Once. Twice. Three times. "Winnie, there is no way you saw Adam. He's still in prison. He went back after getting into that bar fight, remember? I showed you the article."

I vaguely remember her sending me the link to the arrest blotter. The bastard literally got blackout drunk on day two of being free from his sentence and then severely injured the bartender with a broken stool leg when they cut him off.

I'm shaking my head. "I know what I saw, Kourt. He was standing inches away from me, and he *knew* who I was. It had to have been him. He must have gotten out. Maybe there was another overcapacity situation, and they released people."

She's still trying to grasp this as she pulls a little footstool over to sit on in front of me. "I really don't know about this, Win. When jails and prisons get overcrowded, they tend to release the nonviolent offenders first. He's not one of them. Especially not after the bar incident. I still talk to our lawyer sometimes. The last time we spoke, a couple of weeks ago, he mentioned that Adam was locked away and would be for a very long time on attempted murder charges. The damage he did to that bartender was bad. Like, *really* bad. With his record, they aren't going to let him free anytime soon."

It wouldn't be the first time the justice system made a mistake. How many times had he gotten his wrist slapped for drinking and driving before finally getting caught? He'd been involved in *two* different car accidents that injured other people and never got charged with a DWI because he hid for a week after each one. The coward knew if the cops couldn't prove he was drunk at the time of both accidents, they couldn't officially charge him. All he had to pay was a fine for the damage, and his insurance company paid out to the victims.

If he'd faced bigger consequences then, maybe it could have avoided what happened to our parents. Maybe then, he wouldn't have hit them going twice the speed limit while his blood alcohol level was almost triple the legal limit. *Maybe* the Satan incarnate wouldn't have gotten out of his truck at the scene, walked over to the crumpled metal of our parents' vehicle, and then run back to his truck before speeding away until his truck stopped working in the middle of the road. He hit my parents, went over to them, and *left them to die.*

I sniff into the tissue, feeling that sour feeling swirl in my chest. How could going to the bar and getting trashed again be one of the first things he did? What did that bartender ever do to him? I bet they'd only wanted to make sure they both got home safe. Adam Burgess is a cancer to society.

"It's got to be him," I say, jaw quivering. "He looked so much like…" I stop myself, wetting my dry lips and closing my eyes.

He'd aged in the years since, but my gut knew who he was. It screamed for me to go. My fight-or-flight mode kicked in and begged me to get out of there.

Kourtney takes my free hand with hers. "Did he introduce himself as Adam?"

"I—" I frown. He hadn't introduced himself at all. "No. My boss said his name was Ashton when she told me about the meeting. But he could have easily changed his name because he didn't want to be associated with what he did. People do that all the time to save themselves from the problems they created."

My big sister nods, even though it's obvious, she's still not sold on this. "I'll do some digging. Did he approach you at work? Is he a client? Give me something to work with so I have better context. Can you do that for me?"

She's using her motherly tone. The one she uses on Luca and her students. Hell, I've heard her use it on her husband a time or two before.

So, I explain the very short story leading up to my absolute freak out that made me ditch work in the middle of the day. My phone went off at least three times before an onslaught of text messages poured in. All Janel being concerned about me. Not mad at how I ran out. Not judgmental for being unprofessional.

Just worried.

I groan, realizing how I must look to Janel now. She's been trusting me to handle the Moskins case, and all I've done is cross every line possible. "I'm probably going to lose my job," I mumble, drying my face off once the tears stop flowing. "First, I let a client give me an orgasm, and then I ran out of a meeting with his manager like a scared little girl."

"Whoa," Kourtney drawls, gripping my hand tighter. "Did you just say you let someone…?"

I sniff again. "Yeah," I murmur, not even caring that I'm admitting it. There are worse things going on in my life, so who gives me an orgasm isn't the first thing on my mind right now. "Not my finest moment. Neither is the whole running away thing."

She waves that off. "I don't care about the second part at all. Not when you drop a massive bomb like this. You had *sex* with your *client*? The asshole who you said you couldn't kill with kindness? When I told you to show him who is boss, I didn't mean Venus flytrap him with your vagina."

I really hope there aren't cameras in here because I do not need anyone she works with to hear this conversation. "I didn't have sex with him," I whisper-hiss. "Things just got a little heated. And is that all you can focus on right now? Mom and Dad's killer could very well be at my office as we speak!"

Kourtney pinches the bridge of her nose. "I have so many thoughts right now, but I don't know where to begin."

I blow my nose obnoxiously loud. "Can we begin with you referencing my vagina as a Venus flytrap?"

She snorts. "It sounded like the perfect analogy at the time. I kind of want the details, but I also don't. Am I going to be grossed out if I ask how he got you off? Was he good? Is his dick big? Men who are assholes usually know how to use their dicks. It's how women look past their bad personality. How the hell did things go from you loathing each other to him giving you the big O?"

This is not the reason I came here. "We're getting way

off track, considering the monumental event that brought me here."

To her credit, she tries to let it go. "I'm going to reach out to our lawyer and see if he heard anything about Adam. But he knows better than to track us down. Think about it, Win. He's not going to come after the people he's screwed over. If anything, he'll try starting over somewhere far, far away from Fairbanks."

That's what I would have thought, until he got arrested in the town over for that bar fight. "He was only thirty minutes away when he hurt that bartender. We don't know what he's capable of if he's angry enough."

She points out something very poignant. "We didn't do anything for him to be angry about. It wasn't us who convicted him. We were the ones who were hurt the most by his actions. I don't want you to live in fear that he could come after you. I don't want Mom and Dad's deaths to be the reason you stop living. You've got so much potential, Winnie. You deserve the world, and they would have wanted you to be happy."

I close my eyes, trying to refrain from letting more tears fall. "It's not that I think he'll hurt me. It's just that..." How do I explain this? "Up until today, I haven't let myself *think* about him. But when I saw his face, it all came rushing back."

The trial. The pictures they showed. The way his lawyer tried to blame *our* parents for driving recklessly to get his client off easier. I understood why Kourtney told me not to go. Seeing the images on the screen of their mangled car, the very car I rode in only hours before the accident, ripped my heart apart. But nothing, *nothing* could have prepared me for the pictures of Mom and Dad. I held on to Kourtney's hand so tightly, I heard her joints crack from the pressure.

She stands and gives me a tight hug. It's only when she squeezes me that I let myself relax against her and take a deep breath of her favorite lotion that smells like summer and cotton candy. Luca picks it out for her every year for Mother's Day, and even though I'm not sure she likes it, she wears it for him.

"Babes," she says softly, brushing my hair. "I'm sorry you went through that. I really am. And I wish I could have been there to tell you if it was him or not. I'm sad that I wasn't around to give you that confirmation."

I frown against her shoulder. "You can't always be there for me."

"I know. But I want to be," she says, pulling away and swiping her thumbs over my cheeks. "And I'm glad you came here to talk to me about it. Although, how did you get here? Did you Uber? Please tell me you didn't walk."

A laugh bubbles out of me. "I took the bus. The driver kept staring at me like I was about to have a breakdown. I waited until I saw you for that."

She smiles, playing with the tips of my dyed hair. "That's probably for the better. You're not a pretty crier, sis."

I roll my eyes that feel sore from wiping them. "Nobody is. Let's not forget when we watched *Marley and Me*, and you sobbed so hard you had snot coming out of your nose. I watched it slither out like a snake."

She gasps dramatically. "That is totally justifiable! And you were crying too, you little bitch."

We both start laughing, which lightens the weight resting on my chest. Then Kourtney's smile wavers, and I can tell she wants to say something but isn't sure if she should.

I tap my foot against hers. "What?"

She wets her lips. "Adam had a brother," she says carefully, gauging my reaction. "I remember him at the trial. Their parents were there too."

Why don't I remember them? I'd studied his side of the courtroom to see who was there to support him—somebody so blatantly guilty of taking my mother and father away from me. I wanted to know how they felt. If they were going to argue for their son's innocence. But I couldn't bear to look at the people whom I wanted so badly to blame. Their images always blurred, and fury would take over until Kourtney forced me to switch sides with her to block my view.

She hadn't let me memorize them.

But *she* did.

"A brother," I slowly repeat.

She nods gently. "I don't know his name. I wouldn't allow myself to learn it. Why should I burden my mind with useless information? But what I *do* remember is that they looked a lot alike. I think they may have been twins. So, you may not have seen Adam today. Maybe you saw his twin brother."

Hadn't Bodhi asked me if I knew his manager? He'd said his name was Ashton Dessen. And he seemed strange about it. But…

"They don't have the same last names," I realize aloud. Am I losing my mind? Has my lack of sleep finally caught up to me? I bury my face in my palms and groan loudly into them. "I don't know what's happening to me."

Kourtney rubs my arms in comfort. "You've been working a lot, and it's close to their anniversary. It could be triggering things. I think about them a lot this time of year. I wonder what they would have been like as grandparents. If they would like Brad. Don't give me that look. I know you hate him. But he's been good to me."

I refrain from rolling my eyes because that won't end well. I didn't come here to fight with her.

"The point is," she says gingerly, "I think about them nonstop. I miss them. Sometimes, I think I see Mom when I'm shopping. Especially when I pass by the yarn aisle."

Our mother wanted to be a knitter so badly, but she was terrible at it. She'd make us scarves and hats, but they'd have holes in them and fall apart after one wash.

"I didn't hallucinate him, Kourt," I defend.

She frowns. "I'm not saying you did."

"You're totally saying that!"

She sighs. "Okay, maybe I'm insinuating that it's a *possibility*. But maybe you also saw his brother or a close relative. Fairbanks isn't that big. Everybody knows everybody. We're infamous around here, just like the Burgess family is for all the wrong reasons. If he did change his name, I can't say I blame the guy. I wouldn't want people to know who my brother is. There was a lot of media coverage on the trial. They televised it for the local news channels."

I stare down at our conjoined hands and swallow past the lump in my throat. I'd forgotten about the cameras inside the courtroom. There were always reporters outside hoping to speak to us as we'd walk to our car. People would shout questions at us about how we were feeling. I'm pretty sure Kourtney told them to fuck off with their ridiculous questions once. There had been an article in the paper a day later with a picture of her flipping off the camera and a headline about *her* rather than the man who'd taken two lives.

"They would have been obsessed with Luca," I finally tell her, swiping the back of my wrist along my cheek. "Mom always talked about having a grandbaby to spoil."

Kourtney nods, a nostalgic, sad smile on her face. "She always wanted a boy to break up the estrogen fest."

I giggle, remembering her saying that to us. Dad was always quick to agree, adding that he didn't want a grandbaby anytime soon though. If he were still alive, he'd choose to believe we were both virgins. Even if one of us had a baby.

"Sorry for coming here and blubbering," I apologize, frowning. I look around her classroom. "Everything looks cute so far."

She stands, pulling me up. "Since you're here and probably not showing up to work looking like *that* anytime soon, I'll take advantage of the extra set of hands. Come on."

I ignore the backhanded comment about my disheveled appearance and spend the next two hours being blissfully distracted by boring science facts while being directed in a million different directions until Adam, Ashton, and work are the last things on my mind.

Even if there's still a tug that pulls at my gut that says there's so much more to this story that I don't know.

CHAPTER SEVENTEEN

Moskins

MY MUSCLES SCREAM in the best possible way after three hours of grueling conditioning with the boys. I'd forgotten how much I love the competition that arises in the weight room to push three more reps, go ten pounds heavier than someone else, or run two miles more on the treadmill than the person next to you. It's nothing compared to the testosterone fest on the ice when we gear up to practice.

People think we're violent against our rivals, but very few people see the way we slam each other into the boards trying to get the puck. It doesn't matter who we're facing off with; we all want to prove ourselves worthy.

"Christ, it's like you never left," Clarkson says, clapping me on the back once we get off the ice. He gestures toward the bloodied tissue pressed against my face. "How's the nose?"

"Doc said it wasn't broken," I tell him, voice muffled by the packing. I can still taste the faint metallic tinge of blood on my lips from when Jackie Dawson slammed me into the boards and knocked off my helmet, then had Richie Head run into him until my face met the plexiglass.

I'm assuming their aggression is a combination of

adrenaline and the fact that someone named them Jackie Dawson and Richie Head. According to the former, he claimed his mom's favorite movie was *Titanic*, but she wanted her son's name to be unique. Richie's parents just hate him, apparently.

I like both the defenseman though. They're nearly a decade younger than me, and make me feel old as fuck, but they're good players. Rich is a rookie, and Dawson used to play for the Islanders.

Hoffman took me off the ice to get checked by the team doctor, who's far too young and attractive to surround herself with the likes of us and not be corrupted. Something tells me it was Mikhail's personal choice to hire the young blonde who looks a little too much like Winter for my liking. He may give me shit for the things I've done, but he's no better. The only difference is that he's kept his infidelity under lock and key.

Jesse Clarkson bumps my shoulder. "It's good to see you back. I take it things with Yokav are better?"

I'm still not sure what his motive for leaving Pittsburgh is. But considering his pretty brunette stepsister, Belle, is also with him, tells me that's a big part of it. It's a bit surprising that they made the move together, considering she owns a speakeasy bar and restaurant back in the 'burgh. The Penguins used to go there all the time because it was a private place with great food and decent people. Nobody bothered us there. We could go, decompress after long days, and enjoy the music and atmosphere.

When I asked Clarkson why she'd come too, he gave me a half-assed answer about new opportunities and left it at that. A few weeks later, the news reported that Belle's Place was sold to some anonymous buyer. Belle's pride and joy, suddenly just…gone. The grumpy ass standing beside me hasn't said anything about it since. He hasn't even brought up how his stepsister is since choosing to part ways with the business that seemed like it was doing well. There were always people there when we went. Minus a few unfortunate issues with drug users and homeless people hanging around hoping to sap rich fucks out of a few dollars, it was in a decent area.

"Things are as good as they can be," I tell him, walking to the locker room together. "Yokav is smart. He knows he needs a full team with valuable players to stand a chance. If he put a rookie in, it wouldn't have looked good."

Clarkson makes a thoughtful noise that doesn't offer much to the conversation. "Some would say giving a rookie a shot puts him at an advantage in the media. It means giving them a chance to prove themselves."

It's obvious that Mikhail Yokav doesn't care about giving everybody a fair shot. "Maybe," I relent, lifting a shoulder. "What's your deal? You don't seem very happy. I didn't think you'd be kissing my feet or sucking my cock when I came back, but you've barely said two words to me."

He's distracted, glancing at something on a far wall. "What?"

My point exactly. I snort. "Never mind. I've got to change and meet up with Hoffman. He wants to have a heart-to-heart or some sappy shit like that before I leave."

Before I walk to the opposite end of the locker room,

he stops me. "We should get together sometime. Grab drinks. Ideally, where you don't wind up face down on my guest bed or vomiting into my fake plant."

I glare at him. "I did that one time."

His eyebrows lift.

I amend my statement when his skepticism pierces my soul. "Okay, *maybe* twice. But that's because your plants look real."

Clarkson raises an eyebrow. "And you thought your vomit would help a real plant?"

Perhaps the drunk version of me saw the logic in it. "I'd been vomiting all night. At that point, it was just water anyway. You kept passing me glasses to sober myself up, and I chugged them."

He rolls his eyes, realizing he's not going to win this conversation with reason. "Whatever. You still have my number. Let me know when you're free, and we'll plan something. Perhaps dinner instead of alcohol, so I don't have to risk cleaning up after your ass."

It's good to know my drunken escapades haven't turned him off of me. "Will do, Cap. Tell the lovely Belle I look forward to seeing her now that she's got time on her hands."

Clarkson's jaw tics like it always does when somebody flirts with his stepsister. It's become a game that I'm looking forward to our new team getting in on as much as our old one did. He doesn't take the bait and tell me more about why she let go of one of our favorite restaurants, and I'd guess it has to do with financial shit that I have no right knowing. Which is fair.

But I know the fiery brunette is a hard worker. If she left it behind, it's for a good reason. And Clarkson isn't going to let anyone in on that unless he has to.

"I'll get right on that," he grumbles, waving me off and walking to his locker to shower and change.

I chuckle and go about my business.

It takes me no time at all to wash up and put something clean on. By then, my nose stops bleeding, and the only soreness I feel is settled into my thighs from how hard Hoffman worked us. I like the challenge. I like even more how I dominated the ice over everybody else on it. Save for Clarkson, but he's always been better than me. I'm man enough to admit it. To myself, anyway.

Bodhi Hoffman's office is smaller than I expected it to be, considering his position on this team. It's lacking any color, trophies, or personal touches. "Hiding all your medals, Hoffman?" I ask, examining the empty beige walls. He's probably got a case built in his home to store them all in.

He leans back in the chair with a grin. "I wouldn't want to intimidate the rookies," he replies easily, a flash of amusement on his face.

"Intimidate or inspire?" I counter, dropping into the seat and propping my ankle over my bent knee. "When I was starting out, I liked seeing that the coach had victories up his sleeve. It meant that I was part of a winning team."

He nods along, scraping a palm over the blond stubble on his jaw. The man used to be clean-shaven every time I saw him. Now that he's coaching the Fireflies and off the ice, it looks like he's trying to grow out a beard. His hair, which used to always be in a manbun whenever I saw him for games, is just above his shoulders. "Is this new look a cry for help? If you're not careful, you'll start looking like the version of Thor from the last *Avengers* movie."

He snickers at my commentary, patting his flat stomach. "I think I have a ways to go before I turn into Fat Thor. But Honor likes to tell me that dad bods are in." His smile grows. "And to your other point, I think you're forgetting that I was rated a top-five NHL player consistently over the past five years. That has the power to impress more than me flashing medals."

I huff out a laugh. "You fell to eighth during your last season with the Rangers," I point out. How do I know? Because I worked my ass off to get the recognition I deserved and finally scored the seventh spot that year after being number ten for a long-ass time.

He says, "It was because of my shoulder."

I shrug. "Doesn't matter why. I still beat you by one spot. I'm going to hold on to that for a very long time to come."

Hoffman chuckles, taking it lightheartedly. We both know the reason he's sitting behind a desk now is because of his injury. He'd had one too many surgeries and cortisone injections to continue without permanently damaging the mobility in his arm. He chose to retire and be a good father to his daughter over playing professionally. It's a choice I can respect, even if it's probably not one I would have made myself.

"Are we going to have a little kumbaya, or is this supposed to be a little catch-up?" I ask, settling into the chair and stretching my legs out to let my muscles get a break. They cry in relief, and I realize I'll need an ice bath if I want to move tomorrow. I'm good at keeping a workout schedule, but nothing beats the exercise we get on the ice. It works muscles you don't know exist until you wake up the next morning and feel them.

Hoffman crosses his arms over his chest casually. "I wanted to see how things are going. You haven't been around the new players for long, but it seems like you work well together on the ice. Although I think you need to trust some of the younger guys better."

"And why is that?"

"You wouldn't pass," he states.

He's right. "I didn't have to."

"You always have the opportunity to pass," he says. "There were multiple times you could have sent the puck to Dawson or Head. They may be the youngest, but they're good."

I'm not disagreeing with him. "They are, but that doesn't mean I don't have more to prove. My ass has been on the line since signing on the dotted line with this team."

"So you're trying to prove to Mikhail that you belong on the ice," he says with a head bob. "That makes sense. But you still need to work with the others. You've barely had any interactions outside of the stadium with them from what I can tell."

"I've seen Clarkson," I counter. Once in passing, when we were out, but it should count. "If this is you about to tell me how I need to treat my team like family, you're barking up the wrong tree with that analogy. I don't like my family. Don't talk to them either. Personally, I don't know if I buy having to get along with the people you work with. They say it's good to have a work-life balance."

He studies me, unfazed by my cynicism. It isn't like he doesn't know how I am. I'm sure he's heard the same rumors as everybody else. "I don't expect you to have sleepovers with any of them, but I would like you to get along. It's hard to form those connections with people if you show up only for practice or the game and then bail directly after."

For someone who says he doesn't expect me to host sleepovers, it sure as hell seems like that's what he wants. "Do you want me to invite people for a team bonding experience at Dave & Buster's over air hockey and basketball? Want us to do trust falls too?"

My sarcasm doesn't bother him. "I know from personal experience that you keep to yourself most of the time. That's not a bad thing. Frankly, it's probably the best thing you could do given how much your face has wound up in the tabloids this year."

I knew it was only a matter of time before he brought that up.

"But you used to spend time with your former team," he continues pointedly. "You had friends. Clarkson confirmed as much."

"Clarkson is a gossip," I accuse. "And I wouldn't exactly say I was best friends with anybody. I didn't paint their nails or tuck them in after reading them a bedtime story. I tolerated them, especially if alcohol was involved."

I haven't touched a drop since promising Emaly that I

wouldn't wind up in any more headlines. I'm familiar enough with myself to know that one too many drinks leads to an equal number of poor decisions. And, if I'm being honest, I don't want to cross the lines with liquor that my parents did. I'm not afraid to drink, but I *am* afraid of the potential of it going awry.

Mostly, the potential of it leading me to a certain blonde's apartment and banging on her door until she lets me in. Holding her at Our Open Table made me feel things I didn't know I was capable of. It wasn't purely physical. It was more. And I think that scares me more than alcohol does.

"The point is, I want everybody to get along," Hoffman informs me, breaking me from my thoughts. "You're getting a late start to the season because of everything that transpired. But since you aren't being benched, you'll have to work ten times harder to catch up. The guys are already forming bonds. Going out. Making friendships. It would help if you were more open to doing the same. Teach the newer players something. Clarkson mentioned doing weekly dinners—"

"Look," I cut him off, "I appreciate what you're trying to do. But forcing friendships isn't going to work. I'll make them a fucking friendship bracelet with my phone number on it like Kelce did for Swift and see if something blossoms. But that's the extent of what I'm offering. If they want to learn how to be better players, they can watch me. I don't need more people in my life trying to get to know me."

Because there's way too much for them to figure out.

Hoffman's sigh is heavy, like he expected the answer.

He doesn't tell me to play nice or order me to do shit. Probably because he knows that'll only make me want to do the opposite.

Because I like him, I offer Hoffman the only thing I can. "Maybe we can do the charity gala together. Clarkson's presence would make sense, since he's the captain of the team. Mikhail is bound to be there as the owner of the team. Maybe Richie or one of the others can tag along as well. My PR team is scheduling a meet-and-greet session before the gala starts begins so we can talk to people. Let them get to know us or some shit."

If we show up on a united front, the community can see us as a team before they see us in action during the season.

"I'll have to get it approved, but…"

"That's a great idea," he praises, seemingly impressed. "If you need me to contact anyone, I can. I'm sure Yokav wouldn't object either."

Especially if we made it seem like it was his idea. He loves getting credit for shit he has nothing to do with.

My phone goes off, and I take advantage before my head coach starts trying to psychoanalyze or guilt me again into doing something I don't want to. Like hosting a team dinner or something equally as dumb.

When I see Ashton's name on the screen, I groan but answer anyway. "What do you want?"

"We have a situation." His tone is off. It's not bossy or perturbed like I'm used to it being.

"What kind of situation?" I ask, earning a curious look from Hoffman.

My agent pauses, which isn't a very common occurrence with him. He's like me. Blunt and to the point. Not willing to waste time.

"Ashton," I bark impatiently.

Then he says it. "It's Winter."

My fingers clench around the edge of the chair arm. "What about her?"

There's a deep sigh, defeated and something else, before he murmurs, "There's something I should tell you. I should have told you when you asked before."

I stand up and look at Hoffman. "I've got to go."

He doesn't try to stop me, which would have been pointless anyway. As I head out to my car, I tell Ashton, "Talk. Now."

THE ANGER RADIATING through my body could have been avoided if Ashton had told me the truth when I asked him for it weeks ago.

I don't feel bad hanging up on him after he's done explaining how his brother ruined Winter's life, or how he's kept tabs on her since the fatal accident and hearing. I have no interest in listening to some half-assed excuses as to why he thought it was okay to still involve himself in her life like he has a say.

He doesn't.

His brother doesn't.

None of his family do.

Guilty conscience or not, he should have never stepped

foot into her space. Anybody who goes through the loss she did...Christ. I can't even imagine. My family is still alive—still out there wasting valuable oxygen while hers is six feet under. It isn't fair.

I'd known something heavy happened in her life, but I never would have assumed she lost both her parents. Especially not the cruel way she did.

"How old was she?" I growl at Ashton over the phone.

A pause. Then, "Thirteen," he answers in a raspy voice.

When I was thirteen, I'd been getting drunk with my biological father. Every goddamn time my parents got custody of me again, I was sucked back into their world. I was surrounded by alcohol and drugs and vices that made me just as weak as them. I wish I had stayed at any other foster home—even the ones that would lock me away at night and limit my food during the day. Even the ones that clearly only did it for a paycheck, not because they wanted to make a difference. At least if I stayed in my room and kept to myself, I was safe from myself. Safe from *them*. Why do the good people, those who deserve to be parents, go first?

Ashton knows better than to call me back to lecture me about hanging up on him. At least he's smart enough not to break through the thinnest fucking ice he's standing on right now.

There are four text messages waiting for me when I pick up my phone to search for the name I want to talk to.

Hoffman: *Is everything okay?*

Clarkson: *Coach said you walked out like your ass was on fire. You good?*

Ashton: *I didn't want her to find out that way*

Ashton: *I've done everything I can to make up for it*

What way did he want her to find out that his little brother had hit and killed her family? For Christ's sake, did he think a musical number would suffice to reveal that information? Maybe a five-course meal and a five-digit check bonus for all the hard work she's done to better my reputation? In his infinite wisdom, did he think hiring her for the job out of everybody at the company would somehow make up for what happened?

Money can't fix heartache.

I would know.

The hand still on my steering wheel vice grips the leather as I think about the loss I've felt over the years. It doesn't matter how many zeroes are attached to my net worth. It doesn't change the past or how it molded me.

I find Emaly's name and hit the call button, impatiently listening to it ring until she picks up.

Her groggy voice answers on the third ring, so she must have been sleeping. "Is this an emergency? I'm so exhausted, and there's a chance I won't remember anything said in this conversation. I just had an eight-hour surgery on top of a twenty-four-hour stint at the hospital."

"Give me her number," I answer, grinding my teeth the

more I think about everything Ashton told me. "I need to talk to her."

There's such a long pause that I have to peel the phone away from my face to make sure the call didn't drop.

"Did you fall asleep?" I ask, frowning.

But then Emaly says, "Who?"

"Don't play dumb with me right now, Em," I warn her, not in the mood for games. "I know you have her number, and I need it. Ashton fucked up, and I need to make sure she's okay."

That wakes my wife up quickly. Probably because she hates Ashton. Or maybe because she simply adores Winter. "Okay. Is she all right? I'm texting you the number now. Do I need to kick the he-devil's ass? Because I will. I'll use my flight miles just to hit him where it hurts and then fly back to Cali."

"Get in line," I mumble, glancing at the message she sends with the number. "Got it. I'll call you later."

"Is she—"

She doesn't finish her question before I hang up and dial the new number while driving a little too quickly down the interstate.

I don't think Winter is going to pick up when I hear a quiet, "Hello?" come from the other end of the phone.

I'm not sure why the sound of her voice has my muscles easing into the seat, but it does. Even the exhausted tone that sounds heavy and forlorn makes me glad to hear it at all. "Are you home, sweetheart?"

Winter is quiet for a second, the subtle sound of a sharp breath being inhaled the only thing filling the space. Then,

"Thomas?"

"Are you home?" I ask again, gripping the wheel tighter. My throat bobs when I hear the faintest sniffle from her end. "Ashton called me and told me…a lot. I need to make sure you're okay."

Once again, I'm met with silence. I know she hasn't hung up because I can hear her choppy breathing. Is she crying? My foot presses down on the accelerator.

"You don't—" Her words get muffled and hoarse, and it makes me want to beat the shit out of Ashton more than I already do. He isn't the one who caused the accident, but he didn't do her any favors by walking into her life like this. "You don't have to come. I'm fine."

All I say is, "I know you are."

But there's an incessant need inside of me to make sure she's all right, and I won't label what it is yet. I don't expect her to tell me about her past. Ashton told me enough. It makes more sense why she's so close to people in the community. Why Bev and Vinnie consider her and her sister one of their own.

Winter needed them. Her sister needed them. She's passionate about Fairbanks because they helped them put some of the pieces back together.

I pull up to the front curb of her apartment building and waste no time putting the car into park. "I'm coming in. What number is your apartment?"

Another sniffle. "Thomas—"

"What. Number?"

Apparently, the seriousness in my voice makes her realize I'm not playing around. She knows I'll knock on every single door until I find the right one.

"Two," she whispers defeatedly. "It's on the first floor to the righ—"

That's the only words she gets out before I'm barreling in the front door the second someone opens it and veer off in the direction of apartment two.

I hang up the phone, bang on the door twice, and wait impatiently until there's a subtle click of the lock before the wood cracks open.

Winter's face is damp and tear-stricken, and her eyes are red-rimmed and swollen. It's all I need to see before nudging the door open, backing her inside, and wrapping her in my arms.

At first, her body is stiff against me. Like she can't believe I'd hug her *again*. But the second she accepts it, she melts into my chest, and I can feel the tears soak into my T-shirt. I kick the door closed, run my fingers through her hair, and murmur, "I've got you."

I don't know how long we stand like that.

Me holding her.

Her crying.

But I don't mind. Not at all.

"We don't have to talk about it," I begin softly, combing my fingers through her hair and resting my chin on the top of her head. "But we can if you want to. There's no pressure."

It takes her a few moments to collect herself and pull away, using her wrist to wipe at her cheek. "Why are you here, Moskins?"

I shake my head, suddenly hating her using that name.

"It's Thomas to you."

Her throat bobs with a swallow, and she closes her eyes and rubs them with the heels of her palms. "What are you doing here, Thomas?"

I release a quiet breath. "Isn't it obvious? I'm checking on you."

She cracks her eyes open, and there's an emptiness there I want to fill. "I'm not your responsibility. Or your friend. You don't need to do that."

I lift my hand and swipe the pad of my thumb over her cheek to capture a fallen tear. "Just because you aren't my responsibility doesn't mean I can't make sure you're okay."

Her eyes narrow, and the sadness coating her glassy gaze morphs into anger. "Is this a game to you? I'm not particularly in the mood to deal with your hot and cold ass. You're giving me whiplash."

My jaw tics. "Does it look like I'm playing? The second Ashton called me today, the only person I wanted to see was you. Do you think I like feeling this way?"

She throws her hands up. "What way? And why should I give a shit how *you* feel right now?"

She's right. *Fuck.* She's right.

I hold my palms out in surrender. "I'm not trying to make this about me. I just wanted to see you. Not because I feel obligated, but because despite every fiber of my being telling me I shouldn't, I give a shit."

Speaking that truth aloud lifts a weight from my chest that I didn't know was sitting there for so long.

Winter's lips part, but nothing comes out as she stares at me. She's as confused as I am about whatever lingers between us.

Not friendship. Whatever we're classified as goes beyond that. We've crossed lines. Played with fire. And maybe this is us paying the consequences of those actions.

Feeling more than we signed up for.

Being vulnerable when we don't want to be.

We hold each other's secrets. Not to trade, sell, or give away. We hold them so we can finally fucking *breathe.*

Winter doesn't say a word as she walks over to the small couch pushed against a wall. She drops onto it and brings her knees up to her chest and wraps her arms around them.

I follow her in, not sitting, but standing a few feet away to give her space.

She says, "I was thirteen when they died."

I'm silent as she stares down at the floor and squeezes herself for comfort. The information she's offering me straightens my spine, and I cross my arms and ball my hands into fists as she keeps going.

"I found out about the accident hours after they were found by a bystander driving home from work. There was so much damage to the car, the police said the driver that hit them would have been going twice the speed limit when they made impact." Her eyes close, and a shiver rocks her body. "The first time I saw the photos was at the trial."

I push off the wall and kneel in front of her, wanting nothing more than to touch her. To comfort her. To be there in some way. But I force my hands to remain by my sides, fingers clenched into balled-up fists.

She shakes her head as more tears flow down her face

like a waterfall. "You want to know the worst part? The first responders on the scene said they didn't die right away. They said that both of my parents were alive. In rough shape, but alive by some miracle. By the time they got the jaws of life there to c-cut them out of the car, my father was dead. Mom was..." She shakes her head, lips quivering. "During the trial, they showed photos of footprints from a third party leading up to the driver's side, where my dad was trapped by crushed metal. Those same footprints were seen leaving the scene. The person who hit them left them to die, Thomas. Adam Burgess *left* them there. Two innocent people who just wanted to come home to their teenage daughter."

My throat bobs as her voice cracks, and she squeezes herself tighter.

Ashton doesn't talk about his family, and I never gave a shit enough to ask about them. He wasn't hired to divulge personal information about himself, even if he was always up my ass trying to get info on me. Maybe I should have pressed. I should have cared enough to wonder why he was so tightly lipped about his past when he had roots here.

"I didn't know," I tell her. "About any of it. I didn't know my agent had a personal connection to you. That his brother did that to your family."

Her eyes open, narrowing into slits. "But you asked me about him. You wanted to know if I knew him. You obviously suspected something."

Her anger may be pointed at me right now, but I know it's not me she's pissed at. It's Ashton. Adam. The world. So, I brush off the hostility in her tone—the accusation behind it. "Ashton made it sound like he knew you," I admit, watching her nostrils flare with irritation. "But he never said how, and you didn't seem to recognize the name."

Winter's teeth grind. "Because the bastard obviously changed his name."

Ashton mentioned taking his mother's maiden name after his brother was charged because he was starting to get traction in his career. According to him, he didn't want his name to be attached to something as gruesome as a hit and run when he was supposed to be representing well-known people.

From a business standpoint, I get it. He didn't want anyone digging into him and learning what his brother had done. There are repercussions that could impact his clientele, so he had to protect his reputation. But the second Winter was involved, he should have backed away. He should have owned up to the things he was holding back.

I don't tell Winter that I'm sorry about her parents, because what good would that do? They're gone. My condolences aren't going to bring them back or rid her of the trauma.

"I thought he was…" Her words trail off as she shakes her head again, closing her eyes. "I thought he was Adam. I thought he changed his name and came back to taunt me. It wasn't until Kourtney called our lawyer to confirm that Adam was in jail that I realized how ridiculous that sounded."

"It's not," I reassure. "They're twins. You couldn't have

known that."

"I went to the trial," she reminds me dryly. "I saw his family. I should have known. I shouldn't have jumped to conclusions."

Why is she blaming herself? "Ashton shouldn't have bulldozed you with this. He knew who you were and should have gone somewhere else for our business. I don't know why he chose not to. He's great at his job, so I went with whatever he recommended. I should have done my own research."

All she does is lift her shoulders, as if words are beyond her capability right now.

"Your parents' death is the reason you're so close with the community, isn't it?" I guess I now understand why so many people are fond of her.

She wets her lips, nodding as she looks away from me and blinks back tears. "Kourtney had to raise me. She was barely an adult herself. She was in college, working toward a degree, when she suddenly had a distraught teenager to look after. There are times I wish she had just let our aunt and uncle take me in, even if it meant moving. But she was determined to keep me here, where our parents always wanted us to grow up. So, I stayed. I graduated from high school, went to the local community college, and babysat to help her cover bills and schoolbooks. We made it through all the traumas and tribulations. We managed to survive somehow.

"And after a while, I stopped thinking about what happened to my mom and dad. Kourt said it was important to focus on all the good times we had instead. She didn't want me to obsess over them being gone or the man responsible for it. She thought it was more beneficial to show our parents that we could make something of ourselves despite what happened. So she put us both through therapy using some of the money we were given from the will, then she became a teacher like she always wanted to, got married, and had a child. And I…"

Winter pauses, her lips twitching downward for a moment. "And I'm here. In an apartment I can barely afford, with a pantry that's never stocked outside of ramen noodles, and working my first real job that's blowing up in my face. Compared to her, I have no idea what I'm doing."

I shake my head. "This whole thing may be a setback, but that doesn't mean it's exploded."

She deadpans, "The brother of the man who killed my family showed up in my life as the agent to my first client. Fairbanks is a small city, but not *that* small. This is fate bitch slapping me in the face. I stormed out of a meeting and left work like a baby."

"Winter—"

"And don't get me started on all the lines I've crossed with *you*," she goes on, dropping her head back on the couch and staring up at the ceiling. "I'm not like this. I don't run away from things. I don't sleep around. I don't involve myself with my clients no matter how—" she cuts herself off, her face blooming with red.

One of my eyebrows quirks up. "What?"

She shakes her head, pressing her lips together in a thin line and massaging her temples like she has a headache.

But I'm not ready to let this go. I rise up and sit on the

edge of the cushion beside her. "You and your sister didn't deserve the hand you were dealt, Winter. Nobody deserves that. Anybody in your position would have reacted the same way if they had seen Ashton and been brought back to the worst time in their lives. Would you call them babies? Tell them they were weak? That they should have reacted differently?"

She frowns. "No. Of course not."

"Exactly." I move her chin over to make her look at me. "Ashton knew better. He knew who you were and didn't remove himself from this situation. It was only a matter of time before you two crossed paths, and I'm sorry about that. I'm sorry that I brought this on to you. But I'm not sorry for whatever *this* is between us. I'm not sorry for enjoying how we banter. And I'm sure as fuck not sorry for knowing what you look like when you come. If that makes me a terrible person, then so be it. I've been labeled worse."

The red in her cheeks grows darker. "What does that make *me* then?"

I shrug nonchalantly. "Human."

She stares at me, her glassy eyes scanning my face. I don't know what's going through her mind when she draws her bottom lip into her mouth and bites down on it with her top front teeth.

Sitting this close to her, I smell fresh dirt and chopped grass. "Where did you go?" I ask, brushing at the spot. Any excuse to touch her, I'll take.

Winter releases her lip. "When I'm upset and don't know what to do, I go to my parents. I sit in front of their graves and talk. Sometimes about everything, sometimes about nothing. At least until my chest feels less full."

Tension coils in my shoulders as I offer up a piece of information I don't talk to anybody about. "My parents were not good people. They shouldn't have had me. Their lives were a mess before my mother got pregnant, and it only got three times worse after I was born. Their biggest regret wasn't getting addicted to painkillers and methamphetamine, it was having a kid."

Winter stares at me, slack-jawed.

I don't give her an opportunity to say anything before I get to the point. "So, I'm sorry that the two people who very clearly loved you more than anything, who raised two brilliant, motivated women, aren't here. I'm sorry that mine are. Life is cruel. It doesn't make sense, and I hate when people say everything happens for a reason. Because sometimes there is no reason. There is no excuse. We can't always fit every little thing that happens to us into a box. Reality is an ugly thing. But you know what I do believe?"

She wets her lips. "What?"

"I firmly believe that only the strongest people are handed the worst cards. Because we're resilient enough to survive. There are days I have to remind myself that I didn't become like my mother and father. I chose a different path, which is for the best. Things could have been very different for me if I hadn't."

A tiny breath escapes her lips as she studies my face like she's seeing me for the very first time. There's a lot to my story she doesn't know, and maybe I'll tell her. One day.

But not today.

Today isn't about me.

So, she can keep that secret and add it to the others just because I want her to.

"What do you need?" I ask her.

Winter stares and stares and stares.

Then, with a face still damp and eyes still bloodshot, she sits up and turns her body toward me. "This isn't me begging for it," she whispers, voice still raspy from the tears that were flooding her face only moments ago.

I'm about to ask what she means when one of her legs swings over me until she's straddling my lap. My hands instinctively go to her hips, kneading them as she lets out a shaky breath.

"This isn't me begging for it," she repeats, her hands coming to my shoulders and curling her fingers around the tops of my collarbones.

I swallow, fully understanding what she's referring to. *The next time we kiss, it's going to be because you're begging me for it.*

When she rolls her hips over me, I should tell her to stop. I should tell her now isn't the time or place. That she's hurt. That she's sad. That she'll *regret* this.

But then she pins me with those pleading eyes and whispers, "Please."

Please don't stop this.

Please don't turn me down.

She moves over me and squeezes her fingers into my flesh, and all I can think is...

Son of a bitch.

CHAPTER EIGHTEEN

Winter

DEEP DOWN, I know this is a bad idea. But I see the edge of the cliff that will take me far from the pain, anger, and grief rising higher and higher within me, and I leap toward it headfirst.

This isn't me begging for it.

I don't kiss Thomas, because then he'll win.

This isn't about him or the game we're playing. The endless back-and-forth. The banter. The push and pull that builds every time we see one another. No. This is about me and the distraction that will make me feel anything other than the way I do right now.

Heartbroken.

This is for relief. I would rather be full of regret than sink into the endless pit of despair that has been building for over twelve years.

Thomas asks, "What do you want, Winter?"

That's a loaded question. What I want is something simple. Easy. I want to feel free from the chains that have wrapped around me since the day I put white roses on my parents' coffins. I want to have an out-of-body experience where only pleasure encompasses me instead of the emptiness that I pretend isn't eating away at my soul.

I don't just *want* it at this point.

I need it.

I need the shadow to stop casting me into darkness. I need the rain cloud to go away. What I need isn't just Thomas to bring me to a place of mercy. It's to make me feel like a normal girl. Not the orphaned one that people pity. Not the headstrong one people see because she had to overcome her parents' deaths.

What I need is to be the type of person who makes mistakes. Who's giddy and reckless. Who acts out of emotions and not out of logic.

I'm sick of *thinking*.

I'm tired of trying to be *reasonable*.

All I do is pretend to be fine when I'm drowning in choices that don't make me happy. Suffocating on decisions that only get me so far.

But I don't divulge those deep, dark thoughts or desires.

"I don't want to feel this way," I whisper instead, dragging my fingers from where they're curled atop his collarbone to cup the nape of his neck and knead the tense, knotted muscles there.

I close my eyes and inhale slowly, finally letting my lungs get the oxygen they so desperately need.

"I don't want to feel—"

Thomas doesn't let me finish before he's flipping us over, so I'm on my back beneath him. The couch is short, barely large enough to fit both of us because of his bulky frame, but he makes it work without struggle. He's good at domineering his space, no matter how little of it he has.

His presence, authoritative and confident, is both attractive and terrifying because I know I can't compete. We're not on equal footing. My experience is lacking in ways I refuse to admit.

I don't do virgins, he'd told me once.

I swat that thought away like a pesky fly.

"You want me to make you come," he purrs, hovering over me and propping himself up with his arms on either side of my head. "The question is, sweetheart, how do you want me to do it?"

I blow out a shaky breath as he dips his face dangerously close to my mouth. He doesn't kiss me—doesn't cross that invisible line bordering on the brink of our insanity. He knows the second he does, he'll lose his control.

Keeping true to his promise, his lips move to the crook of my neck to press open-mouthed kisses against my pulse. He nips the skin and drags his tongue across the same spot, his bite hard enough to make me suck in a breath. Involuntarily, I arch up until I feel the hardened length under his jeans.

"Do you want me to get you off with my fingers?" he asks into my throat, before moving to pepper a trail of kisses down my neck. He bites into my collarbone, and I hiss at the pain that he licks away with a smile. "Or my mouth?"

My eyelids flutter closed as he lowers his body to press against mine. His weight doesn't feel overwhelming, and I suspect he's holding himself up so as not to crush me. "B-both," I rasp when his teeth sink into me again, this time at the curve of my breast. "More. I w-want more."

He hums against my chest, where he grazes his lips against the spot above my racing heart. I hear the faintest chuckle vibrate against me, undoubtedly because of how hard the organ in its cage drums in reaction to him.

"More, huh?" he muses, his tongue flattening against the bite I suspect will leave a small bruise tomorrow. "What else do you want from me? I'll need you to use your big girl words."

His comment should annoy me the same way it did when he referred to me as a kid weeks ago, but I'm incapable of irritation. His hot kisses and the way his hands roam up and down the sides of my body like he's petting me are setting me on fire. I do want more. I want it all. Everything.

I make a noise when his mouth disappears, and he rises up to look me in the eye.

He pinches my chin and tilts my head. "Look at me, Winter." His voice oozes authority, so I know it isn't a suggestion. I force my eyes open and try calming my beating heart. "Good girl."

Oh God. I clench my thighs at the sound of his praise, and he notices immediately.

"Do you like that?" he asks, with interest sparking in his eyes. The gray-blue color sides more with the latter, making his hues look like a stormy sky. "Do you like it when I call you a good girl?"

There's no room for embarrassment when his hands trail up, up, up until the side of his palm brushes against my breast. After I'd come home from the cemetery, I changed into a worn pair of leggings and a T-shirt, forgoing a bra because I wanted to be comfortable. The shirt is so thin, Thomas may as well be touching my bare skin.

Eventually, I find myself nodding. I'd never been called a good girl before, but the high praise in his tone and etched into his features is a turn-on I never expected to have.

He hums, his hands stilling as he studies my face. "You never answered my question," he notes, his lips curling into a half-grin. "What else do you want from me? Do you want me to touch you?"

The way he asks, in a quiet, sure voice, makes heat rise to my face. "Yes."

"Where?" he asks, his hands moving over my breast and cupping it. "Here? Is that where you want me?"

His thumb caresses my hardened nipple, and I make an involuntary noise over the sensation that dampens my panties. Boys have touched me in the past. Above the clothes, mostly. But they never made me feel like *this*.

Another thoughtful noise comes from him as I wrap my fingers around his wrist and move his hand down my body. "H-here," I tell him, leaving his hand at the elastic of my leggings and not an inch further despite where I *really* want him.

Thomas knows that. "Interesting," he says, hooking a finger into the elastic and brushing his knuckle back and forth along my abdomen. "This is where you want it?"

He's teasing me, knowing that it isn't.

"If you want me to help you forget the pain," he says slowly, his eyes locking with mine, "you need to tell me exactly what you want. More importantly, what you *don't* want."

Kourtney always used to say it was important to have a partner who was open in communication and checked in, especially during sex. I've never experienced that before and didn't think it would be hard to voice what I wanted.

Mostly because…I don't know.

I don't know what makes me feel good or what doesn't. I don't know what will get me off. What won't. What I'm craving.

I shut myself away from the world for years, focusing only on how to be independent. How to be okay with being alone. As lonely as it gets, I know that time by myself has been vital. It means knowing I can survive without somebody stepping in to help.

I've never let boys go farther than this. I always believed sex would complicate things—throw me off track. I couldn't focus on whether somebody liked me or not, or worry if someone found out too much about me. I don't want their sympathy, pity, or judgment.

Shutting down was easier. It's been the only way I operate. Until Thomas.

"I want," I begin in a quiet voice, wrapping my hands around his wrist again, "for you to touch me here."

I move his hand down to cup me between my thighs, where undeniable heat and wetness greet him.

His eyes flash with lust, and that crooked grin grows as he applies more pressure. "Is that all you want?"

He's going to keep making me say it.

My nostrils flare. "I told you. I want more."

"More what?" he goads innocently, watching me. "More of this?"

I gasp when he runs a finger over my clothed center, pressing the pad of his thumb against my achy clit.

"Do you want me to get you off like I did before?" he questions, circling his thumb over me with the perfect amount of pressure. "Or do you want me to sink my fingers into your pussy this time? Would you let me put my mouth on your cunt to taste what I do to you?"

Yes, yes, yes. All of it. The answer is screamed inside my head, but not voiced aloud, because my brain short-circuits as pleasure sends shockwaves down my legs.

As if he knows that, he immediately stops, and a whiny protest comes out of me before I can squash it.

"I want it all," I all but growl at him, the frustration of being so close to something so blissful and having it yanked away grating on me. "I want your fingers and your mouth and your—" The word is lodged in my throat, the truth so close to being revealed but still holding on to my vocal cords like once it's spoken, there's no going back.

Thomas's eyes scan my face, the lust like a fire being fueled by gasoline. "You want my what, Winter? Be a good girl and say it."

No going back.

No going back.

No going back.

"I want your cock inside me," I admit hoarsely, feeling the fire from my core rise up and heat my body like the fire within him is spreading to me. "I want to feel it inside of me. Happy?"

His smile doesn't waver as he works me over my leggings with his skilled fingers. "Very much so. In fact, I think I'll reward you."

Reward—

The thought is cut off when his hand dips inside my leggings and touches me *there*. The blunt tip of his finger circles my entrance before doing a sweep up and down the seam of me as another finger nudges the bundle of nerves that are firing at a million miles an hour.

I arch into him, and he chuckles at the urgency waging a war inside me. I can feel it pulling me toward the brink of orgasm and far from the other emotions still trying to work their way into my consciousness.

But I brush them away and focus on Thomas's fingers. On his palm. On how his mouth dips back down to my neck and kisses, sucks, and bites at my skin until one of his digits finally enters me. He's got thick fingers, and my body clenches around the foreign object, earning a low growl from him.

"I can feel you contracting around me." He groans against my throat, trailing his tongue down to the neckline of my tee. "If it feels this amazing around my finger, I can't wait until I feel your cunt squeezing my cock."

It only makes me squeeze him harder, flooding his finger with arousal. He jerks my T-shirt up high enough to expose my bare breasts and instantly takes one into his mouth.

I've always been a little self-conscious about how small my boobs are. I'd been envious of my sister's chest since she developed them and thought I'd grow into mine one day.

Unfortunately, I wasn't blessed with the same genetics as she was. But Thomas doesn't seem to mind at all. He's practically got the whole thing in his mouth, sucking and licking and biting until—

"Oh my God." I moan, eyes closing as a sudden burst of pleasure racks through my body and quivers down my spine. The orgasm comes out of nowhere, barely giving me time to breathe as he pumps a single digit in and out of me as my strung-out body floats down from the high.

I'm not sure how, maybe magic if that sort of thing exists in the world, but the shirt that had been pushed up my body while he devoured my breasts is now on the floor. Along with it, his.

We're skin to skin, my hard nipples brushing against his chiseled pecs as he continues to play with my over-stimulated clit while his lips hover over mine. They don't brush or touch, but his breath is a caress against my own. Like he wants me to know how good he is at taking over. How much he wants to make that next move.

But he won't. And I won't ask him to.

I gasp, my lips nearly brushing his as my legs shake under his experienced hands. I feel my body shudder as he continues to work me closer and closer to something that feels blindingly good. Too good that I fear this isn't real at all.

"You're fucking soaking my hand," he praises, biting the edge of my bottom lip and pulling it with his teeth. "I can feel how close you are again. Give it to me, baby. Come on my fingers so I can feel you come on my cock next. I'm going to keep this going until you can't take it anymore. Until you're milking me of cum. Understand?"

It's too much. His hand. His *words.*

I lose it for a second time, everything going black for a few seconds. Nothingness greets me in a world outside my body. No sound. No sight. Just this moment between us. This sated, full feeling that outweighs all the others trying to scratch their way in.

When I come to, Thomas is combing his fingers through my hair and watching me. "I thought I lost you for a minute," he muses, a cocky smile curling his lips.

I blush, closing my legs.

"Don't get shy on me now," he says against my ear, nipping at the lobe. The hand that was inside me is now petting the side of my leg longingly. Does he even know he's doing it? His touch seems soft. Thoughtful. Like he's okay with things ending here despite what he wants to do to me.

Unfortunately for me, I'm right.

He massages my hip to regain my attention, watching as I swallow at his intense stare. "Are you sure about this?" he asks in a tone that's a little too soothing. The dominant version of him from moments ago is gone, and the way he looks at me is full of exactly what I don't want.

Pity and caution. Hesitation and sympathy.

I want the other version of him back. The one who isn't afraid to take control. To talk dirty. To demand things and give me everything he gives to the other women he's been with.

His eyes roam over me, studying every inch of my face like he's trying to read my mind. "This isn't something you can take back, Winter. If you haven't—"

"I'm not a virgin," I snap defensively, having had enough of whatever this is. Since when is he playing good guy? That isn't what I want from him.

I want the experienced Moskins that's featured in headlines. The one that women get when he travels. The person everybody *thinks* he is. I want to stop being treated like I'm fragile, as if I'll break at any second. He's never coddled me before, and I appreciate that about him. Because he doesn't treat me like everybody else.

"I never said you were," he replies, hesitation in his tone still. "But as far as I'm concerned, you're as good as one. My finger barely fit inside you. What will happen if I put my cock in you? Will you bleed on me? Will I hurt you? Is that what you want?"

Those stupid, stupid words from before play back in my head. *I don't do virgins.*

My nostrils flare. "I thought *you*, of all people, would be down for an easy fuck. You'll sleep with anybody besides your wife. Why hesitate with me?"

His shoulders tense, squaring back. I notice the smallest tic to his jaw as the words land. As much as I regret saying them, I can't take it back.

"Is that what you want? For me to treat you like the others?" There's a bite to his tone that's so cool it chills the air around us. "Do you want me to be rough with you like them? To *use* you?"

His gaze pierces mine with a surprising level of hurt and frustration that I feel in my soul.

"I..." I wet my lips, squirming under him. How can

one look both set me ablaze and freeze at the same time? "Yes. I do."

If I thought he was angry before, it's nothing compared to now. "Well, you've come to the right whore then."

Without another word, my leggings are being ripped down my thighs and discarded on the floor along with our shirts. My panties are nothing to write home about, but his eyes flare when he sees a sizable wet stain from what he did to me only minutes ago.

When he cages me in again, there's a new challenge on his face. Like he's waiting for me to tell him to stop. Like he *wants* me to, but doesn't at the same time.

"How rough do you want it, princess?" he asks, lowering himself down and rolling his hips into me. He's still half-dressed, but the front of his jeans is obviously tented with an erection that looks…

I gulp at the size. I'd seen part of him at the animal shelter. He'd held his cock as he came, but his hand took up most of it. He was…big. Bigger than I would have imagined.

"Since you've done this before," he goads, "surely you can handle me. Right?"

He's baiting me. Intimidating me.

I suck in a breath and meet his eyes. "Yes," I lie as smoothly as possible, hoping the shake in my voice isn't evident. "You can be as rough as you want to be, Moskins."

"It's Thomas to you," he growls, his mouth so close to mine that I think he may break his promise.

He wants to kiss me, I realize.

But he's teetering on that line of self-control.

He reaches down between us, and I hear the metallic sound of a zipper being pulled down before his jeans slide down his hips until he's out.

And when I look down—

"Oh my God," I whisper, staring at the silver piercing on his shaft.

He wraps a hand around himself and strokes his dick. "Do you like what you see? Women have told me it feels good when it's inside them. You think you'd want that?"

I can't stop staring as he continues to move his hand from base to hilt, watching as precum slides down and coats his hand. "You..." I'm at a loss for words, and I hear the faintest chuckle at my speechlessness.

"Did you change your mind?"

That's the problem.

I haven't.

No matter how many times he offers me an out, I'm in this. I want this. More than anything.

I reach out and drag the pad of my thumb over his tip and watch him shiver at the sensation. I gather the cum and wipe it just under the head and over the piercing until a sound escapes him that sounds like a whispered prayer.

He closes his eyes as I experiment with the silky-smooth skin covering hard steel before brushing against the piercing. "Did it hurt?" I ask breathlessly.

His only response comes out choppy as I play with it. "It was worth it."

I swallow, peeking up at him through my lashes. "I want to feel it. Like them."

Those stormy eyes cloud over at the mention of the

women who came before me. Since when does he not like talking about it? He's never been ashamed of his past or what he's done. Why now? Why be angry about something he's never seemed apologetic for?

"Is that so?" he says, moving my hand away and pinning it to the cushion. "How much do you think you can take before asking me to stop? Do you think I'll fit in your tight, little cunt?"

My free hand grasps his biceps. "Y-yes."

His teeth bite down on my neck, harder than before. If he's not careful, he'll leave marks everywhere, and I'll have to go to work covered in makeup and a turtleneck. "I guess we'll see," he says, before the tip of him nudges my entrance and sinks in.

Another drawn-out curse comes from him as he stops only a fraction inside me. It's a whisper against my skin as he tightens his hold against the wrist still pinned to my side.

"What if this is all I give you?" he provokes, his hold on me flexing as I begin wiggling to adjust to the foreign pressure between my legs.

It's nothing like his fingers, which offered a bite of pain that quickly melted to pleasure.

This is more.

So much more.

But I don't want him to stop.

"What if I just give you the tip?" he asks against the shell of my ear. "Would that still be too much for you?"

My teeth grind. "It won't be." I try moving my hips to take more of him in, but he's quick to stop me the second he sees me wince at the pain.

His grip moves from my wrist to my hip, holding me in place. "Stop," he commands, leaving no room for argument. "If we do this, we do it *my* way. If you want this, you will listen to what *I* say. That's the only way this is going to feel good for you. And whether you want to believe it or not, that's what I want most. For *you* to feel good. For *you* to enjoy yourself. If you're looking for a distraction, you can use me. If you're looking to forget everything you're feeling for a few hours, then I'm right here, baby. But I will not let you hurt yourself, and I sure as hell won't let you keep lying. To me *or* yourself."

The authority in his tone isn't as cold as before. Neither is his expression nor the way his eyes pin me to my spot beneath him.

He wants to give me everything I'm asking for, but he doesn't want to hurt me. He doesn't want me to regret this.

Will I anyway?

Maybe.

But that's a problem for tomorrow.

"Do you understand?" he asks, and I realize he won't continue until I agree to his terms.

So, I nod. "I understand."

"And you'll be a good girl and do as I say?"

Once again, I nod.

He brushes hair away from my face, then traces my bottom lip with his finger. "I think you like being told what to do, don't you? You like not having to be in control one hundred percent of the time."

For a second, my brain falters. Because…is that true?

I'm not sure that's something I even realized myself. But when he puts it like that, he's not wrong. It's tiring having to have everything figured out. To be okay when you're not. To have a logical next step planned.

I want a break from that reality; to give somebody else the reins, even for a little while.

"I…" I pause, blinking up at him as one of his hands begins toying with my nipple. It's still sensitive, still hard, and yearning for his touch. "I do," I realize, swallowing. "I'm tired of always having to figure everything out. I'm sick of always pretending—"

That I'm not hurting.

I don't finish the sentence.

I don't need to.

His mouth wraps around the opposite nipple and sucks hard before he says, "I get it, baby girl. I can give you that. You won't have to think about a thing."

Yes. God, yes.

The way he works his tongue and fingers over me eases the coiled muscles in my stomach until my legs open a fraction wider for him. He sinks into me, his cock moving another centimeter or two at best and stopping to let me adjust.

"There you go," he praises against my breast. "You're doing so good. Stretching so fucking good for me."

I thread my fingers through his hair as his lips move away from my chest and up to my throat. He goes back to the same spot he's kissed and bit and licked before, doing the same thing as his hands roam farther south.

I gasp when I feel his knuckles brush my clit, and I

involuntarily jerk my hips and take him further.

"Tsk tsk," he murmurs against me. "What did I say? No moving. Not until I tell you."

A whiny noise comes from my throat that doesn't sound like me at all.

"Maybe I should pull out," he thinks aloud, his nose grazing the column of my throat as his mouth moves toward my ear. "Maybe I should get you off again. This time with my mouth. Make you ride my face until you're flooding me. Get you good and wet and primed."

I shake my head. "No. I want you like this."

I claw at him as his movements over my nerves quicken until I feel that sensation build in the pit of my stomach again. My fingernails drag along the corded muscles of his back, and he groans and moves forward, sinking into me a little farther. I feel so full, but not full enough, and I know he's barely in because I don't feel his piercing yet.

"For fuck's sake, you feel good." He groans, pausing once again despite how badly I want him to keep going. "I could come just like this. Not even all the way inside you. You have no idea..."

His eyes focus on my mouth as his words trail off, like there's so much more he wants to say but holds himself back.

Part of me wants to know, and the other, more logical side of me, is afraid to hear it.

"Would you let me?" he asks, moving out of me before pushing back in. He doesn't go any further than before; he just repeats the movements. Careful not to thrust. Always aware of every breath, moan, and flinch that his movements create within me.

"Y-yes," I admit, wrapping my arms tightly around his neck and squeezing as I allow my body to adjust to his thick cock. And that piercing…

God, that piercing.

"I bet you'd come again," he murmurs, peppering kisses along my face. My forehead. My temple. The tip of my nose. One cheek, then the other. But never my mouth, and all while moving in and out of me.

Just the tip, and maybe half an inch more.

"I bet I could get you to come all over my cock just like this," he continues, his mouth pressing a dangerously close kiss to mine. His lips land on the corner of mine, a breath away from sealing something between us.

But he keeps going, his mouth moving away to trail along my jaw. My throat. Back up to my ear. The path he creates leaves fire in its wake, overheating my naked body as he pumps in and pulls out.

"More," I beg, unashamed of the need in my voice. My fingernails dig into his shoulder blades again as he moves over me. *In* me. "Please, Thomas. I need more."

A knowing smirk curls his lips. "My girl is a needy little thing, isn't she?"

My girl. I contract around him, my nipples getting harder at the sentiment that should most definitely not get me wet. But it does. Boy, does it ever.

And Thomas knows that.

He *feels* it. "You like that, don't you? Being claimed? You don't even need to answer. I can feel how you react to it." He slips in deeper, and I can feel the piercing nudge me.

I tense for a moment at the idea of it going inside, but

he's quick to hush my worries with soothing praises and pets that have my leg muscles loosening and spreading even wider for him.

Just when I think it's not possible for him to go in even deeper than he already is, he does. I gasp at the fullness—at the way I stretch around him. It's painful, I won't lie. Discomfort settles between my legs at the intrusion that's so blunt that a voice in my head urges me to get it out.

But then he moves his hand between us, settling on my core to work the oversensitive nerve endings to get me to stop panicking. "You can trust me," he promises, his thumb working lazy circles around my clit. "You can let go and let yourself enjoy what I'm giving you. That's it, sweetheart. I can feel you relaxing. You're—" A groan rips through him as he moves his hips forward and his piercing enters me.

And *holy shit.*

A pinch of pain fills me, but is quickly wiped away by the sensation of him hard *there*. He feels way too good—better than he should. Every time a shift brings me even the slightest bit of discomfort, he makes it up to me with his mouth and hands.

Until...

Until...

"Thomas," I breathe out, feeling the telltale sign of tingles shooting down my spine.

"Are you going to be a good girl and come on my cock?" he asks, brushing hair out of my face and cupping my cheek. "Are you going to vice grip me? Answer me, Winter. *Look at me.*"

He gives me no choice but to look at him, and I lock eyes as I teeter on the edge of yet another orgasm that surely won't happen. Not again. "I-I…" Too much. This is too much and not enough, somehow, at the same time.

"Say my name," he demands. "Say my fucking name when you come. I need to see it on your lips."

My eyes start rolling back as he keeps his pace, his piercing scraping against me in the best way possible. "T-Thomas. I'm going to—"

"Come," he commands, and it's like that's all my body needs to let go.

To free my mind. Free my body. Free all those ill feelings woven around my soul that have been that way for over a decade.

Right now, it's Thomas and me.

It's two people who bear heavy secrets.

I may not know nearly as many as his as he does mine, but I can see them in his eyes. The demons that hold them back. All the reasons he lets the world rip him apart.

Just like I just did.

I judged him.

Used him for my benefit.

For *this*.

I'm no better than the people who are quick to assume who he is, when it's obvious that there is so much more to Thomas Moskins than a pretty face and ruthless scowl. So much more than he allows people to believe.

It's sad, and that sadness and guilt slowly begin to creep their way back in until he asks, "Are you on the pill?"

His cock is still sliding inside me, and I can see the

urgency in his eyes as he scans my face.

I nod. "Yes."

"Thank fuck," he replies like it's a prayer. "I need to come in you. I need you to fucking feel me, Winter. I need—"

I lock my legs around him and meet his eyes, not looking away. "Please" is the only thing I have to say before ecstasy takes over his face, and he pumps forward one more time and fills me.

The softness on his face, the warmth he radiates, isn't what I expect at all. He cups my face, his hand gentle, his eyes a calm sea after a wild storm, and…smiles.

But the smile disappears, wavering once like he's trying to hold on to the moment but realizing he can't.

He pulls out, as slow and careful as possible, before moving away from me. His silence soaks into me, thickening the air around us. I don't know what to say as I lie on the couch, letting the cool air caress my naked, sated body.

I watch as he disappears around the corner and listen to the water run. Then I see him come back with a washcloth, and confusion pinches my brows.

"What are you—?" I stop short when he makes quick work of cleaning me up. I suck in a breath as he brushes me, but his expression is blank. Lacking the lust that's been there this whole time.

I hurt him.

"Thomas," I whisper, putting my hand on his forearm to try to get his attention.

He won't look up at me, but I see the way his teeth grind to hold back what he's thinking.

"I'm sorry," I tell him, voice hoarse.

His eyes close, and I feel the muscles in his forearm flex. Then he withdraws, the washcloth with blood and cum on it disappearing with him down the hall to my tiny bathroom.

When he comes back, he collects his clothes and changes without saying another word.

"Thomas," I repeat, voice weak.

He heads to the door, hesitating with his hand around the doorknob. "I'm sorry for what Ashton's brother did to your parents. And I am sorry for how deeply you're hurt. I know what that's like."

Because of his family? "Then tell me," I plead, sitting up and wincing at the pain between my legs. "Talk to me about it. Help me understand. Give me another secret."

When he looks over his shoulder, there's something dark shadowing his features. "Why?" he questions blandly. "I'm just a man whore. What are my problems and feelings to you?"

His words slice into me, and I have nothing to say before he's out the door and shutting it behind him.

I close my eyes and feel my lips waver into a watery frown. But no tears come, because I have none left to spill.

I know then that I messed up big time.

Because if this were something casual between us, I wouldn't feel bad at all. I would have accepted what he'd given me and walked away from the rest.

But I don't do that.

I can't, I realize.

And it scares me on a whole new level.

CHAPTER NINETEEN

Moskins

I HAVE EIGHT missed calls and over twenty unanswered texts from Emaly after hanging up on her yesterday. Apparently, sending her a message on my way home from Winter's apartment saying I was fine and needed time to myself wasn't clear enough for her.

She's always been the one to call me on my shit, but not even she could have calmed the hurricane inside me. If I had talked to her, I would have been a dickhead. Then I would have taken it out on her the way Winter did on me and felt guilty about it for the rest of the night.

I'd told Winter to use me, and that's exactly what she did. She used and discarded me all at fucking once, like I was a balled-up napkin.

The only two times I've looked at my phone in the twenty-four hours since are first, when Jesse Clarkson told me I had to go to Coach Hoffman's house for a team dinner today, and second, when Mikhail Yokav's name appeared on the screen. It isn't often I'm in direct communication with my father-in-law. Usually, he goes through his typical channels to get ahold of me when he needs it. To him, I'm a cockroach beneath his shoe. He wouldn't dare try to crush me and ruin his Versace shoes—he'd let the exterminator do it for him.

So, I wasn't about to let him go to voicemail as much as I was tempted to sulk alone in between all my other responsibilities.

His no-nonsense, "Meet me at my office tomorrow," left no room for argument or interpretation before he gave me a time and hung up the phone.

Which is why I'm pulling up white-knuckled to Yokav Stadium and glaring at the large block lettering on top of the dome roof. They designed it to look identical to the Yokav complexes in Russia, which offers very little humble architecture to the area. It's not fitting for Fairbanks's city, which is designed in old brick buildings with Revolutionary War history, but I'm not surprised they were able to get the plans approved.

All it takes is a large check slid across a mahogany desk for anybody with authority in this town to smile and put a stamp of approval on government letterhead. I've seen it before, and I'll see it again.

Yokav's reputation for getting what he wants is notorious, which is why I soak in the victorious feeling every time he sees me and his daughter together. Because if there's anything he wants less than a losing hockey season, it's for me to have any claim over Emaly.

Because that means *he* can't.

I'd rather be doing literally anything but this today. I typed and deleted at least three text messages to the unsaved number that I've already memorized as Winter's. It took everything in me not to send something to her. To check in.

I'm not your responsibility, she'd told me. Then why the hell did I want to make her mine?

Fists clenching my keys, I walk to the building I've become familiar with over the past week. The security guards at the front entrance greet me with their usual smiles as they scan my badge and wave me through. I've made small talk with everybody I've met here for the sake of civility, even if I'd prefer keeping to myself. Being an asshole ninety-nine percent of the time takes too much effort, so I'd like to think I sprinkle a little normalcy in when I can, despite what my teammates probably think.

How'd that niceness go for you yesterday, dickwad? an annoying voice in my head asks.

I can still picture Winter splayed out on the couch, blood caked onto her thighs, and tears glazing her eyes that made them look darker than normal. She gave me something she hadn't given to anybody. I don't know why she lied about her virginity, but I'm determined to find out.

When she's ready.

Because if what happened between us yesterday proved anything, it's that she's not ready to be honest with herself. I refuse to regret what we did, because she wanted it. She wasn't going to let me leave until she got it. And if being the person who could give her temporary peace is what I could offer her, I'm not going to guilt myself for it.

I just wish her words didn't cut so goddamn deep. How often do I sacrifice myself for those around me? Emaly. Mikhail. The team. *Her.* I've lived a life of torment, and don't want to see anybody else deal with the same problems. The look in her eyes, the pure destruction of her soul as she cried, broke me. It reminded me of everything I've gone through and have been determined to never experience again. It made me want to soak up her sadness and take it all away for good.

I did that for *her*. I let her use me. Take advantage of me. I let her have whatever she needed at that moment. And for fucking what? For her to take out the boxing gloves because she felt guilty for it? Because she was ashamed of who she decided to let fuck her?

Nah. She'll have to deal with those demons on her own and come to me when she's ready to talk about them. I can't help her with whatever internal battle is waging inside her until she's ready to approach the topic herself.

Jaw grinding, I think back to my own demons. They hang out with the skeletons in my closet that date back to my childhood. Bones that I dug up for the sake of relatability. And Winter may as well have slapped me in the face with them.

As I approach the top floor of the building where Mikhail's office spans almost a third of the floor plan, anxiety sinks into my gut. I wish I didn't feel this way whenever he's involved, but I've always had to be cautious around him.

"Come in," he calls out after I knock on the partially open door.

I take a deep breath, roll my shoulders, and enter the space that's far too white and warm to fit the brooding, calculated man sitting behind the desk.

"Hi, si—"

"Sit," he cuts me off, not looking up from the papers he's scanning. Some of them are highlighted. Some of them are redacted. There's ink written in the margins. I don't bother asking what he's doing, because he won't tell me. It's likely a new deal, because he never seems to know when enough is enough. Frankly, ignorance is bliss when it comes to the Russian businessman.

I claim the same seat I did last time, which is far enough away from the desk not to feel overtaken by his personal bubble or the smoky scent of tobacco from the cigars he loves. "Sir, what is this meeting about? If it's regarding the gala, everything is set. I made sure Dawson has a suit, and Clarkson is going as well. Everyone will be on their best behavior."

Usually, I know exactly why he wants to speak to me because it's typically not good. But the only press I've been getting lately is the positive kind, and the mixed reviews that surrounded me have cast me in a better light more often than not. I'm captured with my team and not with women. I keep to myself, living under the radar. There isn't anything for him to complain about. And he's not the type to praise me for my good behavior, which leaves me at a loss for what this entails.

"I don't care about the gala," he informs me.

You'd think he would, since he's a donor to the Historical Association hosting it. When Hoffman spoke to him and Janel about doing a meet-and-greet to gain extra money for the Association and put positive attention on the Fireflies, he seemed to appreciate the idea. I'd told Hoffman to keep my name out of it because he would have shot it down if he knew it was mine.

"My daughter," he begins slowly, still writing down something with his ballpoint pen that has his name engraved in gold lettering, "is hiding something from me. And I don't appreciate it."

There are a lot of things he could have said, but I wasn't anticipating that. "What makes you think that?" I ask curiously.

When his head lifts, there's no amusement on it. In fact, he doesn't offer me any emotion. His face is completely unreadable; save the unimpressed glint to his dark eyes that's a permanent fixture whenever I'm around. Emaly has the same color eyes as her father, but hers are always full of light that makes the brown far less threatening. "How dumb do you think I am?"

His thick accent makes the question sound like a warning, as if I need to be very careful with my answer.

"Is that a trick question?" I reply, tilting my head as I try to relax in my seat. If he sees how tense I am, he'll know how uncomfortable this is for me. Then he'll use it against me, which I have no intention of allowing him to do.

His nostrils flare as he slowly puts his pen down onto the papers scattered across his desk, which means this conversation is about to get messy. "We both know that my daughter's priorities have always been unbalanced."

That's his opinion, not mine. "I think her priorities are hers to focus on alone without any of us stepping in."

Mikhail, to nobody's surprise, does not agree with the sentiment. "When she put herself through college, I didn't stop her because it was clear she'd never make it as an athlete the way Sasha can."

It takes everything in me not to point out why that is, which never seems to matter to him. She's always been sick. For years, nobody could figure out what was wrong with her. When the professionals told her and her parents that it was "simply fibromyalgia," her father accused her of trying to fake her illnesses so that she didn't have to skate. But I saw her—the pain she suffered through. The dizzy spells. How pale she'd get when she tried pushing herself for her parents' approval. She was prone to migraines that would wipe her out for hours. There was more to it than some cop-out diagnosis the doctors slapped on her file and sent her away with.

I was the only one who saw it.

Not her father.

Not her mother.

Me.

Ever since the day I moved in next door to her family, I'd seen Emaly for who she is. Kind, considerate, and passionate. There isn't one day that goes by that she hasn't tried her hardest at something. She wasted years of her life trying to earn her father's approval, only to finally accept that she never would. Before fully acknowledging that her body couldn't handle the physical strain that her brother could.

Mikhail either doesn't see the resentment on my face or doesn't give a shit. "And when she informed us that you two had gotten married behind our backs with no prenup, no ring, and no plan, clearly, there was nothing I could do. Trust me, I tried."

It takes everything in me not to snicker.

Emaly had shown me the texts, voicemails, and emails from her parents after news broke that we'd gone to a courthouse with nothing but a photographer, two friends, and a judge. Neither of our families were there, and they'd found out when the rest of the world did via social media. It wasn't until a few weeks later when we decided to do the engagement photos hanging in my home. Mikhail and Valeria questioned where the proof was of our relationship, because they didn't believe the marriage certificate was enough.

Anybody with eyes could see that Emaly and I loved each other. But only those close enough could see what kind of love it is.

Inevitably, that's why nobody gets close.

Not until Winter came into my life.

Following Mikhail's heated voicemails that used a lot of expletives spoken in both English and Russian, he sent money bribes to convince her to annul the "ridiculous marriage" that she "trapped" herself in. When he realized she wasn't going to change anything about her life, he gave her the silent treatment and threatened to cut her off. It was pointless given her lack of handouts throughout her life. She barely accepted any money from them to begin with, so their control was nonexistent.

Everything Emaly has done, she's done on her own. Not with her family's help, money, or title. When Mikhail realized he had no real sway with her financially, he used the next best thing to keep her around. Emotional warfare.

Which is why I wound up signing a contract with the

Fairbanks Fireflies. He knew if he couldn't get to her directly, he'd get to the person closest to her. And while I'd like to think I'm the equivalent of a gold medal in her eyes, Ronnie's existence pushed me to silver.

But I'll take second place if it means her happiness is intact.

"Do you have a point to all of this?" I ask casually enough not to give away my growing irritation. "Because I'm supposed to meet Coach Hoffman at his place for a get-together with the team."

Something I'm not looking forward to since Clarkson texted me about it this morning to inform me he'd drag me there if I tried skipping, but it's a distraction from what transpired between Winter and me.

"And when she moved forward with med school, I could see the determination on her face clear as day. She is a Yokav, after all. She was not going to let anything her mother and I thought get in the way of becoming a doctor."

Is that a hint of...pride in his voice? He's never acted like she's done anything worthwhile since she stopped skating. With Sasha going on to win medals and become one of the world's best-known Russian figure skaters, Emaly accepted the shadow she was stuck in that would never compare to her little brother.

Once again, I ask, "Is there a point to this history lesson? Out of everybody in her life, I think I'd know the events that occurred so far since I've been the most prevalent person she's shared them with."

He makes a thoughtful noise. "That *is* my point. You

of all people know what's going through my daughter's mind. Even on different coasts, you know her whereabouts and motives. So what *I* would like to know is what she's hiding from me. Because I know it's something."

Something triggered this line of questioning. He's never cared enough to ask about what's happening in her life before. "Why?" I dare ask. "What does it matter to you?"

This man only ever reaches out and pretends to give a fuck when it benefits him. So what is he after now? What control is he seeking? He already has me, and there's nothing Emaly has that can be taken when there's so much he's in the dark about.

He leans forward, the creak in his chair echoing in the room as he pins me with eyes that look nearly black. "You may believe whatever you want about me, but she is still my daughter. And one of my sources said she was seen leaving a neurology office crying like she'd been told she has six months to live. Care to explain what that's about?"

His *sources*? I clench the arms of the chair when I realize what he's implying. "Are you having Emaly followed?"

That's a huge invasion of privacy. I've had people looked into, sure, but never followed. I never even went through with getting intel on Winter because I'd craved the information directly from the source—tit for tat. A trade-off of secrets.

Chances are, whoever is trailing Emaly has a lot more intel than they should. Emaly and Ronnie live together in our San Diego home. They work together at the same hospital. If there is somebody trailing her for Mikhail, they'll probably have seen the patterns. Emaly could easily write off Ronnie as a coworker if she's asked, but I know she wouldn't stoop so low.

Not if it means hurting Ronnie.

Mikhail intertwines his fingers on the desk. "I need my questions answered since neither of you is willing to give me any information when I request it."

The tips of my fingers ache from how hard they dig into the material of the chair arm. "Don't you ever get tired of being this much of an asshole?"

My question barely causes a reaction from him. He doesn't seem pissed or offended by it. If anything, his lips twitch upward.

That is, until I say, "If your daughter wanted you to know anything about her, then maybe you should have made it easier for her to share. All her life, you've done nothing but critique her. Judge her. Tell her she isn't *good enough*. On what goddamn planet do you think that means you're owed any explanation from her when she's finally happy?"

His spine goes rigid as he glares at me. "Is that what she is? *Happy?*" He spits out the word with venom in his tone. "How can she be happy when she's married to a man who can't keep his dick in his pants? Who lives across the country rather than being with her? Supporting her? Who spends more time focused on himself and his own pleasures versus anything to do with his wife?"

I stand and crowd his space, leaning my hands on his desk and getting as close as possible to him with the table between us. "Out of everybody here, I am the *only* one who has ever supported her. Not you. Not your wife. Not your son. The only time you ever have her around is when you need something, and you use that time to tear her down like she's nothing. She is one of the smartest women I know. One of the kindest people I know. She deserves so much better than a father like you."

He rises to match my stance, barely an inch between us, when he seethes, "Evidently, she's not as smart as you claim if she's settled for *you*."

There's a tentative knock at his office door followed by a nervous clearing of a throat. "I'm so sorry to interrupt," a woman's voice says, clearly anxious about intercepting whatever she sees through the glass wall. "But you have a phone call on line two that you've been waiting for. They finally have time to talk, but now is their only slot."

Mikhail doesn't look away from me. "Tell them I'll be on in two."

Heels scamper away quickly, clearly not wanting to bear witness to our spat in here. Especially if I wind up missing and the center of a *20/20* episode.

The next question he asks takes me by momentary surprise. "Is my daughter sick?"

I blink, my guard dropping only for a second before the walls go back up. Because he sounds like he cares for once. Like he's worried. "She's always been sick. You know that. You just chose to ignore it when she told you."

His nostrils flare. "The doctors never found anything when we took her. Do you know how much money we spent on specialists?"

Why is it always about money?

"Well, guess what," I say crudely, squaring my shoulders back. "The doctors you hired were yes-men. They told you what you wanted to hear to get her back on the ice. She never wanted to be there, but you refused to listen. You pushed her and pushed her until she nearly broke. Do you really blame her for not wanting anything to do with you? For *settling* for a man like me if it meant getting away from the person who controlled her like a pawn rather than a human?"

Mikhail does not like that. Not one bit.

His hand grips my shirt, yanking me forward until I nearly lose my balance as my thighs press against the edge of his desk. "There have been Olympic athletes with severe lateral sprains and tendon damage who still competed in the Games and were able to win gold medals. It is not uncommon for people like us to encourage their children to push past the pain. Yokavs are *strong*. We are determined—"

"You are *fools*," I correct him. "You may not have seen what all of your rigorous training did to Emaly, but I did. Sasha saw it too, but was too afraid of you to stand up for his sister. She was hurting every single day. She was struggling every single day. She pleaded with you to stop skating because she couldn't handle it. And you saw that as weakness. Emaly isn't Kerri Strug or any of the other athletes who pushed through their injuries for the sake of a medal. She never *wanted* that life. She wanted to make a difference. What she's doing now *is* her happy place. You're going to have to accept that and back the fuck off."

Mikhail's jaw twitches as he slowly releases my shirt and shoves me away. I stand straighter, catching myself before I stumble. "You did not answer my question."

I did. He just isn't accepting it.

There's a lot that I can't say about Emaly. I promised I would keep her secrets to myself until she was ready to explain them. It was her choice about who to tell and who not to.

So, all I say is, "Yes, she is. But you already knew that. And you're choosing to take it out on me because some illnesses are out of our control. Some of them can't have money thrown at them to cure it. You'll have to live the rest of your life knowing that you continuously pushed your only daughter away when she needed you the most."

He clenches his jaw. "I care more than you think."

I shake my head. "I don't buy that for a fucking second, Yokav. There's always a motive at the end of the day, and it only benefits you. Stop pretending like you care."

"If I didn't," he says, as I walk toward the door, "then why would I ensure you're on this team? The only way to keep my daughter in our lives is through you."

I pause. Is that what he really thinks? I turn to face him slowly. "Most fathers would simply be there for their children for no reason at all. I wouldn't know what that's like, as you well know. My father would probably be relieved if I wound up dead, but the feeling is mutual. If you want Emaly to be in your lives, how about you try being in *hers*? No ulterior motive. No threats. Just because you care, like you claim you do."

He doesn't offer me anything. Not a nod, not a blink, not a single action that shows he heard me or my advice.

I huff out a dry laugh. "Who am I kidding? Some people just aren't cut out to be parents."

I refrain from flipping him off as I walk out of his office, no matter how badly I want to. I hear him say something in a different language, then a loud crash from a distance. I don't stop to see what he threw or hit. I don't care.

Because, unlike him, I can admit it.

I FINALLY CALL Emaly back when I've cooled off from my meeting with her father, but she doesn't answer. She doesn't see the three texts I sent after leaving a voicemail either. It isn't uncommon for us to miss each other, given her hectic work schedule and the time difference between the coasts. She always gets back to me when her shift is over or whenever she wakes up.

When my phone buzzes with an incoming call, I pick up, thinking it's her. "It's about time," Ashton says, sighing. "Are you done ignoring me now, or do you plan on keeping up this charade? We've got things to discuss."

My free hand grips the steering wheel, twisting until it makes an unruly sound against the leather. "I think I said everything I had to the last time we spoke."

Uncharacteristically, my manager is silent.

He's usually the first one to speak up and insert his opinion where I least want it. Hell, it's a wonder he didn't show up at my house after the phone call we had.

When Ashton speaks, it's obvious he's had time to reflect on what happened based on the guilt in his tone. "I wish I could go back in time and prevent my brother from getting in that car. If I could change the timeline of events, I would. I would have tried harder to get him the help he needed instead of brushing him off. I would have enrolled him in a program. He was an alcoholic, and I knew that. But I never, *never* thought he would do what he did."

Nobody thinks their friends or family are capable of killing people. It may have been unintentional, but every choice he made that led to the Brontes' deaths *could* have been prevented. He made all the wrong decisions and has to live with it, just like Winter and her sister do.

"Nobody thinks that," I tell him. "I didn't think my parents were capable of half the shit they were. But we can't control what they're going to do, and we can only help them as much as they want to be helped."

As mad as I am at him, I can't hold a grudge forever. I understand that some people are beyond help. If he'd done more to offer his brother some resources, it would have been better than turning a blind eye. But what's done is done. Even if he had put Adam in a program, that doesn't mean it would have worked. People have to actually try to get better, and it sounds like his brother didn't want to. My mother and father didn't either. It's life.

"What pisses me off is that you knew who Winter was. It makes sense why you never wanted to go to any of the events if she was there. What I want to know is, why go through the trouble? Why lie about who she is to you if you feel so bad about your brother screwing up her life?"

It doesn't add up. One second, he feels bad, but the next, he's taking her off the Furrever Home event that she worked her ass off for. What is his motive?

He says something unintelligible under his breath before another sigh. "Do you think I can just let go of the past that easily? For fuck's sake, Tom. I changed my last name just so my clients didn't have to be associated with my family."

"That doesn't change who you are," I snap back, shaking my head. "Just because you took your mother's maiden name doesn't mean it changes who your brother is or how he impacted Winter. You knew all of that, and you still inserted yourself in business you had no right to."

"It's my *job* to be part of any PR for you," he counters gingerly. "So it *is* my business. Everything about the events pertaining to you and your image is where I need to be. I meant what I said before. I don't want to see her dragged through the mud if she's associated with you in a negative way. You and I both know what the vultures can do if they see her around you. Her life is hard enough without all the press you can add to it. She got enough of that after the trial."

So, is he looking out for her? If he knew exactly who she was when I asked about her, how long did he know she worked for Janel? How long has he been keeping track of what she's doing?

"You knew she was working there, didn't you? That's why you chose Starrs Strategy." It's posed like a question, but I don't need confirmation; I already know the truth. "How long have you been keeping tabs on her, Ash?"

Once again, he pauses. Which means it's probably been for a long time. "Since after Adam was sentenced," he admits. "I needed to know she and her sister were okay. When I found out she'd gotten her degree in a public relations field, I knew she'd probably wind up at one of the few agencies in the area."

"She could have left town," I point out.

"But she didn't," he replies tightly. "She chose to stay because her roots are here. I knew she would stick around because her sister did the same. They're all each other have. Being here keeps them close to their parents."

The fact that he's thought about this pisses me off. Because he knows so much about the girl I've wanted to learn more about since she walked into the conference room with a giant coffee stain across her chest. I knew somebody with that much to prove had to have gone through something unimaginable. I saw right past the facade she'd been wielding because it's so similar to mine.

Our pasts are our biggest motivators, and our trauma is our weapon. The problem is, we usually use those against the wrong people.

"My parents spent the first few years of Adam's incarceration in denial," Ashton admits to me solemnly. "They didn't want to believe their son left two people to die. Eventually, they accepted it. And years later, they chose to never acknowledge it, as if it would go away. But it was never going to. Not for Winter or her sister, Kourtney. Not for the rest of their family either. I refused to pretend as if it didn't happen. Sue me if checking in on her and making sure the girls are okay is a bad thing. Nobody else did. From what I can tell, not even their extended family put that much effort in. After the news stopped reporting on it, very few people acted as if they cared."

Winter never mentioned anything about extended family, so it must be true. If it were really only her and her sister, I could see why Ashton would want to keep an eye on them. He's older, with more money and authority. But how much of that did he use to help them?

So, I ask the question I don't want to. Because then I'll have to figure out if I'm willing to tell Winter the truth or if I'll be just another person who lies to her. "Did you have something to do with her getting that job?"

He's had connections in the industry long before I came into the picture. He'd been new to the scene around the time of his brother's hit and run, but he would have known the key players. And it was *him* who suggested the success rate of Janel's firm with sensitive PR cases like mine. If he played puppet master to line all of this up, he's used us for...what exactly? To make himself feel better or to make Winter better? To get good karma points?

Ashton is silent.

"Ashton," I growl. "Did you—"

"No," he finally says roughly. "I'd made some *suggestions*, but Scott also had a hand in where we took our business. The fact that Winter worked at Starrs Strategy was more of a bonus. She'd be getting good money from the deal because we were offering a bonus for discretion and fast work."

Winter doesn't want handouts. If she finds out that someone associated with her parents' killer gave her this opportunity, I'm not sure she'd handle it well.

Pinching the bridge of my nose, I internally groan.

"Everything I've done is for her benefit," he tells me coolly. "It's never out of ill intentions. Care to explain why you're this invested in the matter? Why you keep biting my head off over this girl?"

This time, it's me who's quiet.

"Thomas, I swear to God. If you laid a—"

"What?" I cut him off through gritted teeth as I slow at the intersection that leads to Hoffman's house. "If I laid a hand on Winter, what would you do? Quit? Bitch me out? Tell on me to Janel? Go ahead. Finish that sentence."

It's a dare.

A challenge.

A warning.

Because we've both done fucked-up things.

I was drawn to her feisty attitude and broken spirit because like calls to like. Ashton has been drawn to her because his family is the one who caused it.

We're not the same. We just have vested interests in the same girl.

"If the wrong people hear about my *vested interests*, it would hurt her more than help her," I remind him. "So if you step in, it isn't going to help. If you even *think* about removing her from this event—"

"Christ, Tom," he grumbles, cutting me off. "I didn't call to fight or listen to your veiled threats. I called to explain myself because I feel bad about all of this."

He doesn't get a response from me because I'm not sure what else I can say. Our motivations are different, even if our end game is the same.

For Winter to be happy.

"Do you want what's best for her?" he eventually asks, voice calmer than before. He knows he won't get anywhere otherwise.

I swallow, thinking back to yesterday.

The redness in her eyes.

The weight on her shoulders.

The words whipped like a weapon until they sliced my skin.

"Yes," I admit into the phone.

Ashton makes a noise.

We fall silent.

For one second.

Two.

Three.

Then, Ashton says, "Then you need to cut it off with her, Tom."

He doesn't list the reasons why, but I can hear them clear as day between the lines.

Because of my wife.

Because Winter deserves better.

I pull up to the front of Hoffman's house, where cars from the other players line the driveway, road, and front lawn. I see Jesse Clarkson outside on his phone before he raises a hand to wave in my direction.

My jaw clenches, teeth grinding at the thought of letting this all go.

You need to cut it off with her.

Problem is, I don't want to.

"I could say the same for you," I point out. There's no ice in my words, but the accusation is there regardless. He knows he can't hold on to the guilt forever. He can't twist fate's hand to make sure Winter and her sister wind up okay for the rest of their lives.

Eventually, he has to let it go too.

He has to let them make their own choices without influencing them. He says he didn't play a hand in Winter getting this job, but I don't think he's being honest with himself. And he'll be just as much of a reason why she's upset if she ever finds out.

Ashton makes a thoughtful noise. "I know," he eventually murmurs. Then an even quieter, "I know."

Knowing there's nothing more to say, I hang up and set my phone down.

There's still no message from Emaly.

None from Winter either, not that I expect it.

Swiping a palm down my face, I lean my head against the rest and close my eyes. "What a shit show," I say to myself.

I startle when the passenger door opens, and Clarkson slides into the seat.

"You trying to bail?" he asks, eyebrows arched curiously.

I make a face. "Wasn't going to." However, it sounds like a great plan now.

"Good. Come on, then."

Neither one of us makes a move to get out.

"Got something on your mind?" he questions casually. He's not pressing. If I tell him to fuck off, he'll shrug and make other conversation. That's how he's always been.

"Do you ever get sick of playing therapist, Clarkson?" I

ask of the captain who's always had a knack for knowing the right thing to say. "You really need to start charging people for all your precious words of wisdom."

I'd watched him offer advice to plenty of people during our time with the Penguins and saw what a difference he made. He's always believed talking it out helps unravel the blocks that get in our way on the ice. Not once has he ever expected reciprocation if it meant strengthening the team. Guess that hasn't changed, even if our jerseys have.

Clarkson raises a shoulder. "If there's something bothering you, I'd rather hear about it now versus seeing it six beers in."

Fair point. "I haven't been drinking" is my only response.

To which he raises his brows in disbelief. Reasonable, considering I tend to wind up so drunk that he has to drag me to a spare room to sleep it off. I've clearly never shied away from drinking, even after watching my parents drink until they're numb. I'd like to think I know my limits better than they do and can stop whenever I want.

But lately…Lately, I haven't wanted to risk it.

Maybe because alcohol doesn't get rid of anybody's problems. It only adds to them. I can drink reality off for a night and wake up to it the next morning with a wicked hangover that only makes it worse. It doesn't make me feel any better than them. Numbing is still numbing, and I'd rather feel the effects of life rather than bury them.

Clarkson's phone goes off, and his jaw clenches when he sees his stepsister's name on the screen before sending it to voicemail. I've been around him long enough to know that's not normal. Unless we're at practice or a game, he always picks up her calls.

"Everything good?" I ask hesitantly.

He and Belle have been tight-knit for as long as I can remember. Nobody knows the depth of their relationship or the history of their family. But he's been protective of her for years, and I have a feeling it isn't because their parents got married.

His shoulders go rigid as he glares at the screen. "Fine," he grumbles.

Clearly, he isn't. "That's a woman's response when she's pissed off. Want to try again, or is this going to be a full-on back-and-forth where I call you out for lying and you deny it? You suck at it, by the way."

His glare turns to me, but all I do is grin.

I'm not sure what he mumbles under his breath, but he eventually sighs. "Belle and I are disagreeing about something. She's being a giant pain in my ass right now."

Is that all he's going to give me? "Hasn't she always been a pain in your ass?"

His lips twitch a fraction upward before neutralizing.

My grin widens. "That's a yes," I muse.

He rolls his eyes. "It doesn't matter. I'll talk to her later. We should head in before the rest of the guys try cramming their way into the back seat."

I snort. "They're too afraid of me to willingly get in my vehicle."

Clarkson knows I'm right because he says, "That's because you always look mad when we're together. They don't want their dicks ripped off if you're in a mood."

I stare at him. "Maybe that's just my face."

"Maybe," he relents. "But I've seen you smile before. There's obviously something going on that's putting you on edge. Don't know if it's the press, your father-in-law, or a combination. But you have more people on your side than you think you do."

Here he goes with his sappy bullshit again. "The team should get used to my resting bitch face. I have a feeling it'll be there for a while."

He tilts his head. "Why?"

"Maybe I also have a stepsister who's a giant pain in my ass," I retort with a smile.

The look he narrows me with is comical. "Watch it."

I raise my palms up. There's his overprotective nature. "I'm just saying, it could be true."

He shakes his head and opens the door. "You coming in or not?"

I sigh and shut the car off, glance at my phone one last time, and mumble, "Yeah. Let's go."

Because I have a feeling that if I don't, I'll wind up staring at my phone all night like a girl waiting for her first crush to call.

CHAPTER TWENTY

Winter

I STARE DOWN at the paperwork that's been in a folder collecting dust since I graduated from college. I'm not sure why I kept the award letters and semester grade reports. Maybe because I was proud to have gotten any scholarships at all. I wasn't exactly an A student, but I did okay. By my senior year of high school, I realized how hard I'd need to work to get money for college because we didn't have any.

Community college wasn't cheap, so any help I could get was better than none. The school guidance counselor helped me apply for some of the scholarships, and I'd researched others. But the one thing I refused to do was use my parents' death as an excuse to earn pity money. My counselor told me not to think of it that way; that my mom and dad would have been happy to help me fund college. It never sat well with me, though. I wanted whatever I got to be because I earned it, not because people felt bad for me.

As I search through the paperwork to find the one I'm thinking of, anxiety bubbles under my skin. I've been out of work for two days now, but I'm doing whatever I can from my phone at home. After hearing Ashton Dessen's explanation, Janel told me to take time for myself, and I appreciate her kindness.

But I don't deserve it.

Ever since Thomas walked out, everything I've done has caved in around me. Not out of regret. Well, not *only* because of that. I'd done something for myself for once. Not because of what was the right choice, but because I needed to put myself first. He helped me do that.

It was the shame that ate at me whenever it got too quiet. And since I haven't been to work, that silence has been deafening here.

Thomas's parting words haunted me, and I knew I was unfair to him. He didn't deserve to be hurt just because I was. My anger didn't justify the horrible things I threw at him like daggers.

And yet, he'd still gone through with it.

He could have left.

He probably *should* have.

But what was it he told me at his place? *Just because you* shouldn't *want something doesn't mean you* don't *want it.* He'd wanted me as much as I wanted him. Maybe even more.

He stayed.

For me.

And I treated him like garbage.

Closing my eyes, I rub my chest where a tight ball is coiled deep inside. It spreads, pressing against my lungs until I struggle to suck in a breath.

Then I remember the other reason there's a weight resting on my chest. When I open my eyes, I look down at the letter in front of me and feel my jaw quiver.

Dear Ms. Bronte,

On behalf of the Marjorie D. Essen Foundation, I am delighted to announce that you have been awarded the Student Excellence Scholarship for the 2018 academic year. This award is granted to students who show exceptional achievement throughout the academic year—

I stop reading when a teardrop lands on the paper and soaks into it. My eyes blur, and I close my eyes to stop more from flowing.

Marjorie D. Essen.

Dessen.

The name had nudged something deep, deep inside of me when Thomas first asked about Ashton. I'd chosen to ignore it because it didn't seem important, and I soon forgot about it entirely until two days ago.

Thomas said Ashton used his mother's maiden name after Adam's arrest. Marjorie must be her first name.

Marjorie Dessen.

I swipe at my wet cheeks and stare at the name harder, as if it'll tell me everything I need to know. There's no way this could be a coincidence. It's why my gut nagged me that day at the diner when I was being interrogated by Thomas about his agent.

My grip tightens on the paper until it crinkles in my fingers, and I have to let go before I rip it.

I want to know why. Why give me a scholarship? Was it randomly selected? I know better than to ask that aloud.

No.

Someone did this intentionally.

Standing, I abandon the papers scattered on the living room floor and go to the kitchen where I left my phone. I've been avoiding it all day because I'm sick of Kourtney's hourly check-ins and threats to come see me with Brad and Luca. I'd love to see them, just not her husband. And she knows it. Which is why I begged her after the sixth "I'm fine" to stop texting me.

She's not who I need to talk to, though.

I dial the number and swallow down the anxiety bubbling in my stomach as it rings.

Once.

Twice.

Three times.

On the fourth, I'm about to hang up with shaky fingers when I hear, "Hi."

The husky voice makes my lower lip tremble as I furiously swipe under my eye again. "Hi." My voice comes out weaker than I want it to, and I mentally slap myself for it.

Thomas is quiet for a second before clearing his throat. "Are you okay?"

The shame from earlier comes crashing back down. I'd said some messed-up things, and he's asking if I'm okay still. Why can't he be an asshole? The version of him that he introduced himself as? It would make this easier.

I don't answer his question. Because I'm not, and I don't feel like lying to him. There are already so many lies and half-truths between us, I can't keep track. Why add to the list?

"I need to speak to Ashton."

I expect him to ask why. Maybe to tell me that it isn't a good idea. But he does neither of those things. He simply says, "Okay. I can make that happen."

No questions.

No hesitation.

I close my eyes again, take a deep breath, and murmur, "It would be easier if I hated you."

He says, "I know."

"But I don't," I murmur.

Again, he says, "I know."

We're quiet for a few heartbeats.

I look toward the other room at the papers on the floor and feel nauseous. No. I've felt that way since Ashton stepped into Janel's office. Despite that, I know I need to face him. No matter how much I wish I didn't have to.

Alone.

Not with Kourtney.

Not with Thomas.

Not with Janel.

It's time I faced this on my own.

I swallow, feeling a buzz of anxiety flow through my veins and shoot tingling sensations up my neck that warm my skin.

I break the silence with, "I'm sorry."

About what I said.

About what I made you do.

About everything.

I wait for his reply.

His next "I know."

But it never comes.

No.

Thomas lets out a quiet breath, a sigh, before saying, "I'll set up a meeting with Ashton and text you the details."

It's my fault that the distance is there. Where it *should* be, but where I don't want it to.

So, I try to bridge the gap I created by offering him another secret. "The day my parents died, I was awful to them. I was thirteen. Young and dumb and annoyed over the stupidest stuff. They told me they'd take away my phone if I didn't clean up my room. I'd thrown a tantrum like a child and told them I hated them."

I close my eyes and squeeze them shut to fight off the growing tears prickling behind the lids.

Only the faintest sound of Thomas's breathing tells me he's still listening.

"I locked myself in my room and stayed there even after I finished cleaning it," I continue, swallowing down the lump in my throat. "I was mad and didn't want to go down and apologize for saying that. I didn't hate them."

"Of course not," he says softly.

"When my dad knocked on my door and said they were going to run errands, they wanted me to come with them." I sniffle, closing my eyes and remembering that night all too well. I was sitting on my bed, stewing in my teenage angst. "I told them I didn't want to. I'd begged them to let me stay home. That I'd behave. So, they agreed. My parents gave me back my phone and told me to call them if there was an emergency. I hugged them both and said I would."

But still, I don't know if I told them I loved them. I

hugged them. I smiled. But did I say those three words?

"I don't remember if I told them I loved them," I whisper, pressing my lips together. "I told them I hated them, but I have no idea if I took it back."

My heart aches so badly that I wonder if it will burst right here. Kourtney will find me on the floor, dead from a broken heart. It was bound to happen after all these years. How much damage can the organ sustain before it gives up?

"They knew you loved them," Thomas says when the silence lasts between us. There's no doubt in his mind. He's sincere. But how can he know? "I don't think you're capable of hate, sweetheart."

My throat thickens. "I hate Adam Burgess," I state through the tears trying to push past the gates they're stuck behind.

He simply says, "No, you don't. You hate what he did. A heart full of hate weighs a person down. It slows you down. Eats at you. You're mad. You're angry. But you don't hate him. Just like you don't hate me."

I sink to the floor and lean my back against the cupboard, bringing my knees to my chest. All I say is, "I'm not sure I know the difference."

And all he says is, "Deep down you do."

We sit in silence for minutes. Only our breathing is heard in the open air. I close my eyes and hug myself. I don't know what he's doing, or why he even picked up.

But I'm glad he did.

After a while, he speaks up. "I'll call Ashton." Another pause. Then, "Thank you."

He doesn't say for what, but I don't think I need him to. He's thanking me for the secret. The one I handed him without him needing to ask. Something for him that I haven't told anybody but my therapist.

I hang up first and stare at my phone as a text pops up.

Kourt: *Are you still okay?*

My eyes go to the papers on the floor.

Marjorie Dessen.

Me: *No*

Kourtney: *I'll be over in 20*

Kourtney: *Alone*

THE ADDRESS THOMAS sends me is on the nicer side of Fairbanks. The swanky neighborhood is gated, and you need a code to get in. I should have known that the pro hockey player would set up a meeting at his house. When the Uber driver, Abel, pulls up to the keypad, I get out and enter it, careful not to let him see. He'd been quiet after he picked me up, listening to some golf recap on his Bluetooth and making commentary about how he needed to improve his swing. I tuned him out the best I could, wishing he'd put music on to drown out the sound of my nerves thrumming under my skin.

Knowing it's too late to back out now, I thank the driver and swipe my clammy hands down my thighs. I stare at the house through the window and all but groan when I see the front door open and Thomas appear.

The driver said, "You're not going to puke in my car, are you?"

I frown. "No." At least, I don't think so.

"Good. Then do me a favor and get out before you do," he says, locking eyes with me in the rearview mirror. "You're looking a little too green for my liking, and I just got this thing detailed."

My frown deepens, but I unbuckle and open the door. Right before I close it, I hear the driver say, "Wait a minute. Is that Thomas Mosk—"

I scurry up the walkway to where Thomas is leaning against his doorjamb and glance up at him through my lashes. "The driver," I warn quietly, as if the man in the car has supersonic hearing, "recognizes you."

His brows lift before peering from me to the man still idling in his car on the street. His hand gently wraps around my arm, tugging me inside and closing the door behind us. "I'll make sure he's not allowed access into the neighborhood after this."

My shoulders tighten. "I'm sorry. I—"

"Don't be," he says plainly, walking down the foyer and toward the kitchen. "It's not your fault your car broke down. Any news on it?"

Is he really making small talk like he wasn't inside me days ago? Yes. Yes, he is. And because I don't know what else to do, I rub the spot on my arm that tingles from his touch and follow him into the other room. "They said it would cost more money than it's worth to fix, and that I should look into getting a different car."

I'd known that was going to be the response, but I held out hope that a miracle would happen. When I told Kourtney, she'd offered to help me get a small loan to find something else. That was after Brad shot her down when she said they'd let me have their car to get something bigger for themselves. Turns out, he was not cool with that idea. Not at all.

"I'm sorry," he says, passing me a bottle of water from the fridge. I fidget with the plastic cap as I stand on the other side of the island, which looks freshly washed. The whole house smells like someone just went through and doused it in disinfectant and air freshener.

I lift a shoulder, looking around the kitchen that I hadn't spent any time in the last time I was here. It's spotless. The counters organized. The refrigerator has a specific place for everything and is full of fresh food. Does he cook?

"It's okay. Fairbanks has cheap transit. The bus schedule is easy to figure out and goes everywhere I need."

His teeth grind, and he looks away like he doesn't like that idea. He'll have to get in line, though. Kourtney has been telling me what a horrible idea it is to ride the bus instead of saving my money to get a used car. But since neither of us has the funds for something new, and adding a small car loan to my name isn't in the cards for me, it's all I have.

"Where is Oreo?" I ask, searching the room for the kitten that may be today's only saving grace. There are a few cat toys scattered on the floor, but no sign of the feline.

Thomas props his hip against the counter. "I assume she's destroying another one of my shirts. Her favorite pastime seems to be breaking into my closet and climbing the clothing until her talons poke holes into the fabric."

I wince, assuming his wardrobe cost him a pretty penny. He doesn't seem like the type to buy his clothes at Walmart. "At least she's cute?" I offer with a tiny smile.

He studies my face a little too closely, his eyes raking over every square inch. It makes me wish I'd worn my hair down to hide behind it. Thomas may not be touching me, but I feel the heat all the same.

After a moment, he nods. "She is."

But the way he's staring at me makes me think he isn't referring to Oreo at all.

I swallow, shifting from one foot to another. The movement makes me wince, and I grip my water a little tighter in my hand until the plastic crinkles under my fingertips.

He steps forward before stopping himself. His palms clench and unclench at his sides. "Are you all right?"

The panic in his voice confuses me when I look up at him.

Then he says, "Are you hurting from…?"

I gape, my cheeks heating when I realize what he means. He thinks I'm hurting because we had sex. "No," I say, a little too forcefully. I stand straighter. "It's not from *that.*"

His shoulders seem to relax. "I'm just making sure. I've heard things can be…tender for women their first time. And I could have been gentler. I *should have* been gentler."

"No," I tell him. "I didn't want you to be." I fight the flames rising up my neck and trying to settle into my cheeks when one of his eyebrows arch. "I got my period," I murmur, not sure how that explanation is any better. "That's why I'm hurting. I'm fine."

There's a bite to my tone that I wish wasn't there, because it tells him that I'm evidently *not* fine.

Thomas simply nods and says, "Okay."

He doesn't push.

Doesn't say anything to embarrass me.

He still doesn't ask what all of this is about.

Thomas walks over to a cupboard full of food and ingredients, and I can't help but ask, "You really cook, don't you?"

He pauses, glancing at me from over his shoulder. "Doesn't everybody?"

I shrug. "Does heating up ramen noodles count as cooking?"

His cheek twitches, and I can tell he wants to smile but stops himself. "I'm not sure that counts. That's like saying you made a cake from scratch when it comes from a box."

I hum. "I don't know. If you're adding eggs and water to the mix and putting it into the oven, you're still baking a cake. Seems to me like you're discrediting a lot of people."

Thomas, despite himself, chuckles. "My mistake. I didn't mean to offend you, chef."

My lips lift a fraction. "You still haven't answered my question. You have a lot of food. I thought you would have done premade meals or hired someone to cook for you."

He shakes his head. "Nah. I actually find cooking to be

relaxing. And when you need to stay in shape, it's better to make everything from scratch so you know what you're consuming. Premade meals have too much sodium to make them last. I have trouble tracking intake when I'm in training mode."

I make a mental note to check the back of the freezer meals next time I go shopping. "My dad used to do most of our cooking, growing up. Kourtney and I usually helped, but I didn't pick up on the skills they did. When it was just us, we lived on eggs, hamburgers, and whatever else was on sale. Cheap stuff."

"Makes sense," he replies easily. "I can teach you, if you'd like. I know how to make quite a few things."

His offer surprises me. "You'd do that?"

He dips his chin. "Like I said, it's relaxing to cook. I've gone back to Our Open Table a few times and helped Vinnie and Bev get meals prepped."

My eyes widen. "You've gone back?"

Once again, a nod of acknowledgment.

"Even when I wasn't there?" I prod, trying to figure out why he'd keep going there.

His lips curl into an amused smile. "At first, I was hoping to run into you. But then it became about something else. I don't always know what to do with my free time—what little I have of it. It seemed like a perfect place to go if I didn't want to be by myself."

He goes to Our Open Table.

No cameras.

No press.

He goes because he *wants* to.

My heart warms, as though it's being wrapped in a hug of its own. "Being around Bev and Vinnie is one of my happy places to go, so I get it. Besides Kourtney, they're the only people who have ever cooked for me. They're...home."

The way he watches me feels too intimate. I have to look away before my heart jumps up my throat and chokes me of my words.

Which is nearly impossible when he says, "I can cook for you. You just have to say the word."

My eyes snap up to meet his.

We stare at one another for a long time.

Maybe one of us would have said something more if the doorbell hadn't gone off. When he sees the way my body stiffens, knowing who's on the other side of the door, he walks around the island and steps up to me.

His touch is gentle, so gentle, as he tips my chin up. He scans my face. My right eye. My left. My nose. My lips, downtrodden in a frown. Then he says the same thing he did at my apartment when he saw me crying. "I've got you."

A soft-spoken promise that I feel all the way to my toes. The pad of his thumb caresses my jaw before he releases me when the doorbell goes off for a second time.

"Impatient asshole," he grumbles as he heads toward the front door.

I didn't tell Kourtney I was doing this when she came over yesterday. I knew she'd volunteer to come, and there was a chance Ashton Dessen wouldn't walk out without some significant damage—whether physical or emotional.

As much as I love how protective my sister is, I know I need to do this alone. She can't fight every battle for me, even if she wants to. So, I stand a little taller, roll my shoulders, and wait to feel the impact of seeing Ashton's face.

And when he steps in, he instantly locks eyes with me. Weary and alert and…sad. Sad for me? Or him? Or does he have the audacity to feel sad for his brother?

Thomas and Ashton exchange words, but they're too quiet for me to hear from the kitchen. Whatever our host says is short and sweet, maybe a warning to behave. Maybe something else.

I've got you.

I believe him.

Wetting my lips, I try not to react as Ashton walks into the kitchen and holds out his hand. He looks so much like Adam.

Staring at the angular face and the almond-shaped eyes that are the color of brown that isn't quite chocolate or golden but a shade in between is a punch to the gut. His features are nothing spectacular. Nothing unique. Yet, I'll never forget that face. Not even when I'm old and gray and have forgotten my own name.

That face—*Adam's* face—will be imprinted in my mind until the day I die.

Because it's the shade I saw when Adam Burgess yelled out to Kourtney and me as he was being taken away in handcuffs. *"I'm sorry. I'm so sorry. I didn't mean to. I don't remember."*

Kourtney and I held on to each other so tightly that

day that we gave one another bruises.

Ashton still holds out his hand, but I don't take it. Not out of spite, but because I can't will myself to lift my palm. I swallow, finding it hard to get past the lump forming deep in my throat as I stare up at him and notice every similarity he shares with his brother.

His throat bobs as he watches me, trying to keep an even expression but not hiding the dim in those brown eyes. "Hello, Winter."

If he's offended that I don't shake his hand, he doesn't show it. He simply lowers it, clears his throat, and slides that same hand into the front pocket of his slacks.

Say something, a voice in my head urges.

The two-letter greeting is on the tip of my tongue when I find myself saying something different entirely. "You look so much like him," I whisper, blinking at the same shape of his nose and lips and the way his jaw is not quite square or round but still a masculine shape. His brother was a little heavier, like he didn't really work out or eat right. He was probably on a liquid diet only, or whatever food was served at bars. Peanuts? Wings?

I wouldn't know. I refuse to step into one.

Ashton's throat moves again. "We used to get that a lot," he answers, voice cautious.

Used to.

But not anymore.

He gestures toward one of the stools at the counter. "Would you like to sit? I'll answer any questions you have. Tom said you wanted to speak to me."

I don't know why, but my eyes go over his shoulder to

where Thomas stands silently just outside the kitchen. He nods once, encouraging me to say what I need to.

So, I find myself sitting down and doing my best not to fidget with my hands or squirm on the stool. If Kourtney were here, she'd be stick-straight and glaring at Ashton to death.

Once again, my eyes dart to Thomas for a microsecond before returning to Ashton's face as he searches for the right words. He knows apologizing isn't going to help. What is he sorry for that would make a difference?

I swallow, reaching into my pocket and unfolding the scholarship award letter before sliding it over to where he stands on the other side of the counter. As soon as he sees the letterhead, he closes his eyes.

The only thing I ask is, "Why?"

I hear the creak of the floorboard by the kitchen, and see Thomas shift as if to see what I showed Ashton. From his vantage point, he has no idea what this is. And that's probably for the better. Because if he knew, then I wouldn't believe him at all when he said he got me.

Ashton lets out a small breath before picking up the paper. He doesn't need to scan it because he knows exactly what it says. Which tells me what I already knew. This isn't a coincidence. "I watched my brother ruin a lot of people's lives because he wasn't learning from his mistakes. I'm as guilty of looking the other way as my parents were, and it led him down a path he can't come back from."

I don't say anything because I can tell he's far from finished. So, I sit on my hands and hold my breath as my heart *thumps* hard in my chest.

Ashton sets the paper down. "I don't want to be like Adam. I want to make a difference. To help people. Not just rich clientele or people Adam harmed, but people in the community who need the extra assistance." His hand flattens on the piece of paper. "My mother, Marjorie, has always been the same way. She's been a part of various foundations and charities that have bettered the community. Her work in the education field primarily focused on Greenwich, where I was born. We were well off, and my mother wanted to use some of our fortune to help those less fortunate. So, she started a foundation called the Marjorie D. Essen Grant, which awarded students scholarships to help pay for their education. She's given out millions of dollars over the years to people who want to better their lives with a college degree."

"So this grant already existed before…?"

Before Adam killed my parents.

Before I received the money.

He dips his chin once in confirmation. "It'd been around for at least a decade before the accident. After my brother went to jail, her personal involvement…waned. I took over to make sure Adam's mess didn't impact more people than it needed to. She cares deeply about people, and the fact that she could raise someone who was so careless hurt her in ways I'm not sure I even fully understand."

I shake my head, staring at the paper and not the man explaining himself. I can't. If I look up at him, all I'll see is Adam. "Did you hand select me to receive the scholarship for college? Did you do the same for my sister?"

There's no hesitation. "Yes." But that answer comes with an explanation that isn't hurried or shameful. "But it wasn't money to silence anybody or heal the wounds Adam caused. I knew better than to think that was possible. My mother's foundation is supposed to encourage people to get a higher education and chase their dreams. You and Kourtney fit that perfectly. Neither one of you was going to let my brother stop you from bettering your lives. You could have, but you didn't. So, I reached out to your school to make sure your names were both on the list of recipients."

A sour feeling enters my stomach and curdles there. "You may not think it's blood money, but it may as well have been."

He opens his mouth as if to argue, but a throat clears from the hall that Thomas stands in. I glance in his direction to see him staring harshly at his agent. This is all news to him.

Ashton sighs, pinching the bridge of his nose and nodding. "I understand why you think that, and I'm sorry for intruding. I only wanted to help you. My parents may have chosen to avoid the past we were all intertwined with, but I wasn't going to do that."

I scoff. "You changed your name to associate it with something positive."

His eyes sadden. "You're right," he agrees. "I did do that. And perhaps the reason was selfish. I was young and wanted to make a name for myself and refused to let Adam drag me down."

"Like he did us?" I question.

This time, he doesn't reply.

I take a deep breath and press my thighs into the hands I'm still sitting on. "What else?" I ask, afraid of the answer. "Did you do anything else to get me where I am? Because you're right. I wasn't going to let Adam take away my ability to live just because he did that to my mom and dad. Kourtney made sure we would be better than him. We were going to make our parents proud. And if you did anything to get me there, it'll feel like—" My voice cracks, and I hate the weakness in it. I take a deep breath and blow it out slowly to ease the tension in my lungs. "It will feel like I cheated to get there. Like I didn't earn this."

The room is quiet, save for the hum of the refrigerator behind Ashton. Somewhere in the distance, I can hear little feet pitter-pattering around. Oreo.

But that's it.

I finally meet Ashton's eyes, not allowing myself to be afraid. "Tell me."

His Adam's apple bobs. "No," he says, nostrils twitching. "It was only the scholarship. I checked in, made sure you two were okay. But that was it. I had very little power to impact your lives in the way I wish I could have."

I stare at him for a long time, trying to determine if he's telling the truth. He doesn't look away, doesn't back down. So, I reach forward to take the award letter back, crumple it into a ball, and throw it in the trash.

Because I wish I'd never accepted it.

I wish I could somehow give it back.

"You *have* earned it," Ashon tells me as I slide off the stool. I can't sit any longer. I'm too anxious—wound too tight. "I've watched my family unravel and become ghosts of themselves for what Adam did. For what he *continues* to do by blowing up his life. You and your sister—"

"Stop!" I cut him off, glaring at him. "Stop talking about me and my sister. Stop saying that your brother ruined your family's lives. At least you *have* one still."

He pales at the comment.

Thomas walks into the room, putting a hand on my lower back as he stops beside me. "I think we need to take a break."

"No," I tell him adamantly. "I'm not sure I need one. I think I've heard all there is to. I get it, Ashton. Your brother royally screwed you. He screwed all of us. But I don't need you picking up the pieces for me. Neither does my sister. We are more than capable of doing it ourselves. We've been doing it for years, no matter how hard it's been. Even the thought of someone who knows Adam trying to make up for his mistakes is…" I shiver, and nausea creeps up my throat. "It makes me sick to my stomach. Blood money or not, it's all the same. And I don't want you, nor do I need you, in my life. I want nothing to do with you or your family or their handouts."

Color comes back to his face, but barely. "I understand," he says quietly.

I hope he does, because I'm not sure I have the energy left to get him to. "From here on out, I want privacy. I want to be removed from whatever vocabulary you use. I'm not your responsibility or your problem, and I'm sure as hell not your brother's."

Thomas's hand presses harder against the skin on my

back in comfort.

Ashton clears his throat. "Okay," he agrees, nodding once. His eyes go from me to Thomas, then down to where his client's hand is touching me. "But I have one thing to say, and it's important."

I can feel Thomas's fingers flex.

"Whatever this is," he tells me, gesturing toward Thomas and me, "is not going to end well. You, of all people, know the circumstances of who Tom is and what he brings to the table. I don't need to remind you about his wife or the very public life he has. All I'm saying is that if you want privacy, you won't get it if you're seen with him."

It's not a threat or warning. His tone is cautious yet calm, simply delivering a message woven in truth. Because, despite what I'm asking him, he still feels guilty. He still cares enough to make sure I don't make mistakes.

But it would be my mistake to make.

Thomas says, "Ashton," in a low tone.

His manager raises his palms. "You and I both know I'm right, Tom."

He takes a step back and looks at me with a softer expression. "For whatever it's worth, I am sorry for what happened. For all of it. I know that doesn't change a damn thing, but it's still worth being said."

That's all he says before walking to the door, stepping on a cat toy that squeaks under his shoe. It gives him pause, making him frown.

Before he can ask Thomas why he has cat toys in his house, the man beside me says, "We'll talk later," in dismissal.

Ashton looks like he wants to say something, but shakes his head and chooses not to. He leaves us, not looking back as he closes the door behind him.

I stare down at Oreo's mouse toys.

Thomas asks, "Are you all right?"

I peek up at him through my lashes. "No."

All he does is nod, pulling me in for a hug and resting his chin on the top of my head. He doesn't say anything else. Doesn't try to make it better. Doesn't press me for how I'm feeling.

We stand like that in silence for a long time.

My arms fold around his waist and stay there, not tight or loose. I soak in the warmth and hard muscle under his clothes and rest my cheek against his pecks. Closing my eyes, I breathe him in and find myself relaxing for the first time since the Uber dropped me off.

I break the silence first. "He's right," I say, hating how the words taste on my tongue. "If there's anything I want more than peace of mind and independence, it's privacy. And I don't know what I'm doing anymore. I don't know why this is so..." My arms tense before dropping back down to my sides, and I take a step back to put distance between us. "I don't know why I'm doing this. I know I don't have a lot to lose, but the thought of losing what little I do have to my name..."

My pride. My job. My independence, no matter how limited it is.

His eyebrow twitches, but he doesn't make a point to tell me I'm overreacting. After all, he's the married one. Not me. No number of excuses he could make would make that okay if it comes out to the public.

"I got what I needed," I tell him hoarsely, clearing my throat. "So, I should go."

He stops me from walking away, and I stare at his fingers wrapped around my wrist. "I'll drive you."

"I can—"

"I know," he cuts me off. "But I want to drive you."

That's not what he's saying at all. He *needs* to make sure I'm okay because he knows that I'm not.

So, I follow him to his garage in silence.

I let him open my door for me in silence.

And I let him go as far as buckle me in.

All silently.

His knuckles barely brush against me as the seat belt clicks into place, but my heart reacts as if we were naked all over again.

I swallow as his eyes meet mine.

His Adam's apple bobs.

I take a deep breath...and watch him pull away as he closes the door and rounds the front of the car.

We don't speak on the short drive to my apartment, or when he puts the car into park at the curb in front of my building.

I try to force myself to speak up, but nothing comes out.

He reaches over and grabs my hand, squeezing it once in acknowledgment. As if he's saying "*I got you*" without saying it at all.

"I was in some shitty foster homes when I was a kid," Thomas says, voice lighter than usual. Distant, but present at the same time. "But I didn't hate it, because it meant I got to escape the people who made my life miserable. I didn't know what it was like to be in a happy household. I didn't know what it was like to be loved. Not until I met Emaly."

He'd told me that before, when I admitted I didn't think I was capable of love. Why is he bringing it up again?

I don't say anything. Don't ask.

Because part of me is afraid to.

He leans against his seat and stares down at our conjoined hands. "I never thought I was going to find somebody who could understand the pain I suffered because of my family. Emaly never could, even when she was ousted by hers. They still loved her enough to be in her life, while mine didn't care if I lived or died. And I hate that your heart knows that kind of pain, sweetheart. I hate that you've been put through hell and back. But I can see how that has transformed you. You're a better person than I could ever be, because you don't let that hate go to your heart. Not really."

His fingers flex around mine before he lets go and lets out a deep breath. "So, here's another secret just for you." His head lifts, meeting my cautious eyes. "I have never felt like I could relate to somebody so wholeheartedly until the day you walked into my life."

We stare at each other.

For five seconds.

Ten.

Fifteen.

My heart drums so wildly I can feel it in my eardrums.

Thump, thump, thump, thump.

I let out a choppy breath. "Thomas…" I swallow, my mouth feeling dry and my heart feeling too full. His words absorb into it, growing far too big for the cage it sits in.

I shake my head, and his brows furrow.

"Fuck it," I whisper, closing the short distance between us in the car.

I kiss him. And I don't hold back.

I kiss him like my life depends on it.

I kiss him like he isn't married.

I kiss him like we're the only two people on this god-forsaken earth.

And he lets me.

His hand cups my jaw, eagerly meeting my lips. He opens his mouth and lets me explore. My tongue brushes his, and my teeth bite into his bottom lip. My entire body buzzes as we kiss and kiss and kiss until I fear I'll explode from the pressure building within me.

I pull away first, my eyes meeting his shyly.

He rests his forehead against mine, brushing strands of my hair with his fingers. "There is so much I wish I could do right now."

I swallow. "I'd invite you in, but I'm on…" Well, I'd already admitted I'm on my period. I blush, like something so natural is embarrassing rather than normal. "I can't."

"Let me make one thing clear," he says, his lips brushing my nose, then my mouth, before gravitating toward my ear. "The only thing stopping me from going inside with you is my respect for you. Nothing would stop me from doing very dirty things to you for a very long time. Blood doesn't bother me."

Oh my God.

"But I'm not going to do that," he informs me, and I'm not sure if I feel relieved or disappointed. "Because you've had a long day, and I want to let you settle and relax. So, I'm going to get out and walk you to your door. Then I'm going to kiss you goodbye and drive home, where I'll probably wind up getting myself off to you in the shower."

Double *oh my God.*

If possible, my face grows hotter.

And Thomas does exactly what he says he will. He gets out of the car, opens my door, walks me to my apartment, and kisses me.

On the temple.

Not the lips.

And I can see that he wants to, but doesn't trust himself not to follow me inside if that line is crossed.

So, I let him go.

And I try very hard not to think about what he may or may not be doing in the shower hours later when I crawl into bed for the night.

The next morning, I wake up to find a bag full of chocolate, pain relievers, and a heating pad at my apartment door.

There's no note, but I don't need one.

CHAPTER TWENTY-ONE

Winter

JANEL'S SMILE DOESN'T look any different from the one she usually greets me with when I walk into her office the following day. Even after six hours of solid sleep, my lips still tingle from the kiss I shared with Thomas.

"How are you?" my boss asks softly as I sit across from her.

I rub the heels of my palms down my leggings and clear my throat. "I'm okay." *As I can be.* "I wanted to apologize for leaving like I did. It was unprofessional, and it won't happen again."

One of her brows quirks up. "Why are you saying sorry? If I were in your shoes, I probably would have thrown my coffee on him."

Her admission makes my eyes widen.

She shrugs. "We're only human, Winnie. I've spoken to Ashton, and he explained everything. I want you to know if I had any clue that he was associated with—"

"It's fine," I say to stop her from saying anything about my parents. I can only handle so much before the dam breaks again. "I mean, it's *not* fine that he withheld that information. But I've come to terms with it. I've moved on."

Well, as much as a person can in such a short amount of time. If I allow myself to stew on the past, it'll pull me under until the current drowns me. I've let that happen far too often.

I don't want to sink. I want to swim.

I want to thrive. Be happy. Be proud.

I will not let Ashton, Adam, or their family ruin everything that I've done for myself. I may be taking baby steps toward a better future, but they're still steps forward.

Janel seems surprised. "Oh. Well, good then." Her eyes move over my face before nodding, as if satisfied enough with my answer. "Since I have you, I wanted to see if there's anything else that needs to be done for the gala. I've been keeping up with the backend of socials for him and working closely with his team to ensure that we filter out any old articles trying to resurface that could derail all the work he's been doing recently. Now it's just organizing the final details for this event."

Every year, the Fairbanks Historical Association hosts a charity gala to raise funds for the city. They split the proceeds among various organizations that benefit the people of the city and the nonprofits within its borders, including a few soup kitchens and food pantries in the area. They host a black-tie event and sell tickets to attend so people can shake hands and take pictures with some of Fairbanks's finest. And since this year is the first one we have a professional hockey team, I was able to get Thomas and a few of his teammates invited to rub elbows with government officials and pose for the public who are bound to attend games at Yokav Stadium later this year. It was his idea to include the others, and I happily went along with it.

More pro athletes means more ticket sales, which means higher funding that can be allocated to places like Our Open Table. And as fall grows closer, it would be perfect for the colder weather and holiday season, when people need food and shelter the most.

"There isn't anything that needs to be done on our end besides having him show up to it," I tell her. "When I last spoke to the organizer, they confirmed that Jesse Clarkson—the team's captain—and one of their rookies, Richard Head, will also be in attendance. Mikhail Yokav is also going to be there since he's a big donor to the Historical Association."

I don't need to point out that the association is a large influence on Fairbanks's infrastructure. If the people running the city don't approve of projects that can jeopardize the historical bones here, that means no stadium and no hockey team. Whatever number Yokav wrote on a check must have been astronomical.

Janel nods along. "Makes sense. He knows he needs to play into people's favor."

More like pay into it, but it's all the same. "I'd say the only thing we need to be concerned about is how Mikhail and Thomas interact. But if the news articles circulating aren't focused on the personal tension between the Fireflies' owner and one of their players, then we should be okay."

She writes a few things down in her notebook, probably reminders about the upcoming event, before looking up at me. "I'm sure both men know what's at stake if things go awry. This will be the last event before the Fireflies' first game, so I doubt Mr. Moskins will do anything to impact him starting."

All very valid points, so I nod silently.

She glances at a Post-it note with a frown. "I could use your help on one thing," she mentions, peeling it off her computer screen and sticking it to her desk. "It's the strangest rumor I've seen yet about Moskins to date and came out of nowhere."

My brows pinch. "What is it about?"

She passes me the paper, and I nearly choke on my spit when I see what's scrawled there. She has a few websites where the article has appeared, as well as the sites that have referenced it.

"Why on earth would anybody say that Thomas Moskins just got out of *prison*?" she asks aloud with a head shake.

I rub my lips together, and I clear my throat. "I don't know," I reply, sounding a little high-pitched. "Probably just someone who thought it would be funny to joke about."

Janel sighs heavily as she gestures toward her screen. "The fact that people believe this garbage is ridiculous. This article says he went to prison for dealing drugs. When has he ever been seen doing drugs? Never."

I wet my lips and set the note down. "You know how people are," I reply, scratching my cheek. "They'll say anything."

She hums. "True." She clicks a few more times before leaning back. "We'll get them taken down. Thankfully, there aren't many reports on it. People must realize there's no evidence to back it up."

I try my best not to fidget as I think about the way the waitress kept staring at him that day in the diner. I'd said what I did—that Thomas had just gotten out of prison as a joke—not for someone to take me seriously. It'd been to get a reaction only. Internally, I flinch.

But do I tell Janel where that rumor started? No. I add it to the growing list of secrets that I'm keeping from her. How long until the basket of lies overflows and she finds out everything?

I swallow, afraid of what will happen. She'll have to fire me. She'll be disappointed in giving me a chance to lead a case only for me to cross the biggest boundary I possibly can.

Janel's frown reappears. "Are you okay?"

God only knows what my face looks like. "I am. Sorry. A little out of it, I guess." I offer her the only semblance of truth I can. "I had to get up early to catch the bus on time. I'm still figuring out my car situation."

Sympathy coats her upturned lips. "I forgot yours broke down. If you need any help, let me know. I know some people who sell decent used cars for cheap."

She would do that for me? I don't know why I'm so surprised when she's never been anything but kind. "Thank you. I'll let you know."

I stand up and head toward her door when she stops me. "I know it's none of my business," she says hesitantly. "But are there any savings you could access to help you fund a new vehicle? I know sometimes people are left money in wills. You've mentioned your student loan payment is high, which tells me you didn't use anything to pay for college. And I see how stubborn you are. It makes you strong. But I don't want that stubbornness to make you struggle."

I've always known that Janel cares about me, but this is the first time I've seen her truly dig for answers I've never offered her in order to help me. Maybe she knows the only person in my way is…me.

I tug on the hem of my shirt before standing a little straighter. "There was nothing," I tell her quietly, unable to look her in the eye. "My parents never had wills drawn up. And everything they had went to pay off debt. The bank took the house and cars. Kourtney and I got some money, but it was barely enough to get us by for the first couple of years after their deaths."

My eyes drop to the floor, and I stare at a speck of dirt on my ballet flat. I wiggle my toes inside them and take a deep breath. "Our lawyer tried to encourage Kourtney to file a wrongful death lawsuit. We were told it was the smartest option because it would help support us financially, but it didn't feel right. By the time we realized he was probably onto something, the statute of limitations had run out, and we couldn't file one. So, we both worked with what we had. We became frugal. We struggled. But we did it together."

That sympathetic smile warms into something else. "I know you still have your sister. You always will. But who else do you have, Winter? Because I worry about you sometimes."

My stomach drops. "You don't have to. I can take care

of myself."

"I have no doubt that's true. But I want you to know that it's okay to let others in. I know I'm your boss, but I like to keep an eye out on people I care about."

My chest tightens, and I'm not sure if it's because my heart is growing or because guilt fills the space around it. "It's easier not to need people, because then the only person you have to blame for your situation is yourself."

Her eyes soften. "Oh, Winter."

I shake my head. "It's the truth."

"It's a sad truth to live."

I lift a shoulder. "It's my truth." I look away, take another deep breath, and return my focus on her. "I appreciate everything you've done for me, Janel. I mean it."

No matter what happens, I'll always appreciate you. I'll always be glad for what you've done. And I'm sorry for what I've *done.*

I don't say any of that, but it's cemented into my head. And I think she knows it without me having to verbalize a word.

"Well, if there's ever anything you'd like to talk about…" Her words fade as she watches me, then she lifts a shoulder casually. "You know where to find me."

A nagging feeling pokes at my stomach, but I ignore it. "I should reach out to our point person for this weekend's event to triple-check that we're still good to go," I tell her, jabbing my finger behind me. "If you need me, I'll be at my desk."

She watches me for a second in a way that feels a little too knowing. Like she can sense there's something I'm holding back. Like she knows all the secrets—both mine and Thomas's.

But if she did, it would be detrimental.

Still, I can't shake the feeling that something is coming. I don't know why or how to stop the anxiety from nipping at my consciousness, so I walk to my cubicle with the weight of the world on my shoulders, feeling ten times heavier.

When I sit down, I see four messages waiting for me on my phone.

Kourt: *Dinner at my place? Brad said he'd get Chinese, and I'll get your favorite*

Kourt: *I'm not going to take no for an answer*

Kourt: *I'll pick you up at 5*

Moskins: *How are you feeling?*

My stomach flops at the last message, and I don't even groan at the idea of seeing Brad. Fingers hovering over the keys on my screen, I hesitate before typing out a response.

Not to my sister.

But to *him.*

Me: *You didn't need to get me anything*

Me: *But it was nice of you*

I'm not sure why my skin buzzes as I wait to see the

responding bubbles dance across the bottom of the screen. Or why my heart drops when I don't see them after a few minutes.

"Stupid," I tell myself, setting my phone down. "You're being stupid."

I startle when Farrah asks, "Are you talking to yourself?"

Hand flying to my chest, I stare over at my coworker, staring strangely at me. "When did you get here? I didn't even hear you."

Her perfectly tweezed brow arches as she gestures toward her heels. Stilettos that look like they could double as weapons. "How did you not hear *these*? I'm offended. Somewhere out there, so is Tom Ford."

I frown. "Who?"

She gasps, mouth open as she gapes at me in disbelief. "You don't know who Tom Ford is?"

Slowly, I shake my head.

Then her eyes trail to my ballet flats, and she winces. "Makes sense," she mutters. Instead of elaborating, she says, "You owe me big time. While you took personal leave, I had to answer the millions of calls you got. Here."

She passes me a stack of sticky notes with her handwriting on them. There are a lot of them, which makes me feel bad for not coming in sooner and soaking up the time Janel gave me.

"If you're going to play in the big leagues," she tells me with an odd look on her face, "you need to keep up. That means knowing designers, because people like Thomas Moskins aren't wearing secondhand items."

If I were younger, I'd be embarrassed by the comment. It isn't the first time I've had people poke fun at the clothes I wear. After my parents' death, I wore a lot of Kourtney's hand-me-downs or whatever we could find cheap at Walmart or local thrift shops. Some clothes were even donated to us. They never looked old or worn down, but they certainly weren't up to date on trending fashions either.

"It's a good thing I don't care what Thomas Moskins, or anybody else, thinks," I inform her with a tight smile.

To which she smiles back, with something flashing in her eyes. "Don't you?"

That's all she says before walking away with a pep to her step that I don't trust.

I shake my head and try to avoid the funny feeling in my stomach. The anxiety bubbling there that reminds me something is off. Something I can't put my hand on.

When my phone buzzes, my heart picks up, and I find myself lunging to check the message.

That's when I know I'm in trouble.

Because it's not Thomas.

It's my sister.

And I'm...disappointed.

Kourt: *Stop trying to think of excuses to get out of it. It won't happen*

Kourt: *Five pm sharp*

Kourt: *Luca says he misses you*

If I felt bad before, it doesn't equate to the feeling now. I'm sad because a man who isn't even mine to claim isn't texting me back. I feel twelve again, waiting for my first crush to finally talk to me.

I type back a reply and force myself to lock my phone in my desk after.

Me: *Tell Luca I miss him too, and I'll see him tonight*

DINNER ISN'T A total bust. Brad is on his best behavior, and so am I. Mostly because I spend the majority of my time in Luca's room watching videos of children playing with claw machines instead of with the adults. I find it more distracting when Luca asks me a million questions about what kind of pulley system and motor I think is inside the machine, and what kind of money engineers make to build them.

I use my phone to Google answers for him instead of obsessing over the unanswered messages I sent to Thomas earlier.

My sister tries to convince me to stay the night because she knows what I'll do when I get home. And she's right. Because after telling her I'll be fine to go home, she drops me off and I curl up on my living room couch that I haven't looked at the same since the day with Thomas.

And the second the silence sinks in, I hate it.

I hate that I can't drown out the noise.

Or the sadness.

Or the guilt.

I hate that I'm not looking forward to going to the gala and seeing Thomas, not because I have nothing to wear—because I don't—but because I have no idea how I'll react around the man I can't stop thinking about.

I kissed him, and he kissed me back and…nothing. Maybe all it took was sleeping with me to get me out of his system. Maybe he just needed to prove to himself that I would cave and kiss him exactly as he expected. Maybe using him the way I did put the final nail in the coffin for us. Not that there is an us, but whatever relationship we were forming. Friendly. More than that.

That's the problem with getting to know people. You start to like them. You start to open yourself to them. And the second you realize you want more—more of their secrets, time, and company—it's too late. You're sucked in, regardless of the consequences.

There have only been a few times in my life that I've truly been scared. The first was when I realized my mother and father weren't coming home. I would never have my father's famous pancakes or hear my mother's angelic laugh when she heard Dad's jokes that weren't even that funny.

The second was when I graduated from high school and had no idea what came next. I had no ambitions like my older sister and no clear path that made sense to me. I felt alone in a world full of billions of people and had nobody to help guide me in the right direction.

And the third is right now, when I realize that I might love Thomas Moskins—a married man with secrets, a wife who loves him, and a life of grandeur that is beyond what

I'll ever comprehend.

This isn't some rags-to-riches story. Because at least Cinderella had parents.

No. I won't be that girl—the one who depended on somebody to give her a better life.

I made a promise at my parents' graves that I would stand on my own two feet and live a life they would be proud of me for.

That can't include him, because he isn't mine to love.

I'm starting to wonder if it can include anyone, or if I've been broken for a lot longer than I thought.

CHAPTER TWENTY-TWO

Moskins

I ALREADY KNOW it's going to be a shit day when I have two missed calls and three text messages from my agent all by the time I finish my run, shower, and hop in the car to go to the stadium for a team meeting.

The first image he sends me is of me pulling Winter inside my home. It's from the other day and must have been taken by the Uber driver who recognized me.

The second one is us at a diner, sitting across from one another in an intense conversation. It looks like it was taken from behind a counter, which means one of the servers must have snapped it. My bet is on Linda. I'd seen the flash of familiarity in her eyes that Winter insisted wasn't there.

And the third is of us kissing in my car outside her apartment building. *Yesterday.* Which means that while I was dropping her off, someone was *waiting* for her. Someone who knew I'd be there.

My jaw clenches as I dial my agent's number and growl, "Kill it, Ashton."

"Good morning to you too, asshole."

Teeth grinding, I roll my shoulders and take a deep breath. "Hi, Ash. Would you be so fucking obliged as to get rid of the goddamn pictures you sent me? You know, like I *pay* you to take care of."

He mumbles something under his breath about Scott needing to step up in his managerial role. Then adds, "I'm working on it, but I figured you'd need to know in case you decide to have anymore *guests* at your house that can't drive themselves."

"So it was the driver," I guess, swiping a hand down my face.

"He took multiple pictures of you and Winter. They're incriminating, Tom. He sold them off to TMZ, which is how I found out about them from our contact there."

My nostrils flare. "Son of a bitch."

"I told—"

"Now is not the time for 'I told you so,' ass wipe," I cut him off. I pinch the bridge of my nose as I pull into the back lot of Yokav Stadium and park in my usual spot. "I've done what you suggested and backed off a little. I'm doing what I can to make sure I don't pull her into my bullshit until I can figure it out."

When she kissed me yesterday, it'd been an unexpected—but welcome—surprise. And that fucking kiss changed everything for me. It made me want to find a solution that gives us an actual chance to get to know one another. It made me want to cook dinner for her and give her as many hugs as she wanted.

It made me wish I didn't have a wife.

And that was a crushing thought.

Because I love Emaly too.

"I'm not trying to be a dick," Ashton says with a lofty

sigh. "We have a standing relationship with our source at TMZ, but we don't always have that at other tabloids. I already bought out the images for a pretty penny, including the other two. You're walking on a very fine line, my friend. Everything you do is under scrutiny, regardless of what good deeds are being done in the community."

I close my eyes and lean back in the seat, letting my body melt into the leather. I've been around long enough to know that I can't control everything, not even with all the money in the world. There will be people, like that damn Uber driver, who will want a piece of that profit to say they got the best of me.

"How much did you have to pay?"

Ashton pauses, but eventually says, "Half a million for five images. You're seen pulling her into your house in two of them. TMZ seemed to think it was a worthy paycheck for that kind of photography."

It doesn't matter that we hadn't done anything more than talk. People will come up with their own narrative, whether it's true or not.

I pull my phone back and glance at the thread I've been avoiding. I feel bad for ghosting her after I'm the one who asked if she was okay. If I'd met Winter first, maybe things would be different. I'd have more ability to make a difference in her life. If she'd let me.

But something tells me she wouldn't.

"You've got to figure out what you want," Ashton says, cutting into the silence.

But it's not *what* I want that he's referring to.

It's *who* I want.

My throat bobs. "Yeah, I know."

"There might be other photos out there, so I'm going to try finding them before any get out. But I can't make any promises, Tom. So while I work on making this shit disappear, I need you to behave at the gala tonight. I won't be there to intercept any of the media bound to be in attendance since they announced you, Head, and Clarkson would be there."

I don't need him to babysit me anyway. "I'll lay low. Just take care of this using whatever money necessary," I say, before hanging up.

Scrubbing a palm down my face, I lean back and stare up at the ceiling of my car. It's not often that I've had to pay out anybody for images. But as time went on, and rumors of my affairs started spreading, more of the media became interested.

I'm not sure why it's all come to a head now. I know some people need to make ends meet, so maybe the pictures are a means of survival. But what are the odds that every person I run into will take a picture and sell it? It's not that unheard of in more populated areas, but not in Fairbanks. I'm too new for it to solely be bad luck.

There's something else going on.

When my phone goes off again, I half-groan, thinking it's going to be Ashton. When I see Emaly's name, I frown. "You good?"

"Shouldn't I be asking you that?" she questions, sounding much more refreshed than she did the last time we spoke. I'd wanted to talk to her about what her father told me, and—

For fuck's sake.

If Mikhail hired somebody to follow his daughter, then my guess is that some of these photos from TMZ were because of him as well.

"I haven't heard from you in days since you lost your shit on me," Emaly says as I move my jaw back and forth and try not to punch something.

I rub my eyes and sigh. "I didn't lose my shit. I was worried because of what your father said, and I thought you should know he got someone to tail you. You're welcome, by the way, since you never thanked me."

I can imagine her rolling her eyes. "I didn't thank you because I already knew. It's pretty obvious when people are following you. He really should have hired someone better."

I wish I could say the same, since I'm fairly positive he's been doing it to me.

But this isn't about me. "So you and Ronnie have been careful then?"

"Don't worry about us. We're good."

"But—"

"I'm calling because you've been moody and I'm making sure you're not about to go postal or something," she informs me, clearly diverting the conversation to safer territory. "It's not like you to go silent on me."

We don't talk every day, but there are weeks when we speak more than others. Mostly because of our schedules. Hers is five times as busy as mine most days, so I try not to bother her. But I know if I use that excuse, she won't believe me. "I'm doing okay. Just keeping to myself and letting everyone live their lives."

She hums. "While that's kind of you, that doesn't seem like the entire story. Want to try again?"

I check my watch. "No, because I don't have time for whatever this is. I'm going to be late for practice and don't feel like having your dad up my ass and threatening to sit me out for next week's game."

She groans. "Thomas, I want to talk to you."

"Then I'll call you when I'm done."

It isn't like I have anyone to speak to these days anyway.

"Do you mean it?"

I don't know. "Yes," I lie. "Talk later?"

"Fine. But if I don't hear from you by the end of the night, I'm calling. And I won't stop until you pick up. And if you dare turn your phone off—"

"I wouldn't dream of it, Dimples," I tell her to appease her from this rant. "I love you, and I'll talk to you later."

There's a frown in her reply when she says, "I love you too." And I don't have time to think about why it's there.

I also don't think about the fact that she called me, which tells me she probably wanted to talk to me about more than what's up my ass.

So, I'll make it up to her later.

I have to.

Or all of this is for nothing.

THE SOUND OF skates scraping against ice and bodies

slamming into the boards is music to my ears. Unless, of course, it's my body being rammed into the plexiglass by a two-hundred-pound man in full gear.

"You good, Moskins?" Hoffman calls out when Dawson releases me with a pat on the back.

Clarkson and a few others were murmuring about Yokav watching our practice from one of the suites. When I looked up, I saw him lurking above us like a king on his throne. And he'd been staring at me.

That's inevitably when Dawson, the asshole, body slammed me for the puck.

"All good," I yell back, smacking the wall as I push off it. At least there weren't any bloody noses today. Yet. The day was still early.

Hoffman gathers us all back in the center of the ice. "Look, I know we all have our own shit going on. But being distracted out here isn't going to help anyone."

He doesn't direct that comment at me, but he may as well have. Nobody else is slacking on their plays or being watched like a zoo animal. Just me. And everybody else probably suspects who the owner of the Fireflies is keeping an eye on.

"Our first game against the Islanders is going to be a good test to see where we stand under pressure. Remember one thing—preseason games may not count toward the Stanley Cup, but they still matter. This is our official introduction to the league. If we want fans to root for us, then we need to prove we're worth it. That means giving it our all from here on out."

Richie Head smacks my chest. "Yeah, Moskins. Hear that?"

A few of the guys snicker, but quickly stop when I shoot them an unimpressed scowl.

Clarkson clears his throat. "We all need to be at our best. I was slower on the last run and screwed up my pass. It threw things off."

He wasn't the problem, and I don't like him taking the blame for me.

I look at Hoffman. "I have no intention of letting New York beat us. Never been a fan."

Hoffman chuckles when I point that comment in his direction. He may not have played for the Islanders, but the Rangers were a New York team too, and a damn good one. He always made sure the competition was tight.

"Fair," Hoffman muses. "And since we have a former Islander"—he looks at Dawson—"we have an insider. If you have any tips on playing their weaknesses, now's a good time to share."

I can see the line Dawson's towing with loyalty as he glances at everybody staring in wait. He started out with the Islanders and still has some semblance of appreciation for them. That's how I feel about the Penguins, so I get it.

Dawson clears his throat. "Their defense is strong," he begins, almost hesitantly.

His eyes roam around us and lock on Clarkson, who nods once in encouragement. It's no wonder that nobody questioned who would captain this team. There's only one answer when Jesse Clarkson is involved.

Eventually, Dawson hefts a sigh and stands a little straighter. "It's the goaltenders that aren't as strong compared to other Metropolitan teams in the Eastern

Conference. Their OG starter is out with an injury until at least next year, and the backups have a lot to be desired."

That's good to know. "And their offense?" I find myself asking, wondering if there's a weakness I can exploit.

My teammate shakes his head. "Not as strong as their defense, but still good. During my last season, it was their forward unit that was considered their biggest fault. They've done a lot of reworking since then, so I can't say what it's like now. We won't know until we play them."

Hoffman nods along. "That's good to know, Dawson. Thank you."

Someone clasps Dawson's shoulder when he's silent, and Hoffman goes on to explain our next formation. It's simple. I've done it a million times before and rarely mess it up.

But when I see Mikhail Yokav with his arms crossed, looking down at the rink with his disdain burning holes into my back, I show him exactly what can happen if he keeps fucking with me.

As much as I love winning, he loves it more.

And if he wants to play with fire, then I'll hold the goddamn gasoline.

I make a point to meet his eyes, not breaking eye contact until Hoffman blows his whistle. We start the drill. I purposefully fall a few seconds short, letting the puck go past me. The other team gets the goal.

We go again.

I go left when my opposer goes right.

Hoffman stops us for a second time.

Do you get it yet? Is what my eyes say to the man still

standing above us.

His arms go to his sides, and he turns to give me his back and walks to his office. He doesn't want me here. He doesn't want me in his life at all. The feeling is mutual though.

"Moskins," Hoffman calls out, sounding exasperated. "Head in the game. We don't have a lot of time left. I've been on the ice with you. I know you can do better."

I snap my eyes away from where Yokav disappears and skate back to my position. "I'm in it," I call back, grinding my teeth.

With Yokav gone, I show the team what I'm made of.

Nobody gets past me.

My team wins.

All while Clarkson's suspicious eyes watch me. When we get to the locker room, he pulls me aside before I can go to the showers. "I don't know what's going on, but it's not fair to the rest of the team if you're playing a different long game."

I meet his eyes stubbornly. "Yokav needs to learn a lesson."

"Well, don't fuck over everybody else just so you can prove some mundane point. There are rookies on this team who look up to you. They want to follow your lead. Learn from you. Don't lead them down the petty path. You're better than that."

My eyebrows raise. "Am I?" I doubt.

"You know you are," he replies easily. "You just like to pretend you're not."

With that, he walks away to change and shower.

Without the game, I have nothing.

I'm sure a lot of these guys feel the same.

So I have to decide what I want more—to win the game and secure my spot on this team, or to shove Yokav's face in the mess he's made to show that he's not free of consequences.

I feel Dawson's eyes on me as I leave, and I can tell he wants to say something. He starts to, but stops himself at the last minute. Shaking his head, he disappears down a different corridor as I head toward the parking lot.

It gives me pause, and I wonder if Clarkson is right. If people do look up to me. I feel bad for every person who thinks I'm worth looking up to, because there are far better people in the world than me.

CHAPTER TWENTY-THREE

Winter

I GAPE AT myself in the mirror as Kourtney fixes the curled pieces of freshly dyed hair. The pink is gone, much to my sister's dismay. And maybe a little of my own. But when Janel told me I was expected to attend the gala, I knew the color would have to be a sacrifice for the sake of professionalism. It can always come back, even if I'm a little sad to see the boring blond that brings me no real joy.

"Wow," I breathe, flattening my hands down the emerald-green velvet dress. There's a small slit up the left side that goes to my knee, and the fabric hugs my body in all the right places. "This is beautiful, Kourt. Are you sure I should wear it?"

She sprays my hair, protecting my eyes as she plays with the loose curls. "Mom would have loved seeing you wear it. I'm just impressed the shoes fit."

I pop my foot out to examine the silver pumps that our mother used to wear all the time. It was the perfect thing for tonight's event. "Why?"

She snorts from behind me, and I meet her eyes in the mirror. "Your feet are massive, that's why. You might as well be wearing the shoe equivalent of those magical pants from that stupid movie you loved so much as a kid."

I gasp. "Don't hate on *The Sisterhood of the Traveling Pants*! The movies were so cute."

She rolls her eyes. "They were about a pair of jeggings that were literally meant to stretch on every body type. And most of those girls were so annoying."

Sometimes I'm sad we're related. "You just don't like seeing Alexis Bledel as anything other than Rory Gilmore."

Kourtney nods once. "Damn right. And I stand by that, especially after you made me watch *The Handmaid's Tale*. I'm still traumatized seeing her like that."

It's my turn to scoff. "She's an adult. She was bound to start taking on other roles. But that's beside the point. I do *not* have giant feet. My feet are totally average."

"Babes, you're five foot three and a size nine shoe," she retorts with amusement. "I'm *taller* than you and only wear a size seven."

I refuse to acknowledge that as anything other than normal. "Whatever. I'm trying to be nice and thank you for sharing Mom's things with me, and you're ruining it."

A small smile tilts her lips. "I'll drop it. Unless you stretch out the shoes. Then I'll never let you live it down."

I try to kick her, but she dodges it and laughs when I nearly fall over.

She steadies me and grins when she gives me a once-over. "You look hot, sis. Like super hot. Your client won't know what hit him tonight."

I wince, and her grin drops. "That's not exactly what I'm going for."

"Why? He already got you off once. Why not let him—Wait!" She studies the flush on my cheeks that has nothing to do with the makeup she helped me apply earlier. "You've totally screwed him, haven't you? Oh my *God*! Did you give someone your virginity finally?"

I'm so glad we're alone because I do not need Luca or Brad to hear this conversation.

"Shut up," I whine, feeling the heat from my cheeks creep up the back of my neck.

"You did," she squeals, jumping.

Literally. Jumping.

And clapping.

I playfully shove her. "You're so embarrassing. Stop! And why do you make it sound like it's a present I hand-wrapped and delivered? I didn't 'give' anybody anything."

She shakes her head. "You let somebody in, and I don't even mean that in a gross sexual way. I've been waiting for you to tell me you did the deed for years. I was starting to wonder if you were asexual. Which is totally fine, by the way. But this is way more exciting than I thought."

My brows pinch. "Why?"

"Because your client is rich. Wait." She studies me for a second. "Didn't you say you were working with him on some sort of scandal?"

I start to answer, but I quickly press my lips together to stop the words from coming out. I've been dreading this since I was dumb enough to let him press me against the wall at Furrever Home. Kourtney is going to lose her shit.

"Win," she says slowly. "Talk to me."

The thing is, I can't. Because the second I start, I'm not sure I'll be able to stop. And I've never been worried that she'd blab what I have to say to anyone. Any NDA I sign may as well have her written in the clause as someone I can share anything with.

This just feels…bigger.

Because Thomas is etched into my skin. My mind. My chest. He's everywhere he shouldn't be. It's not some random fling. It's more. So much more.

"Oh, Winnie." Kourtney breathes out, seeing every emotion wash over my face. She clearly doesn't need me to confirm anything, even if it's obvious she wants to know. "Okay. It's okay. These things happen."

Who is she trying to convince?

I bat my lashes repeatedly to stop the oncoming tears from leaking out and ruining the eyeliner I spent twenty minutes applying. "I messed up," I whisper, voice watery.

She pulls me in for a hug. It's nice, but it doesn't feel as good as Thomas's. And I hate that I even think such a stupid thing. "Yeah, you did," she agrees, not bothering to sugarcoat it. "But it's going to be okay."

I let her squeeze me against her, trying not to hyperventilate. "I'm sorry," I say against her shoulder.

I can feel her shake her head against me before she says, "Don't be. We all make mistakes. I've made a lot of them." She pauses, takes a deep breath, and releases it. "I'm not saying I condone any of this, but I understand. We can't always help who we're attracted to. And sometimes life just…happens."

When she pulls away, she forces me to look at her. It's hard. I don't want to see any disappointment on her face. But when I finally do peek up at her through my painted lashes, there is none.

"I don't regret Luca," she tells me. "You know how much I love him. But sometimes I do regret the choice I made in who to have children with. Brad isn't a bad father, but he's a terrible partner. And I have to live with that."

She never talks about her relationship with Brad. Ever. "No, you don't. Nobody has to settle, Kourt. You shouldn't have to sacrifice your happiness for the sake of Luca. He'll be fine."

Limply, her shoulders lift. "You may be right, but I'm not sure I'm ready for that battle. That isn't the point though. The point is that we all make decisions in life. And those aren't always the best ones for us, but they make for great lessons. We all have to learn things in order to grow. This is your moment to do that."

She sounds like such a mom, it makes me almost smile. "Do you think Mom and Dad would be ashamed of me?"

My big sister gapes at me. "Are you kidding me? No. No way. They weren't perfect either. Do you know how many times I heard them fight? I'd have to put headphones on to ignore them when I still lived at home. Nobody is perfect. If they were here, they would tell you the same thing. They wouldn't love you any less for what you've done."

I know she's right, so I don't fight her on it.

She swipes at my cheeks, which I don't realize are damp. "None of this. You're going to ruin your makeup. We can't have you looking like a trainwreck at the event."

I snort, and the pathetic sound makes her laugh. "Thanks for the pep talk."

Kourtney winks at me. "Always." She gives me another

once-over after we dry my face and touch up some of my eye makeup that a tissue rubs off. "Are you going to be okay? I can come. Consider me your security. I make a great cockblock if you're concerned you may fall onto your client's dick."

I glare at her. "Too soon."

She holds up her hand. "Fine, fine."

I turn back to the mirror and stare at the woman looking back at me in the reflection. "I look so much like her."

She leans against me, her smile warm. "You really do."

Warmth enters my chest, wrapping around my heart like a heated blanket. It's Mom, I realize. Giving me her love. Showing me that she's not judging.

Kourtney touches the strands of hair that used to be pink. "You didn't dye this because of him, right? You're not trying to, like, impress him or anything."

I shake my head, staring at my blond locks and missing the color. "No. This is about me trying to fit in."

"Who says you need to?" she doubts.

I swallow. "I do." My lips fall into a frown as that soaks in. "If I fit in, then things will be easier."

Kourtney's lips match my own. "I don't think it's as easy as that, babes. I wish it were."

It's hard to swallow suddenly as I truly see myself. The girl void of color. The one who has to force a smile. "I'm sorry about you and Brad," I find myself saying quietly.

Kourtney's smile reappears, but her eyes dim a fraction. "Me too, Win. Me too." Her hand finds mine. "I'm sorry you fell in love with a married guy."

I flinch. "I never said I loved him."

She shrugs. "You didn't have to."

THE HISTORICAL ASSOCIATION decided to host the gala in Fairbanks's City Hall, which is one of the oldest buildings in the city limits. Its Greek architecture and large pillars make it look like it should be a museum full of rarities, not local government officials and court proceedings.

Tonight, there is no sign of the people who usually congregate around the historic building to pay fines, deal with speeding tickets, or trying to get special-use permits signed off by the board. There's a literal red carpet rolled out that covers the marble steps, lights wrapped around the Corinthian-style columns, and temporary police bans posted along each side of the road so cars dropping off big-name people can stop curbside in front of the building.

Even though it seems silly to go all out for an event like this, they did a beautiful job. Everything looks so much more immaculate than usual. Government officials who usually wear jeans and plaid button-downs for board meetings are in tuxedos and cocktail dresses, and there's not one work boot or flip-flop in sight.

I glance down at myself, suddenly glad that Kourtney forced me to try on the heels. They're easier to walk in than I thought, considering I'm at least three inches higher than usual, and my go-to shoe choices are flat and hazard-free.

Well, usually. Mom used to say I could trip over painted lines, and she wasn't wrong. I'd get scrapes and bruises just from walking. Once, I fell *up* the stairs. The only good thing that came from that was knocking a baby tooth out of my mouth and getting five dollars from the Tooth Fairy.

I rub my arm as I stand a healthy distance away from the crowd gathering at the front entrance of the building. Janel was supposed to be here, but she couldn't make it because of some other family event she had tonight. I'm a little sad about not having an ally here and wish I'd told Kourtney she could come when she begged me to be my plus one. I'm not even sure I'm allowed one, which is inevitably why I told her I should go alone.

Now I find myself uncomfortable because I can't tell if I'm too dolled up or too dressed down. There are varying degrees of outfits as people pour out of cars and walk the carpet, getting photographed by two men at the top of the stairs. One of them we hired to ensure that Thomas and his teammates would get captured for news outlets and their own social media, and the other must have been hired by the association for their own use.

"There he is," I hear someone say excitedly from a few cars down. A man opens the back door of a black Escalade with tinted windows, and I see someone vaguely familiar step out.

"Mr. Clarkson," a white-haired man greets, holding out his hand for the man in a tailored suit to shake. "We're glad you joined us. I'm Charles Westwood, head of the Historical Association."

I realize after a few seconds of their pleasant conversation that this is the captain of the Fairbanks Fireflies. Which means—

"Thomas Moskins!" a little boy yells out, trying to jump past the rope someone stretched along the staircase to keep locals away from the partygoers. "Can you sign my jersey?"

My eyes instantly find the tall, broad man stepping out of the Escalade after his captain, and I swear my heart flutters for a second like I'm a teenager staring at her first crush.

He looks…different. Good. No, great. If men could be beautiful, I'd even label him that. But the man standing in front of the crowd of people wearing a charcoal gray suit and crisp white shirt underneath isn't the same one I've spent the last few weeks with. This is Thomas Moskins, the hockey star, not the book-loving human being.

This version of him takes up space and makes the air buzz around him. This version dominates the conversations simply by existing, drawing attention from everybody nearby. People stare at him, not in judgment from all the things that led him to be front-page news, but in awe. They're mesmerized by this larger-than-life figure.

I watch as he walks over to the boy beaming up at him with a marker in his hand. I'm not sure what he says to the young fan, but the boy's smile grows three times bigger as Thomas bends down, writes on his shirt, and then gives the kid a high-five.

It's sweet watching him interact with his fans. His softness toward them, especially the children, is another unexpected part of him that I've become rather fond of. It isn't like the closed-off version who masks how he's feeling when he's around everybody else.

I find myself walking toward him without thinking, so I force myself to stop and observe from my carefully chosen spot out of the way of the action. I'm here to make sure he shows up and behaves. That's all.

He's the one who's been avoiding me. He's the one who took my secrets and disappeared with them like they meant nothing.

Calm down, I tell my racing heart.

It doesn't, the traitorous bitch.

Thomas and Jesse Clarkson do that weird bro handshake hug thing and talk to a few of the spectators. All fans, I realize. I'm not surprised. The Historical Association has been heavily promoting its guest list for the past week, hoping people would come and donate to the cause.

As if he can sense me, Thomas lifts his head and finds me within seconds. In hindsight, he can be looking at an array of people near me. There are men I'm sure he'd benefit from rubbing elbows with, and women who definitely fit his type better than I do.

Yet, I know he isn't paying them one ounce of attention. Not like he should be. And as if he wants to make that very clear, he comes walking over.

Thump, thump, thump, thump.

My heart has a mind of its own, reacting despite my best efforts to squash its anticipation.

Thomas doesn't walk over to the beautiful redhead in a tight black dress and heels that make her legs look long and slender. He doesn't go to the man with a fancy watch on his wrist that he's looked at no more than three times in the past twenty minutes solely so people can see the little Rolex label in the watch face.

He ignores them completely, coming to a stop mere inches from *me* in a borrowed dress and shoes with cheap makeup and jewelry on. I don't have to crane my neck nearly as much thanks to my shoes, which he notices.

"You look..." His throat bobs as he swallows with a shake of his head. "You look beautiful, Winter."

Winter.

Not kid.

Not princess.

Not sweetheart.

My hands nervously flatten down the front of my dress. "It was my mother's," I tell him quietly, staring down at my outfit. "My sister lent it to me for the night, so I'd have something nice to wear."

When I peek up at him, his eyes are running over the length of my body. He clears his throat and lifts his gaze back up, narrowing on my face.

"You dyed your hair."

Absentmindedly, I touch the curls that sit loose past my shoulders. "It made sense. Have you seen anyone with pink hair here?"

He frowns at my question. "Who cares? If you like the pink, that's all that matters." He pauses, reaching out as if he wants to touch my hair before remembering better. When he lowers his hand, his jaw tics. "I liked the pink."

A familiar heat rises up my neck and settles into my cheeks. "It'll be back. Or maybe I'll do purple. I haven't decided yet."

His eyes roam over my face. "Purple would look nice."

We stare at one another for a moment that seems far too long before I take a step back and gesture toward City Hall. "You should go in. The schedule has you meeting a few VIP guests in about thirty minutes. Then I'll make sure the photographers get pictures of you with your team. Are the others here yet?"

Working is the only way I can calm my mind and my heart down. It distracts me from the annoying buzz that I feel every inch of me that his eyes go, like he's physically touching me.

"Winter," he says quietly, trying to earn my attention back.

But I can't.

If I look at him for too long, it will hurt.

The truth.

That he isn't mine.

That I can't have him.

That this is all temporary.

An infatuation and nothing more.

"You should go in," I repeat, voice a fraction weaker than before. "You don't want to be late."

I can feel him staring at me.

His body all but radiates warmth and want, and it's a dangerous combination because my soul is cold and needs the heat.

Thomas lowers his voice so only I can hear him. "I'm sorry for not texting you back. I wanted to, but I thought it would be better if I figured some things out first."

Better for whom? For him? For me? For Emaly? For his career? It's probably all accurate. I'm the last person he needs to concern himself with. After all, we've established that I'm not his responsibility. He doesn't owe me a thing, not even an apology.

"It's fine," I tell him as earnestly as possible. I turn away from him to see a few people looking at us with interest. Too much interest. One of them being his teammate, Jesse Clarkson. "People are watching."

It's the only warning I give him before plastering a big smile on my face. The one I use in all my meetings with clients, no matter how much I dread some of them. The one I paint on there that's faker than the pink-dyed tips that used to be in my hair, but gets me along based on professionalism alone.

Thomas's eyes go to my nails. "They're not bright," he notes, almost sadly, when he sees the boring beige color I painted on them.

My eyes go down to my hands that feel naked, stripped of the neon or pastel colors usually painted on the nails. "I'm trying to be more professional."

He shakes his head. "You should just be you, sweetheart."

My heart finds its way to my throat hearing that name. I used to hate it. But now…not so much. And I hate how that makes me feel.

"And who are you, Thomas?" I question. "Is it this version or the one you pretend to be around people so they don't ask questions?"

He swallows, but doesn't answer.

Because he knows he's a hypocrite.

Jesse Clarkson walks over to us and dips his head, offering me a civil smile. "Sorry to interrupt, but we should get going."

Before Thomas can interject, I nod. "I was just telling

him that. You two go in. I think I saw Richard Head go in about ten minutes ago, so I'm sure he's looking for you. I'll be up soon. I have a few things to organize."

It's a lie. Everything is already set, but I need some air before suffocating myself in his presence again.

Thomas doesn't introduce me to his teammate, and I don't bother doing it either. I don't want to. I don't have the energy.

Eventually, Thomas relents and shakes hands with at least twelve different people as he makes his way up the stairs. He gets his picture taken, plasters an even faker smile on his face than the one on mine, and doesn't look back.

I'm glad.

Especially when someone comes up to me a few minutes after he disappears and says, "If you look anymore obvious, dear, you're going to give yourself away."

I don't recognize the accent, nor do I know the large man standing beside me. He's older. Gray hair, aged face. There's a tightness to his smile that seems beady and calculated.

"You should have known better than to get yourself involved with a man like that, Ms. Bronte. Or would you prefer I call you Winter?"

How does he know my name? I stand taller, my guard up, and internal alarm bells going off.

"I don't think we've met," is the only reply I can come up with.

He huffs out laughter and holds out his hand to me. "My apologies. I'm Mikhail Yokav. And I believe you know my son-in-law based on the pictures I've seen."

Everything in me stills.

"Pictures?" I repeat.

He hums, a secretive smile on his face. "I think we need to talk, Ms. Bronte."

CHAPTER TWENTY-FOUR
Moskins

I'M HYPERAWARE THAT Winter hasn't made it inside after twenty minutes of me shaking hands, signing pictures, and posing for photos with fans in front of a Fireflies backdrop spanning at least six feet along the back of the tables set up for me, Clarkson, and Head to use during our meet-and-greet session.

After another five minutes, I'm searching the space as a middle-aged woman tells me all about how her husband recently left her for a younger woman. I nod along, pretending like I'm listening when I actually couldn't give less of a rat's ass. If she thinks I'm going to offer to warm her bed tonight in sympathy, she's mistaken.

"Here you go," I tell her, sliding a recent headshot of me in Fireflies gear toward her. I'd gone in for team photos at the beginning of the summer when the official lineup was made public. Right before the images of me and my bartender friend made their way onto cyberspace, followed by the onslaught of past flings that followed. "If you'll excuse me, I—"

"We haven't taken a picture!" she says as I round the table and walk toward the entrance. "I paid for a picture!"

I'm sure one of her hands would wind up in places that

would get me sued if the roles were reversed, so I don't care about fulfilling her little photo shoot fantasy. "All donations to the Historical Association are greatly appreciated," I call out, eyes scanning the crowd of people mingling and laughing and sharing drinks and stories of God only knows what.

My gut is tight, telling me something isn't right. Winter should have come inside by now, even if she felt awkward being here. Being around *me*. She would have rolled her shoulders, held her head up, and walked in like she owned the place, just to prove that she could. Something must have happened.

A hand grips my upper arm, and a low voice with a thick accent asks, "Where do you think you're going?"

I turn to Mikhail, who showed up only minutes after I arrived, to greet the people getting our autographs. He had to play the proud father role, after all. He's all smiles and friendly conversation as he talks about the upcoming season, but I know he hates this shit as much as I do. Maybe even more. Because his face may be split with a smile, but his eyes are dark, empty pits that offer no friendliness. He doesn't give a fuck about these people. He couldn't care less about Fairbanks. He wants money and power, so he simply pretends like he gives a rats ass about those who could help him get there.

I jerk my arm back out of his grasp. "None of your business."

"It is my business, considering I paid a substantial amount of money for you all to be here," he counters aggressively. "So you need to go back and do exactly what you're supposed to be doing with the fans. We have tickets that still need to be sold for the rest of our preseason games. I expect a majority of those seats to be taken. Do you understand me?"

Everything is about money to him. I'm half tempted to write him a check with seven digits just to get him out of my goddamn face. "I need to make sure that—"

"Your little blond-haired friend left," he informs me with pointed eyes. "She knows this is the last place she should be, which means she's far smarter than you."

My shoulders go rigid as I take a step toward him until our shoes touch. "What did you say to her?"

He scoffs at me, as if the notion is preposterous. "I didn't need to say much of anything. You always do a perfectly good job at fucking yourself and everyone around you over."

What the fuck is that supposed to mean?

Before I can ask, he pulls his phone out of his pocket and shows me an article already pulled up on his phone.

It's a picture of Winter. From *tonight*. She looks shell-shocked as someone takes her photo. And the one printed beside it, under the large bold headline plastered on a famous tabloid site, is me standing a little too close to her, staring at her mouth.

"Shit," I cuss, grinding my teeth as I scan the headline.

> *Thomas Moskin, 35, who is set to begin his new journey with the Fairbanks Fireflies in a matter of days, seems to be a busy man off the ice with a mysterious new blonde. Sources say the woman has been seen entering his new Connecticut residence and spending time in public*

together with him and his wife.

What. The. Fuck.

"This isn't what it—"

"Looks like?" Mikhail finishes for me, no expression on his face. "Isn't that the story you always weave?"

No, it's not. Usually, I openly admit that I'm a scumbag. That I did sleep with the women I've been photographed with. But not this time. This time, it's none of his goddamn business what's going on between Winter and me.

I stare at the image of Winter with Emaly at a café. That must have been when my wife gave her our numbers. "They're friends," I inform him, choosing to move the narrative in a different direction and gesture toward the picture. "Why else would they be hanging out? Not everything has to be about me being a douchebag. Winter has nothing to do with any of this. You know, there are people willing to sell any story for a quick buck, whether it's true or not."

"And what about this?" he inquires, his accent thicker than usual tonight. He seems confident—like he knows where he's got me.

My eyes go down to his phone reluctantly.

There are photos.

So. Many. Photos.

The first I see are pictures of me and Winter at my front door. Then of me pulling Winter into my house and closing the door behind us. These were the ones taken from the Uber driver that Ashton told me he took care of. But how the fuck did he manage to do that if Mikhail is showing them to me?

There are others.

Images of me watching Winter with a little too much interest at Our Open Table.

Photos that look like I'm touching her back at the Food Bank when Kayleigh came over to flirt with me.

Then there are more damning ones—ones that make me ten times angrier than the pictures of us at my house.

These were taken in front of *her* apartment the day I'd found out about Ashton's brother.

Images of me pulling up.

Getting out.

Storming inside the building.

Those could probably be explained. I look angry. Like a man on a mission, ready to burn down the world. It's the pictures taken of me leaving her place with disheveled hair, a flushed face, and rumpled clothes that's the most damning.

There are more. Some of the same ones that Ashton showed me from a "source" that gave them to TMZ. Not just the driver. But Mikhail himself.

"Why are you showing me these?" I ask, grinding my teeth. "When we both know you're the one responsible for them being taken."

He doesn't deny it. "You have continued to make a mockery of my daughter," he tells me under his breath so the people surrounding us can't hear. "And, in turn, me. I will make sure you pay for that."

If I could hit him, I would. But that wouldn't get me

anywhere. "Do what you have to, Yokav. But Winter stays out of it. You're not the only one who can fuck someone over."

His head cocks as he studies me, and something passive crosses his features. "You have the audacity to care about a random woman. Perhaps even more than my daughter."

"I love Emaly," I state matter-of-factly. There hasn't been a day I haven't loved his daughter. "I will always love her. But you know nothing, *sir*. If you don't understand that, it's because you've put the wedge between her and you. Not me. Not my actions. And *not* because of Winter. I will not let you screw over an innocent person's life so you can gain control of mine."

He powers off his screen and tucks it carefully into the inside pocket of his suit jacket. "You have a strange way of showing how much you love your wife, considering these photos exist. How old is she? Nineteen? Twenty?"

My nostrils flare. "She's twenty-five," I hiss to him. "And you probably already know that too. I'm sure you've done your research."

He hums. "She has a sad background. Very unfortunate to experience so much loss. It would be a great shame if she experienced more. I'm sure her boss will not be happy of her current relations with a client. No?"

He's threatening her job. These photos are to put me in my place, but that's not going to happen.

I take a step forward, but he lifts his hand to stop me. "If you do anything to her—"

"I won't," he promises, "as long as you don't fuck up my season. If I see you purposefully do anything to let the other teams win, I will bench you for the season and find a way to trade you faster than you can blink."

So, practice the other day got to him. And just like before, he's going after what I love to get what he wants. "I have to be on the ice."

"My daughter should have a loyal husband," he spits at me before stepping back and adjusting his suit jacket. "Looks like everybody is going to be disappointed by your actions."

"If you wanted positive press, why leak those photos to them?" I ask. "What does that get you?"

He smiles easily. "Control."

"Do you really think this is going to win over your daughter? Emaly considers Winter a friend. You stepping into her life is only going to make her even angrier at you than she already is."

"How can she be angrier at me than you? I am not the one who has chosen another woman."

I snort. "You've chosen everything over Emaly. Sasha. Your businesses. Now hockey. There has never been a moment when you put Emaly first."

His eyes sharpen. "And you are to tell me *you* have?"

There's no hesitation. "Yes. I've done everything in my power to love and protect your daughter in ways you have continuously failed to do."

Mikhail doesn't like that answer. "She will still choose family."

"I *am* her family."

His teeth grind. "You lie."

"The only person lying here is you. And if you fuck

with Winter any more than you already have, I will make sure your entire season is fucked. And if you try to get in my way, I'll break my contract and leave before you even come close to a championship. Because, inevitably, that's what you want more than a healthy relationship with your daughter."

He stares at me. "You would break your legally binding contract for her?"

Winter. Not Emaly. "I would."

His jaw moves back and forth, the vein in his forehead pulsing. "You disgust me."

"The feeling is mutual," I inform him bitterly.

A throat clears beside me. "Everything okay?" Clarkson asks hesitantly, looking between the team owner and me.

I'm about to say "no" when my father-in-law offers the captain of his team a smile. "Yes. We were discussing future plans and where Moskins sees himself on the team."

Clarkson seems a little tense, which means he must hear the slime in his tone the same way I do.

"Come on," my captain says quietly, tugging on my elbow. "Let's go back. We have a few more people to see."

I start to shake my head, but Mikhail pins me with a stare that halts me from arguing. My stomach dips when he says, "If you don't want me to drag her into this, I suggest you go back and make your fans happy. There is very little you can do to get out of the contract you signed."

I want to point out that there's always a way, but I don't. I also don't bother saying the fans won't be happy watching me sit on a bench, but I don't waste my breath. Because as much as I want to shove those words down his throat, I know they won't help.

Not when he's threatening Winter.

He knows he has me right where he wants me, and that smile spreads on his face.

"How does it feel?" I ask him as Clarkson starts pulling me back to the meet-and-greet table.

Mikhail looks at me dubiously. "How does what feel?"

This time, I smile. But it's empty. Void of any emotion, even hatred. "To know that you're going to lose everything because of this? You think you're in control, but you're not."

Clarkson's grip tightens. "Let's go," he warns under his breath.

My father-in-law's eyes flash with rage, but he doesn't get a chance to respond before my captain is yanking me away.

"Care to explain what the hell that was about?" Clarkson asks once we're back at the table, where Dawson is entertaining a group of kids with some cheesy magic trick he tried showing us at practice one day.

I finally meet my captain's eyes. "No. Not particularly. Can we just get this whole fucking thing over so I can go?"

Clarkson studies me. "Who was he talking about?"

I swallow. "Somebody who doesn't deserve what's about to happen to her. All because I was dumb enough to fall in love."

His eyes soften for a moment. "If you need to leave, I'll cover for you."

As much as I want to bolt out the door, I know Mikhail will stick true to his word. He will find a way to screw

Winter over, and I refuse to allow it.

"After," is all I say.

After, I'll make this right.

I'll find a way to fix it.

I will burn the world down for the blonde who I should have never flirted with to begin with, but now don't know if I can live without.

I like her banter too much. Her sass.

I like the way she's blunt. She doesn't tell me what she thinks I want to hear. She tells me the truth, even if I don't want to listen.

Even though I wish I didn't, I'm gone for this girl.

By the time I look at my phone hours later, there are hundreds of notifications littering my screen. Missed calls, texts, social media messages, emails, and news alerts all cover the image of Emaly on my home screen. But I don't pay any attention to them. Not to the twenty missed calls from Ashton, or the five from my agent, Scott, *or* the three from Emaly.

I also don't answer any text messages, especially not the ones with images attached, because I don't have the energy to see what bullshit is being plastered about me now. I've never cared that deeply before. Not until Winter became involved in the whirlwind that is my life.

When I finally find the name that's sunk toward the bottom of my text threads, I click on it and wait as it rings.

And rings.

And rings.

And rings. Until the voicemail picks up and I'm greeted with a generic automated voice that isn't the one I want to hear. *"You've reached Winter Bronte. Please leave a—"*

I hang up and toss the phone into the passenger seat, unbuttoning my suit jacket and loosening my tie so I can fucking breathe for the first time all night. When I see the light on my screen flash, I bolt to pick it up and narrowly miss side-swiping a parked vehicle. I'm sure that would be another twisted headline. *Hockey star side swipes car while drunk driving after charity gala.*

It wouldn't matter to people that I didn't touch a drop of alcohol tonight. I'm sure it would be widely believed solely because I would be the asshole to do something like that.

"Winter," I say, straightening out the car and slowing down as I approach a red light.

"No," Emaly says, voice sounding heavy. "I saw the pictures, and I've been getting calls again."

She means from the media wanting commentary. The fact that they have her number, after the *third* time she changed it, isn't surprising to me one bit. They have weird ways to get the information they need, and it makes me want to punch something. Ideally, one of them.

I pinch the bridge of my nose. "I'll get in touch with the phone provider and see about getting you a new—"

"No," she cuts me off. I'm really starting to hate that word. "Forget about that. I can field calls. I want to make sure you two are okay."

For a moment, I'm quiet. She's not just calling to inquire about me and my dumbass mistake. She's asking about Winter.

I swallow. "I'm not sure," I admit, hating the uncertainty. "Your father approached her tonight. He's been following her too. And me, obviously. I don't know what he said to her, but it was enough to spook her."

This is all my fault.

My fault.

My fault.

My fault.

"I ruin everything," I whisper aloud, forgetting she's on the phone still. "This is my fault."

"It's not," she disagrees. When I don't reply, she says, "It *isn't*, Little Bear." Her tone is firmer than before. Not allowing me to argue.

Maybe my father was right. I get in the way. Of myself. Of everyone. I'm a cancer. Everything I touch is poisoned. Ruined.

I should have known the second I stepped into Winter's life—the moment I realized I wanted to know *more*—it wasn't going to end well. Because that's what happens when people get close to me.

"Listen to me, Thomas Xavier Moskins," my wife all but growls at me. "You are not responsible for this. I am. We both know it. And I think it's time I stop letting you take the brunt of the consequences because all it's doing is hurting us. Seeing you like this is killing me."

It's hard to swallow as I take in her words.

"You care about her," she states. It's not a question. "I think you may even love her. And don't try to argue because I won't have it."

I nod, driving when the light turns green and hoping Winter is at her apartment when I get there. "I know," I finally reply, getting closer to the turnoff that leads to the shitty apartment building Winter loves so much.

"I'm sorry," she offers softly. "I'm sorry for letting this go on for so long. It shouldn't have. Not for you. Not for Ronnie. Not for Winter. We all deserve to be happy."

I want to tell her she shouldn't be sorry.

That it's me who should be sorry.

Sorry for her.

Sorry for Winter.

But not sorry for myself.

I'm the creator of my own downfall.

A cancer to society.

Sickness to everyone who comes into my life.

"You fuck everything up," my father says before backhanding me until I'm lying on the dirty tile floor of the kitchen. He looms over me, reeking of alcohol and cigarette smoke. "You always fuck up everything."

I was six, and it was the first vivid memory I have of the man who looked twice his age because of the pills and booze. Since then, his hand had been a common occurrence against some part of my body when he'd get mad. If I were in his way, which was too often, he'd make sure I knew what an inconvenience I was in his life.

I did my best not to come out of my room unless it was an emergency. Usually, that left me nearly having accidents in my bedroom because I was terrified of going to the bathroom. It wasn't until some of the bruises from my father's anger became more visible that the school stepped in.

Some people were terrified of foster homes and the experiences they had in them. Mine brought me relief, even when I had nothing but a garbage bag full of clothes and a thin mattress to call my own. At least there was peace from the monsters with whom I shared my blood.

And, eventually, my time away from my parents brought me next door to Emaly.

The woman who took me in didn't care where I was as long as I behaved myself and didn't bring trouble to her door, so I made sure to keep my head down. I spent time at the local skating rink in the summer and the frozen pond in the winter, and learned my passion for skating thanks to the young dark-haired girl.

Emaly was my salvation from the harsh words that had always been locked in my mind.

You fuck everything up.

It's a cruel thing to believe your entire life, and Emaly made me wonder if they were wrong. Until, inevitably, I realized that maybe they weren't.

"Little Bear?" Emaly asks quietly. "Are you still there?"

I wet my lips and turn onto Winter's street. I know now where her apartment is and don't see any lights on through the far window. But she could still be there, sitting in the darkness and worried that someone with a long camera is waiting for her out here.

I grip the steering wheel, hating that I brought that into her life. "Yes," I say through gritted teeth. "I'm still here."

She takes a deep breath. "I think it's time."

I'm still staring at the window when I register those words and frown. "Time for what?"

"Time to end this."

I sit back against my seat. "There's no point."

"When it comes to love," she counters, "there is always a point."

And then she tells me she loves me and hangs up the phone.

I don't call her back.

Because I don't want to. Not right now.

I try the front door.

Locked.

I tap on the window.

No response.

I sit on the stoop outside, wondering what to do now. I call her. I text. Nothing.

And then I think about what she told me that day at her apartment.

And I get back in my car and call Ashton.

"Where are they buried?" is the question out of my mouth before he can cuss me out for ignoring him.

"What the fuck are you talking about? We have a serious problem on our hands. We need to—"

"You need to tell me where Winter's parents are buried," I cut him off firmly. "I know you know. There's no way you don't after years of keeping an eye on the girls."

Ashton is quiet, likely trying to figure out if he can win an argument with me right now. He realizes he can't and tells me the cemetery's location so I can put it into my GPS.

"We still need to talk," he tells me, but there's a difference in his tone of voice. "Tomorrow."

He's giving me the night to figure this out.

To finally be the cure, for once, instead of the disease.

So, I hang up my phone and follow the directions until I find myself parking along the driveway of a cemetery.

In the near distance, a blond-haired girl is sitting on the ground in front of two graves.

I don't say anything to her as I approach.

I'm quiet.

Careful not to scare her.

Then I kneel, peeling my suit jacket off and draping it over her shoulders. I don't care about the stains that will wind up on my gray pants or the dirt that will probably get on my white button-down. I sit beside her and stare at the names on the polished granite with moss growing over the tops of each.

Winter and I stay like that for a long, long time. In silence. Simply breathing. Letting the wind rustle our hair.

It feels like forever before she whispers, "I miss them."

I say, "I know, sweetheart."

She takes a deep breath, and I think she's about to say something when she chooses to hold it back.

Then she leans against me, her head resting on my shoulder, and stays like that.

I don't move my arm around her as much as I want to. I don't apologize as much as I need to. I let my body heat warm her, comfort her.

She doesn't tell me to leave, so I stay.

I'll be whatever she needs right now.

I'll be whatever she needs for as long as she'll let me.

Because Emaly was my salvation as a child. She brought me everything I needed when I needed it most.

But Winter…she's the salvation I need now.

The person who makes the pain go away.

"I would have loved to meet them."

Winter doesn't reply. Not right away. But then she says, "My dad hated hockey. He said it was too violent."

My lips twitch into a smile. "That's a shame." I press my mouth to the top of her head in a chaste kiss. "I would give it up."

Her body tenses beside me.

"If it means you can be happy," I tell her, taking a deep breath. "I'd give it up."

She draws her knees up and rests her chin on them. "I would never ask that of you. The game means too much to you. So does Emaly. I get it, Thomas. This is—"

"You do too." I stop her. "Don't mistake this, Winter. You're not the other woman. You're not disposable. What did I tell you before?"

She doesn't answer right away. Slowly, she turns to look at me curiously.

"You're capable of love and being loved."

I don't say the words.

The three words I have no right to say to her yet. But one day…

One day, I'll be able to tell her.

When I deserve her.

CHAPTER TWENTY-FIVE

Moskins

I WATCH WINTER sleep peacefully on her couch, using my lap as her pillow. I shouldn't have come in, especially when I saw the photographers camping out across the street. They know they can't be kicked out for trespassing if they're on public property, so they use their cameras to get what they need from there.

Since the story already broke, I walked into the apartment building with my middle finger up in their direction. They can plaster that on the tabloids next, for all I care. They'd been lucky I didn't flash them my ass and tell them to kiss it while I was at it.

I brush my fingers through Winter's hair as her chest rises and falls slowly. She hadn't told me to go home. Hadn't said goodbye. Hadn't told me to fuck off like I deserved. So, here I am. Watching her sleep and being here with her for as long as I can.

It's nothing like the last time we were on this couch together. The emotions aren't as high or deadly. Not in the same way. She's not whipping insults or demanding anything. She's not using me or expecting anything.

She just…is.

Soaking up the moment.

Getting a moment's peace, if only in her dreams. When she wakes up, we'll have to face this mess together. Because whether she likes it or not, I'm going to be there for her.

My phone buzzes with an unsaved number, so I ignore it. Then it buzzes again with another unsaved number. I almost turn it off when it goes off for a third time, and I see Ashton's name.

Winter stirs, and I try to hush her back to sleep when she murmurs, "You can answer it if you need to."

"I didn't mean to wake you."

The phone keeps ringing.

Ashton. Again.

I pinch the bridge of my nose and answer it, putting the cell to my ear. "I thought you said this could wait until tomorrow."

"It is tomorrow," he states, making me look at my watch.

12:06 a.m.

I roll my eyes. "What do you want?"

"You clearly haven't been online yet," he mutters, sighing. When he speaks next, there's a hardness in his voice. "Why didn't you tell me the truth? All of these years you've been lying to me."

What the hell is he going off about? "Ash, I already saw the headlines earlier. You of all people should know I'm not going to go online to see what people are—"

"Not about you and Winter." He curses, sounding impatient. "Look at your goddamn phone, asshole."

I shake my head and put my phone on speaker, shooting Winter an apologetic look. Then I open up my browser and see the first article in the trending news section.

"Holy shit," I whisper.

"Yeah," Ashton says. "Care to fucking explain?"

Winter is sitting up, eyes alert. "What?" she asks, frowning. Her hand goes to my leg, as if to comfort *me*. "What is it?"

I can't look at her though.

All I can focus on is the headline.

> *Emaly Moskins-Yokav, wife of Fairbanks Fireflies right-winger Thomas Moskins, comes out amidst her husband's latest cheating scandal.*
>
> *The 34-year-old makes a big announcement only hours after news broke of her husband's newest affair.*
>
> *Moskins-Yokav, who has never commented on the press surrounding her husband of thirteen years, has chosen to speak out to clear his name.*
>
> *"I think it's time to be honest with the world about what's really going on, because my husband doesn't deserve the backlash he's continually gotten over the past decade. The world knows Thomas Moskins not only as a skilled hockey player who's helped his team win three Stanley Cups, but as an unfaithful husband. And I'm here to tell you that isn't the truth. My husband has always been the most loyal person I know, who would sacrifice his happiness for the sake of everybody else. And I've selfishly allowed him to do that for too long. So, it's time you knew the truth.*
>
> *"My name is Emaly, and I'm in love with the most amazing woman I've ever met. I met her after I married Thomas and have been with her for the majority of my marriage. If anybody is the cheater, it's me. I love Thomas and the relationship we have, but it's time for him to be happy as well. So I'm asking you all to respect our*

privacy instead of using the photographs online to create a false narrative. Thomas isn't cheating on me. He's free to do what he wants with whom he wants, same as me. Thank you."

I gape at the article until I hear, "...you even listening to me right now?"

Shit. Ashton. "I'm here." My throat is dry. "I didn't know that she was going to do this."

It's time to end this, she'd said to me. I didn't know what she meant—I hadn't asked her because all I could think about was Winter.

"Looks like I wasn't the only one with secrets," my agent bemuses. "This makes a hell of a lot more sense now."

But I don't feel like having this conversation with him. "I'll call you—"

"Tomorrow," he finishes for me. "Go figure. Fine. But we're having a meeting because I'm getting a lot of calls from a lot of people who want to hear your side of things."

That's too fucking bad, because they're not getting it.

When I hang up, I look at Winter. She looks wary, nervous. "It's going to be okay," I tell her, believing it for the first time. I bring my hand to cup her face and run the pad of my thumb along her bottom lip, tracing the shape.

I take a deep breath and watch her, my eyes roaming over her face. Her eyes are glassy still, whether from exhaustion or the tears she shed earlier, I'm not sure. They're red-rimmed and sullen but beautiful all the same.

She wets her lips. "What?"

"You're beautiful," is all I say, letting my thumb move

to her jaw and caress the skin.

She blushes. "We should probably talk about what comes next. Because there's—"

"In the morning," I urge, my eyes locking on her mouth. I've been wanting to kiss her all night, but I knew it wasn't the right time. But things are different now. "I can tell you everything in the morning. Right now, I want..."

My tongue drags across my bottom lip, and she tracks the movement carefully. "What?" she asks, looking as though she also wants one night where we don't have to face the people outside of these walls.

I slide off the couch and kneel in front of her, my lips curling into a sly grin. "Do you remember when I got on my knees for you, Winter? At the animal shelter?"

I see her eyes widen a fraction and her throat bob with a swallow. Is she thinking about that day? About the things we'd done? God, I fucking hoped so.

"Do you remember what I told you?" I ask, running my hands up her thighs. She's in a pair of sleep shorts that she changed into when we got here. Gone are her dress, heels, and makeup, and in their place a freshly washed face, a tiny pair of shorts, and a shirt that looks like it used to have a logo on the front that's long since faded.

Goose bumps pebble her skin as my hands make their way up her thighs. She parts them, whether voluntarily or not, and her eyelids flutter closed for a moment as her head tips back.

I stop at the apex, kneading the muscles there. "Do you remember, sweetheart?" I prod, my grin stretching as she exhales a shaky breath.

She nods. "Yes," she breathes, finally opening her eyes to look at me. "You told me the next time you were on your knees, you'd…"

I flash her my teeth when she's at a loss for words. "I said the next time I get on my knees, it'd be to taste you. And I'm a man of my word."

My fingertips dip into her shorts, tracing the skin beneath it.

"No underwear?" I ask in curiosity, feeling my cock harden at how close I am to her.

Slowly, she shakes her head.

"And your period…?" My eyes flick up to her, finding her cheeks redden. "Not that it would matter to me."

She gapes, not believing me.

But one day, I'd show her I mean it.

"I'm done with it," she whispers.

All I say is "good" before my hands peel off her shorts and toss them somewhere behind me. "If you don't want this, now is a good time to stop me," I warn, looking at her through my lashes.

I wait for the word.

The "stop."

The "no."

But she doesn't speak at all.

Thank whatever God exists in the world.

I grab ahold of her hips and pull them toward me, getting a surprised yelp from Winter. I graze my knuckles up and down her inner thigh, pleased when I see her shiver.

"So pretty," I compliment, nose grazing her core. I can feel the heat coming from her and smell the desire. She's turned on. The anticipation building in her as much as it is me.

When I close the gap, her hand instantly comes to my head. Her fingers weave in my hair and pull as my tongue drags across the seam of her lips. A noise escapes her, and her thighs try to close, but can't, thanks to my body.

I move her legs to rest on my shoulders, before my hands go to her ass and knead and massage the plump skin. She tastes incredible. She tastes exactly as I imagined. Sweet and sultry and *mine.*

Her fingers remain in my hair as I lap and suck and lick until her legs begin to shake. Her spine arches, pushing her pretty pussy into my face and giving me better access. She needs the release, and I want nothing more than to give it to her—to let her body finally let go of all the bad feelings from today.

The pressure.

The negativity.

I use my mouth and fingers to bring her closer and closer to that edge that she needs to jump from. Her thighs cage my head in, and I love it.

I love every moan. Every shaky breath. And when she says my name like *that*, like she's claiming *me*. I nearly come in my goddamn jeans.

"Thomas," she moans, both hands in my hair and holding me against her.

"Let it go," I tell her, tongue moving upward to the nerves that are firing on all cylinders. I suck her clit into my mouth, and that's all it takes.

Winter detonates, arching off the couch with a silent

orgasm taking over her. I wait it out, pressing kisses along her inner thighs as they quiver from the comedown until she's sated and still on the couch.

"Oh my God," she whispers.

I chuckle against her before pulling away to look at her. Her body is sunken into the cushions, her eyes closed as she catches her breath.

Then she yelps again when I pull her up, tossing her over my shoulder and walking us toward her bedroom.

"What are you doing?" she asks, holding onto my shirt.

I kick open the door and deposit her onto the bed, her half-naked body draped along the mattress. I watch her, licking my lips and still tasting her on them. "We should sleep," I say, still watching as she squirms.

She bites into her bottom lip. "Or…" Her words fade as she looks up at me.

"Or…?" I repeat slowly.

Winter stares up at me, her bottom lip still tucked in by her front teeth. Then she sits up, grabs the hem of her shirt, and peels it off her body until she's completely naked.

She's fucking gorgeous spread out before me.

"In the morning," she begins, "we'll figure everything out. But I need this. I need…you."

Her voice is so quiet, I almost don't hear her at all. But the statement hits me as if she screamed it aloud. It soaks into my body the way her secrets did, wrapping around my heart and squeezing it.

Winter has never admitted to needing anybody, but she needs *me*.

Slowly, I crawl over her onto the bed. I'm still fully

clothed, hardly on an even playing field. But all in due time.

"Say it again," I tell her.

Her lips brush against mine as she says, "I need you."

Three words.

But not the ones that most people's hearts will hold on to like their lives depend on it. No. These ones mean more to me.

She knows it too.

Because she says it again as she unbuttons my shirt. And again, when she takes off my pants and discards them onto the floor with our other clothes. And once more, when her fingers slowly peel the boxer briefs down my thighs.

I need you becomes my favorite phrase, and I want to hear it for the rest of my life. Because being wanted is one thing—a lot of people want me. But being needed by someone like Winter is a whole different game.

She can take care of herself. She *has*.

But at this moment, she's choosing me to take care of her.

And my heart reacts to that.

It thumps hard in my chest, beating in sync with hers when I press my body against her and guide my cock to her entrance.

All my thoughts wash away when I enter her, like nothing around us matters. Like the world stops for us.

Every single day, it's non fucking stop.

The noise. The demons. The past.

I don't catch a break.

I busy myself to drown it all out.

I refuse to acknowledge it so it can't touch me.

But not with her. With her, I allow it to surround me rather than hide from it. I don't pretend the past doesn't exist. I don't let it suffocate me. Around Winter, I can breathe. I can be the foster kid with shitty parents *and* the hockey player with a top scoring average. I can share my secrets like their currency and not worry about them being used against me.

I've always allowed Emaly and my career to bury the things I don't want to deal with. I let one version of myself out at a time.

Winter gets it all.

Every one.

I whisper four words back to her on the brink of my orgasm. "I need you too."

And apparently, it's her undoing too.

Because she breaks apart for a second time around me.

CHAPTER TWENTY-SIX

Winter

I WAKE UP to an empty bed and a note on the nightstand that says there's a surprise waiting for me in the kitchen. After yesterday, I'm not sure I want any more surprises. But I find myself going anyway, smelling something faintly like…bacon in the air.

Then I see a piece of paper taped to the microwave. Walking over, I tear it off and scan the words written in ink.

I'll explain everything today.
Don't look at your phone.
There's breakfast in the microwave for you.
Everything will be okay.

~ T

He can't promise that today will be okay, yet I find myself…trusting him. It's an odd feeling, one I'm not sure I've ever felt before.

Because I refused to feel it.

I need you, I told him last night. And for the first time ever, I realized that I meant it. I need somebody other than Kourtney—a person who isn't obligated to love me because of blood, but because they *want* to.

Opening the microwave, I stare silently at the plate of food. Eggs, bacon, sausage, and toast all greet me as I pull it out and set it on the counter. None of these things were in my kitchen before he came over. Which means that Thomas had to have gone out and bought the ingredients, brought them back here, and cooked them.

The dishes are washed and in the drying rack.

The counters are clean.

Only the smell lingers.

I swallow.

Thomas cooked for me.

My heart feels warm all of a sudden.

I pull my phone out of my pocket and get ready to text him when I see a new message from Janel.

And that warmth grows cold quickly.

Janel: *We need to talk. Come to my office when you get in, please*

My appetite leaves in an instant. I knew this was coming. Last night could only last for so long before reality came back. Thomas made sure every second was worth it, though. My body is sore in the best ways possible.

I force myself to eat the entire plate of food because he put in the effort to do this for me when he didn't have to. I shower, change, and look at myself in the mirror.

I'm not sure I know who the girl looking back at me is. She's different, but not in a bad way. I miss my pink hair and my bright nails, and I have every intention of getting them back. Hopefully, I'll still have a job so I can buy new hair dye and nail polish.

It'll be okay. I have to believe Thomas is right, because if I don't, then I have no idea what comes next. I can't make him fix the problems I created for myself; I have to own up to them. Take responsibility.

Which is why I find myself knocking on Janel's door not even an hour later. I have to remind my heart not to beat out of my chest when I see her.

"Shut the door, please," my boss tells me.

The only positive thing is that her office lacks an HR representative. Maybe they'll come in *after* she breaks the news that I'm being fired. I wouldn't blame her for whatever she has to do. She had to let go of Cody, so it's only fair that I serve the same fate.

It feels like an eternity stretched into two before Janel lets out a long breath and pinches the bridge of her nose. "I don't need to tell you how bad this is," she begins, looking exhausted from God only knows how many calls and emails she's gotten since the event.

This reflects poorly on her and her company. She's worked too hard to let someone like me come in and bulldoze it.

"I'm—"

"Don't." She stops me, making me press my lips together. I wait for her to give me *the look.* The disappointed one because the person she spent a year training did her dirty. But…

It doesn't come.

"I need you to listen to me," she says slowly, meeting my eyes with a firmness on her face that's all seriousness. "I like you, Winter. I like what you bring here. I like how authentic and headstrong you are. You're resilient. And, for the most part, unproblematic."

Internally, I wince at the last bit.

She clearly gives me too much credit.

"That's why I need you to lie."

I start to reply, thinking she's about to explain why I'm being let go. Then her words sink in, and I slowly close my mouth.

Because... *what*?

Janel clears her throat and intertwines her fingers together on top of her desk. "I need you to lie to me, Winter. Because what I'm seeing doesn't look good, but it doesn't have to be damning. Not when you have so much potential."

I'm struck speechless.

She wants me to lie? To deny everything?

"I..." I wet my lips and shake my head. "I'm not sure I understand, Janel. Cody was just investigated and let go for—"

"Sexual harassment," she says with a singular nod. "Cody was let go because he was creating an unsafe work environment for his peers. He was engaging in acts that made both coworkers and clients uncomfortable. You, to my knowledge, have not done that."

She gives me a pointed look.

There are so many things I had expected her to say. I'd gone through every scenario possible as I showered this morning and on the bus ride here. Each one led to me being told to pack up my things and leave. I'd anticipated it because I deserved it. No ifs, ands, or buts.

However, *this*...I don't know how to respond at all. "Janel," I try to say again, voice raspy. "I screwed up."

Once again, she dips her head in acknowledgment. "You did," she agrees, but there's a lightness in her tone that doesn't seem angry or judgmental. "But to be completely transparent, so have I. If you think you're the only one who's dabbled in adultery in this practice, you'd be mistaken."

My jaw drops before I can stop it. *Janel?* But she always talks so fondly of her husband. Well, maybe not fondly, but she never speaks badly of him. Not once. "Oh?" It comes out unintentionally as a question.

I'm not sure what else to say. What does one reply when their boss admits to having an affair with a client? That it's sweet she can relate to me? Do I thank her? Ask follow-ups? I'm not sure I want to know.

"I don't want to know," she continues, "what happened. I don't need to know either. I've seen the photos circulating, and they can be easily explained. You and I are both trained to dispel rumors, so that's how we'll treat this."

She's really not going to fire me? Penalize me? Put me on probation? I ask one question out of the thousands I have. "Why?"

Janel's lips tug up at the corners. "A few reasons. One, I've seen some of the photos even before they were broadcast. Why do you look like that? You should know I have sources. They felt the need to give me a first look. And you know what?"

I don't answer. Because...*what*?

"I've seen the way you've changed. Your shoulders seem lighter. You walk with confidence. You smile more. I didn't know what it was at first. But now I think I know exactly what brought you to life."

All I can do is gape.

"Thomas Moskins brought something out of you that I haven't seen before." She shrugs casually, like I'm not on every tabloid headline right now as an adulterous whore. "I've always known you've had it in you, but he's the one who allowed you to be...you. And I don't know why that is, but I'm certainly not going to complain."

I'm about to shake my head, to deny it, but she won't let me.

She pins me with a look. "I'm not saying that this isn't problematic, Winnie. It is. And again, I don't want you to tell me the details because I'd rather not have to report it to HR. Ignorance is bliss, after all."

I have to stop her before she keeps going, because none of this makes sense. "I'm grateful for everything you've done, Janel. Truly. But I don't deserve this second chance."

"Why not?"

"Because..." Isn't it obvious? "There are policies. Rules. Rules that I—"

"Nope," she says, eyeing me.

Right. Lie. "Rules that are in place for a reason," I say carefully until she's satisfied. "I broke your trust. I—"

"Winter, who are you trying to punish?" she questions suddenly. The curiosity in her tone is almost alarming to me. "Because it seems to me that you want me to fire you.

You *want* to be punished for this."

She acts as if this is a small thing. "It's not about what I want. It's about what I deserve."

Janel offers me a small, warm smile. "Don't you think that, above all else, you deserve to be happy?"

Once again, I'm staring silently at the woman who must have fallen and hit her head on the way to work this morning. Maybe this is all a dream. I'm going to wake up and realize that I'm assuming the best-case scenario for myself. When I really go to work, Janel will have security flanking her door ready to escort me to my cubicle, just like they did for Cody on his last day.

Except this *isn't* a dream. I check, pinching my arm just to be sure. I hide the wince from the stinging pain and rub the spot all while under the watchful eyes of my boss.

Thankfully, she doesn't call me out for it.

"Why should I be happy when I've done inexcusable things?" I counter with a frown, feeling that weight in my stomach.

"Have you?"

"Have I what?"

"Done something inexcusable?"

She is obviously kidding me. "Janel."

"No," is the answer that comes from somebody at the door that I hadn't heard open.

I spin to see two women standing there.

"Emaly?" I ask, standing as she steps in.

The woman behind her is as beautiful as she. Her blond bob fits her sculpted face and bright blue eyes. She's taller than Emaly by a handful of inches and seems like the exact opposite of the dark-haired woman.

My eyes go between the two of them, who are both smiling at Janel and me. And when my gaze trails down to their conjoined hands, something deep inside me clicks into place.

"Hi," Emaly greets, releasing the blonde's hand and stepping over to me for a hug. It's so quick, I don't have time to return it. "I'm sorry for interrupting, but it's important."

I'm so confused as I glance briefly at the stranger in the room before looking back at Emaly. "What are you doing here? I thought you were in California."

She lifts a shoulder. "I got on a red-eye because I needed to be here to make sure I made things right. I didn't want you to pay the price for something that you shouldn't be punished for."

I start to ask what she means when Janel clears her throat to regain our attention. "Does this have to do with the media alert that came through on my phone last night?"

Media alert? I pat my pocket but realize I must have left my phone at my desk when I dropped my bag off when I got here. Is it the one Thomas saw last night? I'd asked him about it, but he just kept saying he'd tell me everything today. And, truthfully, I was okay with that. Because I was scared of the truth.

"Probably," Emaly admits, smiling at my boss. She walks over and reaches her hand out for a shake. "I'm Emaly Moskins-Yokav. It's nice to meet you."

"Janel."

Emaly turns to me and gestures toward the quiet blonde still standing by the door. When the other woman walks over, they link hands again.

"Winter," Emaly says in a tone I've never quite heard before. It's soft and warm like usual, but also full of…love. "This is Ronnie. My fiancée."

My eyes widen into what I can only imagine are saucers as they shoot down to her hand, which has a beautiful gold ring and a green gem on it.

"That's…" I blink slowly as I study the gorgeous, round gem. "It's beautiful. I'm…"

"Speechless?" Emaly muses.

Her fiancée, Ronnie, swats at her. "You just dropped a massive bombshell on the poor girl. Let her soak it in."

Once again, Janel cuts in, "While I offer my full congratulations on this very spontaneous news, I think there needs to be some explanation as to why this is coming out now. No pun intended, of course."

Emaly snorts. "I like you," she tells my boss with a grin. "And I think the reason is perfectly clear." Her eyes turn to me. "Thomas fell in love."

Everything in me stills, and my heart drums wildly in my chest. "W-what?"

With her free hand, she squeezes my wrist gently. "My husband has sacrificed so much for me, Winter. He's let his reputation take a nosedive time and time again because of me and what I've been keeping from my family. But it's not fair to him, and he'd never agree to let me put myself out there with the truth for people to pick apart and judge. I realized something though. I don't care what they think. I don't care what my father thinks, or my mother, or my brother. The only person whose opinion affects me is Ronnie's, and hiding her was hurting her, and lying was hurting Thomas. I refuse to keep allowing that to happen when I have the power to stop it and change the narrative."

There is so much unfolding right now that it hurts my brain.

"This would have certainly changed things months ago when we first inquired about the case," Janel pipes up, still sitting behind her desk and watching us closely.

Emaly nods, almost sadly. "It would have, and I suggested telling the truth when Thomas was first being put through the wringer after getting caught with his ex from Seattle. But he didn't want that, and I let him convince me to keep quiet. It's time, though. It's time to end this so that everybody can move on. He deserves to be happy."

Emaly's eyes are on me as she delivers that last sentence. "And I saw it in your eyes the first day I met you, Winter. I saw the hurt and the loneliness even before you ever admitted it. It's the same thing I see in Thomas. I can't offer him the kind of love he needs, but you can. Because you deserve it too. You two are so alike, and that means you have the chance at filling in the holes left in each other's hearts."

The room is quiet as I swallow and take a deep breath.

"I'm sorry for lying," she tells me. "But I'm not sorry for being one of the reasons you were able to meet Thomas. In a weird way, I'm glad. He needs someone like you."

Someone like me?

She can see the question in my eyes. "He needs somebody who will challenge him."

Janel laughs lightly. "From what I've witnessed, I have no doubt she's capable of that. I knew the second that boy's eyes lit up during our first meeting that you had no clue what was coming."

I turn to her with my mouth ajar.

All she does is wink at me.

I'M STILL TRYING to wrap my head around the events of this morning when Farrah appears at my desk looking as cross as usual. Honestly, I'm surprised she didn't come harass me sooner. Being in other people's business is one of her favorite pastimes.

"What, Farrah?" I ask tiredly, rubbing my eyes. My work phone and cell have both been going off nonstop all day, and the only person I've willingly spoken to is Kourtney because I know she'd come here if I didn't.

She sits on the edge of my desk and puts her hands in her lap. "How does it feel to be the favorite? If any of us pulled the shit you did, we'd be gone quicker than you can blink."

I knew this was coming. "Can we not do this right now?"

"Oh, are you busy?" she asks, studying my blank computer screen. "You've been working on *one* case, and I'm sure it's not a hard one considering you're fucking the only client you have. That's bound to get you some deadline extensions."

I swipe my palms down my face and take a deep breath. In my wildest fantasies, where I have no consequences for any of my actions, I kick her really hard. Maybe even borrow one of her pointy heels to do it. But that's bound to get me a first-class ticket to the unemployment line, so I bury that temptation deep, deep down.

"What? Cat got your tongue?" she muses, pulling out her phone and scrolling through something. She laughs, but it's dry. Then she shows me an image of me cradling Oreo at the food bank. "This cat, perhaps? Looking a little too cozy, Winter."

I roll my eyes. "That was at a work event. He brought his cat. You would have done the same thing."

All she says is, "I hate cats."

Somehow, that doesn't surprise me. I'm sure the second she tried reaching out to Oreo, the feline would hiss and bat her hand away just like she did with Kayleigh.

My shoulders slump. Why do I miss Oreo right now? I could use some warm cuddles and rumbling purrs.

"I don't know what sob story you told to Janel to let her keep you, but it's not going to work on the rest of us. Your woe-is-me tale doesn't make you any more important than the rest of us. You aren't owed opportunities because you were orphaned as a kid."

I pale at the harsh words spoken to me. "How did you…?" I stop myself, already knowing the answer.

When I pick up my phone, I scroll through all the alerts and images being sent to me. Including the article deep-diving into the life of Thomas Moskins' new lover.

I'd gag if I had the energy, but I don't.

My shoulders slump as I scan the article, wincing when I see the timeline some amateur reporter put together. Some of it is painfully accurate, while other pieces are disgustingly wrong. And the worst part of it all? They name my sister.

I slam my phone down onto my desk. "Can you please go? I'm sure you've said everything you want to now."

"Hardly," Farrah spits. "In fact—"

"Go," a man says.

My spine tingles at the familiarity of those words spoken so firmly that I can't help but pick my head up. I have déjà vu, picturing Cody standing where Farrah is while Thomas stands there stick-straight and glaring at my coworker.

And behind him is Ashton.

"Shocking. Your protector has arrived," Farrah murmurs, standing up and flattening out the wrinkles from her pencil skirt. She gives Thomas a once-over. "It's a shame, honestly. You're wasting so much time on someone who doesn't know the difference between Prada and Walmart."

Ashton's hand wraps around Thomas's arm to stop him from stepping toward the mean girl, who has never really liked me that much. At least she was better at hiding it before.

"It's best if you walk away," Ashton suggests dryly. "For your sake."

Farrah's eyebrows lift. "Is that a threat?"

"No." That comes from Thomas. "It's a promise."

She scoffs as she starts walking out of my cubicle, purposefully brushing against Thomas's side in the process. "I guess all men have a savior complex. A real rags-to-riches story."

Thomas leans down to her and, through gritted teeth, says, "I'm no Prince Charming."

Farrah snorts. "That much is obvious."

She flicks her hair over her shoulder and walks away, leaving Thomas's nostrils flaring with anger.

"She isn't worth it," I tell him, almost defeated by the truth. But she isn't. Her nasty words aren't unjustified, even if they're not entirely accurate. She'll never know that I tried keeping my past on lockdown solely so it didn't afford me a single thing. I don't want pity or sympathy to make people give me things that I don't earn. I have every intention of working for it. And if I make mistakes, to pay for them.

"Now isn't a good time," I say, not looking at either of the men who linger mere feet away.

"Now is the perfect time," Thomas says. "I think we need to talk."

Slowly, I turn my chair toward him. "About what? About your *wife*? About her *fiancée*? About the media somehow knowing every little thing there is to know about me and publishing things I'd never wish on my worst enemies?"

My words catch, and I have to stop talking for a moment to gather myself. I count to three and try to ease my shoulders from the stiff, guarded squares they are. "There have been so many secrets, Thomas. I've always known you were holding back, and I didn't press. Because then I'd have to offer my own demons in trade, and I wasn't ready.

Not fully. I offered you parts of me that—" Once again, my words get crammed in my throat, and I hate it. I hate how shaky they are and how weak I sound. "That I haven't given to anybody before. And now the world is divulging details about me for everybody to pick apart."

Thomas walks over and kneels in front of me. "I never wanted that. I've only ever wanted you to tell *me* those secrets, and now you know the biggest one of all."

Emaly.

"I want to tell you everything," he says. "I'd prefer to do it elsewhere, if that's all right with you. Ashton is going to speak to Janel about the next steps, but there's a lot that's going to happen now that Emaly went to the press. You can ask me whatever you want, and I'll be honest."

I stare at him for a very long time. So long that Ashton clears his throat and excuses himself, probably to go to Janel's office.

Then I sit back in my chair, cock my head, and ask the one thing that comes to mind. "Was it all a lie?"

There are so many ways he can answer.

So many lies he can spew.

But his eyes soften, and vulnerability takes over his face as his lips twitch upward into a sad smile. "No," he says quietly. "Not all of it."

He could elaborate on which parts, but he doesn't need to. His face says it all. His need for me to hear him out. The way he stayed with me last night without pressing for a conversation.

Thomas Moskins doesn't just love his wife.

He loves me too.

I stand up, gather my bag and jacket, then deposit my phone into my pocket without checking it as it rings. At this point, I don't care who's on the other end, because the person I need to speak to most is right in front of me.

"Then let's go."

CHAPTER TWENTY-SEVEN

Moskins

IT'S HARD TO figure out where to begin when Winter settles onto the couch with Oreo draped across her lap. She focuses solely on her, cuddling into the cushions as the feline nuzzles her for more affection.

"I was put into foster care for the first time when I was six," I begin, only then earning her attention. Her eyes meet mine, but there's no sympathy there. Only a desire to listen. "I've told you that my parents were—*are*—shitty people. They're drug addicts and alcoholics who should never have had a child. In their minds, I ruined their lives by existing."

Winter stares at me with gaping, somber eyes, but remains silent.

I shift in the armchair I occupy across from her, because being close to Winter isn't a good idea. I would want to touch her. Comfort her. There needs to be space if I'm going to tell her the sordid tale of my past. "My father used to beat me whenever he'd be coming down from a high or in between twelve packs, so the school called CPS when the bruises became harder to hide. I was put in a home for four months before my parents were awarded custody again. They behaved well enough not to warrant any suspicion from the system, so eventually, the social worker wrote the case off and closed it."

But that was far from the end of it.

I learned over the next year to lay low. To not make much noise. To stay out of sight whenever I could. Because if I didn't, chances were I'd be on my father's bad side again. And my mother would be too far gone to step in or do anything about it. She may not have done most of the beatings, but she certainly didn't care enough to intervene when they happened.

"The second time I was taken away was two and a half years later," I explain, looking down at a random spot on the rug beneath the coffee table. "I spent my ninth birthday locked in my bedroom alone. And maybe I should have been sad about that, but I knew it was a gift on its own. I may not have gotten cake or presents like most nine-year-old kids on their birthdays, but I didn't have to endure the shit my parents put me through. I was given some semblance of peace, and I found myself enjoying the time alone. It gave me time to think."

Winter lets out a tiny breath. "What could a nine-year-old possibly have to think about?"

I lift a shoulder. "The future," I answer easily. "I thought about what I was going to do when I was old enough to control my life. I dreamed of better days and better things when I didn't have to answer to anybody. I thought about what freedom would taste like, and how I wouldn't take advantage of it once I got it."

Her brows furrow, and her frown deepens more than it was moments prior. "That's a sad thing for a boy to concern himself with."

I don't deny it. "Oddly, it gave me something to work toward and look forward to. Especially when I was sent back home. Apparently, there was some error, and the case against my parents was dropped. I went home and watched them fade away, drowning in liquor bottles and taking pills. There were some days they didn't even know I was there. There were some days I didn't eat unless I had school. And when my mother found the food I'd snuck into my room and hid under the bed after some of it went bad and started rotting and smelling, she took it all away and locked the cabinets and the fridge, so I didn't waste anything. They spent most of their money on drugs, so they couldn't afford to have me wasting what little food we did have."

I'd lost so much weight that I looked skeletal from the time I was ten until I was thirteen. Puberty hit, I grew at least a foot and a half, and you could count each one of my ribs. Teachers would ask me if I wanted to speak to them about anything, and counselors would try getting me to talk about my home life, but I never would. What was the point? I knew by then that the foster system was flawed, and even if I were taken away, I'd be back again soon enough.

I wet my lips and lean back in the chair stiffly. "The last time I was taken from my shitty childhood home was when my mother overdosed on the front lawn. Our neighbor called because he thought she was dead. There was still a needle hanging out of her arm. The medics revived her, sent her to the hospital, and sent me to a new home in a better part of town. I was almost fourteen."

Sometimes, I'm sad that the paramedics gave her Narcan. What kind of fucked-up thing does that say about me? But it's true. Both of my parents would overdose so much that they had their own Narcan kits at home. Once, my mother made me use it on my father after he'd taken too much fentanyl. And for the briefest moment, I hesitated to administer it. I kneeled there over my father's body across the kitchen floor, wondering what it would be like if he weren't there. Then my mother started screaming and crying and *begging* me to help him, so like an idiot, I did.

Shortly after, CPS came for the final time and took me to the house that would be the beginning of a fresh new start I didn't think I'd ever get.

"The woman who took me in lived in a huge house in a nice community. Apparently, she couldn't have children of her own. So, she and her husband used to foster them. Before me, they'd only taken in babies and toddlers. Then the husband, who was a well-known cardiologist, passed away. From a heart attack, ironically. And the wife continued to take kids in need because she had the money, time, and space. She wasn't the nicest person, but she was nice enough. She didn't lock me in my room, limit my food, or give me strict rules. I think her heart was broken after losing her husband, and she wanted company in the house that was far too big for one person. All she asked was that I stay out of trouble, so I did my best to do that.

"I soon learned that the house next door belonged to a very wealthy family who split their time between the United States and Russia. I'd seen a girl around my age coming and going with ice skates hanging from her arm, so I followed her down to a pond behind our houses one day. It was the middle of winter, so the water was frozen over. I kept my distance as I saw her skate and spin and fall and get back up again. Over and over and over. She'd go every single day, so I watched her whenever I was home. Then, one day months later, she called me out on it."

I smile to myself, thinking about the dark-haired girl looking directly at me from where I stayed on the hill. She'd yelled, *"Aren't you finally going to come down and join me?"*

At first, I thought she'd been talking to somebody else. Maybe a friend. A family member. There was a boy who I'd seen at their house too, but he never joined her on the pond. He usually went with one of the adults somewhere else, typically for hours at a time, while the girl stayed home.

But she wasn't talking to anybody else.

"Yeah. You! Come on."

It'd taken me a long time before I eventually slid down the hill and walked over to her. There was a second pair of skates beside hers that looked much bigger than hers.

"They're my brother's old skates," she tells me when she sees what I'm staring at. "But don't worry. He has new ones, so he won't miss these. Put them on."

I stare at her dubiously. "What?"

She points to the skates, like I'm dumb. "The skates. Put them on your feet. Like shoes. All you have to do is lace them up. I'm pretty sure you're the same size."

Shaking my head, I swallow. "I don't know how to skate."

She blinks at me. "Really?"

Sheepishly, I shrug. I've never thought much about skating, but it does look freeing whenever I see her on the ice. It's like she's flying. Free.

She watches me for a minute before nodding to herself. "Okay. I'll teach you. I've been taking lessons since I was four. I'm not the best, but I'm okay. You'll learn the basics at the very least."

Why is this stranger being so nice to me? She doesn't call me out for watching her for months like some weirdo. She's friendly. Welcoming. A little bossy.

"Why?" I ask with a frown.

She looks up at me because she's much shorter than I originally expected. "Because you look like you need a friend. And so do I."

As I retell the story of Emaly and my first meeting, Winter gets a small smile on her face that matches my own. "We became fast friends after that," I recount thoughtfully. "We spent a lot of time together. As much as we could. And when I learned I wasn't going to be sent back to my parents' home, it gave Emaly and me even more time to bond. We grew close. Closer than I thought I'd ever be to someone. She taught me how to skate and suggested I join the hockey team at my school. Turns out, her father sponsored the athletic departments at a lot of the local schools, so his money was what afforded me equipment and jerseys. When I wasn't at practice with my team, I was on the pond with her."

"That's sweet," Winter says softly, still petting Oreo, who's fallen asleep on her new favorite human. "It sounds like you needed her."

I dip my chin in acknowledgment. "We needed each other. Her parents were very strict and had expectations of her future that she didn't fit into. She wasn't as strong an athlete as her brother, but they pushed her to be. Her aspirations were never to follow in her mother's Olympian footsteps or her father's business-oriented mind. She enjoyed the idea of helping people and would often talk to my foster mother's late husband before he passed about the medical field. The older she got, the more she realized she wanted to go to school for that."

"And her family didn't agree," Winter guesses, sounding sad for the girl who got me through so much growing up.

I nod. "Her father is a very tough man to please. He has plans for everyone and expects the people in his life to follow his orders and do as he says without complaint. But Emaly isn't like her family. She's full of love and loyalty, but she isn't the type to bend at will. She's always supported her brother's love for skating and his success, but never received the same in return. To her father, going to college and med school was an act of treason against the Yokav name. He disapproved of the path she was taking, so he told her he wouldn't pay for any of it. Not school. Not housing. Nothing. He thought that would stop her, but it didn't."

Winter's lips twitch up higher, and mine do the same. Emaly has always been strong-headed. She's hardly the type of person you can boss around. If anything, she's the one doing the bossing. In a loving way, but still.

My smile slips. "One of the reasons that Emaly couldn't become a professional figure skater is that she's always been sick. As a kid, she'd constantly get colds. Her immune system wasn't strong enough to fend off viruses. Then she started getting pains. Small ones at first. The doctors thought it was from all the exercise she did and suggested physical therapy and ice baths. But none of that helped. Her body wasn't in any condition to train the way she was being forced to. It was draining her, and the doctors couldn't figure out why."

I take a breath and think about the defeat in her eyes whenever she'd come back from another appointment that led to a whole lot of nothing. I hated how she wanted to impress her parents, especially her father, to no avail. She'd make herself show up every day on that ice until she literally collapsed in the middle of it and started crying uncontrollably.

Emaly is not a crier.

I knew something was wrong that day.

Even her mother, as emotionally absent as she tended to be, could see it.

"Her father cut her off in so many ways, and I hated that. It wasn't Emaly's intention to disappoint him. She simply wanted to do what would make *her* happy and successful. She spent a lot of time at my foster home, speaking to my foster mother about her husband's schooling, and even got a reference letter that helped her get into college. She managed to do all of that on her own with loans, scholarships, and organic connections she made in the community. Em thought if she could prove to her father that she could make a name for herself, he'd be proud of her."

Winter wets her lips. "But that wasn't the case."

"No," I murmur, fisting my hands. "It wasn't. And I'm not sure if it was the stress of it all or something else that made her ten times sicker than she'd ever been. We decided to room together in a two-bedroom apartment that we could barely afford when we were straight out of high school. We both went to college and tried to help each other as best we could. I got a decent athletic scholarship, and her grades earned her an academic scholarship that covered a solid three quarters of her undergrad tuition. But she was starting to deteriorate in front of my eyes. Losing weight. Losing sleep. Losing hair. She'd get headaches all the time. Stutter. All of these strange things that had never happened before. The pain came back, but worse. She was losing focus and struggling in school, but she didn't have any health insurance because her father took her off of his as punishment for going her own way.

"I worked a shitty job that had decent health benefits, so I told her I wanted to help. She didn't agree at first. In fact, she told me my idea was ridiculous and foolhardy. But then..." My jaw clenches. "Then I got scouted and eventually signed as a rookie to the Pittsburgh Penguins and had to start traveling for training camp and preseason games. I wasn't around as much. She was still in school, so she stayed behind. I felt bad and talked to her every day to check in. But one day, I got a call from a neighbor who sounded frantic, saying she had found Emaly on the ground outside our building. She was having a seizure. The first one ever. And I wasn't there, and I couldn't be there for hours."

I close my eyes and relive that fear, having no idea what I would have done if something worse had happened. If she'd hit her head on the stone pathway or fallen down the three small steps and broken something.

It'd been déjà vu for me, remembering the way my mother's crumpled body had been lying on the ground outside our house. The difference was that I wasn't there to save Emaly. To call 911. I wasn't there, and I hated myself for it. Because, unlike my mother, I'd *wanted* to save my best friend.

I'm glad our neighbor was there and called for help, but I still beat myself up for not being the one who found her. Who encouraged her to get checked out sooner when she always complained about her head hurting and having dizzy spells.

"When they found a tumor on her brain, she finally agreed to my plan. Regardless of how ridiculous it was. So, we got married. She needed health insurance to cover all the scans, bloodwork, and specialists so that it wouldn't bankrupt her. She was already paying for her own schooling; she didn't need the medical bills to pile up too."

Winter stares at me for a long time, her hand pausing over Oreo's back until the kitten mewls in protest. "You married her for health insurance," she whispers, more to herself than me.

All I reply with is, "She's my best friend. I would do

anything for her."

I'm not sure why, but Winter closes her eyes as if looking at me is too painful. Maybe it is. This is a lot. The truth has been something I've held on my shoulders for years, not saying it to a soul. I needed to protect Emaly—needed to protect myself in ways too.

Until…I couldn't.

Because I *would* do anything for my best friend, but that didn't mean I wasn't lonely. I wanted companionship. Love of my own. Things that she couldn't give me on the levels I desired them.

For a long time, I didn't think I deserved it.

But I want to believe I do.

And when I met Winter Bronte on that first day with a giant coffee stain on her shirt and an attitude that stirred something in my chest, I felt something click into place.

"That doesn't explain Ronnie," Winter says, finally opening her eyes.

Ah. Yes. "Emaly and I never talked about relationships. We'd never entertained one between us, and she never spoke about her sexuality. We were friends, and that was that. We talked about everything *except* dating. I didn't think much about it because we were both young and busy with building our futures. I chalked it up to a lack of interest in getting into a relationship and nothing more."

Maybe that was naive of me, and there were signs I missed. But I've thought about it over the years, and she kept that part of her locked away for a long time. I assume it's because she refused to accept it, knowing it would be another problem for her father, and that's just sad.

"She met Ronnie during her residency," I tell Winter, remembering the way Emaly would light up whenever she video-called me to tell me about her day. At first, I assumed it was because she was excited about the next phase in her career. I quickly learned it had more to do with the pretty blond girl she worked with. "She likes to refer to it as a *Grey's Anatomy* worthy meeting. They were both surgical interns trying to make it in the medical world. That's when Emaly admitted that always knew she liked women, but never acted on it. Not until Ronnie came into her life and things clicked into place for her.

"I won't lie, Winter. There was a time when I was younger that I thought I had a chance with her. Mostly because she was all I ever knew. She was kind, caring, loving, and I felt as though she was the best I could do because she was familiar. I loved her; I still love her. But it was never more than friends, and it took me a while to understand the difference."

Winter stares down at the cat, her lips twitching downward only for a microsecond before neutralizing again. "I think there can be more than one type of soulmate in our lives. She's one of yours."

And are you another? It's a question I don't ask, because I don't want to scare her. But the pull I have toward her makes me answer the question for myself.

"Emaly's father is a very traditional man," I continue, the thought souring my mood. "He barely tolerated her marrying me. But a woman…Well, that's certainly not what he had planned for her. As much as I encouraged her to be honest about who she was, she didn't want to. Not to her father, mother, or brother. To my knowledge, nobody knows or suspects a thing, except for a very tight-knit group of their friends in California. And that secret lifestyle worked for a while for her...until things started getting serious between her and Ronnie. They were on and off for a while, mostly because of our situation, but it was obvious that they're each other's person. She found the love of her life and has risked it every single day because of her father's opinion."

And now...

Now it's out there. Now she's going to face the wrath of Mikhail Yokav, and I don't think she cares anymore. And as much as I wish she'd given me more warning, I'm happy for her. I'm happy for Ronnie and what that means for them. It's been a long time coming. I just don't think she knows what she's in for. The media will praise her for being brave enough to come out and attack her for lying at the same time. There are always two sides to every story, and allies for each of those narratives.

I've been fine being the bad guy, but I don't want a single person to view her in that role.

I take a deep breath, scrub the side of my neck, and release the air slowly. "I made a lot of promises to Emaly over the years. Our story wasn't only mine to tell. Everything we did, we did for her. It wasn't my right to offer up the information to anybody, no matter how much..." My throat bobs as I let the words fade.

Winter pierces me with a look.

"No matter how much what?" she presses, the same way I did with her when she wasn't being entirely forthcoming with her feelings.

I try to come up with an answer that's honest, no matter how scary it is.

"You told me you'd tell me whatever I wanted to know," she says, eyes still pinning me to my seat. "I want to know what this is, Thomas. Because it's terrifying me. I'm scared, and I don't know what's going to happen now. You were right when you said I didn't like always having to be in control. But I *need* control. I *need* answers. I need to know it's going to be okay because I haven't been for so long."

Her fear hits me right in the chest and grips it with sharp talons. "You're not the only one who's scared, sweetheart. This is terrifying for me too. Because I've never had to be real for anybody. I could be surface-level and unimportant, knowing whatever I had with them was temporary. But this isn't that. And I think you know it, which makes it even scarier."

Her throat bobs with a swallow.

"And I will do everything in my power to make sure that it *will* be okay. I don't know how. Not yet. But I'll be right here, right beside you, if you'll let me."

Please let me.

If she tells me she doesn't want that, I'll respect it. If she insists that this is too much, I'll let it go. Let *her* go. But I will never be the same.

I dig my fingers into the arm of the chair when the silence wraps around us until I can't take it anymore. "One more secret," I tell her, throat bobbing. Her eyes lift again, meeting mine with hesitation. "I've always accepted that being alone is easier than sharing my life with someone. I have a lot of wants that I've suppressed because I knew it wouldn't matter if Emaly and I were going to keep this charade up. But I'm going to say them now, because I'm tired of pretending like they don't matter."

I close my eyes but feel her gaze on me all the same. I take a silent, deep breath and exhale slowly. "I want to love somebody the way Emaly loves Ronnie. I want somebody to come to my games. I want somebody to celebrate my birthday with, even if it's a homemade dinner at home. I want to stop being the villain in everybody's story, because I'm tired of it. I'm tired of feeling like I have to play a role rather than be myself. I want to play hockey and surround myself with people I love. I want..."

My eyes find hers. "I want you," I admit, shrugging. "I want you to give me a real chance. I want to take you on dates. Not in a corner booth at a dark restaurant, but somewhere nice where I can hold your hand and kiss you in public. I don't want any more secrets, because they've been crushing me slowly since the day I told my best friend 'I do' in that courthouse. I want to be free to love someone out loud."

Saying those words feels like something is being lifted off my shoulders—like I can breathe properly again.

The only thing that can put it back is if she tells me she doesn't want that at all. If she does, I'll respect her decision. Even if it kills what little hope I have left inside me.

Winter's voice is watery when she finally says, "I need you to understand something first." There's a firmness in her tone that makes me nervous about what she's going to say. Until she speaks. "I'm never going to be the person who relies solely on somebody else. I can't be. I have to stand on my own two feet. I have to work and earn the things I have. I don't want to be handed anything just because of who I'm with or the things that have happened to me in my past."

She eyes me, and I quickly nod. "Done."

Her tongue drags across her bottom lip. "And I know I can't be on equal ground as you—"

My brows pinch, and I can't help but ask, "Who says you can't?"

Winter deadpans, "I know what you make, Thomas. I'm never going to be where you are, and that's fine. I've never dreamed about being the breadwinner. I've only ever wanted to pay my bills and have a little left over for hobbies or food or…I don't know. *Something.*"

I lift a shoulder. "Fine. Easy." Her skeptical expression doesn't seem to agree, so I offer her a smile. "Winter, I know you can take care of yourself. I'm never going to get in the way of what you need to do. If you want to pay for dinner, then fine. If you want to pay for groceries. Have at it. I'm not trying to take away your independence, sweetheart. I'm simply trying to love you."

It's out there. The possibility. The endgame that's so close, but could go away in an instant if she denies me.

Winter sucks in a shaky breath.

Stares at me.

And then says, "Okay."

One word.

Not three. Not *those* words.

But it's the start of something new.

"But if I'm paying for dinners, we're not doing steakhouses. You're going to have to downgrade from your usual," she warns seriously.

I hide a smile. "Deal. I'd be happy with McDonald's if it meant going with you."

She doesn't comment on that. "And I don't really understand hockey," she admits, nibbling her bottom lip. "But I can go. I can watch if it means that much to you. I just may need to watch some YouTube videos first to figure out what's happening."

My hidden smile wavers into a bigger one. "I can give you a crash course," I offer.

She nods for a moment, thinking. "And I'm not the best cook or baker, but I do okay. I can make a birthday cake as good as anyone. As long as it's from a box." She adds the last part quietly, but I appreciate it all the same.

"Sounds good to me, sweetheart."

And I mean it.

Winter watches me, only looking away once to glance at the sleeping feline still curled into a ball on top of her.

Her next words wrap around my heart and remain there. "Then I want that too."

I don't stop the smile from forming this time.

And when she sees it, that pink color creeps back onto her cheeks right before her lips curl up at the corners to match mine.

I think, *I love this girl.*

But I don't say it.

Not yet.

CHAPTER TWENTY-EIGHT

Winter

I STAY AT Thomas's place solely for the security it offers. According to Ashton, my apartment building is swarming with reporters who want to hear *my side* of the story, whatever that means. Something tells me it's bullshit. If I show up, they'll yell out their questions and accusations and take a million pictures that I don't consent to. They'll run with whatever story makes them the most money.

And, okay, I also stayed because Oreo fell asleep on me and I quickly followed suit.

The truth is, I don't have the energy to go home or deal with the people who want the next big headline. I don't want to be the freakshow that they use to get a big paycheck, especially when they have more vital things to focus on. My past doesn't deserve to be front-page news, and I won't let anybody make a spectacle of me because of it.

I texted Kourtney yesterday after no fewer than twenty missed calls from her, ranging from "Are you okay?" to "I'm tracking your location and busting down the door." The latter is when I realized I needed to tell her not to get arrested for breaking and entering, not that I think Thomas would mind.

The explanation I left her with was vague, and I felt bad for not offering her more information. But I…couldn't. I could barely process the way my life was unfolding. Trying to explain it to my sister was even harder. The last conversation I had with her before falling asleep was an apology for our past becoming a viral moment that is nobody's business.

Me: *I'm sorry you got dragged into this. I'll make it up to you*

Kourt: *How do you propose that?*

Me: *IDK. Groveling?*

Kourt: *If you stay with the rich guy, then you can afford me a better present than that*

Me: **glare emoji**

Kourt: **angel emoji* *eggplant emoji**

Me: *You're gross*

Kourt: *You're the one having sex with a married guy *wink emoji**

Kourt: *Although I'd be lying if I said I didn't like him way more after seeing what he did for his wife*

I didn't have to tell her I agree. His friendship with Emaly is nothing like I've ever seen. He loves her the way she loves him—unconditionally, without fail. He was ready to live the rest of his life as a villain if it meant she could be happy with her person.

Kourt: *If you're actually doing this with Mr. Married, then I need to meet him. No arguments*

Kourt: *Also, now we know someone who can buy Luca a vending machine*

Me: *Kourtney!*

Kourt: *He looks strong enough to move it too…*

Me: *He's not buying Luca a vending machine *glare emoji**

Kourt: *We'll see about that*

I wake up to the last message because I'd fallen asleep before she responded. I can't help but snort, because I have no doubt she'll try getting the professional hockey player to buy her son a vending machine. She has no shame.

I hear animated voices coming from the kitchen when I leave the empty bedroom that Thomas guided me to last night. We hadn't done anything. He hadn't even tried. He gave me something to wear to bed, tucked me in, and kissed me good night. I'd woken up to Oreo sleeping stretched out beside me and the owner of the house gone.

Some of the voices talk softly, while others…not so much. The one that sounds particularly angry has a thick accent that immediately puts me on full alert. It's the same voice that approached me at the gala.

Mikhail Yokav.

"—is not the place for this," a feminine voice replies. It's Emaly, I realize. When did she get here? That must be why Thomas wasn't in bed.

"And where *is* the place, daughter?" the angry man spits venomously. "Because your current residence is across the country with a woman I have never met in my life that you're allegedly engaged to."

I have no idea what to do. This isn't my place or my business. Or is it? I'm definitely involved in ways I really shouldn't be, but it's too late to go back now.

"I am engaged to her," Emaly corrects him smoothly. "There's nothing alleged about it."

Thomas is the next one to speak. "Perhaps if you had the kind of relationship that welcomed the truth, we could have avoided all this."

There are whispered words spoken in a language I don't understand between Mikhail and Emaly, but it's safe to say whatever Russian is being thrown around probably isn't light-hearted.

"Father," Emaly says in English, voice firmer than it was before. "That's uncalled for. And, frankly, Thomas isn't wrong. I tried telling you years ago, but you never listened."

There's a scoff. "You never told me *this*. You only spoke of a better path for you. You complained about skating, not...not..."

"Men?" Thomas offers coyly.

There's a choked laugh from someone that I can only

imagine is Emaly. Then she says, "Let me be as clear as possible so you understand me perfectly. I'm a lesbian. I'm not bisexual or heterosexual or asexual or any other thing. I'm in love with a woman. I've always preferred women. But I finally found the one I want to spend the rest of my life with. I'm as sure about Ronnie as I am about being a doctor. And we are *going* to get married."

It's silent for a long, tense moment. Suddenly, I feel like I should be somewhere else.

"You are already married," he points out. "If memory serves, I told you not to, but you did it anyway. What do you propose to do about that?"

"And *I* told *you* not to mix business and pleasure by buying him out," she counters. "You did that anyway. So maybe I am more like you than I want to admit."

"Is that such a bad thing?"

Simultaneously, Emaly and Thomas say, "Yes."

There's more Russian spoken and I have a feeling they're curse words.

"Thomas is my best friend, whom I love dearly and platonically. I can't speak for him, but I'm pretty sure he's in love with a woman too. Specifically, the one in the other room. I owe him so much, Father. Without him, I wouldn't have gotten this far in life. He's endured far more than he deserves, and I've allowed it to happen for too long. But I'm putting a stop to it right now."

"Emaly," Mikhail warns.

I take a deep breath and peek over the edge of the wall to look into the open kitchen across the hallway.

Emaly walks over to Thomas and stops in front of him,

reaching to cup his cheek. She smiles widely, lovingly, up at him. "Thomas, my love," she begins, stroking her thumb over his jawline, "I want a divorce."

More curses ring out in Russian, and Emaly looks in my direction as if she knew I was here this whole time.

She winks at me before dropping her hand and taking his to squeeze it once. "And you should take Winter on a proper date. Not one disguised as a business meeting."

Thomas laughs. "I think I can do that. As long as she'll let me."

Emaly's smile widens. "Oh, she will. Trust me on this."

Mikhail continues speaking rapidly in Russian until Emaly turns back to the figure I can't see because of the wall in the way.

"And, Daddy?" she adds innocently. "If you ever do anything to hurt me, Thomas, Ronnie, or Winter, I will find a way to destroy everything you have. Don't think I don't know how. There's a perk to being a wallflower. It means we see everything. Even the things you don't think we do. I've watched how you run your businesses, and there are people who I'm sure would love to know the things I do."

I'm not sure what the threat entails, but if I were her father, I wouldn't want to find out.

"You are a disgrace," he tells her coolly. "Your mother and I will never forgive you for this."

Emaly shrugs. "What's new?"

The tall man darts past her and Thomas and toward the other side of the kitchen, where a hallway leads to the foyer.

Before he goes, he says, "Everything I've done is to keep this family together."

Emaly rolls her eyes. "You've done everything but actually try," she counters. "If I'm done lying, maybe you should do the same."

I hear the front door open and slam closed with a brute force that rattles the pictures on the wall. Apparently, he didn't like that suggestion.

Thomas leans his lower back against the counter and crosses his arms over his chest. "That went about as well as expected."

Emaly grins. "Better, I'd say." She pulls her phone out of her pocket. "Ronnie wants to know if you'd like to have dinner with us. We're thinking sushi. You and Winter should come."

Thomas thinks about it. "Rain check. I think I want some time alone with Winter. When are you going back to Cali?"

"I'm not sure yet," she admits, typing out a reply. "Soon, probably. Ronnie has patients to check on, and there's an important surgery for one of them scheduled in a few days. And I need to speak to my boss about…a lot."

I'm not sure what kind of silent conversation is happening between them, but there's understanding.

Thomas pulls Emaly in for a hug. "Thank you," I hear him say. His voice is softer than usual, his words lighter as he squeezes her once before letting her go.

I'm not quite sure what he's thanking her for, but she does. "I want you to be happy, Little Bear. It's time."

All he does is nod.

Then she turns to me and says, "Treat him well, Winter. The ones he chooses to love are truly the luckiest people in the world."

With that, she walks out and leaves Thomas and me alone in the large home.

He pushes off the counter and walks over to me, stopping a few inches away. "Are you okay?"

"Shouldn't I be asking *you* that?"

One of his shoulders lifts as he tucks his hands into his front pockets. "I'm free," he answers easily. "Relatively speaking, of course. Ashton is bound to come here and start preaching about damage control now that Emaly has aired all of our dirty laundry to the public. But he's giving me space. Mostly because, for once, this isn't because of something bad I did. Even he knows that this can't be twisted into something negative."

I find myself nodding, looking at a speck on his shirt because meeting his eyes seems too intense. "I have a feeling you're about to have a lot more followers once they realize you did this for your best friend. Your jersey sales are about to skyrocket, and I'm sure you'll get a lot more female fans wearing your number in the stands for your first game."

His chuckle draws my attention upward, only enough to see the tilt of his lips. "I don't care about what they're wearing."

I'm expecting a dirty joke to follow, but that's not what I get.

Instead, he says, "I want *you* in my jersey."

I'm now gaping at him. "What?"

"But first, I think I want dinner."

Dinner.

"Okay…"

"Together," he amends.

I blink.

"I'm asking you on a date, sweetheart. Although I don't think going out right now is a great idea. We'd hardly be left alone. So, let me rephrase. I'd like to cook for you. Tonight."

He wants to…cook for me?

"I'll even make leftovers for you to bring home," he adds, a secretive smile dancing on his lips. "Because I know I can't convince you to stay here, even if I sweeten the deal with Oreo."

He's accepting my independence, even if it means me going back to the apartment that's half the size of his kitchen. "Although, I'm hoping one day to convince you to get out of that shithole. There's no security and there are water stains on the ceiling. There could be mold."

There probably is, but I don't voice that suspicion because it wouldn't help my case. My apartment isn't much, but it's mine. It's cluttered and small, but I love it. One day, I'll get something better. Maybe with him. Maybe on my own. I guess we'll see what the future holds.

"I should have never told you about the food thing," I grumble instead.

His smile spreads. "It's my intention to ensure you never need to go out on dates for food again. I actually enjoy cooking, and I don't do it often enough. So, I'd like to cook you dinner and spend time together. Maybe we can go to Our Open Table and see Bev and Vinnie this week. If we're going to be followed by the press, we may as well get their organization some more attention."

He wants to go to Our Open Table.

Together.

I swallow. "What's for dinner?"

He moves some hair out of my face. "Whatever you want, sweetheart."

Whatever I want.

I shake my head. "I'm not sure how we got here," I admit. This feels like a fever dream.

He presses a kiss to my temple. "Neither am I, but I'm sure as hell glad we are."

CHAPTER TWENTY-NINE

Moskins

I'M NOT SURE I ever knew the definition of love until I met Winter Bronte. I'd experienced different levels of the four-letter word, but it never sank in the way it has its grasp on me whenever the blonde is nearby.

But when I see the blonde and her sister in jerseys with my name and number on them from the friends and family suite at our first game, almost a month later, that feeling blossoms in my chest—a warmth so deep that I barely feel the cold of the rink.

She spent the last week watching videos on how hockey works and asking me questions each time we saw each other to better understand the game so that she would be prepared.

Then, two days ago, she showed up at my house with a pan covered in tinfoil. It smelled like chocolate and sugar, and I couldn't help but grin when I saw what was inside.

A cake. Chocolate. *"For your sweet tooth,"* she'd said. There were two number-shaped candles that made a larger number I silently hated because it meant I was another year closer to retirement. But until then, I'd embrace thirty-six like I embraced everything else. With pride and vengeance.

Since Emaly's threats toward her father, he hasn't tried

benching me. I'm not sure what she has on him or his business tactics, and I don't think she'll ever tell me. That'll be her secret to keep unless he warrants it to be told. And it won't be to me, but the media contacts she has now.

Maybe when I'm a free agent, I can move on from the Fireflies. Hell, maybe by then I'll be ready to hang up my skates and do something else with my life. For right now, though, I have no intention of letting Mikhail, my age, or anybody else get in the way of what I want.

To win.

To be on the ice and feel the cold on my face.

Every time my blades meet the frozen surface, I'm reminded of the very first time I ever stepped an uncoordinated foot onto that frozen pond as a pre-teen. Emaly held my hands as she helped me learn how to stand, balance, and turn on the borrowed skates. She came to my high school games. She cheered me on the way Winter is doing right now.

And for the first time in my life, I'm the happiest I've ever been.

A hand comes down on my back. "Tongue back in your mouth and boner in check, Moskins," Clarkson orders with a knowing grin. "We've got a game to win."

One of my eyebrows quirks up as I gesture toward the scoreboard. We're in the lead.

By a lot.

"I don't think we have to worry, Cap," I bemuse. "But I'm grateful you're concerned for the state of my cock. He appreciates it."

He rolls his eyes. "Head in the game, jackass."

I salute him. "Always."

I give another cursory look at the crowd. "I don't see Belle. Did your stepsister have better things to do?"

His nostrils flare, and a passive expression crosses his face. Once again, he says, "Head in the game." But with a bite to his tone.

There is definitely trouble in paradise.

"And Moskins," Clarkson says as he starts skating away, "It's about time you pulled your head out of your ass."

I can't help but laugh and lift my gaze to the blonde with red streaks in her hair. She'd asked her sister for help dyeing the strands and wouldn't let me see the results until today.

It's the same red as her jersey.

Red for our team.

I lift a hand to wave and wink in her direction, not realizing there's a camera on me that's cast onto the large screens hovering above us so the crowd can see everything better.

Kourtney, a spitfire who doesn't mince her words, nudges Winter with a grin on her face as the crowd reacts to my flirty grin.

I like her sister. Not only because she watches out for Winter, but because she doesn't play with words.

The first time I met her was two weeks ago, and she'd jabbed her finger into my chest and heeded a warning. *"If you break my sister's heart, I'll personally rip yours out of your chest and feed it to your cat."*

To which Winter turned red, yelled at her older sister, and made a comment about how Kourtney needs to stop holding a grudge against cats just because she didn't like Melvin, whoever the fuck that was.

But that didn't stop her sister from turning back to me with a mischievous grin and say, *"I also am going to need you to look into vending machines."*

Their dynamic is strange but loving. And because I don't want to mess with the all-encompassing force that is Kourtney, I'll start looking into vending machines as soon as I drop her and Winter off after we win our first game.

EPILOGUE

Winter

THE CHUCK E. Cheese parking lot is packed full of cars when Thomas pulls in to one of the last remaining spots. "Whoa," I breathe out, staring out the window. "You really meant it when you said the team shows up for people."

When Luca met Thomas for the first time almost two years ago, he'd been a little shy. For at least thirty minutes, anyway. After that, he asked Thomas no fewer than fifty questions. Including if he knew how claw machines worked, why the sport he played is so violent, and if he knew anybody selling a vending machine.

They became fast friends when Thomas told him that he *did* know how they worked, and entertained Luca by watching whatever video my nephew showed him. They were mostly showing the inner mechanisms of claw machines, and Thomas never complained. It didn't matter how long the videos were, he watched from start to finish and asked questions that he knew Luca would know the answer to.

That friendship rapidly grew when Thomas gave him VIP treatment at a Fireflies home game. He introduced the lanky boy to all of his teammates, where Luca asked them a similar line of questioning as he did the right-winger, and then he then invited every single person to his nineth birthday party.

Today. At Chuck E. Cheese.

Thomas puts his car into park. "I told you almost everybody on the team RSVP'd. Hoffman told me yesterday that his daughter was excited to come play with Luca again."

I smile instantly. His head coach's adorable daughter, Gemma, had a playdate with Luca almost a year ago now. Since, they've insisted on meeting up every chance they get. Whenever Luca tags along with Kourtney, and a reluctant Brad, to games, he always finds Gemma and spends most of the time with her.

"He's got a crush," I tell Thomas, my smile growing. "Apparently, he's always asking Kourt when they can see each other again."

He chuckles. "From what I gather, it's mutual."

I should have known it would happen. The last time I went over to Kourtney's, Gemma and Luca were in his room watching videos of kids playing claw machines. Gemma told Luca all about the prizes she'd won from them in the past and made me drive them to the nearest store that had one so she could prove it to him.

She won them both stuffed animals.

I'm excited for their future wedding.

"I still can't believe you got him a vending machine," I grumble, getting out of the car. It's been two years of the ongoing joke, and Thomas finally found one. "You did it just to piss off Brad."

Thomas grins. "Of course I did. The dude is a prick."

I roll my eyes. "Luca is going to officially crown you his new favorite person, and Kourtney will no longer like you. You've been warned."

He grabs my hand, interweaving our fingers, and walks me toward the front entrance. It took a long time for me to be comfortable with the public affection. Even something as simple as holding hands made me cautious. People would watch, some a little too closely. It wasn't until about a year after truly giving this a chance that I stopped caring. Inevitably, so did they.

Thomas and I weren't new news anymore at that point. He was happy. I was happy. His ex-wife and her *new* wife were happy. Whatever the press came up with to get a quick buck stopped mattering because people were rooting for us, not condemning us. There was no story and there were no villains.

"I'll find a way to make it up to her," he tells me, breaking me from my thoughts.

I eye him. "How?"

He shrugs. "Do you think finding her a good divorce lawyer and paying for everything would do?"

That makes me snort. "Good luck. I've been trying to make that happen for years."

He hums but doesn't have a chance to speak more about it when we walk in and see everybody spread out. His teammates all greet him with handshakes and high-fives. A few of them give him a half-hug and back clap before hugging me and pointing to where the birthday boy is showing Gemma a game. Puck, Honor's service dog, is sitting on the ground beside her while looking in our direction.

Bodhi Hoffman and Honor, who I've come to adore, are watching their daughter with a similar smile as mine. "Are you guys picturing their wedding too?" I ask, sidling up beside them.

Honor laughs at the twisted face her husband makes. "I'm pretty sure Luca is the only boy Bodhi will approve of."

"As he should," my sister says, popping up from who knows where. "My son is amazing."

Bodhi sighs heavily. "He is," he replies, almost sad by it.

I get it, though. Kourtney tells me all the time that she's sad how quickly Luca has grown. I'm not even his parent, but it feels like yesterday when I held him as a baby in the hospital.

Honor leans her cheek on Bodhi's shoulder, wrapping her arm around his. "Are you going to be this way with your other daughter too?"

I stand straighter, looking between them with a huge smile on my face. "Are you pregnant?"

I've gotten to know Honor since 'officially' dating Thomas, and I've learned her battles with PCOS and infertility over the years. They've talked in depth about having a child if they could, but I never pressed them on it because I know it's a sensitive subject.

Honor bites down on her bottom lip, peeks at her husband, and then nods as she meets my eyes again. "We are."

Thomas claps his head coach on the arm. "I didn't know. Congrats, man."

Bodhi smiles. "Thanks. We're very excited about it. Gemma is too. It's a wonder she hasn't told more people. She decided to announce it to her class during show and tell by taking the ultrasound in."

"At least she didn't draw a picture showing how the kid was made," Thomas muses.

Kourtney snorts. "That would have been hilarious."

"And mortifying," I murmur.

Honor seems to agree with me. "I wouldn't be able to show my face again."

Bodhi rubs her back. "Thankfully, we don't have to worry about that. She still thinks the stork brings babies in baskets."

"She's going to be disappointed when a bird doesn't show up at the front door," Honor tells him.

To which Bodhi chuckles. "I think she'll be fine so long as she has a baby to play with. She's already trying to convince me to let her bring her sister with her to school."

Kourtney sighs. "That's so cute. Luca asks about a sibling all the time."

My brows shoot up. "He does?"

A distant look passes over her face, and I know it well. It's not sadness or disappointment, it's defeated reluctance. "Yeah. I told him we'll see what happens in the future."

Which means no.

I look around, brows pinching as I try finding the person I've been dreading seeing since I woke up this morning. "Where is Brad anyway?"

My sister shifts from one foot to another. "He isn't here. I told him not to come."

Thomas and I share a look before I ask, "Is everything okay?"

Kourtney rubs her lips together. It takes her a moment to say, "I asked for a divorce."

Everybody gets quiet. Kourtney and Honor have become friends since their kids have grown closer, and I know they've discussed Honor's previous marriage before. I wonder if that has anything to do with this new revelation. If it is, I'll have to get Honor a present.

She clears her throat. "But that's a conversation for another day. Today is about Luca."

I walk over and squeeze her hand. "I'm sorry," I tell her softly.

She shakes her head, trying to hide the glaze in her eyes by rapidly batting her lids. "Don't be. It's time."

I hate that she always masks her emotions, but I understand. Now isn't the place to let the tears shed. "I can come over later," I offer. "We have to deliver a giant vending machine anyway."

Her eyes go from me to Thomas.

They stare at one another.

Then, my sister laughs. It's a little watery and surprised, but happy. "He's a keeper, sis."

Her approval makes my heart grow. "I think so too," I tell her, giving her a hug.

In my ear, she whispers, "Mom and dad would love him. Especially because he's a good cook. Dad would be begging him for recipes."

My arms tighten around her as a choppy laugh bubbles from me. She knows how much that means to me.

So, I repeat, "I think so too."

My voice is as watery as hers. When I pull back, there are tears in both of our eyes.

And then Luca comes over and says, "Can I open my presents now? None of them are big enough to be what I want, but I'm sure I'll like them anyway."

Bodhi chuckles from behind us.

I ruffle his hair while Kourtney sighs. "Yes, we can open presents. But you need to thank everybody for them as you go."

He thinks about it, then shrugs. "Okay." Then he turns to Gemma and says, "Come on, Gem. We're going to open my presents! You can have some of them."

I beam as they walk over to the table covered in wrapped boxes. "They're totally getting married," I tell Kourtney.

All she does is nod, but her smile returns. "I'd be okay with that."

ACKNOWLEDGMENTS

This book wouldn't have happened without my bestie Jessie Halley listening to my ten-minute voice notes talking out the plot. Thank you for never telling me to shut up and for offering advice whenever I'd get stuck on the plot. You're the best.

Aida – thank you for another adorable cover and character art.

Marla – thanks for polishing up my baby and fixing the dumbest mistakes I've ever made. Sometimes, I wonder how I'm allowed to do this full-time.

To the readers, I love you. I appreciate you. And I'm so excited to begin the third installment of the On Ice Series.

Until next time,
B

ABOUT THE AUTHOR

B. Celeste is a new adult and contemporary romance author that gives voices to raw, realistic characters with emotional storylines that tug on the heartstrings. She was born and raised in upstate New York where she still resides with her four-legged feline sidekick, Oliver "Ollie" Queen, and her goofy golden retriever Murphy. Her love for reading and writing began at an early age and only grew stronger after getting a BA in English and an MFA in English & creative writing. When she's not writing, she's working out, binge-watching reality game shows, having an internal debate on what takeout to order for dinner, and spending time with her friends and family (but mostly her pets).

Website:
authorbceleste.com

Facebook:
AuthorBCeleste

Instagram:
@authorbceleste

TikTok:
@authorbceleste

www.ingramcontent.com/pod-product-compliance
Lightning Source LLC
LaVergne TN
LVHW100501110826
845146LV00002B/473

* 9 7 9 8 9 9 0 9 2 4 3 8 3 *